GREAT WARRIOR
THE SHERLOCK HOLMES DIARIES
1901

by Geri Schear

Paperback ISBN 978-1-80424-421-0
ePub ISBN 978-1-80424-422-7
PDF ISBN 978-1-80424-423-4

Published by MX Publishing
335 Princess Park Manor, Royal Drive,
London, N11 3GX
www.mxpublishing.com

Cover design by Brian Belanger

There is a Victoria Cross gallantry which leads to nothing save personal decoration, and there is another and far higher gallantry of calculation, which springs from a cool brain as well as a hot heart, and it is from the men who possess this rare quality that great warriors arise.

The Great Boer War by Dr Arthur Conan Doyle,

Undershaw, 1900

CHAPTER ONE

Sunday 17 February, 1901

My sleep was shattered at some ghastly hour by the sound of a brief but piercing scream. Then I heard harsh, relentless sobbing. It took a few minutes for my brain to process that the sound came from within 221B.

Since I had staggered into my bed not two hours earlier, my first sleep in more than two days, (thank you, Mycroft) I swore at whoever had awakened me, no doubt because of some domestic issue. I cried out, "For the love of God, Watson, see what's the matter." I pulled the bedcovers over my head and tried to go back to sleep, but to no avail. The caterwauling continued.

Bleary-eyed and in no good humour, I eventually managed to sit up on the side of the bed and struggled into my dressing gown. Belatedly, I remembered that Watson was again working in the clinic. Beatrice had also abandoned me, being in much demand by the royal family since the death of the queen. Thus left to my own devices, I stumbled down the stairs to investigate the fuss and, more to the point, to see if I could make it stop.

I found a chaotic scene. The hallway groaned with all the maids, two policemen, and Mrs Hudson. Most of them were talking at once, and our housekeeper continued to wail.

"For heaven's sake," I cried, "what is the matter?"

"Mr Holmes?" one of the policemen said, "I am Sergeant Thorne from Division D. I'm afraid I just had to give some bad news to this lady. A woman believed to be her niece, a Miss Reid, was found dead this morning."

"Oh."

I am not often so lacking in manners, eloquence, or wit, but my fatigue severely impeded my usual acuity.

"What happened?" I managed.

The sergeant gave the distraught housekeeper a concerned look and led me towards the door. In a soft voice he said, "Stabbed and battered, I'm afraid, Mr Holmes. Nasty business."

"She has been identified?"

"Not officially. The lady in question had a letter in her handbag addressed to a Miss Megan Reid at this address. Mrs Hudson says the young lady had gone to church this morning around seven o'clock."

"What time is it now?" I asked.

"Seven-thirty." The policeman looked unhappily in Mrs Hudson's direction, and he lowered his voice. "From the lady's description, I'm afraid it seems likely that our victim is Miss Reid. Were you acquainted with her, Mr Holmes?"

"Only slightly. She recently returned from South Africa and remained convalescent for several weeks. Since her health improved somewhat, she began to help her aunt around the house. I am afraid I did not have much in the way of conversation with her."

"Do you think you might be able to come to the site? When we saw the address on the envelope, we did hope you might be able to help us."

The policeman gave me a dubious look. No doubt my appearance did not quite match that of the elegant and alert detective of my flatmate's fiction.

"Yes," I said, "Of course I would like to examine the scene. I am much obliged to you for preserving it for me."

At this, the policeman seemed less bemused. "Would you also be able to identify the body?" he continued. "The lady — ah, Mrs Hudson — is so distressed, and the body is in a bad way. Unless she has other family who might be able to do the job?"

"I believe her parents and other close relatives live in Scotland." I suppressed a moan and tried to convince my legs to move. "Very well, I need to get dressed. Please come upstairs. It's difficult to think in all this noise."

I turned back to the staircase but before I could put a foot on the first step, Mrs Hudson clutched my arm and cried, "Oh, Mr Holmes, you will find out who did this to poor Meg, won't you? Please, Mr Holmes."

What could I do? Without Watson to fill his role as comforter, I found the poor woman in my arms, sobbing against my chest, while I patted her ineffectually on the back.

"I will do my best, Mrs Hudson. Come now, do not distress yourself. We cannot be sure it is Megan yet. I will take care of everything, I promise."

I escaped at last. In my room, I bathed quickly, but the effect of cold water on my face felt less salutary than I had hoped. I dressed and joined the two policemen. They had a carriage waiting, and we were soon on our way through Marylebone to Portman Square where the body had been found.

We travelled in silence through the darkness and the gusting rain. With the combination of the hour — not yet eight o'clock on Sunday morning — and the appalling weather, the streets looked deserted. Fortunately, we reached the murder site within a few minutes. Any longer, and I should have fallen asleep again.

They had not moved the body, and I could see that the scene had been carefully preserved. A uniformed officer stood guard, stoic in the freezing downpour. A tarpaulin covered the corpse, preserving both the evidence and the dignity of the unfortunate victim.

"She's been savaged quite dreadfully, Mr Holmes," Thorne warned as he drew back the covering.

The destruction to the human being that had been Megan Reid made my gorge rise. The body on the pavement bore no resemblance to the gentle and thoughtful young woman who served our coffee. Someone's powerful fists had rendered her features to pulp. In addition to the vicious blows, I observed a number of stab wounds and slashes to the chest and abdomen. The face and throat had been so deeply slashed that I could see the bone in places. The blood that had not yet congealed ran with the rain into the gutter. The stench of blood and viscera made me swallow hard, despite my familiarity with ghastly death. To see someone I had known, albeit slightly, thus reduced to a battered corpse, challenged my ability to retain my sangfroid almost beyond limit.

Despite the awful destruction, I could recognise the dead woman by the mostly undamaged right side of her face, her wild red hair, and the silver cross around her neck that she always wore. Her calloused hands, worn from her years of nursing as well as the work she performed for her aunt, and the distinctive crooked little finger on her left hand made her identity indisputable.

"Yes," I said, "this is Megan Reid. *Was* Megan Reid. The rain has washed away most of the signs of the killer, I fear."

Thorne released a long breath. "I hoped you could advise us, Mr Holmes. Truth to tell, we have little to go on. It seems like a random killing. Who would want to murder an innocent young woman?"

"There were no signs of robbery? I see her cross is intact, though I cannot imagine it's worth much."

"We found ten shillings and sixpence in her purse," the policeman replied. "Her skirts do not seem to have been disturbed, but we will not know for certain if she was violated until we hear the surgeon's report."

"No, of course." I studied the street and the area immediately adjacent to the body, but I saw nothing, nothing. Only the frozen rain and the dark street. I took a breath. I needed to ignore the fatigue and, yes, outrage, and work past them. It is at times like this when Watson is so invaluable. He makes some comment or asks some question that helps me to focus and allows my skills to shine.

"The light is not good," I said. "No doubt we will have a better idea of her injuries after she is taken to the mortuary."

"Yes."

I could hear the distaste in the policeman's voice. I did not blame him. For all the complaints I and many others have made about those facilities over the years, nothing has been done to improve them.

My mind could not seem to stop drifting.

Stop. Focus. Remember, she's just a victim. Not Meg. Not the girl whose lilting accent made Watson laugh, and who called Mrs Hudson, "Auntie-darling." Oh, God, Watson. Mrs Hudson. What do I tell them? That I found her mutilated almost beyond recognition?

Focus.

I knelt down and examined the young woman and forced my mind to go through its usual steps.

"The killer is male, well-built, probably aged between twenty and forty. He wears a signet ring on his right index finger. You can clearly see the imprint of it here, on her face where he punched her. Hard to tell what that image is in this light, but it looks like a lion's head. He is medium height, no more than five foot six or seven. And he is right-handed."

The policeman made a note in his book and waited for my elucidation. "From the bruising and the angle of the knife wounds we can estimate the height of the killer. There are no fewer than three bruises on the side of Meg — the victim's face. You can see the imprint of the ring quite clearly here. The damage is primarily to the left side indicating a right-handed killer. His sex, age, and fitness we can deduce from the violence of the blows. The light is too poor for a more detailed analysis; I shall go to the morgue later today to take a closer look. I cannot do a thorough job here on the pavement in the rain and the dark."

5

I straightened my back. "What brought her out in this dreadful weather?"

"According to one of Mrs Hudson's maids, Miss Reid made a habit of attending St Thomas's Church in Bryanston Street to help prepare for the matins. She left a few minutes after seven and about seven-fifteen a Mr Tobias Jarvis discovered her body, as you see it."

"Did he offer a reasonable explanation for being out on such a day?" I asked.

"Yes, Mr Holmes. He claims he visits his mother most mornings and it's his habit to cut through the square. He raised the alarm at once, and Constable Burke took over."

The pudgy, spotty-faced fellow nodded in agreement. (When did the Metropolitan Police Force start hiring children?)

"That's right, Mr Holmes," the infant officer said. "I noticed at once that, even in this weather, she still felt warm. I would have kept the witness here for you to question, sir, but given the hour and the inclement weather, I let him go. We have his name and his mother's address — he means to spend the day with her — so we can follow up with him when we are ready."

He handed me the information written on a page in his notebook. I had to admit that he had done well in preserving the scene and identifying the corpse. Still, "You have only his word for it that he is staying with his mother," I pointed out. "For all you know, he may be the killer."

The constable shook his head. "Not he, sir. Reedy-looking chap. Looked fairly green at the sight of the corpse. He dressed immaculately, and I couldn't see a drop of blood on him. Also, his hands looked delicate. I doubt he'd ever used them for anything more savage than adding perfume to his bath water."

The sergeant chuckled. "No way this milquetoast is a killer, Mr Holmes, but I did have a constable escort him to his mother's home, to verify the address and relationship."

"Excellent," I said. "Did the witness see anyone? If the victim still felt warm, she must have died within minutes of his discovery, given the temperature."

"Jarvis says not," Thorne replied. "What with the weather, and, I reckon, because it's Sunday, the street's deserted. That's what Jarvis told Burke, anyway." The constable nodded in agreement. "At this stage it looks to me like a random attack. Poor soul."

"Well, there is little enough we can do for her now, other than dispensing justice." I managed to suppress a yawn.

"I am going to pay our friend Mr Jarvis a visit, Mr Holmes," Thorne said. "Would you care to join me?"

I hesitated. I confess, despite my outrage at the horrific murder of young Miss Reid, my body craved sleep. I consoled myself with the thought that the interview with Jarvis should not take long and, besides, it had to be done. Best to take care of it at once before the fellow's memory failed. And so, I agreed.

Jarvis's mother lived in Edwards Mews, a mere stone's throw from Portman Square. Our witness answered the door himself, a white apron tied around his waist, and a rose-decorated teapot in his left hand. His tall, thin frame was topped by a long narrow face. His jaw, though large enough to appear impressive, hung loosely, giving him the look of an unhappy Basset hound.

"Oh, it's you, isn't it?" he gushed in a high and tremulous voice. "Mother," he called over his shoulder, "We have a celebrity come to call on us. Come in, do, Mr Holmes, Sergeant."

Ignoring the policeman's snort of amusement, I followed the fellow into a small and stifling room, a dizzying confection of lace, embroidery, and chintz fabrics. The sergeant's amusement seemed even more intense, and he attempted to cover a guffaw with his handkerchief.

"Mr Sherlock Holmes," the old woman said. I almost missed her as her gown looked as gaudily decorated as the room. Only her snowy hair distinguished her from the other gewgaws.

"We love Doctor Watson's stories about you," Jarvis cooed, "don't we, Mother?"

She nodded and raised a heavily veined limp hand. I couldn't say if she meant me to shake it or kiss it. I chose the former.

"I will be sure to pass along your compliments," I said in as firm a voice as I could muster. The sergeant's amusement nearly unsettled me, and it felt incongruous compared with the scene we had just left. I could hardly blame him, however; distress must find release in some form after all.

"We need to ask you about your experience this morning, Mr Jarvis," the policeman said, managing to sound as pompous as Lestrade at his best.

"Oh, awful," the witness exclaimed in an appallingly gleeful voice. "So much blood! I told Mother — didn't I, Mother? — that the ground around that poor girl was just covered in it. A red lake! I think I got some on my shoes."

He glanced down in a peevish way at his feet, and realised he was wearing his slippers. "Oh yes, I took them off. Wouldn't want to track it through Mother's house, would I, Mother?"

"Sad situation," the woman said, "but, there, no better than she ought to be, I'll warrant."

"She served as a nurse," I snapped, "and just came home from South Africa. She was on her way to church when she was murdered."

The old woman mumbled something that might have been an apology. I ignored her and proceeded to fire a series of questions at the man.

No, Jarvis had seen nothing either immediately before he found the body, or after.

No, he had not heard any cries in the moments before he reached the corpse.

No, indeed, he most certainly had not touched her. Oh, the thought! He would have nightmares for ever.

The sergeant offered his brisk thanks and followed me out of the house. I felt too angry to even acknowledge the awful pair, the mother as grotesque as the son.

"A bad day all round, Mr Holmes," Thorne said. "Can I give you a lift home?"

Under normal circumstances I would have opted to walk. Calming down before I faced Mrs Hudson would no doubt be the wise thing to do. However, I doubted my legs could manage even so brief a journey, so I accepted his offer.

As we rode in his carriage to Baker Street, I said, "By your leave, Sergeant, I shall see what I can learn from Mrs Hudson. Perhaps Megan said something to her that could suggest a motive for the murder. At this stage, however, I suspect that you may be right when you described this killing as a random attack. To that end, I shall see if I can find out about anyone with a mental instability who has been roaming the area of late."

"There are no small number who have come back from the war," the sergeant said, shaking his head. "May the Lord have mercy upon them. God knows what they saw over there, fighting the Boer. Well, after I drop you off at Baker Street, Mr Holmes, I shall return to the station. The body will be at the morgue this afternoon if you'd like to follow up."

"I shall. Thank you, Sergeant. Oh, by the bye, I assume you will be handing the case over to Scotland Yard?"

"That is correct, Mr Holmes. I will pass on all the information to Inspector Lestrade. It will be up to him if he wants me to continue with the case or not."

*

9

Mrs Hudson had calmed somewhat by the time I returned. That is to say, she'd stopped screaming hysterically, but sat at her kitchen table, weeping. She grasped my hand and tried to speak when I entered the room, but words were beyond her. Still, I knew what she tried to say. I sat beside her and said as gently as I could, "I am so sorry, Mrs Hudson. I'm afraid there is no doubt that it is Meg."

She leaned forward and rested her head upon my shoulder as she surrendered to her dreadful sobs. I cannot think when I last felt so helpless. At least her weeping remained mostly silent. I put my arms around her and patted her back. I have no idea if she found it helpful, but at length the terrible sobbing slowed.

"Who?" she managed to murmur as she regained her self-control. "How?"

"We have no answers as yet, but I assure you, I shall not rest until I have learned everything I can about this outrage. I will use every skill I possess, and I give you my word, I will uncover the truth."

She patted my cheek with a damp hand and nodded. I wanted to leave and escape to the peace of my room, but I could think of no way to do so without seeming a bounder.

"Perhaps a little brandy will settle you — yes, yes, I insist." I nodded at one of the maids and she scurried to do my bidding. Not for the first time that morning I wished Watson or Beatrice was present. I am ill-equipped to deal with weeping women.

The maid returned with a glass of brandy, and I waited until my poor landlady had sipped a little before saying, "I do not wish to distress you, my dear Mrs Hudson, but do you feel able to answer a few questions?"

She nodded. "If it will help you find whoever did this to poor Megan," she whispered in a husky voice.

"Thank you, I know she recently returned from South Africa, and has only been here for a few weeks. Yes?"

"Yes." She sipped a little more of the drink and cleared her throat. "Yes," she said more clearly. "She has been a nurse for ten years. She trained in Scotland and worked in a hospital there for a long time. People used to stop my sister in the street and tell her what a kind and thoughtful young woman she had raised.

"Later, when the war with South Africa started in '99, she volunteered to serve and left with the first group. She spent most of her service in Bloom— Boom—"

"Bloemfontein?"

"Yes, that's it. It sounds so pretty, doesn't it? But from what Meg said it was dreadful. She didn't mind the hospital, which is where she worked most of the time, but she wept when she told me about the camp, concentration camps they call them."

"Why did she come home?"

"Because of her health." She took another sip of brandy before continuing. "She had such a terrible time of it. Not just her, of course, all those poor girls went through so much. Such long hours they had to work, and what little food they had doesn't bear mentioning. With one thing and another, Megan came down with dysentery, and she just couldn't get better. A few months ago she suffered a heart attack, and the doctors told her that she would probably never fully recover; certainly she would never be physically able to manage the terrible labour of nursing. A few weeks later she had a second heart attack, a much more serious one. At that point, the doctors said her health had deteriorated too much, and they sent her home."

Even her swollen red eyes could not disguise her anger. "Do you know, Mr Holmes, that when she left South Africa, she lost all the medals she had been awarded and her pension. I suppose they don't matter now. Meg felt so dreadful about leaving, oh, not because those things were important to her, but because she knew the desperate need for good nurses."

11

"Why did she come here to London and not go home to Scotland?"

"My sister and I discussed it when Meg wrote to tell us to expect her," Mrs Hudson replied. "Scotland is fierce cold this time of year, and her village even more so. Meg had become used to the heat of South Africa, though she says — said — it gets terribly cold there at night. Not only that, but Braemar, where my sister's family lives, is the very devil to get to, if you'll pardon the expression. Anyway, given the lass's poor health, we felt she would do better here in London, at least until she felt a little stronger. She hoped to go home by Easter if she felt well enough, and if the weather improved enough. Now, though…" And the tears began anew.

Again, I struggled against an urge to leave her to her grief, but I could not in all conscience do that. Only a coward would flee from a woman in such distress. A coward or a cad. Besides, I still had a number of questions. Yes, I could wait until she calmed, but that would not help my investigation, nor, in the long run, would it help her.

"I am truly sorry to trouble you at such a time, Mrs Hudson," I began, but she made a supreme effort and patted my hand.

"My dear Mr Holmes," she said, through tears, "if you could only know what a comfort you are. I cannot imagine how I would face this terrible day if it were not for you."

"Thank you," I said, bewildered. I had not done anything worthy of such commendation. "I need to know a little more about Megan. It is entirely possible the person who attacked her did not even know her. On the other hand, if the killer were known to her, the more I know about her, the greater my chances of finding him."

"But who would want to harm such a good soul?" the poor woman said. "A nurse, a young woman recently returned from serving her country, God-fearing, gentle, and in ill-health, to boot. You met her, Mr Holmes."

12

"I did. A fine young woman, and everything you say. But we all have enemies, even if those enemies are deluded in their thinking."

"If Megan had ever upset anyone, she never spoke of them. She would never intentionally hurt anyone, you know, Mr Holmes." She fell silent a moment before adding, "Would you like to look in her room? I believe she kept some letters from people she served with. Perhaps they may tell you something. If you don't mind, I should probably get back to work."

"Oh, my dear Mrs Hudson, you cannot possibly work today. You must go and lie down. No, I insist. I am sure the girls can manage everything. You have them so well-trained, you know."

After a moment's hesitation she nodded. "Well, I suppose you are right. I could use a lie down."

The dead woman's room sat half-way under the stairs. Despite being small, it possessed a charm. The floral wallpaper and brass bed spoke of comfort, as did the eiderdown quilt and the handmade floor mat. Everything looked clean, neat, and well ordered. The pillow still bore the indentation of the head that lay there only a few hours ago. A fire smouldered in the grate; presumably Miss Reid lit it before leaving early this morning on her benevolent mission. Though the fire had died down, the room remained cosy enough.

Beside the bed was a dressing table on which stood a lamp, a well-worn leather-bound Bible, and a photograph of a group of people outside a cottage: her family, I presumed.

I sat on the bed and went through the drawers. The first contained items related to her nursing service: her caps, pins, cuffs, and so forth. In the second, I found about five or six dozen letters. Most were from her family, one from a hospital in Scotland, and several from unknown people. All but a handful had British stamps; the exceptions had been sent from

13

South Africa. In addition, I discovered several dozen postcards, most with pictures of nurses on the front, and all from someone who signed themselves 'E.' Any other time, I would have sat and read them all, but I felt too weary and could not risk missing something important. I could not find an address book. I must remember to ask Mrs Hudson about it.

With the stack tucked under my arm and satisfied that I had recovered as much as I could, I left the silent and empty room to its ghosts.

In the hallway, I almost collided with Maisie, one of Mrs Hudson's newest maids.

"Begging your pardon, Mr Holmes, sir," she said, "but I just left your breakfast in your room. Oh, and I meant to tell you something. Uhm…"

I waited, losing patience. "Well?"

"Sorry, sir, I forgot. It'll come to me."

She scampered away and left me feeling even more muddle-headed than I had before. I realised that I had hardly eaten in the past few days, any more than I had slept, and despite Watson's fiction that I don't eat when I am on a case, I do find it necessary to replenish my reserves from time to time. That being the case, I went up to my room to eat before facing the bitter winter day again.

To my surprise, Watson sat at the table, doing fair justice to eggs, toast, coffee, and all the other delights the staff had prepared.

"Oh, there you are, Holmes," he said. "Good grief, you look rough. That wretched Holland case of Mycroft's, I suppose?"

"You suppose correctly, at least for the most part. I am pleased to see you, Watson."

"I am pleased to be seen, even by eyes as red as yours. I told Maisie to let you know I had returned."

14

"She forgot. Never mind. It seems an age since we last stood together under this roof. I have felt your absence keenly, I confess. I fear the clinic is taking every minute of your time."

"It would keep me busy if there were three of me," he said with a wry smile, "though the staff are excellent; I even managed to sleep for a couple of hours last night. Each day we get new patients, and all of them in dreadful condition. I shudder to think what would have happened to them if Beatrice had not opened the clinic. We are doing good work, Holmes."

"I have no doubt of it. All the same, you cannot continue to manage virtually single-handed."

"Oh, tosh, I am not working alone. We have almost a full contingent of nurses, all of them Nightingale trained, and there are some new doctors that I hope with start in a couple of weeks. As a matter of fact, Michaelson started this morning. He's an old army war-horse like myself, so he knows how to treat wounded soldiers."

I refilled his coffee cup and mine and said, "I hope that means you can take some time off. You look utterly exhausted, old chap."

"That's the plan. Now, what has been happening here? I heard there has been some upset this morning. Maisie said you'd tell me all about it."

As I sipped my coffee, I said, "I fear so. You have met Mrs Hudson's niece, have you not?"

"Miss Reid? I should say so. Charming young woman, and very obliging." He suddenly paused, the toast not quite to his lips. "Why? What has happened?"

"I am sorry to tell you that the police found her body this morning. She had been murdered."

"No!" he cried. "Oh, Holmes, what a terrible thing. I am truly sorry to hear it. Poor Mrs Hudson must be distraught."

"She is. I lent what comfort I may, but I fear that is not my forte."

15

"You do yourself a disservice, my dear fellow," he said, rising and tossing his napkin onto the table. "Where is she now?"

"I gave her some brandy and sent her to lie down."

"Excellent. You handled it beautifully, Holmes. I shall go check on her, and let you eat your meal. Then we shall find who did this monstrous thing."

"You mean to come with me?" I did not even try to hide my pleasure. "You are so tired."

"And you are exhausted. But for Mrs Hudson, Holmes. Come, man, finish your coffee. The game, as they say, is afoot."

CHAPTER TWO

"I am glad to have you with me," I said, as we hurried down Baker Street.

Even with half his face obscured by a thick woollen scarf, I could see his look of pleasure. I made a promise to myself to be more vocal in my appreciation of the good fellow. Perhaps Megan's death has made me maudlin.

In an alley not far from 221B we found Quinn, one of the brightest and most recent of the Irregulars. He stopped his game of "hockey" with some of the other lads, using sticks and a tin can.

"Whatcher, Mr Holmes," Quinn said. "Cold enough for you?"

"Quite," I replied. "Where are the other boys?"

"Ferret ain't here. He and Little Mac are on that other case for you. Checking up on that bloke with the peculiar name."

"Qualtrough. Yes, I know. I have another job for you boys." I related what I know of Meg's killer. A man with a savage temper, possibly showing signs of madness, who may have been wandering the streets during the hours of seven to eight or nine o'clock this morning. I gave them the brief description I had shared with the police.

"Usual rates?" Quinn said.

"Double the usual rates this time," I replied, "given the severity of the temperature and the price of coal."

"We'll get right on it," he said, and the lads shot off as if several of the official force were at their heels.

"That's one task accomplished," I said, "Though I don't hold much for their chances of finding the man we're after. If there were such a fellow in our neighbourhood, I feel certain I should have heard something about it."

"More than likely," Watson agreed. "Where are we going now?"

"To the church. Services should be over, I believe. I'm hoping the vicar can tell us something about our victim."

"But we've met her, Holmes. And Mrs Hudson has shared so much about her. Perhaps you're too exhausted to remember, when she received the letter telling her that Meg agreed to stay with her for a while, she talked of nothing else."

"I do remember. But Mrs Hudson is unquestionably biased. I want to hear what an outsider made of her."

The Reverend Dr Cyril T Cleghorne looked as tall, thin, and grey as the stone walls of his church. His conversation, too, had a distinctly dusty tone. "Yes," he said, "Miss Reid, charming young woman. Such a shame she had been invalided out of the nursing services in South Africa. The good lady has a heart that burns to serve. Oh dear, I hope she's not fallen ill again?"

"I'm afraid she's dead," I said. I tried to be as gentle as I could, and from the look of approval on Watson's face, I think I did a good job.

"Oh dear!" the Reverend said, his grey face losing what little colour it had. "Oh dear! I am sorry to hear that. She has become such an asset in the weeks she's been here. I hope she did not suffer."

"I'm afraid it's a case of murder," I said.

"Oh my!"

"Mr Holmes is looking into the case," Watson said. "Any help you can give us would be most welcome."

"Of course! Oh, of course. Anything I can do. Such a lovely young woman, and so young."

"What can you tell us about her Sunday morning routine?" I said.

"Well, she usually arrives around a quarter-past or half-past seven. It isn't necessary to be here so early, of course, but she likes to spend some time alone in prayer and

18

contemplation before she begins to prepare the church for the service. Always so anxious to be of use. It didn't surprise me when she failed to appear this morning. Her health is not good, you know, not good at all."

As he spoke, he led us from the bitterly cold chapel into a small sitting room. A fire burned merrily in the fireplace and the room felt quite cosy. We sat in the large armchairs, and I suppressed a smile as Watson unwound the scarfs, removed the gloves, and generally restored himself to a proper gentleman. Despite the hour, we accepted the finger of whisky Reverend Cleghorne gave us, "to keep out the chill."

"I understand she had a bad heart?" Watson asked, though he knew her medical condition better than anyone.

"That's right, and she had several other illnesses too. Ah, she didn't want to worry her family about the severity of her various maladies and so she tended to minimize her problems, but I gather she had a rather wretched time of it in South Africa. Good girl that she was, she soldiered on, as they say. When she suffered that first heart attack, they told her she'd never be up for the rigors of nursing. Still, she continued with her duties, despite everything."

"Her aunt only told us about the dysentery and the two heart attacks," I said.

"Two heart attacks, with a collapse between them," Cleghorne said, "and those on top of a fungal infection, malnutrition, exhaustion, enteric fever, and any number of other problems that were never properly diagnosed. Eventually, her condition deteriorated to the point that they sent her home. Such bitter tears she wept as she told me about it. I tried to console her that God undoubtedly had another task for her to do here at home, and I think that did lift her spirits a little."

He downed the whisky in one go and added, "A terrible irony that she might still be alive if she'd stayed there in South Africa. God works in mysterious ways."

19

"So do I, Dr Cleghorne," I said, possibly too tartly. Watson frowned at me, and I realised I should modify my tone. No point antagonising the man.

"When did you see her last?" Watson asked.

"On Friday. I thought she looked rather peaked. She told me she planned to come to service this morning. I suggested she would be better staying in bed if she felt unwell. She promised she would do so if she felt no better. God rest her poor soul."

"During any of the times that she attended services, did you observe anyone watching her, or following her? Or did she herself mention such a thing?"

"No, indeed. I never saw anyone follow her, and she certainly never mentioned such a thing to me, no."

"Did she mention anyone who frightened or worried her?"

"No, nothing of the sort."

Watson met my eyes, and I could read his discouragement.

"Do you get strangers here in the church?" I asked.

"From time to time, especially when the weather is as bad as it has been lately. No one stands out, however."

"Did she spend time with any other parishioners?"

"I'm sorry, but no. She seemed to like everyone, though I admit she seemed esteemed rather than liked." He hesitated. "I don't mean anyone disliked her, you understand, just that her degree of faith, some might call it religiosity, can be intimidating to the more, ah, moderate believers."

That seemed to be the extent of the man's information. As we turned to leave, however, he added, "She did once tell me that some people did not deserve to serve their fellow man. That doing so is a privilege and they should see it as such. I do not know if that is of any help to you."

"I cannot say at present," I said, "but who knows where it may lead. Thank you."

By the time we stepped out onto the street, the rain had stopped, though the wind continued to howl.

"What do you make of it, Watson?" I asked as I flagged down a cab to take us to Scotland Yard.

"Only that I agree with the sentiment. I cannot see how it helps us resolve the case, however."

"Nor do I. Well, let us see if Inspector Lestrade has had a chance to look at the evidence."

After the cold and damp misery of the journey, I felt my cheeks tingle with the heat of the Scotland Yard building. Several of the officers greeted us warmly as we made our way up the back staircase to the detective's bureau. One of them, young Garvey, said, "He's like a bear with a sore paw today, gentlemen. Good luck!"

We found our old friend in his poky office, overloaded with files, papers, and clearly irritated. Watson and I exchanged astonished looks to see him in such a disarray. For as long as I'd known him, he always seemed an orderly and fastidious fellow. I sank into one of the visitor's chairs and waited patiently.

"Mr Holmes, Doctor," he greeted us without rising.

"Lestrade," Watson said, "Good heavens, man, what's the matter?"

"Hm? Oh, a bad back. I've been meaning to go to the doctor, but we're so short of men at present. Sit down, gentlemen. How can I help you?"

"Lestrade," Watson continued undeterred, "it is we who must help you. You look dreadful." He began taking the man's pulse, making the unfortunate policeman stick out his tongue and raise it up to his upper lip.

"You are jaundiced, Lestrade," Watson said. "We need to get you to hospital —"

"Hospital!" the policeman exclaimed. "No, no! That isn't necessary. It's just a little twinge."

The pained expression on his face belied that.

21

"You may be contagious, man," Watson pressed. "It isn't a matter for debate. Come on, up with you."

It spoke of the fellow's condition that he hardly protested as Watson helped him with his coat and hat, then down the stairs and into a cab. As Watson climbed in beside the poor man, I felt, I confess, abandoned again. Pure sentimental nonsense, of course.

"I'll look after Lestrade, Holmes," Watson said. "Why don't you check in with Gregson? Perhaps he knows something about the case. I'll meet you back at Baker Street."

I found Gregson in his office in the opposite corner of the large room. A pane of glass allowed him to monitor the expanse where most of the detectives worked. His desk, like Lestrade's, creaked beneath a stack of papers, files, and other documents. I suspected he could find everything, despite the apparent confusion. I work in a similar manner.

"How is poor old Lestrade?" he asked. "I saw you and the doctor taking him out."

"He is not well," I said. "Doctor Watson is taking him to the hospital for a proper examination. In the meantime, I wondered if you were familiar with the Megan Reid case."

"Yes, Mr Holmes. Lestrade handed the file to me a short while ago. Between ourselves, he has been unwell for some time; I tried to persuade him to seek medical attention, but you know how stubborn he is. I'm relieved that you and the good doctor are taking care of him. I wouldn't call him a friend, but I should be sorry to lose him.

"Anyway, as to the Megan Reid case, I have Thorne and his men scouring the area for witnesses, but I have heard nothing back yet. Of course, we don't really know what we're looking for, which doesn't help."

"No indeed," I agreed. "I, too, have been busy."

I related the events of the morning, and my activities.

"So, she came home due to ill health, only to die in London. Poor woman," the inspector said. "We do not seem to have much to go on."

"Who knows what we may yet learn, Gregson," I said. "Has the surgeon seen her yet?"

He rifled through his paper. "Not as yet, Mr Holmes. We're still waiting. I doubt he'll get to her before morning."

"Thank you, Inspector, I shall head over to the morgue to see what I may learn."

*

It didn't take long for me to get to that stone and stern building. I made my way down the steps. The surgeon, Dr Wells, nodded by way of greeting and continued his examination of a cadaver, an elderly man with blackened fingertips and feet.

"Diabetes," Wells said by way of greeting.

"Of course. Megan Reid?"

"Over there in the corner."

I removed the sheet that covered the body and began to examine the corpse. In the cold morgue light, the home of the dead, her red hair set her apart, and her wounds stood out against the terrible pallor of her skin.

The body had not been touched beyond the removal of her bloody garments. By my estimate, she had been dead for at least four hours. Rigor, by now, impacted almost the whole body, and this added to the difficulty of my examination. I learned little beyond what I had already determined. A right-handed killer, medium height, who wore a signet ring on his index finger. She had not been violated. (A ridiculous phrase; what violation is worse than taking a life?)

The left side of her face had received the first blow, I thought. Her assailant had stepped out of the shadows and delivered a sudden, unprovoked punch with his fist. I could

23

see the imprint of his knuckles and fingers clearly. His ring left its imprint clearly on her white skin. The profile of an eagle's head. The blow felled her, and then the carnage with the blade began. I counted twenty-seven cuts all over her body. I estimated the blade as at least seven inches long and sharpened on both sides. Most of the knife wounds came in the form of punctures, but there were slashes too. In addition, I found numerous bruises and, I suspected, fractured bones due to his kicking and punching. A shame Watson did not come with me; I would benefit from his professional opinion. Then again, I thought the sight of her in this state would cause him too much distress. I suspected Megan died even before the carnage began; That bad heart of hers may have been a blessing in disguise. We would not know for certain until after the autopsy. I decided to keep that thought to myself; we would never be able to prove murder if a canny defence attorney got wind of it. I must warn Mrs Hudson and Watson to keep mum about this speculation.

I quietly removed the cross from around the dead woman's neck and slipped it into my pocket. At least Mrs Hudson would have something to remember her by. If I left it here, it would be gone by nightfall.

My task complete, I stepped back and returned the sheet over her face.

What sort of a man could do this? I wondered. Who could unleash such violence upon a young woman, barely five feet tall, unable to defend herself?

I had a brief word with Dr Wells and explained my concerns.

"Leave it to me, Mr Holmes," he said.

With that, I left the morgue, and gratefully breathed in the dank air of the London streets.

CHAPTER THREE

As I opened the door in 221B, I beheld Mrs Hudson in the hallway. Though she had stopped weeping, she looked pale. Her eyes were still red-rimmed. She grasped my hand as soon as she saw me.

"Oh, Mr Holmes," she said in a cracked and whispering voice. "Any news?"

"Not a certainty, Mrs Hudson, but a strong probability that Meg died instantly and never felt anything but the first blow that knocked her out. The surgeon conducting the post-mortem will let me know if my suspicions are correct, but I will be surprised if he finds otherwise. Now, I do need you to keep that to yourself. A rascal of a barrister might argue that she died of natural causes, and the killer would get away scot-free. You may, of course, tell her mother, but I'm sure you'll want to wait for the post-mortem verdict."

"That's a relief. Thank you, Mr Holmes, I cannot tell you what a blessing you are."

"It is early days yet, of course," I replied, "but you may be sure Watson and I are giving the case all our attention and efforts. In the meantime, I have something for you."

I pressed the cross into her hand, and her fingers closed over it. I feared she would begin weeping again, but she managed to contain herself.

"Thank you, Mr Holmes," she whispered as if she were in the presence of something holy. Perhaps, for her, it is.

As I rose to leave, she said, "When can I see her? My sister won't be able to come to London, but I would like to be able to tell her something."

"I understand. You know, it would be better to remember her alive."

"I don't doubt that you're right, Mr Holmes. But I owe it to Sheila — my sister."

"I shall ask the officer in charge of the case to let you know, and he shall also inform you and her sister when the funeral arrangements may be made."

I hung up my wet coat in the hallway and went upstairs. The sitting room, other than being tidier than when I had left it, looked unchanged. No sign of Watson. I sat by the fire and ruminated over all I had seen and heard that morning.

As is my practice, I allowed my mind to revisit everything I had seen from the time I examined Megan's body on the dark Marylebone pavement to the moment I left the morgue. On the face of it, a random stranger seemed the most likely probability, but would a stranger's attack be so ferocious? Perhaps Miss Reid disturbed someone in the park as she cut through on her way to the church, and that simple choice saw the end of her life. I cannot rule out the possibility of madness. Still, I can think of several other possibilities, and I would be remiss if I did not explore them all.

I picked up the bundle of Miss Reid's letters and forced my bleary eyes to begin reading them.

Most of the correspondence came from a Miss Alice Dixon. I gathered that the two had met in Bloemfontein. Dixon had returned to London and now lived in Hampstead. The first couple of letters struck me as vivacious, and surprisingly bawdy. I found myself smiling as I read them. However, after I'd read a dozen or so, I began yawning at the repetition.

The postcards offered no further information, save that 'E' whoever he or she was, did not care for letter-writing, and preferred to send cards instead.

A footfall on the stair caught my attention, and I arranged my features into a serious mien. Watson entered and flopped down in the seat opposite me.

"You look perfectly exhausted, old friend," I said. "How is Lestrade?"

"Very rough. We think there's a blockage in his gallbladder. I hope it's merely gallstones and nothing more sinister. He's scared to death, poor chap, and who can blame him? I stayed long enough just to get him settled." He sighed and cracked his neck. "I cannot believe it is only two o'clock. This day seems to go on forever."

After a brief tap at the door, that girl, what's her name, Maisie, brought in some coffee.

"Begging your pardon," she said, "But Mrs Hudson said to say are you gentlemen ready for lunch? We're a bit at sixes and sevens, but there's a good beef stew and bread."

"Excellent," Watson said, before I could reply. "Bring it up, please, as soon as you can, Maisie. I'm famished."

We sat at the table and dined heartily. I confess I felt hungry. The past week, working around the clock on Mycroft's troubling case, meant I had eaten little. I devoured the meal. Watson, too, paid attention to nothing but the food. Not until we finished dining and sat back with our coffee, did we turn our attention to other matters. I told him my theory about Meg possibly dying of a heart attack with the first blow. Watson nodded, "That would certainly make sense, Holmes. I pray it was the case."

"By the way, Holmes, Lestrade is going under the knife tomorrow afternoon. He's terrified, of course, but trying to be stoic. It would be a kindness if you could pay him a visit."

"If I have time," I replied. At his disapproving glance, I added, "Forgive me, Watson, I am not unmindful of the inspector's condition, but I am exceedingly busy at present."

"Do you think Miss Reid's case will take so much time?"

"I cannot say for certain. We do not have much information as yet; I hope it will not prove as difficult as this business of Mycroft's."

"Ah, the mysterious Holland case. Do you progress?"

"Slowly, my dear Watson, too slowly. I am still working my way through the list of Mycroft's most likely suspects."

"And Qualtrough's at the top?"

"Quite so. As my brother's primary secretary, he has greater access to the files than the rest of the staff."

"I can certainly understand why he is a suspect, but none of what you've said makes him a traitor."

I responded with a dry laugh. "My brother has never liked him, though, of course, he would never admit to any personal animus."

"But treason, Holmes?" Watson said. "Would a high-ranking civil servant resort to such extremes?"

"That is the question," I agreed. I refreshed my coffee before continuing, "I have spent much of the past week following the fellow and keeping watch outside his home. As of yet, I have found nothing to incriminate him. If anyone but my brother had marked him down as a spy, I would be persuaded that they had made an error.

"In any case, Mycroft arranged for him to be assigned to the Foreign Office this week, then next week he will be in the country as a guest of Lord Beecham."

Watson lit a cigarette. "Ah, Lord Beecham. The affair of the missing sovereign. He's as wily a man as I've ever met. I doubt anyone will get up to any mischief in his presence."

"Yes, indeed. A simple enough case, but not without interest. I think Beecham's Manor will be a good place for the fellow to stay, at least for now. His Lordship doesn't have access to the sort of documents this spy has been going after."

"Something to do with a submarine, didn't you say? What is it with spies and submarines?"

I managed a chuckle. "They are 'the future of warfare' according to Mycroft. The J.P. Holland plans have the Ministry excited. There will be the devil to pay if those documents fall into the wrong hands. With any luck, I will be finished with Meg's case before our suspect returns. Perhaps

28

I will even have the spy identified. In the meantime, I have a couple of the Irregulars keeping an eye on his house."

"And what if he isn't the man?" Watson said, oh, so reasonably.

I ran my hand through my hair as if the act could stimulate my brain.

"The Irregulars are keeping an eye on Mycroft's other suspects; they have found nothing of note yet." I fell silent for a moment, pondering, not for the first time, the inconsistencies in this case.

"From my brother's perspective, the timing could not be worse," I continued. "Ever since the queen died, there have been undercurrents of turmoil within the government."

"I would have thought your brother would be above all that," Watson said. "Not only because of his temperament, but also because of his lofty position."

"He is uncertain where he stands with the new king, and while his position does protect him somewhat, a scandal such as having a spy in his department could destroy his career. Between that and the Boer situation, he is under considerable pressure."

"I understand," he replied as he yawned and stretched. "But aren't they planning a reshuffle of his department soon? After that, it may no longer be his problem."

"He oversees all such activities, no matter what the department. Besides, we need to determine if the spy presents a genuine threat, or if he's a dilettante merely looking to amuse himself. Something about this case perturbs me. On the surface it seems straightforward enough, but there is an undercurrent." I poured another cup of coffee but before I took a sip, I said, "What of you, Watson? Do you need to spend so much time at the clinic?"

I sometimes regret that Bea opened that clinic; it is causing Watson to work himself to exhaustion. On the other hand, if she had not, he would have gone to South Africa with his friend, Doyle, and heaven knows what might have happened to him. And me.

"I have a few shifts coming up later in the week," my friend replied, "but the new doctors and nurses will be starting soon, so that should take the pressure off."

Reading my mood as he is often able to do, he said, "Any word from Beatrice?"

"She writes daily. She is bored to death, as you can imagine. She has never aspired to a royal life. However, our new king makes much of her advice and enjoys her company, so I do not imagine she will be home any time soon."

"The king has always been fond of her, I think."

"Yes, indeed."

I found myself staring at the rain still pouring down the windows. I thought about Bea, and wondered if she felt as wretched as I, and I wished for an end to winter, war, and my miserable mood.

"Don't you agree, Holmes?" Watson said.

I started, for I had not been listening. "Forgive me, dear fellow. What did you say?"

"I said we should get a few hours' sleep. We'll both do better for some rest."

"Yes, I have no doubt you are right."

I lay down upon my bed and gave myself to Morpheus. Perhaps a couple of hours sleep shall clear my mind.

*

18th February

I awoke with a start to realise from the thunder of traffic that it was morning. Feeling disoriented after my long sleep, and more than a little vexed, I lit a cigarette and swung my legs out of the bed. Had I slept all afternoon? My clock, unwound for who knows how many days, had stopped at six. Surely I did not sleep through the night? The smell of coffee, toast, and bacon insisted otherwise. As soon as I finished my cigarette, I rose, donned my warmest dressing gown, and stumbled into the sitting room. Watson, after rinsing his mouth with a little coffee, took a break from his meal to greet me.

"Ah, good morning, Holmes," he said. "I trust you slept well?"

"Rather longer than I had intended," I replied, a little tersely.

I sat at the table and poured a cup of coffee. "Have there been any messages?" I asked.

"I'm only just out of bed myself," Watson replied, "but I don't believe there has been anything."

"I've lost the entire night," I grumbled as I buttered some toast. "I should have been out, keeping watch on the streets."

"You cannot work twenty-four hours a day, my dear fellow," Watson replied. "Even the great Sherlock Holmes must eat and sleep sometimes. At least now you can face the day refreshed and you will be all the better for it."

"You may be right, but I resent the loss of precious time."

At that moment, I heard a knock at the door below, followed by a thunder of footsteps on the stairs.

"Quinn!" I cried, leaping to my feet.

The young boy stumbled into my room with a mischievous grin on his dirty face.

"Watcher, Mr Holmes, Doctor," he said.

"You have news?"

"Well, good news and bad news, like," he replied.

"Go on."

"Don't care which I give you first? Right. Bad it is. First off, ain't no one seen no crazies around the area. Miss Reid, she weren't well-known, not being long in the area, like, but them that did know 'er said she were a right nice lady."

"That, I suppose, is your bad news," Watson said. "And the good?"

31

"Well, seems there were a bloke in Portman Square that mornin'. 'e passed through the park about ten minutes before we reckon Miss Reid arrived. Anyways, 'e spotted a fellah lurking there, not doing nuffin', just standing there like 'e were waiting."

"Did the man get a good look at him?" I asked.

"Decent enough. Bloke's somefink of an artist and 'as what you might call an eye. He can give you a proper good description like."

"Where can I find this gentleman?"

"Don't know that I'd call 'im a gentleman," the boy replied with a grin. "'e's Irish, name of Gallagher. Peter Gallagher. You can find 'im at number 14 Seymour Mews."

"Good lad, Quinn."

I handed him a handful of shillings and reminded him that I expected him to share with the other lads and grabbed my coat.

"Holmes, do finish your breakfast," Watson implored.

"I've eaten my fill," I replied, as I wrapped my scarf around my neck. "Are you free to join me?"

"Not this morning, alas. I have to meet with Sister Berger to discuss the new hires' schedules. I should be free by about three o'clock. Shall I meet you here?"

"Hm? Oh, yes, three o'clock. That should do." I had my hand on the door, prepared to rush out, when his voice called me back.

"Holmes—"

"Oh, what is it?" I cried, irritably.

"Please don't forget about Lestrade. He's in St Bart's."

"Oh, really, Watson."

"You may not get another chance. He faces the knife this afternoon, and he is terrified, poor fellow. Please try to make the time."

"Since you ask it, I shall try," I replied, and fled.

Seymour Mews is less than a five minute walk from Portman Square. For all its cramped structure, the inhabitants keep it clean and neat. Not the usual squalid alleyway one might expect from the name. I have often observed that places called mews are either the height of fashion or the worst of slums. This one obviously leaned towards the former.

Number 14 seemed more appropriate for an industrial setting than a home. A squat building of three stories that resembled a factory more than a dwelling, its grey stone façade boasted half-a-dozen small windows overlooking the narrow lane. Thanks to the horse stables that sat adjacent, my nostrils were filled with the stench of manure.

Finding the door to number fourteen ajar, I entered. Mr Gallagher, the artist I sought, occupied the top floor, according to Quinn. I hurried up the stairs and knocked at the door.

"Mr Gallagher?" I said, when the door opened. A young man, aged in his early thirties, with black hair and dark eyes, nodded in assent.

"You'd be the famous Sherlock Holmes?" he said in a lilting Dublin accent. "Come in, please. Excuse the mess."

I could see no sliver of space in the entire apartment that was not strewn with canvases and art materials. The man himself wore a once-white cotton vest and dark worsted trousers such as a working man would wear, all of it, the man and his room, spattered with paint. The artwork that consumed the space caught my eye, and I took my time examining the pieces. Their colours gleamed under a huge skylight that covered most of the ceiling.

"You are remarkably talented, Mr Gallagher," I said. "You have made the Impressionist style your own."

"Thank you," he said. He hugged himself, partly due to nerves, and partly for warmth, I thought. I could see my breath in the frigid air.

"Do you sell your work through a gallery?"

"I do, aye. McNichols on Bond Street, and Jacobson's in Golders Green."

"Highly esteemed establishments. I'm surprised you don't live in a more fashionable part of town, if you'll forgive me saying so."

He made a swaying motion, as if his body could not decide what way to react. "I could, it's true, but moving would disrupt my work. Nothing must disrupt my work." Even at that moment, his long fingers twitched, and I could see he ached for his brushes and paints.

"Please do not let me keep you from painting," I said. "I am sure you can talk and work at the same time."

"I can, aye. Thank you for understanding." His entire being seemed to relax. He turned to face the large canvas that sat on a waiting easel, a painting of Oxford Circus in the snow. I found myself transfixed by the image, and it took me some effort to draw my attention away from it.

"Yesterday morning, you were in Portman Square. Can you describe to me what happened?"

He paused in the act of mixing a touch of vermillion into raw sienna and flake white with a palette knife. "I went for a walk," he said. "Sometimes I can't sleep. Often, I can't sleep. I get up and I walk. I look for things to sketch and paint."

"Even in poor light?"

"It doesn't matter. I just need to be in places, to get the feel. It's hard to explain."

"No, I think I understand. Many artists on the Continent have taken to painting in inclement conditions."

"That's it," he exclaimed. "That's it exactly. Monet, Manet, and, oh! so many of the Impressionists paint in snow, rain, after dark."

"I think I understand," I repeated. "Please, go on."

"I wandered around for a while, but nothing caught my eye. The cold started to get into my bones, and I knew I should head home. Just as I reached the Square I saw him, a man standing in the trees on the Baker Street side, like he were waiting for someone. He caught my eye because I saw no one else, and something seemed odd about him."

"Odd?"

"Furtive. He turned his collar up when he saw me and bent his head. It looked to me as if he didn't want me to get a proper look at his face."

"How far were you from him?"

"Not far. Say twenty feet."

"What can you tell me about his appearance?"

"Well, with the dark and the pelting rain, I can only give you a general description, you know. I'd put him at about five foot seven or eight, wearing a long dark coat, black or dark blue, I'd guess, and a scarf with lots of colours. The light from some unfortunate cab passing by caught the side of his face for an instant, and that's the image I saw. Very fair hair; aye, more white than yellow, and it hung straight and reached his collar. He wore no hat."

"Excellent; that is clear enough. Could you estimate his age?"

"Youngish, as I say. Under forty, but that's a guess based on the fluid way he moved rather than his features."

"No, it's an astute observation, and no less reliable than facial features. Can you describe the scarf?"

He closed his eyes and thought. "Well, it seemed big, more like a sheet or a cloak than a scarf. The fabric looked lightweight, perhaps cotton or silk. It folded easily enough as he wrapped it around his neck. I caught a glimpse of bright green and orange stripes, but I fancy there may have been other colours, too."

He turned his attention back to his painting, rapidly applying paint to canvas now. The matter of the man in the park all but forgotten.

"Did you speak to him?" I said.

"No." He hesitated, and his fluid rhythm of movement over the canvas halted. "I didn't like to draw his attention. Something about him made me uneasy." He turned to face me, his eyes dreamy, and his expression far away. "When I was a boy growing up in Dublin, a neighbour of ours had a dog. The mangiest mutt you ever saw, and the meanest dog you'd ever have the misfortune to meet. He had the entire street terrified of it, and one day it savaged a child and killed her. I'd walk a mile out of my way to avoid that beast. That's the feeling I had from that man."

His dark eyes, troubled and sad, met mine and the depth of the disquiet I saw there unnerved me more than his words had.

"Thank you, Mr Gallagher, you've been extremely helpful. Just a few more questions: Did you hear anything as you walked back to your rooms?"

Before answering, he took some time to consider. "I can't be sure," he said after several moments, "what with the howling wind and the hailstones battering down. I may have heard a thin scream, but that could have been the wind. Or it could even be my imagination now that you put the idea into my mind."

"It's of no consequence. Were you, by chance, acquainted with a young woman recently invalided home from South Africa? Her name was Megan Reid."

He pursed his mouth as he thought. "I don't know the name. What did she look like?"

"About twenty-six years of age, stood five feet, with a pale complexion beneath her tan, and dark red hair. She spoke in a soft voice, with a lilting Scottish accent."

"God rest her soul," he said, and crossed himself. "No, I can't say I have seen her, and I have a good memory for faces. I'm that sorry to hear it, Mr Holmes. May her family find some comfort in her memory."

The depth of feeling made his voice break, and tears hovered in his expressive eyes. "Who would raise their hand to an innocent maid like that?"

"I suspect the man you saw may be the killer. If we catch him, we shall have you to thank for it. I appreciate your time, Mr Gallagher. You have been enormously helpful."

"I hope you find him soon, Mr Holmes," he said, ardently, as he shook my hand. "A man like that — if he took one life, you may be sure he won't stop there. You have to catch him before he kills again."

CHAPTER FOUR

After I left Gallagher, I returned to Portman Square, annoyed that I'd lost so much time sleeping, letting the case go cold when I should have been investigating. On the other hand, I probably could not have expected to find much since that morning — was it just yesterday? — when Meg died.

Gallagher had drawn a map for me of the site indicating his position vis-à-vis the suspected killer. I examined the muddy ground and found a couple of excellent boot prints, size eight, under the cover of the trees. Who but the killer would have stood there in such deplorable conditions? The shoe size confirmed Gallagher's estimation of the killer's height, around five-six or -seven. A small number of wood shavings suggested the individual had whittled with his blade while he stood waiting. I found nothing else, however, no cigarette butts, no matches. I made a sketch of the footprints' position, appearance, and size.

Meg had died only a few yards away, but nothing remained to mark the site of the savage crime. The police had removed the body and all other traces. What the police and the public had not seen to, the rain and wind had.

Dispirited, I left, and, mustering up my resolve, went to St Bart's Hospital to visit the unfortunate Lestrade.

I found the inspector lying flat on his back in a narrow bed. His complexion spoke more of bile than blood, and from his expression, I surmised that he felt as dreadful as he looked.

"Mr Holmes," he said, startled, as I reached his bedside. "What a kindness, you coming to see me."

"Of course," I said, suddenly regretting the resentment that had carried me the whole way there. "How could I do otherwise, knowing my good friend Lestrade lay in a hospital bed? I would have brought you something to eat, but Watson said you're not allowed to take any food at present."

"Not a morsel," he said sadly, "I'm under the knife in a couple of hours. I doubt I could keep it down, even if I did have some grub. But never mind my troubles, tell me, you have a case?"

I glanced at the man in the next bed who appeared to be asleep, pulled up a chair, and quietly filled the policeman in on the details of Miss Reid's murder.

"That's a rum thing," he said. "Who'd want to do a good woman like that to death? I gave the file to Gregson, didn't I? Who's working the case locally?"

"A sergeant by the name of Thorne."

"Ah, young Bill. Good lad. Very eager. He'll do well, you mark my words. He's the future, Mr Holmes. My time has passed. I'm a relic."

"Oh, no, Lestrade, that's harsh."

"No, it's not. Come, Mr Holmes, you've always known." The laugh he wheezed out sounded hollow and mirthless. I had a sudden flash of the future which no doubt he saw, a future where I stood at his graveside; and I realised with a shock that I would miss him sorely were I to lose him.

Damn it. I have always sworn against rank sentimentality, yet it seems to cling to me at the most inopportune moments. That is the only excuse I can find for the fact that my hand reached for his and squeezed. Thank heaven Watson need never know. No doubt he would take this as yet further evidence of my "great heart." Such twaddle.

I turned the conversation to other things: the war, changes in the way policemen are now trained, and recent rumours that a telephone system is to be installed in Scotland Yard.

Despite my best efforts, I could see his mind wandered from our conversation. The thought of surgery, "the knife," remained uppermost in his mind.

I patted his arm, and saw, with considerable relief, that Mrs. Lestrade had just come into the ward.

"I will come and see you again after the surgery, Lestrade," I said. "Is there anything I can bring you?"

"Just seeing you is treat enough, Mr Holmes." He squeezed my hand. "You will say a prayer for me?"

Seeing such hope in his eyes, the fear, I felt I had no choice but to say, "You may be sure of it, old friend. I shall see you again in a day or two."

Pausing only to exchange pleasantries with the newly-arrived Mrs. Lestrade, I hurried from the hospital and made my way to Scotland Yard. I found the unfortunate Gregson almost buried by the stack of papers and files on his desk. I found our conversation highly unsatisfying and desultory as every few seconds some officer or other interrupted to ask yet another question. However, I gathered that Sergeant Thorne had made little progress. Gregson requested, nay, implored, that I pass my information along to the Marylebone policeman.

"I am up to my tonsils here, Mr Holmes. For all my complaints about Lestrade, I would never deny he works hard. I don't think I appreciated how busy he keeps until his load landed on my desk. And that on top of some of our more experienced men signing up to serve in South Africa." He glanced at the clock. "How is Lestrade? Have you heard? I should try to stop in and see him, poor beggar."

"He's having surgery this afternoon," I said, and saw Gregson pale before my eyes.

"Is it serious?"

"Serious enough. If you're a religious man, Gregson, you might remember him in your prayers."

"I will indeed."

As I left Gregson to his burgeoning files, I thought how little I had valued Lestrade's organisation and methodical approach to his work. What often seemed to me as unimaginative plodding, I now appreciated masked a keen ability to manage his men and to track every occurrence under his remit.

I took a cab to Marylebone Street. Thorne took my information with quiet attention and interest. I surmised that Lestrade may be right; Thorne represented the future.

"Green and Orange scarf, hm?" he said, making a note of it. "Sounds like a Fenian."

"Gallagher said there were other colours, too. I would not be distracted by the scarf, Sergeant."

"No. No, of course not. Best to keep one's mind open pending more evidence."

"Quite," I agreed.

"I confess I am stalled, Mr Holmes. I shall, of course, have the officers keep their eyes open for the man with the scarf, but I'm sure you will agree it is a vague description, at best. Said scarf is probably in the bin by now. Even if we find the fellow, we are unlikely to have enough evidence to lead to a conviction."

"I agree," I said, reluctantly. "Well, we can but try. I will keep you informed, Sergeant."

"And I shall do likewise, Mr Holmes." We shook hands, and I returned to Baker Street feeling I had done all I could for the moment.

I found a letter from Beatrice waiting for me upon my return. I sat at the table and read it as I ate a late lunch. As Watson was still out, I enjoyed her correspondence in solitude.

My dear Sherlock, she wrote.

Things continue apace here, though in such exacting measures one might be excused for mistaking them for inertia.

Bertie — His Majesty the King, I should say — continues to insist that I attend his dreadful meetings. Every detail of the coronation must be discussed. It will not surprise you to know there are experts in the most extraordinary items of minutia. The colour of one's braid, the height of a hat, and even the correct fold for a handkerchief must all follow some ridiculous protocol. I confess I sometimes amuse myself by telling jokes in Latin, something Bertie (alone) enjoys.

In addition to the tedium of these meetings, one must endure measurements for his coronation robes, the crown must be adjusted to fit his head (not a difficulty in his case), and any number of speeches written.

My presence is tolerated for the king's sake, but any comments I may choose to make are greeted with indifference, at least until Bertie approves and then everyone else chimes in with agreement. The Lord spare me from foolish old men.

Slightly less irksome — very slightly! — are the government meetings. At least I am privy to policy discussions and analysis of the war. The PM is not amused by my presence, feeling I compromise security, but that has made the king even more determined that I should attend. At first, that noble gentleman satisfied himself by addressing me as 'Bee-ah', rather than 'Bee' as a proper Englishman should do; not, you understand, that I had given him permission to address me so informally. I retaliated by telling him rather tartly that he may address me as 'Lady Beatrice.' Oh, did his face turn red! Am I wicked to take pleasure in his annoyance?

I have just this moment heard the news about Mrs Hudson's niece and, oh! what a terrible thing. I am very sorry to hear it. Meg seemed such a sweet girl, a bit conflicted between the compassion of humanity and her own rather orthodox religious beliefs, but one can hardly disparage the intentions of anyone with so kind a heart. Please let me know how the case progresses. I shall write my condolences to dear Mrs Hudson.

I wish I could be there with you for oh, so many reasons. I hint daily that I must return home, but the king and his family plead with me to remain. The queen is particularly anxious that I should stay for as long as her dear husband needs me; otherwise, she might have to step into my role, something that fills her with dread.

I am, therefore, essential to His Majesty's happiness, it seems. I should rue the day I was born with wit!

Stay safe and well. Please write soon with all your news.

All my love to John, Mycroft and, of course, your dear self.

B.

I immediately took advantage of my solitude to reply:

My dear Bea,

As always, I am happy to hear from you. I wish I had better news to relate, but as I am sure you can imagine, the general mood is deeply unhappy. Mrs Hudson is, of course, bereft. She weeps constantly and has taken to her room for the most part. Fortunately, the maids know their business and life continues with little change. The only thing that rankles is that the new maid, Maisie, is forever, in Watson's quaint words, 'away with the fairies.' As far as I am concerned, the fairies can keep her.

The case progresses about as speedily as one of His Majesty's meetings. I have the beginnings of a description of the suspect thanks to a talented Irish artist called Gallagher, and, of course, my own reasoning.

I returned to the site this morning and found footprints at the scene. It is evident someone stood in that spot for some time, given the depth of the prints. However, the motive behind the woman's murder remains a mystery. Though I would not

*dare to suggest it to Mrs Hudson, the fact
that the killer stood waiting for some time,
in terrible weather, until Megan arrived,
suggests his attack had purpose.*

*Mycroft's business continues to consume
much of my time, and I suspect our focus is
incorrect. Despite my brother's insistence
to the contrary, coincidences do happen. I
cannot say more in a letter, as I'm sure you
understand, but I will gladly tell you all
when you return.*

*In other news, Lestrade is undergoing
surgery this afternoon; his gall bladder
needs to be removed. As you can imagine,
he is sorely distressed and convinced he
will not survive. It is a difficult surgery,
Watson tells me, but the bigger issue is
whether or not there is a malignancy
present. It occurred to me when I visited
him that I would miss him should he fail to
come through. No doubt I am becoming
maudlin in my maturity. Between you and
Watson, I am almost a sentimentalist.*

*That said, I hope you come home soon.
Even Mycroft misses you.*

Yours, as always,

S.

Around three o'clock young Little Mac came to report. He
learned that Qualtrough wanted some work done on the lights
in his study. The arc lamp he'd been using burns out too

quickly. He wants it replaced with something that will last longer.

I clapped my hands in delight. This might be the very opening I needed. "Splendid, Little Mac! And in his study too! When is this work to be done?"

"Tomorrow, if you're free. Mind you, 'is butler, Mr Nosey Parker, will be breathing down your neck every minute."

"Then we shall have to arrange a distraction," I said, smiling. "Are they interviewing?"

"Naw, job's yours. I said my uncle Charlie was a master 'lectrician and could do the job lickety-split. That's you, by the way. Charlie Jones. Anyway, the butler bloke said for you to go over there in the morning and 'e'd give you a try."

"Which I suppose means if I'm cheap enough. Who's the butler?"

"Bloke by the name of Smothers."

"What can you tell me about him?"

The boy's forehead concertinaed as he thought. "Not much," he said. "Beady-eyed geezer. Likes 'is cigars, the stinkier the better."

"Splendid, Little Mac. Meet me here in the morning, and you shall be my apprentice. In the meantime, I have another small job for you."

*

Watson still had not returned by seven o'clock, and so I sat to a quiet dinner on my own. As I ate, I returned to Meg's correspondence, starting with the letters from Alice Dixon. Yesterday, the mere sight of them made me yawn. My attempt to get through them had resulted in nothing but sore eyes and bewilderment. As I returned to the task, I groaned in anticipation of such banality. The entire content reads as, *Oh, Meg, what a pretty bonnet I bought today!* (Lengthy description ensues). *I met such a handsome doctor at the*

Langs' dinner yesterday, a little old for me, alas, but I believe he has a younger brother. And so forth, ad nauseum.

In any event, I struggled on, fighting the wretched fatigue. The price of hats and the features of any number of handsome gentlemen soon lost any allure with repetition. Just as I decided to set them aside for the evening my eyes caught a paragraph that made me sit up straight in my chair. The letter in question was dated just three weeks ago.

"My dear friend," Dixon wrote, "you must not distress yourself over that incident in Bloemfontein. Blame there may be, but none of it lies with you. Blame the war, blame the lack of staff and provisions, blame me and our fellow nurses, if you must, but never yourself."

The letter went on to other matters, but this unnamed incident seemed to suggest that something had happened in South Africa that weighed upon the dead woman's mind.

Setting the letter aside, I went downstairs to find Mrs Hudson.

"Oh, Mr Holmes," she greeted me, as I stepped into her parlour, "Any news?"

"It is early days yet, Mrs Hudson. I do have some more questions, if you don't mind."

"Of course, if it will help."

"Did your niece ever mention her experiences in South Africa to you?"

"No, she found them painful to discuss. I did once try to broach the subject with her, but she said 'Oh, dear aunt, you would have to be there to understand.' I did not try again. Sometimes she mentioned something she'd learned in South Africa, ways of making a broth, or a new way to administer a compress, but that's all."

"Did she ever mention a woman called Alice Dixon?"

"Yes, Alice served in South Africa. She and Meg often worked together in Bloemfontein. Meg said Alice was a lovely girl, but she could be flighty and easily led."

"What of someone with the initial E?"

She frowned in thought for some moments before shaking her head. "I'm sorry, Mr Holmes. She had so many friends from all over."

We turned as the front door opened, and I realised Watson had come home at last.

"I should see to the doctor's supper," Mrs Hudson said, rising.

"One last question, please," I said. "Did your niece ever say that she felt as if she had been followed, or did she mention being accosted at any time?"

Mrs Hudson turned and thought for several moments before she replied, "No, at least, not directly. She did mention something about looking forward to when it gets light earlier in the day. She said the streets made her afeart — nervous — to walk in the dark. That it would make a body imagine all sorts. But she shook her head and laughed, as if she were being silly. She said London was hoachin' compared with the wilds of Scotland and the South African veldt. I tried to suggest she stop attending the services for now, especially with her health so poor, but she just laughed and said God would protect her. Maisie offered to walk with her but said she couldn't stay at the church because of her duties. I wouldn't have minded, but I think the girl felt uncomfortable because she's of the Roman faith."

"Quite understandable," I said.

"Mr Holmes, does this mean he'd been following her? The man who—"

"That's by no means certain, Mrs Hudson," I dissembled. "I am just trying to consider all the possibilities."

With that, I left the good woman to her duties and joined Watson in our rooms. He looked utterly spent.

"You've had another difficult day, my dear Watson," I said.

"In many ways, but a happy conclusion, I am glad to say."

48

"You went to the hospital after the clinic?"

His eyes met mine and I read his confirmation. "Did you participate in Lestrade's surgery, or merely observe?" I added, not commenting on the distinctly clinical odours that clung to him.

"I'm too tired to ask how you know. To answer your question, I assisted. No malignancy, thank God. We removed a gallstone as big as a golf ball. He tolerated the surgery very well, all things considered, and I left him in safe hands."

"That is excellent news," I said. "How did you like working in the operating theatre?"

"Well enough, though I had forgotten how hard it is to stand for a long time. Still, Mr Eddows, the surgeon, did not linger and we were soon wheeling Lestrade back to his ward."

He rubbed his bad leg, and I could see the swelling around his ankle. "What about you, Holmes?" he continued. "How did you get on? Was that artist able to help you?"

"Gallagher, yes, he gave me some information we did not have previously. He has excellent powers of observation, and is an exceptional artist, to boot.

"I have viewed the corpse but did not learn much there. I wondered, in light of Megan's poor health, do you think it's possible she died before most of those wounds were inflicted?"

"There's no way to know for sure, not without an autopsy. But I do think there's a good chance of it. Indeed, I pray so. Did you learn anything else?"

"Yes. See what you make of this letter."

I showed him the epistle in question, and he nodded. "I hear dreadful reports from the soldiers who have returned from that wretched place. War is a filthy business, and no mistake, but to send inadequate supplies and personnel is reprehensible. Meg told me she served primarily in one of the Bloemfontein hospitals and even spent time in the nearby concentration camp. I'm sure you've read the reports about those vile places, Holmes."

I nodded, remembering. "I thought a visit to Miss Alice Dixon might prove illuminating. Would you care to join me?"

"I should be delighted, as long as it's not too early. I need to go to the clinic in the morning, and I should like to check in on Lestrade, too."

"I have plans myself in the morning. Shall we aim for two o'clock? We can meet here."

"Excellent. That will suit me well."

CHAPTER FIVE

19th February

The day broke savagely cold but dry, and the paltry sun cast a faint sheen upon these grimy London streets. I rose around seven and reached Qualtrough's Mayfair home by eight, Little Mac at my side. The house sits in the middle of a line of exquisite terraced houses in Mayfair in the richer end of Culross Street not far from Grosvenor Square. We entered through the tradesman's entrance and met Smothers, the butler.

"You'd be Charlie?" he said, studying me closely from my flat cap to my well-maintained shoes. Everything I wore, though old, was spotlessly clean and any repairs neatly made. I looked every inch the respectable workman. The butler's eyes lingered on the cigar that peeked out of my breast pocket. He made no comment, however, but merely nodded his approval. His expression changed when he noticed Little Mac. "We had budgeted only for one man."

"Perfectly understandable, sir. The lad's my sister's boy. I am trying to teach him the meaning of learning a trade and earning his own living through hard work. He's my apprentice, so I shall be responsible for him."

"A noble endeavour, Mr Jones."

"These boys are our future," I said. "I cannot abide how some of these lads behave. No respect for anyone. It starts with respect for one's own self, in my opinion."

Another approving nod. Another glance at the cigar, this time it lingered a moment longer.

"Quite right, Mr Jones," he said, nodding fervently. "Listen to your uncle, lad. He will steer you right."

"Yes, sir," Little Mac said, his tone so meek, I almost laughed.

"Would you like to have a cup of tea before you start work?" Smothers asked.

I sensed a trap.

"It's good of you to offer, Mr Smothers, but I'd rather get on with it, if I may. I have another job to attend at one-thirty, so I would like to get to work."

For a moment, I thought he would not take the bait. However, he succumbed at the last.

"Forgive me for asking, Mr Jones," he said, "But I could not help noticing your cigar. Is that a *Por Larrañaga?*"

"I believe so, yes, Mr Smothers. Would you like it? One of my customers gave it to me in appreciation of my work. I'm not much of a cigar smoker as a rule."

"Oh, I couldn't deprive you..." He licked his lips, and I casually handed it to him.

"Please, I insist. I'm sure you'll appreciate it far more than I would. I understand Morris's on Bond Street got a new supply in. If you are interested, tell them that Mr Holmes sent you and they will give you a generous discount. You'll need to get there before ten, though."

"Will they, by Jove?" He glanced at his pocket watch. "Let me show you into the study..."

We followed him into the room at the back of the house.

"The master isn't happy with this," he said, waving a contemptuous hand towards the offending item. "It doesn't last long enough. Can you fix it?"

"Oh dear, oh dear," I said. "You're lucky to be alive. That's an arc light, Mr Smothers. Dangerous things they are and out of fashion. The problem is the filament; it only lasts a little over fourteen hours, you see. Better to change it for one of the newer Edison light bulbs. Much safer, and they last about 1200 hours."

"Splendid. Ah, will it take long?"

"Not too long, Mr Smothers. I need to examine the wiring, and run some safety checks, so about an hour, I should think."

"Oh, that's excellent. I, uh, need to run an errand. If you need anything, Mr Jones, let cook know. You'll find her in the kitchen."

"Right you are, sir," I said.

After he left, I set various tools on the desk, and studied the offending lamp.

"Are you sure you know what you're doing, Mr H?" Little Mac said.

"Of course," I told him. "I read an article."

I took the precaution of seeming busy because only a minute after I began to search the desk, a maid sauntered in. A pudgy girl of about twenty with a shiny red face and lank, mousy hair. In between constant sniffs, she introduced herself as Nancy. She made no secret of her nosiness about the room. As the staff are usually forbidden entry, I could understand her inquisitiveness.

Her indolence and boredom made it easy to persuade her to discuss the household. She whined about the dull Mr Smothers, and her mistress, Mrs. Qualtrough — "An invalid. Hasn't left her bed in the two years I've been here. Bad heart, they say. Doctor's here every month to examine her. Her da dotes on her. Sir Nigel Royston is his name. Bigwig of some sort.

"He's got a woman in Soho or someplace. Mr Qualtrough, I mean. He's hardly ever home. You hear the missus whining for him to spend time with her, but he's always saying his work keeps him busy."

"Not right, being away from his wife so much," I said. "Rich people — they're not like us, are they? Hand me that screwdriver, lad."

I acted as if my work demanded my attention. Little Mac, reading the signs, made a point of asking me questions. I reeled off a number of terms, some of which I remembered from the article, and some I had picked up from Watson's medical terminology.

"We're going to exchange the old arc light for the newest Edison. I need to evaluate the wattage and create a mitral dissection here at this junction. We can't risk a cerebral aneurysm or there will be a Swan overload…"

The girl, overwhelmed by my babble, turned to leave. Just as she opened the door she said, "Oy, is it safe to do all that without turning the power off."

"Ah, I had to check the power lines here, first," I said, in a show of confidence. Fortunately, she missed Little Mac rolling his eyes. "Now that's done, you're quite right; I should turn the power off."

I followed her out into the hall, and she indicated the fuse box under the stairs. I asked her to let the staff know that the power would be off for a short while. I congratulated myself that I had watched the engineers convert 221B to electricity not so long ago. I remembered how this bewildering box worked. I nonchalantly turned off the power and returned to the study.

"Cor, you're deadly, Mr H," Little Mac said, his voice a mixture of wonder and uncertainty.

"Let's get back to work," I said.

The office measured approximately nine feet by eight, and the book-lined walls made it feel oppressive. None of the volumes looked as if they'd ever been touched, not even to make a secret hiding place between the covers. The mahogany desk, too big for a room of this size, dominated the space. This, too, proved disappointing. However, predictably, a wall safe squatted behind a woeful painting of a Dalmatian.

I had it open in thirty seconds. Few of the documents were of interest, other than his recent bank statements. I found a passport, a few hundred pounds, some financial papers, and a ring of keys. A curious set of keys with a red ribbon tied to the bow. I quickly made a wax impression of each and returned all the items to their proper place.

Next, I had to replace the lamp. Fortunately, I had brought some items with me and in a matter of a few moments exchanged old for new. No sooner had I finished than Mr Smothers returned and declared himself well-pleased with our "work." This did not encourage him to add to his payment, however.

A little after ten, Little Mac and I left. I handed him the full amount of the fee we had been paid for our morning work. He stared at it in delight.

"What, all of it, Mr H?"

"You did a fine job, Little Mac; but make sure you share with the other lads. Ask Quinn to see what he can find out about that woman in Soho, will you? Dawson might know her."

"No worries, Mr H."

*

By the time Watson returned, Sherlock Holmes and not Charlie Jones sat in his customary chair reading the newspapers. I told my friend about my good morning's work, and the progress I'd made in Mycroft's case. I also had a brand-new set of keys in my pocket to show him.

Watson's morning had also been productive. Three patients were well enough to be discharged, and most of the other patients were recovering to his satisfaction.

"We received the references for the new doctors. They have no experience to speak of, but they are eager to learn. We all had to start somewhere, and they will experience far more in six months at the clinic than they would in the same number of years in a typical office."

Maisie served us lunch and managed not to spill the coffee. She blushed at Watson's sincere thanks and scurried away.

"How fares Lestrade?" I asked.

"Still quite tired after the surgery, in some pain, but relieved that everything turned out all right. He sends his regards."

"That is splendid news."

"Yes, I think I can say I had a good morning. What about you, Holmes?"

I told him about my examination of Qualtrough's study and gave him the set of keys. He looked bewildered.

"It's a set of skeleton keys," I explained, "the type that thieves use."

"Ah. That's odd. Why would a man like that need such a thing?"

"Why indeed?"

A moment later, Watson added, "Of course, it's possible there is a perfectly innocent explanation. It may be something he found and held onto."

"Why tie a ribbon around it? Why keep it in his safe?"

I could read the progress of his analysis in his clear eyes. I waited and kept my amusement from my features.

"Do you think this proves he's the spy?" he said, finally. "Perhaps it does; I'm just saying there may be another explanation. For instance, is it possible that Qualtrough has an, ah, lady friend?"

"I doubt she's a lady, but yes, he does. I am told she lives in Soho. I have the Irregulars checking it out."

"Well, that could explain everything. Perhaps they are the keys to her home."

"Why would she not have given him her house or flat key? No, no. This is a complete set of skeleton keys, Watson. I cannot imagine he needs anything so elaborate to access the home of his paramour. On the other hand, if he is the spy, it may explain how he got into Mycroft's desk and his safe."

"Yes, I see. I take it these are copies?"

"Yes, I don't want to alert him that he is under suspicion."

Watson downed the last of his coffee and wiped his mouth. "Did you discover anything else of interest this morning?"

I gave a succinct account of my morning, then concluded, "According to his bank statements, he has amassed a large number of debts."

"Keeping two homes and two women is expensive business," Watson said, drily.

I chuckled. "I can only imagine."

Watson repositioned his cushions and lit a cigarette. "I knew about his wife's illness, of course," he said. "Baxter's her doctor, and he consulted with me about her medication a few months ago. He told me the poor woman suffers from a chronic heart condition. I had no idea of her relationship to Sir Nigel. Isn't he one of the richest men in the kingdom?"

"He is, indeed. According to Mycroft, Sir Nigel is devoted and generous to his daughter, and her husband has no objection to spending her wealth. Or, rather, he would have no objection, but the lady is known to be parsimonious in the extreme."

"I take it they have no children?"

"It seems not, though I cannot be sure he has not sired offspring elsewhere."

"Oh, what a tangled web we weave," Watson said.

"Shakespeare?"

"Certainly not. A great Scotsman by the name of Sir Walter Scott. 'Oh, what a tangled web we weave when first we practice to deceive.'"

"Most apropos. As to Qualtrough, I have no idea if he is guilty of anything more than an illicit *affaire de cœur,* but I cannot rule out any skulduggery too."

"The two are often linked."

"Indeed. I hope to put an end to this business soon. Between the war and the queen's death my brother has been under considerable stress. Well, shall we go?"

*

We hailed a hansom in Baker Street and headed to Hampstead Heath. Watson still rubbed his injured leg now and then, and I did not want to add to his discomfort. Besides, the day remained gloomy and cold with frequent heavy showers. We alighted outside an address in Pilgrim's Lane at the Heath end.

"This is not far from where that odious Charles Augustus Milverton dwelt, isn't it?" Watson said.

"Yes, indeed. Church Row is but a short distance in that direction. Now this, I believe, is Miss Dixon's home."

The house sat back from the street, with a low wall and a small front lawn. I called it a tribute to middle-class banality only to be hushed by my friend.

We walked up the short path and knocked on the door. Several moments passed before it opened. A pale and distracted looking maid said, "Yes, sirs?"

"Good morning," Watson said, "I am Dr John Watson, and this is Mr Sherlock Holmes. May we speak to Miss Alice Dixon?"

To our astonishment, the girl cried, "No, sir!" and slammed the door shut.

We stood on the step, looking at each other in bewilderment. Just as I raised my hand to knock again, the door swung open. A tall woman dressed in black said, "You must forgive Mable, she's, I mean, the whole household. You are Mr Sherlock Holmes?"

"I am," I replied. "And this is my friend and colleague, Dr Watson. You are Mrs. Dixon?"

"Yes. Please come in."

We followed her into a small, ornate parlour, in which not one square inch was free of some ornament or embroidered cloth. Black crepe draped the mirrors, and the curtains were still drawn. A roaring fire crackled in the hearth, adding to the cloying atmosphere.

"May we get you some tea, gentlemen?" Mrs. Dixon asked. "It is a bitter day."

"Thank you, that would be most kind."

She gave instructions to the sniffling maid, who, blessedly, made her scurried exit.

"I apologise for disturbing you at a time of grief," I said, gently. "Do you feel able to answer some questions?"

"Yes, yes, of course." She sat stoically on the armchair facing me, her features set. "You are here to ask about Alice?" On the last word her voice cracked.

"Yes. Can you tell us what happened?"

"No one seems to know for sure. She left early yesterday morning for an interview at the local hospital. She did not return. At first, I did not worry; I thought she had met some friends and started talking. She's a great one for talking—was, I should say."

"When did you learn about the, ah, incident?"

"Someone found her body on the Heath. She had been…" The woman's hand went to her mouth. After a moment, she recovered herself and said, "Someone beat her and stabbed her to death. My beautiful little girl, so full of life and laughter."

"I am truly sorry," Watson said. "Do you know if the police have made an arrest?"

She shook her head. "They have nothing to go on, I understand."

"When did this happen, Mrs. Dixon?" Watson continued.

"Yesterday. Just yesterday morning I spoke to my darling girl, kissed her goodbye." Her voice broke and we gave her time to steady herself. After some moments she said, "I must beg your forbearance, gentlemen. We are none of us at our best, I am afraid."

The maid returned with a tray and Mrs. Dixon poured tea for us.

"Thank you, Mable," our hostess said. "That will do." As soon as the door closed, she said, "I am quite forgetting my manners. Please tell me how I can help you."

"You are already helping us, Mrs. Dixon," I replied. "I came to speak to your daughter in connection with the death of another nurse, a Miss Megan Reid."

"Oh!" she exclaimed. "Oh, that's dreadful. Alice thought the world of Megan. They served together in South Africa, you know."

"So I understand."

"Did she die, I mean, was it the same way?" She could not elaborate.

"I am afraid so," I replied. "When did Alice return home from South Africa?"

"The end of October last. The 28th."

The same time as Meg. Why, I wondered.

"You may be sure Mr Sherlock Holmes will not rest until the man who committed these terrible crimes is found." Watson was at his best, comforting the bereaved and lending solace to women. That sounds disparaging, but I do not mean it so. He is truly gifted in this area.

"You believe the same man killed both girls?" Mrs. Dixon asked.

"It seems too great a coincidence for Alice to die the day after her friend. Though, of course, we need to speak with the police and learn more of the specifics before we can say anything for certain."

Watson said, "What can you tell us about Alice's time in South Africa? Did she talk about it?"

"She said the nurses endured terrible conditions: cramped tents, snakes, and diseases, and not enough food. They had to eat soup made of horse meat. There weren't enough nurses and so the ones who were there worked incredibly long hours looking after patients who not only suffered from terrible injuries but had diseases."

"Yes," Watson said, addressing himself to me. "Enteric fever and typhus are killing more soldiers than the enemy, from what I hear."

"That's what Alice said, too. She went in October, '99 and at the time there were only eighty sisters to deal with a massive number of sick and wounded. There are now more than a thousand, but that is still not adequate to the task."

"I hear there are twenty or more hospitals, each with about five hundred patients so, no, I cannot imagine a thousand nurses would suffice. Even with help from the army, they must be run ragged."

"And that doesn't include the nurses who are serving in the concentration camps," Mrs. Dixon continued, her anger unmistakable. "They must deal, not only with the sick, but with snakes, scorpions, poisonous insects, and who knows what else. Alice, bless her, didn't tell me the full extent of the horror. She never wanted to worry me. The living conditions and poor food took its toll on many. I believe Nurse Reid was one such."

"That is our understanding," I replied. "Did Alice speak of Megan to you, Mrs. Dixon?"

"Oh yes, we had no secrets. She said no matter how tired Megan felt, or how difficult the circumstances, she did not stint in her care of all the patients, and spent herself, probably more than she ought, given her poor health."

"And Alice, did she spend herself?" Watson asked.

"She did her duty," came the brusque reply.

"Why did she return home?"

"She was sick in spirit," she replied, rising from her chair. "Gentlemen, if you'll forgive me, I feel I must lie down. It has been a terrible day and I am weary."

"Of course. One last question—do you know the name of the policeman handling your daughter's case?"

"Inspector Morton. I believe he is attached to the Metropolitan Police."

"Thank you, Mrs. Dixon. We apologise again for disturbing you at such a time."

Her waspish mood seemed appeased by Watson's kindness. "I am glad to help, if I can."

"May I make one last request?" I asked. "May we borrow any correspondence Alice received from Miss Reid? Also, her address book so we can follow up with her other colleagues."

"I shall see what I can find and send them to you, Mr Holmes."

I left feeling somewhat disgruntled. Watson, perceiving my mood, said, "You didn't expect her to let you rummage through her daughter's belongings not twenty-four hours after her murder, did you, Holmes?"

"Why not?" I asked. "Mrs Hudson did."

"Mrs Hudson knows you. You're a stranger to Mrs. Dixon."

"I suppose that's true," I reluctantly agreed though, truth to tell, I didn't see why it should matter. It's not like the woman had never heard of me, after all.

CHAPTER SIX

It didn't take us long to reach the police station on Rosslyn Hill. Watson introduced us to the desk sergeant and explained our purpose. The officers could not have been more helpful. Although the Heath has its own constabulary, in light of the serious nature of the crime, they were happy to hand the case over to the Metropolitan Police. The officer who had been first on the scene of Miss Dixon's murder took us to the site. We rode in a carriage across the Heath, and the officer, Constable O'Brien, led us to the spot.

"We found her here," he said, indicating a flattened clump of grass a few feet away. "There is still blood on the ground."

"Yes. What can you tell us about her condition?" I asked.

"She had been beaten savagely and stabbed multiple times. I doubt a bone in her body had not been broken." He glanced at me, "I cannot imagine anyone committing a murder with such ferocity if he were not in a towering fury. It's my belief he continued to beat her even after death."

"Why do you say so?" Watson said.

"I saw boot prints on her face and hands, clear prints that suggested she was not moving when he stomped on her. If not dead, she had to be close to it."

"You make an excellent point, Constable O'Brien. I agree; it does sound like fury. Did you find any witnesses to the attack?"

"No, Mr Holmes, I'm afraid not. She still felt warm when I got here, and I saw blood dripping from the body. A man walking his dog found her just a few moments earlier. He claims he saw no one."

"Ah, what would we do without our hardy dog-walkers?" Watson said.

"Old Mr Davenport," O'Brien replied, smiling. "Nothing would keep him from walking Kipling, his bulldog."

"Elderly?" Watson pursued.

"Ancient," O'Brien replied with a chuckle. "Both of them."

"I don't suppose you found any other witnesses?" I said, disconsolately.

"I'm afraid not, Mr Holmes. Not many folks about, given the bitter winds. The ones I did find claimed they saw nothing."

"Did anything else strike you?" I asked.

"Yes, sir, it may not be related, but I told Inspector Morton. Over there, behind yon oak, I found some pared wood shavings and a coin. They both felt dry, so they had not been caught in the rain that fell the previous night. The inspector took them as evidence."

"Excellent, Constable! What sort of coin?"

"That's the queer thing, Mr Holmes, I couldn't tell. It had no markings on it at all."

We walked towards the oak, an ancient beast of a tree, and O'Brien pointed at the spot.

"Right there, Mr Holmes. That's the very spot where I found the thing. I took care not to disturb the area, but I can't say with any certainty that no one, man or animal, hasn't been here since."

I knelt down and examined the spot. The outline of a pair of heavy boots were clearly visible a few feet away.

"What size boot do you wear, O'Brien?"

"Size twelve, Mr Holmes."

I measured the prints. "These belong to a much smaller man, size eight, I believe. Did you make note of these prints, Constable?"

His eyes, downcast, met mine. "No, Mr Holmes. I regret to say I did not. It's possible Inspector Morton did, though."

"Don't look so glum, Constable," I said. "You have done exceedingly well. I will say as much to the inspector."

"You're most kind, Mr Holmes," he replied. "But may I ask, those footprints are almost hidden by the undergrowth, yet you seemed to expect to find them. How did you know they would be there?"

"Watson?" I said.

"The wood shavings suggest someone stood there for some minutes, presumably waiting for Miss Dixon to come by. Holmes expected the killer would have left some traces behind the tree."

"Quite so," I said.

O'Brien's face concertinaed into a frown. I wondered if he had anticipated my next observation. A moment later, the good man proved himself worthy of my approbation.

"The killer likely followed her from her home to the nursing facility in South Hill Park Gardens."

"Almost certainly," I agreed. "Mrs. Dixon told us that her daughter had an interview there yesterday morning."

"Yes, for a permanent position," O'Brien said. "The inspector and I spoke with the matron yesterday. She told us that Miss Dixon worked occasional shifts, but she hoped to obtain a permanent position."

"Interesting," Watson said. "I'm surprised they didn't hire her for a full-time position right away."

"Yes, we wondered about that, too, the inspector and I. We didn't have much luck with her, the matron, I mean. Not what you'd call a forthcoming individual. She claimed that they didn't have any full-time positions available."

"Interesting," Watson said. From his expression, I could tell he found this a pretty rum business.

"The facility is in Hill Park Gardens?" I said. "Would it not have been an easier walk for Dixon to keep to the road?"

65

"Easier perhaps, but longer," O'Brien said. "A lot of locals cut across the heath, which is what Miss Dixon did. Saves time from going all the way around."

"What time was this?"

"Seven o'clock. Matron said that was the only time she could see her."

"And I suppose the killer assumed — correctly — that she would return the same way and so he lay in wait for her," Watson added. "He'd have had a long wait if she'd stayed for a full shift."

"Day shift starts at half-past eight," O'Brien said. "It's possible that he knew that."

"Something is still puzzling you, Constable," I observed. "What is it?"

"Yes, Mr Holmes. It's just, this murder would have left the killer covered in blood, so how did he leave the heath without being seen?"

"How indeed?" I replied. "The first murder — that we know of — took place in darkness and torrential rain. Possibly, the worst of the blood was washed away from him by the time he reached his lodgings. Here, though, there should have been sufficient light given the time and weather conditions."

"First murder?" O'Brien said.

"To the best of our knowledge, this is his second murder. Indeed, Dr Watson and I called on Mrs. Dixon this morning in hopes of speaking with her daughter regarding the first killing. A woman by the name of Megan Reid was beaten and stabbed to death on Sunday morning. There is little doubt that the killer is the same man."

"The brute!" O'Brien exclaimed. "He may have been following Miss Dixon for days. He knew who she was. But why on earth would a man want to murder two young ladies? What did they have in common?"

66

"They had served as nurses in one of the hospitals in Bloemfontein, South Africa. As far as we know, that is the only thing that linked them. I think I should update your inspector, and perhaps he will arrange to speak further with Sergeant Thorne, as he is in charge of the Reid case.

"In the meantime, Constable, it would be helpful if you would question people who live on the periphery of the Heath to see if they saw the killer. Apart from being covered with blood, you can describe him as being approximately five-foot-seven, with fair hair, and possibly wearing a scarf of various colours, including green and orange. He probably headed back towards the road."

"I will, indeed, Mr Holmes." He paused. "Is it possible he had a horse? He could have traversed the heath, possibly to his lodgings."

"I did not see any hoof prints in the area," I said. "Did you?"

In other circumstances, the policeman's disappointment would have made me laugh. "No, I did not," he admitted.

"Given the first description we were given, I do not think the fellow is wealthy. Horses cost money and I do not think he would risk arrest by stealing one. No, more likely he walked back to his lodgings, wherever they may be. He is obviously in good health, given the ferocity of his attacks, so walking a few miles will not bother him."

"What makes you think he isn't wealthy, Mr Holmes?" asked O'Brien.

"The witness who saw him described him as having fair hair."

O'Brien immediately saw my point. "He didn't have a hat! Few men would go bareheaded in this weather."

"Excellent, Constable! I have high hopes for you."

He flushed. "I will begin investigations at once and let you know what I discover, Mr Holmes."

"Thank you, Constable, but make sure you report first to Inspector Morton. It would not do to bypass the hierarchical order of the police force."

Before he left on his task, O'Brien dropped us off at the Rosslyn Hill station. We found Morton poring over a stack of police reports. "Mr Holmes," he greeted me with a smile, "A pleasure to see you so hale and hearty. And you, too, Dr Watson. Please, have a seat, if you can find one, and tell me what I can do for you."

Briefly I recounted the Megan Reid case, how the Hampstead findings suggested the same killer.

"O'Brien is an excellent police officer," Morton confirmed. "He is energetic, and he takes pains. There's a good mind at work there, too. Yes, I have that curious coin he mentioned."

He opened his drawer and drew out a singular coin. About the size of a penny, with a hard ridge, but completely blank.

"Have you ever seen the like, Mr Holmes?" Morton asked.

"I have not," I replied. "But I know someone who might be able to shed some light upon it. May I borrow it? I shall return it as soon as I have identified it."

"Well, since it's you, Mr Holmes." He handed it to me.

We left the police station a little after five. The darkness and the bitter wind gave the heath a forbidding air.

"Where to now, Holmes?" Watson said as he tightened his scarf.

"I think a brief visit to the nursing facility in South Hill Park Gardens. I should like to hear what that matron has to say."

Taking our cue from the locals, we cut across the grass. The bitter cold made me glad I had remembered my gloves. The orange sky cast gold and purple streaks over the heath and already in the distance I could see the lights of the city appear.

As we walked, Watson said, "By the way, Holmes, how can you be sure our killer did not own a hat? Some men simply dislike wearing them."

"True. It may be that the fellow is just such an individual, though few men are so hardy they would expose their bare heads to such savage elements. However, I suspect he followed the two nurses from South Africa. Likely he had not anticipated such a journey and he may not have had access to sufficient funds before he left. It is supposition, I admit, but it does stand to reason."

"A man could easily pick up a hat for a few pennies at a bazaar or sale of work."

"If he is a foreigner, he may not know that. Besides, I suspect he's trying to remain as inconspicuous as possible."

*

The redbrick monstrosity called Hampstead Health squatted on the hill. The scattering of bare trees that surrounded it did nothing to alleviate its air of institutional despair.

We were shown into the administrative office by a harried nurse. After waiting some twenty minutes, the matron finally joined us, a veil that resembled a swan in flight fluttering on her head. She exuded all the warmth of a cadaver.

I introduced us and she sniffed in disdain. "You, as a physician, Dr Watson, should know better than to arrive at a health care facility during dinner. I can give you ten minutes. What is it you want to know?"

Watson tersely explained our purpose. If I had expected any easing of the woman's martinet behaviour, I was mistaken. Her replies were brief, specific to that which had been asked, and she volunteered nothing beyond that. She would have fared well on the witness stand.

"Matron," I said, seeing Watson losing patience, "You scheduled Nurse Dixon's interview for seven o'clock, I believe."

"Yes."

"But I gather she did not leave until around eight. Did the interview take so long?"

"I needed to take a report from the night shift first. My interview with Miss Dixon lasted no more than twenty minutes."

"Did you mean to offer her a permanent position?"

"I did not."

"May I ask why?"

For the first time, she hesitated. "Miss Dixon had worked a few shifts for us on occasion. I found her clinical skills lacking, her concern for her patients limited, and her interest in the physicians unladylike. In short, Mr Holmes, the girl epitomised sloth and frivolousness. Furthermore, I found her explanation regarding her early return from South Africa, well, inadequate."

"What did she tell you?" Watson pressed.

"That she had concerns for her mother's health and felt her first duty lay with her."

"That sounds plausible enough, surely?"

"She had no references. One from her training hospital, but nothing from the Bloemfontein hospital where she had last worked. Of course, there may have been some administrative error, which is why I gave her the opportunity to prove herself with a few shifts. She confirmed my worst suspicions. Now, if there is nothing more, I have duties to attend."

She swept out of the room, the swan veil fluttering behind her, while Watson and I stood in a startled silence.

By silent consent, we waited until we were out on the pavement before we spoke.

"Charming woman," Watson said in his driest tone.

"How ever did the gentlemen of her acquaintance let her get away?" I added. We burst into laughter.

"Heaven help the young women who work for her," Watson added. "Nasty old crone."

"Oh come, Watson. It's not often one sees a cadaver walking around!"

We laughed again more resembling naughty schoolboys than esteemed crime investigators. I smiled to see Watson so merry; the weeks since he started working in the clinic have worn heavily upon him.

"I know you're in a hurry to get to the morgue, Holmes," he said when he had recovered his equanimity, "but do you think we might get something to eat first?"

I didn't have the heart to deny him, and so we found an inn on the periphery of the heath, and he ate heartily. At his urging, I managed to consume a bowl of soup.

With his appetite sated at last, we took a cab to the morgue.

The temperature there was no better than the freezing cold outdoors, though it still felt like a haven of comfort compared with the matron's presence. Alice Dixon lay upon a slab. Her soft golden curls forming a halo around her head. Someone had done a good job of cleaning her up, but the bruises stood out lividly against the alabaster skin. The boot prints on her face and neck, the slash across the throat, the many bruises and stab wounds in her body.

"She had been such a pretty girl," Watson said. "All that brightness and hope and vivacity cut short, and for what."

I bit back a sharp comment about his poetic observations, and reminded myself that this was simply the way Watson coped with the horrors of violent death.

"Let us try to find justice for her at least," I said.

In terms of wounds, Miss Dixon's corpse mirrored that of her friend. She looked about twenty-two years of age. In contrast with the delicacy of her appearance, her hands were

71

roughened, and the nails that had not been broken in her fight for life had been cut short.

"The hands of a nurse," Watson said. "Odds are she has evidence of back strain, too."

The surgeon arrived and nodded at us. "Let me know if you need anything," he said.

We nodded and continued our examination.

"Villain," Watson muttered as he examined the boot prints on the icy white skin. I counted thirty-two knife wounds, most of them between five and seven inches deep. Unquestionably, they had been inflicted by the same weapon that had taken Meg's life. I estimated the blade as at least seven inches long and sharpened on both sides.

"Perhaps a bayonet, rather than a standard knife," Watson suggested.

"A modified bayonet," I corrected. "Carrying around a full-sized weapon would invite curiosity. Besides, it is reasonable to suppose he used that same blade for his whittling. Impossible to do so with a full-sized bayonet."

"I didn't see Megan's body, Holmes; were the wounds similar?"

"Almost identical: the same weapon, the same savagery. Miss Dixon fared slightly worse, no doubt due to the improved weather and visibility, not to mention the more desolate location. Besides which, me must not ignore Factor X."

"The unknown?"

"Precisely. Perhaps whatever his desire for revenge, he may believe Miss Dixon more culpable than Reid; or he didn't like the colour of her hair, or her hat."

"Doctor..." I said, addressing the surgeon.

"Andrews," said the fellow, looking up from a stack of papers.

"Have you determined the cause of death?"

"The blade nicked the aorta. She'd have bled out in any case due to the massive damage."

"Any other observations that might help us?"

He wiped his hands on a towel and said, "I found tissue beneath the fingernails, the ones that were not ripped off. She fought for her life and possibly left her mark on the killer."

"Thank you," I said. "That is helpful. Well, there is nothing more to learn here. I have one more stop to make before we return to Baker Street."

As we started up the stairs, the mortician said, "Oh, and I do not know if it's relevant, but her hymen was ruptured."

"She had been violated?" I said.

"No, no; there is no evidence of bruising or tears. Indeed, I cannot say whether she was *virgo intacta* at the time of death or not; so many ladies these days rupture the hymen through a number of unrelated activities, horse riding, athletics, and so forth. I should add, however, that I also found scarring on the uterus — usually caused by childbirth, abortion, surgery, infection, thickening of the uterine wall. I'm sorry, but I cannot be more specific."

"What do you make of that, Holmes?" Watson asked when we stepped back out onto the street.

"We shall remember it. At present, there is no way of knowing if it is pertinent or not."

"Where now?"

"Mycroft. If anyone can explain this curious coin, it is he."

"Ah. I wonder, would you mind if I go back to Baker Street? I feel as if I'm flagging a bit."

CHAPTER SEVEN

Mycroft was in a meeting when I arrived, and so I spent a short time chatting with Gillespie, his ancient front door man. Ancient, but deadly, as I have learned.

"Any word from Lady Beatrice, Mr Holmes? When last we spoke, you said she'd been fair cut up over the queen's death."

"The news did hit her hard," I admitted. "For all their occasional squabbles, she held the queen in great affection. She is still with the royal family, but she writes regularly. Our king relies upon her good judgment, so he says."

"I wouldn't doubt it. She is a remarkable young lady and even your brother esteems her. I have heard said that the king is a genial fellow. He certainly seems popular with the public."

"The new broom that sweeps clean," I said. "Bea is encouraging him to modernise the country; the navy in particular."

"Excellent. They do say the king is easily influenced by a pretty face. At least Lady Beatrice's influence will lead him in a positive direction. I wonder he did not invite you to stay, too, Mr Holmes."

"He did," I replied, "But I felt I needed to stay close to home for anyone who needs me."

Gillespie's telephone rang, and he answered. After a brief conversation, he said, "Your brother is free for the moment, Mr Holmes, if you'd like to go up."

I found Mycroft at his desk though I could scarcely see him thanks to the stacks of documents and maps before him. It seems half the country is in danger of death by paper avalanche.

"Forgive me interrupting you at an inopportune moment," I said. "I can return, if you wish, but my business is brief."

"I can spare five minutes for my only living blood relative," he replied with a shadow of a smile. "What is on your mind, Sherlock? Do not ask me again to encourage the king to send Beatrice home. I have little influence in that quarter."

"It is nothing to do with Beatrice; you have made your opinion on that particular topic plain. It is clear I must be patient. No, there are two issues. First, I wanted to inform you that I had the opportunity today to examine Qualtrough's office."

Mycroft's eyes sparked interest in the lamplight. "Anything of note?"

"A set of skeleton keys. I made copies."

I handed the ring to him, and he studied the keys carefully. "I always said you would make a fine burglar," he commented with a smile.

Over the next several minutes we tried each key on his desk and the safe, but with no success.

Mycroft sank back in his chair in disappointment. "A shame. Oh, well. What an odd thing to possess. Did you find any papers?"

"Not the kind you mean. He is in serious debt and is overdrawn on his bank account. I found no evidence that he has or ever had your documents."

"That's something, anyway. Thank you, Sherlock."

"I'm sorry, Mycroft. I know how worrying this is. I should mention that our friend has a mistress. I am looking for her; perhaps she knows something. He has those keys for some reason, and I cannot imagine it is an honourable one."

"Hmph. Still, thank you, Sherlock. I am not so senile as to assume there can be only one possible suspect. You said two matters?"

"Yes, I wanted your opinion on a singular coin found near a murdered woman's body."

"Tsk," he replied. "The country at war, half the men away in service to the king, and you spend your time dabbling in petty domestic matters." From the smirk he gave me, I could see he was merely amusing himself at my expense.

He took the coin and tossed it back to me almost instantly. "It is South African," he replied. "Last year — June, I believe — the government in Pretoria issued a batch of blank pennies and released them into circulation before the evacuation of the city. There were blank gold coins produced, too, if memory serves."

"Thank you; you have but confirmed my suspicions."

"Is there anything else?"

"Not at present. Thank you, Mycroft. Is there anything I can do for you?"

"No, Sherlock," he replied. "Just keep an eye on the Holland affair, if you would be so kind."

Before I rose, I returned to a matter we had discussed before. "If this is more devious than mere treason —"

"I know, I know, but it changes nothing."

As I reached the door, he called me, "Sherlock, she will be home soon, I have no doubt. Indeed, I would expect her sooner, rather than later."

If it had been anyone other than Mycroft, I would have pleaded for more information, but my brother is a veritable sphinx even at the best of times. Therefore, I merely thanked him and left.

*

I saw no sign of Watson when I returned to Baker Street. Since his coat hung in its usual place, I deduced that he decided to lie down for a spell, I therefore took advantage of the peace to read the newspapers and catch up on the news I had overlooked during the past week or so. I read the reports of the two murders, but they told me nothing new.

I had finished reading the news, the gossip sections, and the classifieds by the time Watson joined me. He sank into his usual chair and sighed with relief.

"Did you take some rest?" I asked.

"A little, then I went downstairs to check on Mrs Hudson."

"Oh. How is she?"

"She is getting over the shock. I must say, the maids have been very good to her. I updated her about Alice Dixon. That's all right, isn't it?"

"Yes, of course. I intended to do so myself in any case."

We lit our cigarettes and relaxed in that peace that comes only from being in the presence of one's most trusted friends.

"How did you fare with Mycroft?"

"Productive. Which is to say, he confirmed what I already suspected." I tossed the unprinted penny to him.

"It's South African?" he said.

I smiled, pleased, as always, by his perspicacity. "It is, indeed. I suspect our killer's scarf is the flag of the Transvaal. Called the *Vyfkleur*, or the 'Five Colours', it contains green, orange, red, white, and blue."

"That certainly matches the description that artist chap gave you."

"Unless I am twisting the facts to fit a theory. I do not believe I am, though. South Africa is the one thing these two women have in common."

"Not true, Holmes," Watson protested. I looked at him in some alarm.

"What have I missed, Watson?"

"They were nurses. They may have trained at the same hospital or have worked together in Britain at some point."

"Ah, I understand the difficulty," I replied. "You have not read the letters."

"Letters?"

"The correspondence from Miss Dixon to Miss Reid. I have not yet perused all of them, but the dozen or so I have read make it clear they did not know each other until they met in Bloemfontein."

"Then I withdraw my objection," he said.

"Your caveat had merit, Watson, and I am grateful to you for making it. In point of fact, I would consider it a great favour if you would find some time to look at their correspondence, too. I would welcome a second opinion, and none is more valuable to me than yours, dear fellow."

"If I can be of assistance, of course."

"Excellent. I find much of the content tedious, relating, as it does, to domestic matters. You have far more patience with such things than I. Oh, you do not have to begin at once!"

But he was already making himself comfortable on the sofa, the stack in his hand. Within minutes he was immersed in the task.

As the night drew in, the cold became far more intense, and a gusting rain rattled our windowpanes. I read some scientific journals that had been awaiting my attention for several weeks and tried to ignore the restive feeling that seemed to have settled in my bones.

A little before ten o'clock, young Quinn stopped by with some news.

"Bugger of a night out there, Mr H," he said, shivering. I smiled at his epithet and asked Maisie to bring him a mug of hot cocoa. He sat at the fire, a blanket around his shoulders, and slurped away at the contents of the cup. The look he gave me, a look of complete happiness, made me chuckle. Nothing ever seems to get these boys down, although most of them have hideous stories to tell.

With the cup empty, Quinn set it carefully down on the side table and wiped his mouth with the back of his hand. "Cor, I'll last till morning, now! Thanks, Mr H."

We got down to the business for which he had come.

78

"So, I went down to Soho and did a bit of snooping, like you asked. Found that lady — well, 'lady' ain't the word, if you get my drift. And she don't live in Soho, she's in Covent Garden. Brydges Place, and not the good end, neither."

"Does Brydges Place have a good end?" I asked.

"I never heard of it," Watson said. "Where is it?"

"It's near St. Martin's Lane," I said, "just off Chandos Place."

"The narrowest lane in London," Quinn said proudly, as if he were responsible for its construction.

"In point of fact it is not," I said. "Brydges Place is one foot, three inches wide at its narrowest point, but Emerald Court is narrower."

"Oh, I know Emerald Court," Watson said. "It's not far from Barts. I remember a standing joke about Mulligan, the porter, being too fat to be able to walk through it."

"Yes," I said, ready to move on. "Continue, Quinn."

"My mate Dawson 'angs out in that part of town, you know what 'e's like for the theatre, and 'e reckons 'e's seen a bloke what matches your Qualtrough man's description two, three times a week, like. 'e comes to visit your one."

"She isn't married?" Watson asked, setting aside the letters.

"Oh, she is. Dawson says she's hooked to some fella who works for the railway. Gone for long spells, if you get me."

"Dawson's a good lad. He knows theatreland better than most. Do we know anything else about this woman?"

"Name is Mabel Burns, 'bout thirty, no nippers. Dawson reckons she's bored. I reckon she has ideas above 'erself, like. She lives in number ten."

"How well does Dawson know her?"

"Well enough, does the odd job for her here and there."

"Good work, Quinn. Pass on my thanks to Dawson. As Qualtrough is away for the week, you can focus your attention on looking for the fellow who murdered Mrs Hudson's niece."

I updated his information, adding what I knew about the man.

"He has blond hair, almost white, which hangs straight. He's not tall, about 5'7. Gallagher described him wearing a coloured scarf, possibly a South African flag which contains the colours green, orange, red, white, and blue, but I cannot be sure that he's still wearing it. He would have been thoroughly blood soaked in both murders."

"Both? You mean there's been another one. Cor!"

"Yes. He is exceedingly dangerous. Make sure the boys use all caution. If anyone spots him, on no account should they approach him. Just let me know at once."

"'Course, Mr H. You know us."

"I do, that's why I'm saying it. Finally, he probably doesn't have much money, so I suspect he's staying in a cheap hotel or boarding room somewhere in the city."

"We're on it, Mr 'olmes," Quinn said, as he stood and donned his still-steaming coat.

"Given how dangerous this fellow is, not to mention the inclement weather, I shall add a shilling to the usual terms, and an additional crown to the boy who finds him." I poured a handful of coins into his hand. "Make sure you share," I admonished. "And this half-crown is for Dawson."

He grinned broadly at me. "I'll see he gets it. This should cheer the lads up."

After Quinn left, I sat staring into the fire, trying to sort my way through the twin riddles of Mycroft's spy and the nurses' killer.

A sudden exclamation from Watson roused me from my thoughts.

"There's a third nurse!" he cried.

"I beg your pardon?"

"I just started on a new batch of letters with different handwriting. At first, I thought it came from a longstanding acquaintance of Megan's, but I see now that this woman is another who returned from South Africa. Her name is Kathryn Lysander. See, here, she writes:

> *No, my dear Meg, I fear I have heard little from any of our former colleagues, other than the odd note from Alice. Is it just me, or has she become even more of a ninny since our return? I suspect her mother's influence does her no good at all. She seemed fairly empty-headed in Bloemfontein — which is quite a feat, I must admit — but at least she showed the occasional moment of backbone. Not often, I'll grant you, but on occasion. But since our return, all her communication is about men, hats, men, parties, men, and, once in a while, just for the sake of variety, her quest for a nursing position."*

"Show me," I said and scanned the letter for myself. "It certainly suggests that all three women returned to England at the same time. But, why? This is dated nine days ago!" As my mind ran through the implications, I cried, "Where does she live?"

Watson already had the Bradshaw in hand. "Haworth in Yorkshire," he replied as he thumbed through the pages.

At my look of horror, he added, "Let me see, yes, all right. According to the Bradshaw, we could leave tonight; there is a train at ten and another at half-past-eleven, but we would arrive in the early hours of the morning and have to wake the village while we looked for her."

He ignored my dissatisfied expression and continued, "We can get the quarter to six train to Keighley tomorrow morning and be there by eleven-fifteen," he said. At my scowl, he added, "There is nothing we can do this evening, Holmes."

"Well, I suppose you're right. I shall telephone Morton and ask him to arrange for the local constabulary to post a guard on the woman and ensure her safety. I am afraid, Watson, very afraid that this Boer may be ahead of us."

I went downstairs to the hall and telephoned the Hampstead station. Inspector Morton answered almost immediately. He gasped when I told him the news. He agreed to alert the Bradford constabulary immediately to the dangers facing Miss Lysander, as Bradford oversees the Haworth area. He said he would let Thorne know.

I returned to our living room and found Watson half-asleep on the sofa.

"Perhaps you should go to bed, old man," I said.

"Yes, I suppose you're right. We have an early morning, and a long day ahead."

"You do not have to accompany me, Watson. I know you are in pain, and the steep hills of Yorkshire may put unnecessary strain on you."

"Can I be of assistance?"

"Always! You need not ask. I merely wish to avoid causing you unnecessary discomfort."

"If I can help, of course I shall accompany you. I'm sure we can get a carriage to avoid the worst of the hills."

"As long as you are sure. I admit, I would be glad of your company. Sleep well, Watson."

I sat up for a time, thinking, and a little after eleven, I heard a knock at the door below. I went down to answer it, the household having already retired. Inspector Morton and Constable O'Brien stood in the hallway.

"Gentlemen, you have news?" I said.

"We do, Mr Holmes," Morton said. "Forgive the late hour, but we saw your light —"

"Think nothing of it. Please, come up to our rooms."

They followed me, and I poured a measure of brandy for the pair.

"That'll keep the chill out," Morton said. "Your health, Mr Holmes."

I nodded but felt uneasy. Their late arrival did not bode well.

Morton began. "I'm afraid the news is not good, Mr Holmes. I sent a telegram to the West Yorkshire police, as you suggested, but they replied that Miss Lysander died a week ago. Murdered."

"Damnation!" I cried. "And with her, our last clue. It is conceivable that our killer is already planning to leave the country, if he hasn't left already."

"I have already alerted all the ports and have given them a full description of our man," he replied. "You need have no concern on that score."

"That is something," I conceded. This new breed of policemen continues to surprise me with their diligence and perspicacity. "By the bye, here is the coin you let me borrow. I confirmed it is of South African origin."

"So at least we can be reasonably certain that the fellow is a Boer. Thank you, Mr Holmes. And we do have some marginally better news. Constable?"

O'Brien placed a wrapped bundle on the table. "Following your suggestions, Mr Holmes," he said, "I checked all the areas surrounding the heath. The St. John-at-Hampstead Church reported a broken window. I thought there might be a link with the killer and went to investigate. I found traces of blood in the sink and these things stuffed in a bin not far away."

The bundle contained a makeshift scarf that had once been the flag of the Transvaal, and a black woollen coat. I took them into my hands. They felt stiff with the dried blood. I examined them closely. Even in such a state, I could tell that

83

the coat would fit our suspect. Sadly, I found the pockets empty.

"A man small in stature, but muscular, if these shoulders are any clue," I said. "He broke into the church, cleaned up, and changed his clothes."

"He anticipated the amount of blood," O'Brien said, "and brought a change of threads with him. Further proof that he planned this murder in advance."

"With three bodies, we need have no doubt of that. Who is handling the case in Yorkshire?"

"The first constable on the scene is Ernest Dalton. So far, no inspector has been assigned to the case, but it's being followed by the Deputy Chief Constable, a man also named Dalton. I'm not sure if there is a relationship there, but more than like." Morton shook his head. "How will you proceed, Mr Holmes?"

"Dr Watson and I had planned to take the five-forty-five train from Kings Cross, but there is no need for haste now."

"If you take the seven o'clock from King's Cross," Morton said, "you can change at Leeds and connect from there to the train to Haworth. Dalton will meet you and take care of you from there."

"It sounds as if you know Yorkshire well, Inspector," I said.

"Aye, my good wife hails from those parts. We visit her kin at least once a year."

"We will do as you suggest, then."

"Excellent, Mr Holmes. I shall send a cable to Dalton telling him when to expect you."

"Thank you, Inspector. By my reckoning, we should reach Haworth before noon, at the latest. We will see if we can learn anything of worth, though a week after the murder, I am not optimistic."

"I am sure Dalton will lend you every assistance," Morton said, "but do not expect the same quality of policing that you find here in London, Mr Holmes. Officers outside the metropolis are thin on the ground, and few have much experience in real detective work, so I am told."

"I am sure we shall manage," I said. Watson would no doubt be impressed that I kept my sarcasm to myself, though I confess I made several tart rejoinders within the privacy of my own thoughts.

The two policemen downed the last of their brandy and rose to their feet.

"Well, the hour is late, and we have the early shift tomorrow. We will bid you goodnight, Mr Holmes."

"Thank you, gentlemen, for your assistance," I said. "I shall let you know how I get on."

"We would appreciate it."

Morton picked up the bundle of bloody clothes and the two men left, looking quite companionable. I speculated that it would not be long till Constable O'Brien joined Morton in the detective classes.

I left a note on the hall table alerting Mrs Hudson that Watson and I would be leaving early in the morning and would not need any meals for at least the day. That done, I tiptoed into Watson's room and reset his alarm. I left him a note saying Miss Lysander was already dead, and we would take the seven o'clock train to Haworth instead.

CHAPTER EIGHT

20th February

I did not retire until the early hours, and I slept poorly, my dreams beset by images of bloody nurses and a distraught Mrs Hudson. Watson woke me at six, and I dragged myself out of bed. The staff had prepared a hot breakfast for us, which I had not expected.

"That's Maisie's doing, Mr Holmes," young Betty said, when I asked her. "She saw your message to Mrs Hudson and thought you gentlemen would like a hot meal before you left."

"She's a good girl," Watson said. "Thank you, Betty, and please thank Maisie for us, too."

She bobbed a little curtsy and left.

Watson and I ate quickly and by six-thirty we were in a cab on our way to Kings Cross. We had the carriage to ourselves, and Watson fell asleep before we trundled through Finsbury Park. I watched London flicker past the window. Hornsey, Wood Green, Friern Barnet. Slowly, the sturdy houses and municipal buildings became fewer, replaced by open fields, trees, and, at last, the sooty structures of Yorkshire. Somewhere around Peterborough, I, too, fell asleep, and awoke with a jolt as the guard called "Leeds! All departures for Leeds!"

Feeling unpleasantly groggy and addled, I followed Watson off the train. Thanks to his quick eyes, we found the platform for the Haworth train, and soon we were aboard for the final leg of our journey.

A young policeman met us at the railway station. He stood a couple of inches taller than Watson, with sandy hair and mutton chops. I took him to be about thirty, though his demeanour was that of a man twice the age. He stood at sharp attention, as if we were visiting commanders and he, the solitary trooper.

"Mr Sherlock Holmes?" he said.

"I am he. This is my friend and colleague, Dr Watson. You are Constable Dalton?"

"Yes, sir. Inspector Morton asked me to meet you and offer you any assistance you might need."

"Thank you," I said. As we followed him out of the station, I added, "What can you tell us about Nurse Lysander's death?"

"Not much, I'm afraid, Mr Holmes. I myself found the poor woman's body. She had a bit of a reputation locally, so I knew her by sight."

"What sort of reputation?" Watson asked.

"She was quarrelsome, always cross and fighting with someone. She got it from her father, I think. The temperament, I mean. Anything she saw as injustice or against her rights set her off."

"And her father?" Watson said. "What did he fight about?"

"Anything and everything. Always fighting with someone over nothing. Beat his wife and daughter every time he had a drop, and he allus had a drop.

"This used to be my dad's division, and he has many a tale to tell about old Lysander."

We reached the carriage, and he helped us stow away our meagre baggage. We climbed aboard and, as we trundled along out of the station, he continued his tale.

"He fell down a flight of stairs and broke 'is neck. Kate would've been about twelve at time."

"An accident?" Watson said.

"Who knows? I wouldn't be at all surprised if he'd had help. From what I hear, no one missed him. Then, old Mrs. Lysander passed about four years later.

87

"A few weeks after, Kate ups and goes, and no one hears any more about her until a few months ago. She'd changed over years, and not for better. Skin and bone she were, and her temper worse than ever. On top of it all, I heard that she'd started drinking. Unfortunately, she didn't limit her intemperance to gin; she went through a fair number of gentlemen, ah, companions, too."

"Let us speak plainly, Constable," I said, becoming irritated. "Was she a prostitute?"

"Well, that's the local gossip, like."

"How old was she?" Watson asked quickly, seeing my expression.

"About twenty-five or -six, I reckon, but you'd believe her a good twenty years older, if you met her. She'd a hard life, I suppose. Many of the residents from these parts could say the same."

"And her war experience, too," Watson added.

"I wouldn't know about that, not the actual experience, like. I heard she were a nurse and been to South Africa." The carriage made a turn and rattled on the cobbles as we climbed a steep hill. "Welcome to Haworth," Dalton said. "Unless there's somewheres else you would like to go first, Mr Holmes?"

"Either the place where she died, or the home where she lived before her death," I said.

"I'm afraid house has already been cleared, Mr Holmes. That landlady, Mrs. Merriweather, isn't one to let the grass grow, if you take my meaning."

"Could I speak to Mrs. Merriweather?"

"Aye, I can take you to her, but she didn't live on the property, like, so I don't know how much she can tell you."

Despite this caveat, he instructed the driver who immediately drove us in his rattling carriage to a cottage on the outskirts of Howarth. The woman who answered the door studied us with poorly veiled contempt.

"Mrs. Merriweather," Dalton said, "These gentlemen are Mr Sherlock Holmes and Dr Watson up from London, investigating death of Miss Lysander. They'd like to ask you some questions."

"I don't know nowt," she said, folding her meaty arms and glaring at us with naked contempt.

"Perhaps not," I said, "But if you could spare us a few minutes of your time we would be exceedingly obliged." I waved a sovereign before her.

She stepped back from the door and let us enter. As I suspected, she would do nothing for the sake of justice, but for some "hard brass," as she would call it, she had no scruples.

"How well did you know Nurse Lysander?" I began.

"Just to collect rent. Hardly spoke more'n five words to her."

"Would you call her a good tenant?"

"Fair. Never complained about owt. Paid rent on time."

"Did you know she had been a nurse in South Africa?"

"I heard summat of sort. No business of mine."

"Would we be able to see her rooms?"

"What for?"

Watson said, "To see if we can find out any clue as to her killer. After all, Mrs. Merriweather, if a killer is on the loose in Yorkshire, it's in everyone's interests that we find him."

That caught her in her tracks. She stared at him, but he held her gaze, good man.

"Ain't nowt there," she said. "I burned everything. But you can see for yourselves if you like."

She handed us the keys and gave us the address. In return, I handed her the sovereign. I held it for a moment before she could snatch it from my fingers. "What about her personal possessions, her clothing, reticule, letters?"

"All burned," she said, her greedy fingers grabbed the coin and clutched it tightly. "Didn't think it would matter."

Back we climbed into the rickety old carriage. I hunched down in my seat, pulled my scarf up around my face, and tried to find some warmth. The bitter cold in our northern shires always catches me unawares. I find that it gets into the bones far more than even the worst weather London can offer. I felt poor Watson shivering beside me.

We rode through undulating roads lined with rows of identical soot-coloured houses. In the distance, the land rose into bucolic, sunlit pastures, a sharp contrast to the grim buildings. The terraced houses eventually turned into a scattering of individual cottages. It seemed we were leaving the town, if town it could be called, and headed towards the country. The sheer wind brought tears to my eyes.

"Where are we?" Watson asked, his words almost unintelligible due to the thick woollen scarf that almost covered his face.

"We're on the road to Miss Lysander's home. It is just on the outskirts of the village," Dalton said. "It shouldn't take too much longer."

Nor did it. Less than ten minutes later we turned in to yet another small street flanked on either side by a row of dun-coloured terraced houses. The doors and windows were all closed — hardly surprising given the inclement conditions — and the street looked not only deserted but hostile. The silence was broken only by the howl of the wind over the moor.

We inched up a hill, not savage by Yorkshire standards, but it would have proved unpleasantly challenging for Watson had we been walking. I hoped he would not have to put too much strain on his legs and come to regret his decision to accompany me.

As we rode to the building in question, I said, "Did you examine Nurse Lysander's rooms, Constable?"

"Uh, not more than a cursory glance, I'm afraid, Mr Holmes. We reckoned she'd been done in by one of her, uh, gentlemen friends, like."

Although I did not expect much, I found the small house a disappointment. It was tidy enough; the windows sparkled, and the bare floorboards had been swept. However, to call the décor Spartan would be an understatement: a wooden dresser, stained and unlovely, slouched against the wall; a crooked table matched by two crooked chairs sat by the window; and a couple of long-past-their-prime armchairs lolled drunkenly by the fireplace. I felt that chill one finds in buildings long empty, as if even the soft glow of life itself has long been extinguished.

I searched down the backs of the armchairs, in the dresser drawers, and even under the bed, but all that remained of Kathryn Lysander's existence was the ash in the grate.

"I'll return the key to Mrs. Merriweather later," Dalton said. "Where would you like to go next?"

"I would like to see the site where you found Miss Lysander's body, and if you could fill us in on the details of her death, I would be grateful."

We returned to the bitter street and the waiting carriage. As soon as we were back in our seats, Dalton said,

"Not much to tell, I'm afraid. I found her about five, half-past. 'Twere nitherin' like today, though 'twere dry, and she were cold to touch. She'd been battered and stabbed summat wicked. I brought you the post-mortem report."

He handed it to me, and I skimmed the details before passing it to Watson.

Miss Lysander, it seemed, had several defensive wounds on both hands and arms. Bones in her knuckles were broken, suggesting she'd struck her attacker, and blood and tissue found under her fingernails indicated she had scratched him. She had not surrendered without a fight. The thought made me feel oddly proud of her. The surgeon noted 42 various stab wounds, contusions, and broken bones. A knife through the heart finished her. I saw Watson grimace as he read.

"I reckon she were walking home from railway station," Dalton continued. "Station master remembered seeing her around half-four and said she were alone."

He stopped the carriage a mere stone's throw from the Haworth railway station, and we alighted outside one of the houses. From the corner of my eye, I saw curtains twitch in the house directly opposite.

"There," Dalton said, pointing. "Half-way on the road. That's where I found her."

I had little expectation of finding anything of worth at the murder site, the event having occurred a week earlier. Still, I have been surprised before and have discovered clues at more than one crime scene several days old.

"Did you interview the neighbours, Constable?"

"As many as would speak to me, Mr Holmes. The watchword here is, 'hear all, see all, say nowt.'"

"Given that Miss Lysander grew up here," Watson said, "I would have thought they'd want justice for her."

"I'm afraid her recent reputation did her no good, Doctor. Yorkshire folk have their own ideas about how a woman ought to behave. I don't say they wished her ill, but they would have seen her death as God's own judgment."

"Many Londoners are no less harsh in their opinions," Watson said.

The street revealed nothing. Whatever secrets it had witnessed had been swept away in the rain and the wind.

I crossed the road and knocked on the door where I had seen the curtains twitch. After three knocks and a full five minutes of waiting, the door finally opened and a woman with grey hair and a faded pinny stood before me, her muscular arms were folded, and from the odour, I wondered if she had recently bathed in a vat of furniture polish.

"Good afternoon, ma'am," I said, removing my hat. "I apologise for disturbing you, but I wonder if you might be able to spare me a moment or two to talk about a woman who was beaten to death here ten days ago."

"I don't know nowt," she said and made to close the door.

Nonchalantly leaning against the jamb, I continued, "Perhaps not, but if you would indulge me. We have reason to believe that the man who killed her also murdered two other nurses. One of them a God-fearing woman who sacrificed much in order to tend our injured soldiers. If not for Miss Lysander, at least for the other two women, we need justice. This man will kill more people if we do not catch him. He is monstrous, Mrs.—"

"Wayne," said the woman. "Judith Wayne."

"Pleased to meet you, Mrs. Wayne. I am Sherlock Holmes. This is my friend and colleague Dr Watson. I'm sure you know Constable Dalton."

She gave the policeman a disdainful look and sniffed. "That Kate Lysander were no better than she ought to be. Still, the other lass were an innocent, you say?"

"Two other women, Mrs. Wayne. Blameless nurses, wanting only to do God's good work in caring for the sick and the wounded. Any help you might give us — to bring a killer to justice, you understand."

"Might be a reward in it," Dalton added softly.

The woman remained silent for a moment, before saying, "Reckon you best come in, then."

For all the grime of the exterior of the building, the inside sparkled. We were not invited to sit down, which distressed me on Watson's behalf, but I hoped we would not be there long and focused my attention on our hostess.

"Anything you can tell us, Mrs. Wayne," I repeated.

"'Tweren't much," she said. "I heard some argy-bargy going on outside and looked out the window. I saw that lass on the ground. At first, I think she were being helped by the lad with her; allus had a new man every day of the week. Trollop. But I saw him raise his hand and punch her. She were already on the ground, and he were kicking and slapping at her. Not right. No matter how bad she were, there be no cause for him kicking a lass. I went and opened the door, but he ran off before I could say owt."

"Did you check on the woman? Help her?" Watson asked.

"She were dead, like. Nowt I could do. I went to bed." She stood glaring at us, silently defying our condemnation.

"Did you get a good look at the man?" I kept my tone as unruffled as I could.

"At first, I thought he were a youngish lad, but when I got a better look at him I saw he were thirty if he were a day. Hair so fair I first thought t'were white. He'd a scarf, lots of colours in it, and a black coat. He were brazen, like, attacking her in open like that, and it still light enough a body could see, though I suppose he thought it safe enough, what with it raining so hard. He touched her neck for a moment before he ran off, and he spat at her and shouted something I couldn't understand."

"Why couldn't you understand?"

She gave Watson a long-suffering look, as if he were dense. "'Twere foreign, weren't it?"

"I see. Thank you. Do you have any men living locally who have returned from the war?"

"Most of 'em would be in infirmary, but you could try Mr Jessup in number 19; he's been home a month or two now. Don't know how they're goin' get on an' all. Her with five bairns and him losing a leg."

"Thank you, Mrs. Wayne. You do great credit to yourself. If we find this villain, I have no doubt we will have you to thank for it."

Watson gave me a look and I wondered for the moment if I'd gone too far, but the woman puffed out her chest and preened with all the modesty of an opera singer.

"One last question, if I may?" I added.

"Well, if I can be of help, like."

94

"You are invaluable, I assure you. Now, do you think Mr Jessup might be home now?"

"Reckon so. Don't go out much 'cos of 'is leg."

"My dear Mrs. Wayne, thank you so much. Your assistance has been invaluable."

"Just doin' my duty, like. I know what that is, unlike some." At his she gave the constable a scathing look.

I handed her a few shillings. I half expected her to test each coin with her teeth, but she merely dribbled them into her apron pocket.

We left the house and walked up the hill to number nineteen. I glanced at Watson, and saw his face set in determination, so I refrained from asking if he could manage.

It took several minutes before the door to number nineteen opened. The man who greeted us bore a face etched with pain, his eyes sunken into his head. He leaned heavily on a crutch and said, "What do you want?" in no friendly voice.

"Mr Jessup," I said, "My name is Sherlock Holmes. This is my friend and colleague Dr Watson, and I am sure you know Constable Dalton. I wonder if you can spare us a few minutes to discuss your time in South Africa? Your neighbour Mrs. Wayne said you were the very man."

"Well, I don't know…" His eyes glanced from one of us to the next. Before he could demur, Watson said, "Perhaps you'd let me look at your leg, Mr Jessup? I'm a retired army doctor. I've seen a lot of wounds. Perhaps I can help."

"Well, damn thing hurts like a son of a — well, that is, it hurts. Yeah, you can take a look all right. Come in."

The house mirrored Mrs. Wayne's in size and dimension, but in nothing else. Where the former woman's house gleamed, this looked unkempt and disorganised. Mrs. Wayne's silent home evinced no sign that anyone but herself and a presumably long-suffering spouse occupied the dwelling; Mr Jessup's home rang with the sound of children, none over the age of ten. At the stove, a weary woman tried ineffectually to cook and keep the children in order.

She packed the children upstairs while Mr Jessup sank into his armchair. With exquisite care, Dr Watson sat on a small footstool and unwrapped the yellow bandage from the fellow's left stump.

"Didn't they give you a prosthetic — a leg to help you bear weight — while you were in the hospital?"

"Damn thing never healed properly," Jessup said. "They said I mun wait till thing knitted over afore they could give me one."

"You have an infection in the stump. How long has it been like this?"

"Ever since the ruddy thing got shot off."

"Thou should have gone back to doctor, Fred," his wife told her husband, and added to Watson, "I did try to tell him, but some folk just can't be told."

"Doctors cost money." Suddenly, with alarm, he said, "Here, how much will tha be charging?"

"Not a penny, Mr Jessup," Watson soothed. "I consider it my duty to help all other soldiers, be they in service or no."

"That's reet grand o' tha, Doctor," said Mrs. Jessup.

Watson, no stranger to British idioms, rightly interpreted this as 'that's very good of you.'

"Have you tried soaking this wound in salt water?" he asked his new patient.

"Nay. They say t'keep dry, and I have done."

"Only until the sutures were removed." He frowned and leaned forward, peering into the wound. "When did the stitches come out?"

"Don't recall taking 'em out, do you, Sheila?"

"No."

Watson peered closer to the wound. "Well, that might be part of the problem; there are stitches still in there and they've become infected. I'm going to take them out and redress the wound, Mr Jessup. Just having those stitches out should help a lot. In the meantime, you try soaking that leg three times a day. Ordinary warm water and table salt."

"We can do that," Mrs. Jessup said, putting her hand on her husband's shoulder.

Watson removed the old sutures with exquisite care and proceeded to clean the wound with some liquid he had brought in his bag. Next, he applied some gauze padding and rewrapped the stump with a fresh bandage.

"This is the way to do it, Mrs. Jessup," he explained, demonstrating. "The idea is to keep pressure on the bottom and the sides of the leg. You see?"

"Aye, I can do that," she said.

"Feels champion already," Jessup said, smiling at his wife.

"What have you been taking for pain?" Watson said.

"He won't take nowt," Mrs Jessup said. "Says it makes him feel dopey."

"Laudanum will do that, all right. To be frank, Mr Jessup, you're probably better off without it. You can get codeine from the chemist. It isn't quite as powerful, but at least it won't make you sleepy."

Watson continued to explain about the medication, the wound, and so forth. The Jessups listened intently, nodding their heads, and asking questions. Not for the first time, I marvelled at my friend's patience. At last, he concluded, "I'll leave a message for the doctor at the infirmary. He'll make sure you are fitted for a proper prosthesis. Once that leg is healed, you'll be able to walk around pretty easily. You'll probably need a cane, but it depends on how you get on."

"Tha's reet kind of you, Doctor," Mrs. Jessup said. "Poor Fred's hardly got a minute's rest with the pain since he came home. Can we get you gentlemen something? A cup of tea?"

"No, we'll be going to get something to eat shortly," he cast a hopeful glance in my direction.

97

"Indeed, we shall," I confirmed. "In the meantime, Mr Jessup, would you mind telling us a little about your experiences in South Africa?"

For the next half hour, the man regaled us with tales about his experiences, all of it horrifying. None of it seemed pertinent to our investigation, however.

"I wonder, did you ever go to Bloemfontein Hospital?" I asked.

"Not as a patient, thank God, but I went to visit a friend of mine there, chap by the name of Carmichael. Nice lad, though he were from Lancashire." He chuckled; his mood vastly improved by Watson's ministrations. "You know what us Tommies call Bloemfontein? Bloeming-typhoid-tein. Not pretty as names go, but truthful."

"What can you tell me about it?"

"Well, 'twere a dreadful place, and that's t'truth. Carmichael were in Hospital Number Nine."

"How many patients were there?" Watson asked.

"Eighteen-hundred, I were told. I believe it, too. Men jam-packed together like sardines."

"Did you see English nurses there?"

"Aye Doctor, and Scots, and a few Aussies, too. Still, there were only a handful to cover the entire hospital and over three shifts. One lassie who were looking after my mate said she hadn't had a day off in three week and she working up to eighteen hours a day. Not right to treat them like that, but I suppose they were like gold dust, so rare and precious as they were. God bless them all."

"I'm sure the nurses must have had some leisure time," I suggested.

"A little, I believe. There were always tales about some of the lassies running a bit wild, it being their first time away from home, and them being a bit giddy like. I did hear that some went running after the officers and the doctors. We enlisted lads didn't get a look in." He glanced at his wife and smiled. "Not that I minded for myself, like, but some of the other lads resented it."

"A woman who had served as a nurse in South Africa died here ten days ago. A man beat her to death in the street outside. It would have been early evening during the rain. Did you hear or see anything?"

He thought hard for a moment. "With the kids in here, Mr Holmes, to tell you the truth I can hardly hear myself sometimes. I'm sorry. Sheila?"

His wife shook her head. "No, sir. Can't hear a thing with that lot gallivanting around."

I waved a genial hand. "Not to worry, Mrs. Jessup, Mr Jessup. Thank you for your time."

"Make sure you fill this prescription, Mr Jessup," Watson said, "and I'll have one of the doctors from the infirmary call upon you in a day or two."

He handed the man the square of paper folded around a guinea. Since I was not meant to see it, I took pains putting on my gloves.

CHAPTER NINE

"Well, Constable," I said as we stepped outside, "perhaps you can recommend an inn where the doctor can have a well-deserved meal?"

"You're welcome to sup with us back at the station, gentlemen," Dalton said.

Watson smiled. "This is just Holmes's way of saying he wants to sit somewhere and think about the case."

"Watson knows me too well," I said. "An inn will do nicely."

"Would you care to join us, Constable?" Watson said, smirking. He knows full-well I do not enjoy having my processes interrupted by strangers.

"Thank you, no. I should check in with the station. Why don't I drop you off at the inn in Haworth and come back for you in an hour or so?"

"Actually, we need to call in at the infirmary after we eat," Watson said.

"That's in Shipley," Dalton said. "You can take the train, and the infirmary is about fifteen minutes' walk from station." A moment later, he added, "May I ask one question, Mr Holmes?"

"Please do."

"Well, the killer, he followed her from the railway station. Why didn't he attack her in her home where he wouldn't have any witnesses? Why kill her in the street?"

"An excellent question, Constable," I said. "Though I cannot say with complete certainty, I believe the answer lies in the surgeon's report. No doubt you observed that Nurse Lysander bore a number of defensive wounds on her face and arms. I believe she realised someone was following her and

100

she confronted him. She seems to have been a forthright young woman, not given to hysterics. Once she challenged him, he panicked, or his fury overcame him, and he attacked her right where she stood."

"Yes. Yes, that makes sense. Thank you, Mr Holmes."

We climbed back into the carriage and resumed our bumpy journey through the cobbled streets of Haworth. We passed the railway station and only a few moments later came to a pleasant looking inn.

Dalton gave us directions to the infirmary on Fell Lane in Shipley before he departed. He assured us that he would be available if we needed further assistance.

*

My cheeks tingled as the warmth of the inn touched my cold skin. The soft yellow lamp light felt oddly soothing after so long travelling around the harsh Yorkshire streets. A low hum of conversation filtered from the corner where a small group of men, regulars by the looks of them, sat drinking their pints. They nodded in response to my "good day," and then resumed their conversation. Their eyes continued to observe us over the tops of their drinking glasses, but they otherwise ignored us as befits good Yorkshire men with strangers.

Leaving Watson sitting at a table near the fire unfurling his scarf, I went up to the counter to order. The innkeeper, a jovial, rotund fellow with a bald head who waddled rather than walked, served us a couple of glasses of hot rum, and, in response to my questions, said his wife would be happy to put together a meal for us.

The food, when it came, smelled meaty and tasty, and Watson did justice to it.

"It's excellent," he said. "You sure you don't want a plate?"

"This soup is perfectly adequate," I replied. I did not have to add that I would not have ordered even that much except to avoid his usual chiding.

As Watson concentrated on his meal, I pondered everything we had learned so far about the killer. What hate had compelled him to travel all the way from South Africa to England, I wondered. What sins, real or imagined, had those nurses committed to inspire such fury?

When at last Watson pushed his empty plate away, he said, "This journey seems to have been a waste of time. We haven't accomplished anything."

"On the contrary, Watson," I said, "We have confirmed the killer is the same man. And you did much good for Mr Jessup, I have no doubt."

"Poor chap. I hope so. There but for the grace of God, Holmes."

After a robust cup of coffee, sated, and sufficiently thawed, Watson and I ventured back out into the hills of Haworth. The innkeeper agreed to store our bags until we returned, so at least we would not have to worry about carrying them about.

Fortunately, it took no more than a few minutes to walk to the railway station. Dalton had been prescient enough to provide us with a rudimentary time table and, as a result, our wait for the next train to Shipley took no more than five minutes. The train journey took not much longer. Soon we alighted on the platform in Shipley, following the constable's precise directions.

We found the infirmary located in a wing of the workhouse. It dominated the road, a forbidding, mid-eighteenth century brick structure with sharp, pointed roofs and tall chimneys. I thought it as unappealing as any institution of its sort.

The porter at the gatehouse directed us and suggested we ask for Dr Olivetti, the physician primarily responsible for the care of wounded soldiers.

The open Nightingale ward housed maybe thirty beds, all nestled cheek-by-jowl. Watson said, *sotto voce*, "Terribly unsanitary. Such a risk of infection."

Every bed was occupied. The patients, all of them young men under the age of thirty, lay with shattered bodies, moaning, weeping, pleading for help. Worse were the ones who lay in blank-faced silence, nothing but the shells of their broken bodies remaining.

Instantly, Watson began to move around the ward, lending whatever comfort or aid he might. I stood, feeling rather useless, in the doorway, until a harried nurse asked if I needed help.

I asked her where Dr Olivetti could be found. She nodded her head towards the end of the ward. I observed a weary man who seemed rather more weathered than his years, hair as grey as his hollowed cheeks, and a short, pointed beard. He was busy examining a legless soldier, assisted by a young woman dressed in the traditional garb of the Nightingale nurse, a dark gown covered with a white apron and a white veil on her head of brown hair. I waited until he completed his examination.

"May I help you?" the doctor asked, not even looking up from the notes he was writing in a chart.

"I am Sherlock Holmes," I replied. "I am looking into the murder of Nurse Kathryn Lysander."

He shook his head sharply. "I cannot speak to you now," he said. "My attention must be on my patients."

"I understand. Perhaps after your shift? My colleague, Dr Watson, and I would be happy to take you to dinner, perhaps in Haworth? We shall be staying in the inn near the station."

The threads on the cuffs of his jacket and the worn appearance of his shoes assured me a free dinner would be welcome. As I expected, he nodded.

"My shift ends at seven o'clock. I could meet you at the Haworth Inn a short while after. Forgive me if I am late; my shifts tend to be unpredictable."

"I quite understand. My friend, Dr Watson, is also a physician. I am used to the demands upon his time. In the meantime, may he and I visit with your patients?"

"Yes, they would be happy to have visitors. Most of them never see anyone but the staff, I fear."

"Thank you, Doctor. We shall see you this evening."

I returned to the ward and observed Watson changing the dressing on the stump of some poor fellow who had lost not only a leg but his sight. It occurred to me that this is what my friend deals with so often in his work. No wonder he has lately been so fatigued and down in spirit.

Not having his skill, either medical or social, I helped the nurses change bedlinen, turn patients, and even managed to feed a couple of the poor blighters. As I did so, I endeavoured to make conversation, though this is not my forte. Although Dr Olivetti had urged me not to discuss the war, several of the men seemed unable to talk of anything else. I didn't need to ask questions; the information surged from them.

They formed a cluster, talking over one another, agreeing with statements and adding their own stories. They spoke of their companies and the companions who had fallen at their side; the terrible campaigns, Ladysmith, Mafeking, and Pretoria; and the hideous heat and environment of South Africa. They spoke of the butchery of the Boer, the poisoned bullets they used.

"What was the medical care like?" I asked.

"All right for what there was of it," one of the fellows said. "Just not enough staff. Had to wait for days to be seen by a doctor when I was brought to the aid station."

104

"That's this ruddy war," another piped in. "Never enough of anything."

"The medical trains were first rate, though," a tow-haired lad added. "And the boat coming home."

"Still," said a third, a red-headed young chap with a mass of freckles on his ghostly white face, "the nurses were angels, every man-jack of them. Worked like dogs they did, too. Filthy jobs they had, cleaning wounds with maggots, fellows with limbs blown off and full of infection, and not a word of complaint from any of them."

"Lying around with open wounds," said the first fellow, "and the flies everywhere. I'm surprised any of us survived."

"Were you in any of the hospitals there?" I asked.

"Aye," said the redhead. "I were in Bloemfontein, God help me. Too many patients, not enough staff."

"There was a nurse who worked here as well as in Bloemfontein, Kathryn Lysander," I said. "Did you know her?"

"Nay, lad. I were shot up too bad to pay much heed of anyone."

"Is that yon lass who were murdered?" said the bigger man. "Aye, I knew her. Knew of her, I should say. Got sent home in some scandal. Very hush-hush it were."

"A scandal?"

"Something to do with dereliction of duty. A few of them there were, all sent packing because they'd gone to some do the officers were having. Poor things. After working their backs to breaking, I warrant a little dance would be just what they needed."

"Aye," put in the third man, "But that weren't at the hospital; that were at one of the camps."

"Do you know which one?"

He shook his head. "It were just gossip, like."

By late afternoon, I could see Watson flagging. Over his protests, I insisted we leave. I suggested that we find a place to stay for the night and that he should rest before we met with Dr Olivetti.

The members of the nursing staff were vocal in their appreciation of our assistance, though I felt that I, at least, had done little enough. Silently, we trudged back up the blustery road to the railway station and caught the next train to Haworth. Fortunately, the inn had a pair of rooms available for the night, and we sat drinking mulled wine as they were prepared for us.

"Poor blighters," Watson said, remembering the patients. "I am sick of death and disease and being unable to alleviate the misery in men's lives."

"You made a difference today, Watson. You improved the lives of those men immeasurably, not to mention how much you helped poor Jessup; he and his wife will never forget your kindness. And that's to say nothing of how invaluable you are to me."

He nodded and continued to sip from his glass. He cleared his throat before saying, "That's kind of you, Holmes. Thank you."

The innkeeper, at that moment, informed us that our rooms were ready. Upstairs we found a charming sitting room, with a hearty fire in the grate, and two single bedrooms on either side.

"What time is it?" Watson asked.

"A few minutes to six."

"I think I will lie down for a bit. I'll see you at seven, Holmes."

Although I did not feel tired, I, too, lay down on the comfortable bed in my room for a time, letting my mind lift and examine each element of the case that we had learned thus far. As often happens when my mind is engaged, time passed with extraordinary speed. Within a matter of moments, it seemed, Watson knocked on my door and said we should expect Olivetti shortly.

Downstairs, we found a table near the window and ordered mulled wine. The wind rattled the signs outside the shops and howled as it sought the moor.

"Wuthering," Watson muttered.

"I beg your pardon?"

"The wind. It's called 'wuthering' in these parts. You know, like *Wuthering Heights*. I know you've heard of it, Holmes. Mrs Hudson spent an entire week talking about it last Easter."

At my annoyed expression he merely chuckled. Before I could respond, Dr Olivetti arrived, grey-faced and haggard. He eased himself into the seat facing the window with the wincing stiffness of a man twice his age.

"A long day," Watson said, sympathetically.

"They're all long," Olivetti replied.

"I hope you will be able to relax and enjoy the evening. What would you like to drink? Indulge yourself; Holmes is a generous host."

I sucked in my cheeks, but I was not truly annoyed.

We ordered our meals and the two doctors talked about medicine and some of the latest innovations as we waited.

"As I mentioned at the infirmary, we are looking into the murder of Nurse Lysander," I told him. "I believe you knew her?"

"Yes, a little. She worked on my ward most of the time."

"Did she work full time?" Watson said.

"No. I think she had some personal problems. I suspect her experiences during the war caused her considerable distress. Many found her quiet to the point of being taciturn, and she could be argumentative, but the patients adored her. She seemed to genuinely care about them, and they could tell."

"The ones we spoke to today didn't seem to know her," Watson said.

"Most of them arrived since her death; we have a high turnover of patients. As soon as we get them stabilized, they are discharged. Also, many patients don't know the names of the night shift nurses. Often, they have nicknames. They called Lysander 'Darling Katie.'"

"She worked nights by choice?"

"Yes. She told me once that she had difficulty sleeping so she might as well work. I suspect she suffered from nightmares."

"Not unusual for anyone who has been on a war front," Watson said.

"I understood she'd been on her way home from working an evening shift when she was murdered," I said. "I presume that she had not worked the previous night shift?"

"She worked a double; that is, two shifts back-to-back, from 9 p.m. the night before, to 4 p.m. the following afternoon. She always seemed short of money. There were rumours that she drank, though to be fair, I never saw signs of it when she worked. In any event, she had been glad of the extra hours."

"Did she have any particular friends; someone she might have confided in?"

"I'm afraid I have no idea. As I'm sure you know, Dr Watson, the night shift is not popular among staff. Consequently, we seldom have the same nurses on for more than a week at a time. It doesn't really facilitate the forming of friendships, though that may have happened eventually. In any case, Lysander tended to be truculent. She had no patience with staff who did not properly understand the conditions in South Africa."

"Did that include you, Doctor?" I asked.

"I'm afraid so," he said, smiling. "She told me once that since I had not served in South Africa, I could have no real understanding of the needs of the patients."

"I cannot in good conscience disagree," Watson said. "One may understand the mechanics of the wound or illness, but without having spent time in a war zone, one cannot fully comprehend the enormous toll conflict has upon the combatants, like the poor fellow Holmes and I met today."

He proceeded to relate the difficulties faced by Jessup. Olivetti, to give him his due, readily agreed to look in on the man and provide whatever care he needed.

Seeing Watson becoming far too engrossed in his memories of his own war, I made a concerted effort to change the subject. Happily, the two doctors were racing enthusiasts, and before I knew it, Watson was regaling his new friend with the story of 'Silver Blaze' and the small part I had played in his recovery. Happily, the evening ended on a much more cheerful note.

*

21st February

Whether because of yesterday's long journey, the bracing weather in Haworth, or the bedtime glass of brandy, I slept unusually heavily. Watson, too, seemed better rested than I have seen him in several weeks.

After we dressed, we decided to have breakfast at the inn before returning to London. We had just missed a train, and it made more sense to sit in the warm inn, than to spend an hour in a freezing railway station.

We returned to the same table from the night before and ordered a substantial meal for Watson; toast and coffee for me.

We had scarcely begun our meal, when a middle-aged woman approached us.

"Mr Sherlock Holmes?" said she.

"I am Sherlock Holmes; this is my friend, Doctor Watson. How may we be of assistance, Miss—?"

109

"Mrs. Elsie King," she replied. "Dr Olivetti mentioned this morning that you were looking for someone who knew Kathryn Lysander. I probably spent more time with her than anyone else. If you have any questions, I will do my best to answer them."

"We would be most grateful," I said. "Please join us. Can I get you some coffee or something to eat?"

"No, thank you. I shall have breakfast when I go home."

"You work at the infirmary?" I said.

"Yes. I am night sister. Nurse Lysander and I often worked together."

"Did she talk about her experiences in South Africa?"

"Not often, but once or twice she made some reference to it, such as if a wound reminded her of one that she had seen in Bloemfontein, either in the hospital or in one of the camps there. She seldom discussed the subject other than in passing, except once."

"She worked in the camps as well as the hospital?" Watson asked.

"From what she said, I gather that a few of the nurses did. I don't know if it was standard practice or a temporary measure. From what Nurse Lysander said, I gather the number of Boer, mostly women and children, arrived in large numbers every day. Unfortunately, many of them were ill and needed medical care. As a result, some of the nurses who had been assigned to Hospital Number 8 were sent to the camp. As you probably know, they both have a dreadful reputation, but that's not the fault of the staff, I am sure."

"No, indeed. I have a friend who volunteered to work as a doctor over there. He reports that everything is in short supply: Food, medicines, staff. Impossible to deliver appropriate care in those conditions. And these 'concentration camps' seem utterly wicked, though I suppose they were well-intended at the start."

110

"Quite so," Mrs. King said. "The way things are going, that camp will soon be bigger than the entire town of Bloemfontein. Nurse Lysander said that all the staff hated working there. Compared with the camp, the hospital seemed like a bastion of civilised healthcare. In addition to the widespread diseases — dysentery, typhus, and so on — they had little food and too many patients."

She fell silent, and I gave her time to organise her thoughts. She impressed me as an intelligent and insightful individual. Watson, too, seemed absorbed in the conversation.

"One morning about a month ago," Mrs. King continued, "I invited Nurse Lysander to stop home with me for breakfast. Poor woman looked stick thin, and I worried that she did not eat enough.

"As we ate, she seemed to relax. She commented that my kitchen reminded her of her late mother's. I thought for a moment that she would cry, but she did not. I've never known a stronger woman, nor one who endured more suffering. I believe her ability to feel so deeply the pain of others is what made her such a compassionate nurse."

"Did she tell you anything about why she returned from South Africa?" I asked.

"She said the service discharged her for abandoning her post. I admit, I found her confession surprising, but, then, I never knew her to be less than forthright. Apparently, she and a couple of other nurses had been invited to a dance. As they had worked for more than three weeks straight, often sixteen-hour days, they felt entitled to a break; however, their supervisors said they could not be spared. Lysander swapped shifts with another nurse for that evening, but unbeknownst to her, that nurse changed her mind and did not work. In any event, not only did the three attend the event, but they were gone for much longer than anyone expected. They did not return until the following afternoon."

"I'm surprised they found the energy," Watson said.

111

Mrs. King nodded in agreement. "Indeed. Lysander said she and another other girl, Meg, I think, were too exhausted to do much dancing, but a Nurse Dixon seemed to find new energy in the entertainment.

"Unfortunately, while they were away, several people died, including a woman and her young children. It caused a terrible fuss, and the nurses were charged with abandoning their posts and sent home. Lysander said that people died in the camps every day, and their presence would not have made any difference."

"Why were they gone so long?"

"According to Lysander, they were all so exhausted that they fell asleep. They returned as soon as they awoke. Well, once they found someone to give them a lift back to the camp."

"Was there a court-martial?" Watson said.

"I do not believe so. I assume the nursing corps wanted to avoid a scandal. There has been talk for some time about making nursing a professional body, and this event could damage those efforts. Besides, an argument could have been made that the nurses themselves were victims of impossible working conditions. In the end, I believe the women were given leave to resign."

"Did Miss Lysander know the names of the people who died?" I asked.

"If she did, she did not say so."

After our visitor left, Watson and I enjoyed another cup of coffee before walking back to the train station. Fifteen minutes later, we were on our way chugging back to London via Leeds.

"At least we know where the alleged incident occurred," Watson said. "And we have accounted for all the nurses. That's something."

"True."

I could not muster up any enthusiasm. For all my efforts, I had made no difference to the outcome. The three nurses were still dead. Nor did I have any clue as to the identity of the killer.

"You've done all you could, Holmes," Watson said. "With any luck, the police will pick this fellow up at the border."

"Perhaps."

"Oh come, my dear fellow. The information you gave the officials about this man's appearance, plus the additional facts about his scratches and bruises, should help identify him."

A short time later, Watson fell asleep, and I sank into reverie. All that kept me from plunging into deep despair was the hope that the Irregulars might have something to report, and that there may be news from Beatrice.

I sighed with relief when our cab dropped us at Baker Street. Back in our sitting room, Watson and I sank into our armchairs and drank the coffee one of the girls brought.

"I should go to the clinic," Watson said after his second cup. He made no effort to move, however.

"I see my role is to talk you out of it," I said, smiling as he harumphed. "Well, by all means, let me implore you, my dear Watson, do please stay and rest. You know, it is a curious thing, but I have often observed that travel is exceedingly fatiguing. Even when one does nothing but sit in a train carriage."

I had to laugh at his scowl. "Truly, my dear fellow, let me urge you to leave your work until tomorrow after you have had time to recover from our trip. I am sure you and your patients will be all the better for it. You can catch up tomorrow."

"Well, I am rather tired. There are enough staff to manage, and they will call me if they need help. Perhaps, Holmes, while I am at the clinic, you would be good enough to visit poor old Lestrade."

With a heavy sigh, I said, "I suppose I could visit Lestrade, if it would help you, Watson."

"It would," he said, smiling broadly. I suspected I had walked straight into his trap.

An hour or so later, Mrs Hudson brought up our dinner, some sort of curried mutton dish. We ate at the table, but Watson could hardly stifle his yawns.

"This is an excellent meal, Mrs Hudson," he said when she came to clear the table. "I wish I were able to do justice to it."

"You're worn out, the pair of you," she said. "Was this journey related to my Megan?"

"Yes, Mrs Hudson," I said. "We have learned that two other women who served with your niece in South Africa were also done to death."

"Oh, that's dreadful!" she exclaimed. "So someone sought her out?"

"It appears that way," I said as gently as I could. "We have, at least, a description of the fellow we believe is responsible, and it has been circulated around the ports. We are hopeful he will be apprehended soon."

"Thank you for all your efforts, both of you," she said. "I know you're doing all you can.

"Poor Megan hated the war, you know. She felt so sorry for all the people in her care, the Boers as well as our boys. I know she saw some dreadful things there, but she made wonderful friends, too."

"Such as Nurse Dixon and Nurse Lysander," I said. "Were they particular favourites?"

"She certainly spoke of those two ladies with great sympathy." She stopped abruptly. "Oh, don't tell me those were the poor women who died?" Her hand, clutching a white handkerchief, went to her eyes.

"I'm sorry, Mrs Hudson. Perhaps I should not have told you."

"No, no, Mr Holmes, I want to know the truth. It does no good to hide from it, no matter how painful it is. Oh, while I think of it, you received a parcel yesterday."

She handed me a small package, neatly wrapped.

"Ah, it is from Mrs. Dixon. No doubt it contains Megan's correspondence that we requested."

Mrs Hudson picked up her tray and turned to leave, but at the door she stopped and turned around. "I almost forgot," she said. "You had a visitor just after lunchtime. Lady Beatrice was disappointed to miss you, but said she'd return in the morning. She asks for you to telephone her if you will not be available."

CHAPTER TEN

22nd February

Beatrice is home.

I had somehow, foolishly, expected her to look different after her absence, but she is precisely the same. I confess to a sense of relief, but whether that is because she is unchanged, or because she is home, I could not say.

"You look well, gentlemen," she said to me and Watson, as she stood at the door scrutinising us. "Though, John, you have been working too hard, and you should know better than go walking up steep hills. Yorkshire?"

I laughed. It felt as if all the gloom and dreariness of the past few weeks were swept away in her presence.

"I suppose you deduced that from some remnant of mud on my shoes," Watson said, trying to sound grumpy, but failing miserably.

"No," she said, smiling, "Mrs Hudson told me."

"How fares our new king?" I said, when I at last stopped chuckling.

She sat on the sofa and removed her hat. "Torn between delight in his new role at last, and utter terror, I think. He has begun to doubt everyone and clings to old and trusted friends in hopes that they will lend him wisdom. Sir Francis Knollys, in particular. He is an excellent fellow, and the king knows him well."

"I am surprised he permitted you to come home, Bea."

"Oh, I am on notice that I may be recalled at any time. I am irked to find that while I have been held hostage in the palace, you have been having adventures without me. Oh, how selfish I am! It is such awful news about Megan. Poor Mrs Hudson is distraught. All that keeps her going is knowing

116

that you, Sherlock, have promised to find the culprit. How does your investigation proceed?"

I told her what I had learned about the case so far. She paid close attention and questioned me closely about every aspect. I have not been cross-examined so forensically since the last time I faced Marshall Hall in court. Bea expressed doubt that Meg would have been sent down in disgrace.

"None of us had a chance to get to know her," I observed.

"That's true," Bea said. "She arrived, when? The end of October, and she died last week? Not long at all. Plus, you and I were away in Sussex over Christmas, Sherlock."

"And I, for my sins, went to Scotland," Watson said with an exaggerated shudder, making us laugh.

"We must return to Sussex, Sherlock, when you have the time. Our holiday was rather curtailed by the queen's illness. Perhaps when the weather improves. John, you should come with us."

"Yes, indeed," I said. "It's a charming cottage, Watson. Though I should observe, Bea, that I have never heard of a fifteen-bedroomed cottage before."

"Fifteen!" Watson exclaimed. "Good gracious!"

"It used to belong to the royal family," Bea said. "The late queen gave it to my father."

"I'm lucky to get new socks for my gifts," Watson said with mock sadness.

"Oh dear," Bea said, wiping the tears of laughter from her eyes. "Again, John?"

He smiled. "Very nicely knitted, as you might expect. It's my own fault. When I served in Afghanistan, I once wrote home about the terrible state of my socks. It's been raining socks ever since."

"You do sometimes get scarves," I pointed out.

"And there was that, ah, interesting jumper," Bea added.

Watson couldn't even pretend to be annoyed. He laughed as loudly as we did. "Well, I suppose I should be grateful to be remembered."

We took a break for luncheon. To celebrate Her Ladyship's return, Mrs Hudson spared no effort in serving the best, the most delightful items in her culinary repertoire. Bea seemed a little embarrassed by the fuss, but she behaved graciously as always.

"You set a better table than the palace, Mrs Hudson," she said to our housekeeper's delight. "Indeed, if the king hears how well you spoil us, we shall hardly be able to keep him from our door. He has a fine appetite, you know."

"Oh, I'm sure it's nothing so special," Mrs Hudson spluttered. Her face turned pink all the way to her ears. She hurried away, all a-fluster, leaving Maisie to stare open-mouthed at Bea, until a sharp, "Maisie!" sent her scuttering after our housekeeper.

As we dined, Bea told us about her time at the palace. The king had insisted she attend any number of meetings with him. Despite her assertions of finding these boring, I had a feeling she rather enjoyed having a front row seat to such important events, and seeing her old friend finally adjust to the crown that he had waited so long to wear.

By the time we had finished our meal, Watson and I were breathless from laughter. Bea's anecdotes about the stuffy politicians and how they each tried to wrangle for position kept us entertained. After our meal, Watson excused himself and returned to the clinic. Bea and I sat by the fire, and she asked me about Mycroft.

"In your letters — thank you — you made several cryptic allusions to a case you are handling for him," she said. "Do I take it that your brother suspects he has a spy in his office?"

As I reviewed the salient points of the Holland case, Bea listened in attentive silence. Thank goodness she is not a woman who prattles.

"On the 25th of January, Mycroft received an extremely important document. He read it and locked it in his safe. As I'm sure you recall, this was just three days after the queen's death; only a handful of staff were in the office. Though Mycroft continued to work over the next few days, he had no occasion to open the safe until the following Monday, 28th. It was then that he discovered the document was missing.

"Before he could take any action, he needed to attend a meeting regarding some particulars of the queen's funeral. When he returned to his office later that afternoon, he opened the safe for some other reason, and found the missing document in the middle of his papers."

I could see Bea following me closely. She did not ask if Mycroft had simply overlooked the paper during the first search; she knows him too well to make that error.

I continued: "Mycroft had the locks changed on his office door, the cupboard in which the safe is kept, and the safe itself.

"On the 8th of February, he received another document on the same subject. He placed it in his safe, under a stack of papers, and even went so far as to conceal it in a different folder. The following Monday, he observed that it had been tampered with. Someone had removed it from the folder and placed it on top of the other documents.

"At this point, he asked for my help. 'You enjoy this unseemly business of investigation, brother dear,' he said. 'I can only promise you than I am not going senile, and I have a clear memory of my handling of the two documents. I can only conclude that someone has gained access to my office, not to mention my safe, and is taking these papers for some nefarious purpose.'"

I paused and I could see Bea's clever mind at work. "What is the nature of these papers," she asked. "Or can you not say?"

"They are related to the building of a top secret submarine, the A-1."

"That's the John Philip Holland project, isn't it?"

I felt alarmed that she had heard about it, and I wondered about our national security.

"The king," Bea explained, seeing my concern. "He talked to me about it at some length one evening. But I interrupted you. Pray, continue."

"You are perfectly correct. Any power in the world would be glad to get their hands on them. Thus far, there is no evidence that the documents have fallen into foreign hands, but that may mean nothing."

She looked bemused. "Why steal documents only to return them? Yes, the traitor may simply be photographing them and hoping to replace them before they are missed, but, forgive me, do you think something more subtle is afoot? Perhaps an attempt to undermine Mycroft?"

"That is what troubles me," I admitted. "Mycroft, too, though he will not admit it."

"How many suspects do you have?"

"The primary people on Mycroft's list are Henry Ambrose Qualtrough who is my brother's private secretary and has unrestricted access to the office, though not the safe; Edward Wainwright, the senior clerk; and two of the newest hires, a pair called McDuff and Burnett. They were the only staff in the office that day. I have looked into all of them but have found nothing definitive as yet."

"So, how is Mycroft handling this unpleasantness?"

"Stoic, as always, but I can see he is distressed. I had hoped to resolve the issue quickly. The longer it drags on, the harder it is on him."

"We will help him, Sherlock. Whoever this villain is, we will find him. You know I will help you any way I can."

"I know. I confess, I am very glad you are home, Bea."

She put her hand on my arm. "Worrying about Mycroft, then Meg's death following so swiftly, Watson being so preoccupied with the clinic, and Lestrade falling ill, I can understand why you have been feeling overwrought."

"A little, perhaps."

"I can imagine. I felt rather neglected myself. That sounds foolish, does it not? How can one feel neglected living in a palace with one's every wish fulfilled instantly? Almost every wish."

Refusing to succumb to the sentiment her soft eyes suggested, I proceeded to tell her about my exploration of Qualtrough's office and my findings. She uttered a theatrical sigh before replying.

"If he is the spy, you'd think he would have more money in the safe, or evidence that he had paid his bills," she said. "The keys are suspicious, though."

"Unless he plans to flee once he has amassed enough cash and leave his unfortunate wife to handle the debtors."

Though we did not verbalise it, I could see the same thought troubled us both: unless he had merely moved the documents to discredit Mycroft.

Bea nodded her consent as I took out my cigarette case.

"What have you learned about the other men?" she asked.

"Edward Wainwright, the senior clerk, does not have access to the safe, but he could have copied Qualtrough's keys. My brother says that his behaviour has always been irreproachable, but he was there both days in question. He is also one of the few who would know the importance of these particular documents.

"McDuff and Burnett are the most recent hires, which makes them suspect. They are giddy young fellows, part of the Eton set. They spend more time discussing tennis than matters of work. Neither has access to Mycroft's office, desk, or safe, nor are they privy to high-level meetings. As the most junior, however, they were ordered into the office on those days to handle routine matters."

"When were they hired?" Bea said.

"Three months for McDuff, four for Burnett."

"What do you know about them?"

"McDuff is the only son of Sir John McDuff, the financier. It seems that gentleman does not have much respect for his son which is a problem because junior is his heir. Unfortunately, McDuff had what might generously be called a decidedly average career at Eton, and he followed this with a dismal one at Cambridge. Sir John arranged for him to work in Mycroft's office in the hopes that this would help him settle down."

"And has it?"

"No. As soon as Burnett started in the office a few weeks later, all hopes of McDuff learning how to focus were lost. The pair are as giddy as a couple of schoolboys, but with less sense.

"Burnett had hopes of becoming a champion tennis player but suffered an injury to his ankle and that ended those ambitions. At his father's insistence, he took the job in Mycroft's office. My brother thinks he would have done well enough if he had not encountered McDuff. Other than his frivolous nature, I have learned nothing bad about him. He is genial, intelligent, and capable of competence, if not excellence, if he could settle down and pay attention.

"Despite my investigations, the worst I can accuse these fellows of is indolence and an obsession with tennis."

"It isn't even tennis season," Bea observed.

"Which suggests their flightiness might be a cover," I said.

"Yes, I see. So much for the staff; what about visitors?"

"The only ones who were present on both occasions were Lord Walton, Secretary Baines, Sir Cuthbert Redmond, and Malcolm Amberley. I am investigating them too."

Bea gave that some thought and said, "What about the people who wander through the building at various times, members of the public and so forth?"

"The office remained closed upon the queen's death except for those people I mentioned."

"Dear Mycroft," Bea said. "I imagine he's castigating himself constantly. A plague on the house of the villain who put him through this ordeal. How is he?"

"Unhappy. Not just because of this matter, but I fear the queen's death unsettled him."

"Yes. I saw him, of course, when he came to the Isle of Wight to see Her Majesty during her final illness. Unfortunately, circumstances did not lend themselves to much conversation."

"He told me that he saw you. Indeed, he believes that he had you to thank for the invitation to pay his last respects."

She did not respond, and I knew that she would have denied it had that not been the case.

"Thank you," I said. "I know it meant a lot to him. He's been feeling rather *persona non grata* of late."

"It's unsettling to lose a monarch who has reigned for so long. I suspect a great many people are feeling out of sorts. However, I know for a fact that our king is well aware of Mycroft's worth, and yours."

"Oh, my dear Beatrice, I am glad you're home," I said.

"So am I, I have missed you. I must say, you do look tired. All this running around cannot be doing you any good."

"You're making excuses for me." I said, trying not to sound pleased.

"No, I'm reminding you that while you may be the great Sherlock Holmes, you are also a human being who is, on occasion, fallible, especially when you are getting inadequate sleep and food."

"Oh, there is no lack of food," I said. "It seems everyone I know wants to feed me. It is vexing."

She laughed. "Poor man. People worrying about him and trying to feed him. Well, let's see if I can offer something of more use. How can I help?"

123

As Bea agreed to take over reading Meg's endless correspondence, I went to the Stirling Club, a favourite of Walton and Amberley. Since it isn't far from Covent Garden, I decided to cut through Brydges Place. While, as I had told Watson, it is not the narrowest thoroughfare in the city, it is, nonetheless, exceedingly narrow, inducing a sense of panic in many of the more sensitive people who use it. Of course, it does widen somewhat in the middle, but the height of the old buildings means there is only a sliver of sky visible in most parts.

By some good fortune, I happened to encounter Mabel Burns as I strode through. She stood lounging by her front door, taking the air, she said. I doffed my hat and bid her good day.

Smelling money, she asked if I'd like to step in for a cup of tea.

I apologised and said I had to go to a meeting, but I would otherwise have been happy to accept.

"Nice cuppa with a spot o' gin," she said with a wink. "Might make it worth missing your meeting, eh?"

"A tempting offer, especially when I consider what a dry old fellow my accountant is. Still, with so much money at stake..." I smiled winsomely (at least, I hope I did), and insinuated I would return the same way after my meeting.

"That's no good, love," said she. "My old man will be home in an hour. Not even my boyfriend is able to see me on a Friday night."

"Well, aren't you the popular lady," I exclaimed. "I'm surprised you would have time for another chap."

She laughed heartily. "Oh, they don't take much in the way of time, if you get me," she said.

"So, why do you hold onto them?"

"Well, the old man is b'cos I love 'im. Honest to God. That surprises you, don't it? Surprises me an' all. The boyfriend is rich. Oh, not as rich as 'e tries to make out, but 'e makes up for it by bein' generous. 'e keeps telling me 'is ship will be in soon, and we'll be 'unky dory."

"What's he planning on doing," I said, "robbing a bank?"

"Wouldn't put it past 'im; 'e's a tricky sod. But nah, 'e'd never rob a bank, too much risk, and 'e wouldn't be arsed to get 'is 'ands dirty. Nah, reckons 'is missus isn't long for the world. At death's door, to 'ear 'im tell it."

"Well, you be careful your husband doesn't find out about your young man."

"Oh, 'e knows. Not wild about it, a course, but a woman 'as 'er needs. Still, I'm all 'is when 'e's 'ere."

"He's a lucky man."

With that I went on my way. I had a great deal to think about.

*

The Stirling Club is on Regent Street, not far from Jermyn Street. Everything speaks of the richness of the name, from the sumptuous dark green carpet, the enormous silver-framed mirrors, and the illustrious clientele. It's not a place I visit often, and then only when I am in pursuit of some villain. Whether Lord Walton or Amberley qualify for that role, I could not say.

I sat at a table with my back to the window and let my eyes sweep the almost-empty room. The fellows on Mycroft's list probably would not show for another hour. The bartender, Josiah, brought me my usual watered scotch, I handed him a pound note.

"How can I help you, Mr Holmes?" he asked softly.

"Lord Walton and Malcolm Amberley."

His eyes swiftly scanned the room before he answered, in the same quiet voice.

"His Lordship just sold the company founded by his father, Walton and Son. Made a fortune, apparently. I hear he's retiring in a month or two. His daughter got married last year, and she's expecting twins. His Lordship plans on spending as much time as he can with the little ones. Funny, isn't it, how a man can have no time for his own children, but the minute a grandchild shows up it's a different story?"

"Quite. What of his son?"

"Young Eric? Joined the navy some time ago. Looks like he's on the fast track to high office. If His Lordship shows up tonight, you won't be able to get him to stop talking about how proud he is."

Well, that took Lord Walton out of the frame. He would hardly compromise naval safety with his own son an officer.

"And Amberley?" I asked.

"That's a different story altogether, I'm afraid. Got a bad diagnosis some weeks ago. Stomach and throat. Taking laudanum round the clock and still in dreadful pain. Won't live to see the summer, by all accounts."

"But he still comes here?"

"Not as much as he used to, but, yes, from time to time. You wouldn't recognise him, sir. Thin as a matchstick and half as lively."

Not for the first time, Josiah had been a font of information. I have never known him to be wrong. That being the case, neither of these men seemed viable suspects. My list is shrinking, but where do I go from here?

CHAPTER ELEVEN

When I returned to Baker Street, Watson had not yet come home from the clinic, but Bea remained at the table, working her way through the pile of letters. She happily joined me by the fire while I updated her on my discoveries and my theory.

"That would certainly explain a great deal. You had a productive afternoon," she said. "I wish I could claim the same. These letters are tedious; I'm not surprised you were glad to pass them over to me."

I chuckled.

"I am pleased you are home, Bea, and not only so you can take over the reading. I was thinking about what we were discussing earlier today, about feeling adrift. As I said, I have missed all of you, but even more — and I realise how nonsensical this sounds — I have missed myself, that is to say, I have missed my usual acuity and focus. They seem to have failed me of late."

"Fatigue —" she began, but I cut her off.

"No. I know it is what people think, and while that is undoubtedly a factor, it is not the heart of the matter. It is anger, Bea; it is fury. I think of Meg lying in a pool of her own blood, the savage wounds. I remember and I am filled with outrage. Seeing Alice Dixon's body, and reading the autopsy report of Kathryn Lysander's wounds, they fill me with fury. I pride myself on my ability to think rationally, on being detached and clear in judgment, but this situation has shaken me to my core." At her nod of consent, I lit a cigarette and took a couple of deep drags on it before adding, "Having to comfort Mrs Hudson on my own was extremely uncomfortable for me."

"I can imagine, but Mrs Hudson hasn't stopped telling people how kind you were, how she wouldn't have known how to cope if you hadn't been there. My dear Sherlock, there is no doubting the extraordinary powers of your brain, but I think you too easily dismiss the greatness of your heart." Observing my embarrassment, she changed the subject. "What about your new theory? How do you proceed?"

"I believe I know my next steps, but I need Watson's professional opinion first."

Watson did not return until after Bea and I had eaten supper. He sat down to a plate kept warm by Maisie and thanked the girl for her consideration. She seems a different person in his presence; the worried face replaced by smiles, the stammering silliness no longer in evidence. It's quite a talent he has to reveal the best in the fair sex.

I couldn't bring myself to burden him with my questions, therefore I asked him to stay a little later in the morning so we could talk. He merely nodded and shuffled off to bed.

23 February

Watson joined me for breakfast and listened carefully as I explained what I had learned yesterday and the theory I had formed.

"Oh, splendid, Holmes. That would explain a great deal." A light burned in his eyes as he considered the implications of what I'd told him. "But what a frightful notion if you are correct."

"We need to test the theory, but it's imperative we proceed with all caution."

"And take care not to alert the bounder. I agree. How do you want to proceed?"

Between us, we hashed out a plan. Although I longed to rush into action, I know the need for patience. I ruminated over our strategy for several minutes after Watson left for the clinic. His seat was not cold when Bea took his place.

At her insistence, I ate my breakfast. She entertained me by talking about a new piece of piano music she had been learning.

"The composer is an American called Scott Joplin," she said. "The piece is 'The Maple Leaf Rag.' It's a lot of fun; I shall play it for you sometime."

We were debating whether "ragtime" could be considered classical music or not and this led to a series of jests about other names Bea thought could be used to describe musical styles. A "ping" for stringed instruments, a "pling-plong" for a piano solo, and so on.

By the time Mrs Hudson came up to clear the breakfast things, we were in an extremely giddy mood. However, when our housekeeper told us that she had just spoken to her sister in Scotland, we immediately sobered up.

"I'm sorry it took so long to get in touch with her, Mr Holmes. It's such a rigamarole, you see. No one in the village is on the telephone, so I have to send a telegram to the nearest post office with a telephone service, and they send word to Braemar that I want to speak to my sister and arrange a time and day, and I telephone at that time. Well, it's a bit of a to-do, as you can imagine. Oh, hark at me, rabbiting on. Anyway, she will send all of Meg's letters to you as soon as she can. She says not to get your hopes up, though. Meg never mentioned anything unpleasant to her."

I walked the good woman to the door, thanked her, and firmly shut the door behind her. She's an excellent person to be sure, but she certainly can talk.

Bea remained at the table, continuing her tedious reading. Her puzzled expression drew my attention.

"There is something odd about these letters Mrs. Dixon sent," she said. "From that look on your face, I suspect you know what I am going to say."

"I think you are about to tell me that Alice's mother has withheld several."

129

She made a rude face. "You noticed that the ribbon had been re-tied."

I chuckled, delighted she had spotted it for herself. The bundle had arrived tied together with a ribbon, but I could see that said ribbon had been undone and re-tied into a smaller loop in an attempt to make the removal of some correspondence less obvious.

I sat at the table opposite her. "You can be such a child," I teased. "And yes, of course I observed the ribbon."

"Well, I have explored a little further than that," she said as she handed me a neatly written list. "You will observe that I have documented all the dates when the letters were sent. As you can see, Megan wrote to Alice every Sunday, yet there are at least three dates missing."

I saw at once what she meant. However, playing devil's advocate I said, "Isn't it possible that she had nothing to write during those times?"

"I thought of that, but as you will see, Meg referenced some of those missing letters in subsequent correspondence."

I went through the documents and compared the dates with Bea's list. She was correct, of course.

"There's something else," Bea said. She laid the exchange out on the table in chronological order, not only the notes from Megan to Alice, but the replies, which Mrs Hudson had given us. "You see," Bea pointed out, "It shows us the dialogue between the two women." She indicated four items in particular.

"In this one, dated the 11th of November, Megan says, 'I understand your regret; indeed, it does you much credit, but do not forget, dear Alice, the good you did, too.' As you can see, not only is Alice's letter prior to this missing, but so is the one that follows."

"The one dated the 18th. Yes. It appears someone found a subject too indiscreet to preserve in writing."

Bea added, "The question is, did Alice destroy those notes herself, or did Mrs. Dixon withhold them?"

"The re-tied ribbon suggests that Alice saved everything from Meg, and Mrs. Dixon removed several missives before she sent the bundle to us."

"I agree, though in the case of the note from Alice missing from Meg's collection, I suspect Meg destroyed it at Alice's request, but I have no idea why."

"Curious," I said, seeing Bea's point immediately. "What so occupied their minds? What did they, or, at least, Alice, deem too dangerous to be preserved in writing?"

"Perhaps Meg's correspondence to her mother will be more revealing," Bea suggested. "After all, a girl is more likely to confide in her mother than in an aunt, be she ever so kind. Also, we will have the advantage of following her thoughts during the period in question."

"Well, Mrs. Reid did not think they would be helpful, but who knows?" I said, standing. "We should receive them tomorrow."

Bea returned her attention to the correspondence, and I continued to go back over every detail of the case that I had learned thus far. So, for the next few hours we focused on our own tasks in easy silence.

I had finally finished reading all the crime reports, viewing the accompanying pictures, and studying the autopsy records when Watson returned.

"I thought you were going to take it easy today, John," Bea said.

"I couldn't rest until I made sure the men at the clinic were looked after."

"And once you got there, you couldn't help yourself from working for a few hours." She chuckled.

As Watson made himself comfortable on the sofa, he said, "How are you, Beatrice?"

"Glad to be back," Bea said. "I have felt of far greater use in the past day than I have in the whole of last month."

"Well, I am delighted to have you here with us again. Holmes has been like a bear with a sore paw without you."

"What utter rubbish," I exclaimed.

She smiled at me. "So, you didn't miss me at all? If I'd known that I could have stayed at the palace a little longer."

"I did not say so," I replied. To my consternation, they laughed.

"Oh, you make it too easy to tease you, my dear Sherlock," Beatrice said.

"I am glad to amuse you," I replied, my voice a little dry. I am not fond of teasing; I suppose I am not accustomed to it. However, I know it is not meant unkindly, and so I let the matter drop. Fortunately, my two friends settled down. Watson made himself comfortable with the cushions and began to read the newspaper; Beatrice continued to analyse the correspondence.

"Sherlock," she said about half an hour later. "Read this."

I took the page she handed me. It had been written by a woman in an elegant copperplate hand. She did not seem to be any of the identified victims. I read the content with increasing interest:

--entitled? I know what we all signed up to, and I have no issue with that, but you must admit that we faced far worse than anyone told us.

I am not one of those who believes nurses must be plaster saints. We are women. We are human. What we faced was difficult enough, without all that nonsense being added. Do you know I had one sister tell me that I should consider my hunger a penance and offer it up to God? What utter rot!

I'll admit, some in our group, Meg, for instance, was the very essence of the dedicated nurse. Alas, she is too nice for me to hate her! I jest, of course, but you will own she functioned on a different level to the rest of us. You, Kathryn, and I were just ordinary women.

"Where is the rest of it?" I said.

"There doesn't seem to be any more. I've been through these papers twice, Sherlock, and I cannot find another page with the same writing. I found this folded in the bottom of the envelope, as if it were an addendum added by the sender."

"Odd."

"Decidedly."

I fell silent, lost in my thoughts, trying to determine what had happened. My reverie splintered when Maisie came into the room bearing a laden tray.

"Ah, luncheon!" Watson said, rubbing his hands together in delight.

"It smells wonderful," Beatrice said, as she scooped the papers up from the table.

"Beef barley soup and some fresh bread, Miss. I mean, My Lady," Maisie said.

After the girl scrambled away, the three of us sat at the table and began our meal.

Bea and Watson were uncharacteristically quiet as they ate. Before I could open a conversation, Bea said, "Did the report of Alice Dixon's death appear in the newspapers?"

"Yes," Watson said. "We still have them, if you want to read them."

"What are you thinking, Bea?" I said.

"Just this: If a colleague of Alice's should have read of her death in the newspaper, it would be simple good manners to pay her mother a visit."

The idea resonated in me, and I smiled. "Simple good manners, as you say. You will need to know as much as possible about Alice and South Africa."

"I have kept up with the war news, perhaps more than most because Bertie — His Majesty, I should say — often discussed the subject with me. I can assay the part of the dilettante newly returned from South Africa well enough."

"And what about Alice?" Watson said.

"Oh, I will admit I did not know her well, but I shall say how kind and compassionate we thought her."

"Why those virtues?"

"Why, John, as a doctor, I am surprised you have to ask. She became a nurse."

He snorted. "Not every nurse in my experience is either of those things, though I concede that the Nightingale nurses are a breed apart."

"It doesn't matter; every mother believes her daughter to be virtue personified. Besides, I have read all those letters from Alice to Megan. That gives me a good idea of her character."

"An excellent idea, Bea." I leaned forward, eagerly. "There is some secret being kept, and I think this is the best way of uncovering it. I do not foresee any peril, but we cannot know for certain."

"I am willing to take whatever risk there may be," Bea said, "and I promise to be careful."

I felt by turns amused and concerned by her enthusiasm. I confess, I also enjoy donning a disguise and becoming someone other than Sherlock Holmes for a time. It is liberating. Bea, even more than I, I suspect, loves the chance to become someone else. Indeed, before our unusual marriage she often ventured out in the guise of a young man or a boy in her pursuit of a life less shackled than that of a privileged young woman.

We spent the afternoon making plans. Bea sent a message on her elegant "Lady Beatrice" stationary requesting a chance to meet with Mrs. Dixon tomorrow afternoon. The reply came to Bea's Wimpole address by return messenger. Mrs. Dixon would be delighted.

Around ten o'clock, young Quinn arrived.

"Watcher, Lady Bea," he said, bowing with an exaggerated flourish. "Nice to see yer back."

"Hello, Charlie," she said. "Have you been behaving yourself?"

"'Course! Proper gent, me."

They laughed in easy camaraderie.

"Do you have any news for me, Quinn?" I said.

He sat by the fire, warming his hands. "Not much," he said. "Ain't no sign of the South African, and we've checked high and low. We're moving our way along the docks."

"I think that's a good idea. If he's still in London, he's probably hoping to get a boat back home."

"Unless he's not done with his killing," Quinn said with that ghoulish humour so typical of the youth.

"I think if there were more victims to come, we would have heard about them by now. The police departments have sent word around the country to be on the alert.

"What about Qualtrough?" I added.

"Only that 'e's back from 'is week away and pretty glum 'e looked about it, an' all."

"Keep close watch on him, Quinn. In particular, I want to know his routes to and from his office, as well as any night time trips he might take. Get the other lads to help you. Around the clock observation."

"Right you are, Mr H."

24th February

This morning, after a leisurely breakfast, I went to visit Lestrade. As Bea accompanied me, the event seemed less disagreeable than it might have been. She arranged for her carriage to pick us up, which eliminated the quest for a cab. Soon we were on our way to St. Bart's Hospital.

We found the inspector in a bed at the end of the big ward. He beamed when he saw us.

"Lady Beatrice," he said in that awed tone he seems to preserve only for her. "I am so honoured to see you. Such a kindness! And Mr Holmes, too!" He wiped his eyes. "I am a lucky man to have such friends."

"Dear Lestrade," Bea said, sitting and taking his hand. "How sorry I am that you are unwell."

"Her Ladyship would have come sooner," I added, "but she spent the last several weeks at the palace at the behest of our new king."

"Imagine," he exclaimed, "spending time with the king. He must think a lot of you."

"You know, I think he does," Bea said. "He's a kind man. Many's the time he spoke up for me when I had a disagreement with his mother, may she rest in peace."

"Is that a fact! Of course, the queen was your godmother, wasn't she?"

"She was indeed, and she took her responsibilities seriously. Of course, as a child, I didn't like having my freedom curtailed. Our new king understood that.

"Anyway, enough of my nonsense; tell me, how are you feeling?"

"Oh, not so bad. Some pain of course, but that's to be expected. It's just so dull, lying here. You know, as a copper, I thought I'd seen it all, but I was an innocent until I came in here. The things you see in a hospital. Shocking! Just shocking!"

"I can only imagine," she said. "Are you being looked after?"

"Oh yes. The staff are lovely, I have no complaints there. And I've been lucky to have my share of visitors. You know who your friends are when you're sick, don't you? Some of these poor wretches have nobody. Damn shame — begging your pardon, Your Ladyship."

"Oh, don't worry about it." She patted his hand and smiled. They both looked at me and I felt helpless. Fortunately, Bea came to my rescue. "Did you hear about this awful case that Sherlock is working on?"

"Oh yes, Mrs Hudson's niece. Poor woman."

"And now we've discovered there were two other nurses who were murdered in the same fashion."

"No!" Lestrade managed to sit up a little straighter and his eyes glowed with an eager light. I confess, I recognised the symptoms. "Were they killed just because they were nurses?"

"No; they served together in South Africa," I said. "In Bloemfontein."

"That hellhole? Oh, I've heard horror stories."

"Have you?" I said.

"Oh yes. My neighbour, Mr Kyle in number eight, he was shot in South Africa. They treated him in Bloemfontein. He came home a few months ago, but he'll never be the same. He has some stories, I can tell you."

"Do you remember precisely when he came home?" I urged.

"Let me think, some time before Christmas, I know that. Yes, around the time young Roach got married, so that would be late October, I think. Does that help, Mr Holmes?"

"I think it could be the very break we need. Thank you, Lestrade. Do you think Mr Kyle would mind if I were to call on him?"

"I think he would be delighted. He spends most days alone, poor chap."

137

We left Lestrade looking very cheerful. As we left the hospital, Bea glanced at her pocket watch. "I should head to Hampstead if I am to keep my appointment with Mrs. Dixon."

I hesitated. I did not care for the idea of her going alone to see the bereaved woman. Not that I thought Mrs. Dixon dangerous, but something about her troubled me.

As if she read my thoughts, Bea said, "You really mustn't worry, Sherlock. I promise I shall be careful."

I looked at her, trying to see her the way others might: Tall, handsome, dressed in an expensive but understated grey suit, a stylish grey hat with a dotted veil, and over it all, a coat of finest sable.

"I haven't seen that outfit before, have I?" I said.

"No. It's new. French. My namesake, Princess Beatrice, had it made for me by her vendeuse. It gave us something to do. Something to cheer me up after my mourning period ended. Thank heavens I only had to wear black until the 22nd."

"Do you think you might do better wearing something less, ah, extravagant?"

"No. From everything you have told me about Mrs. Dixon, I suspect she is a snob. Her daughter Alice seems to have been a rather flighty girl; I shall present myself in the same manner. A dilettante in South Africa looking for excitement. She may despise me, but that will lead her to underestimate me." She smiled in her most fetching manner. I am, of course, impervious, but I confess I felt my anxiety slip away. "I promise to be careful," she repeated.

As we went down the stairs, I said, "If you behave, I shall treat you to coffee on the Strand."

She laughed. "And if I misbehave, you'll treat me to dinner."

I could hardly argue the point. Bea's behaviour is always unpredictable. It is one of the things I like about her. Odd, because it is Watson's unshakable dependability that I like about him. What a curious thing is a man; even the best of us is inconsistent.

"You have that pondering look on your face," Bea said as she pulled on her gloves. "Forgive me, did I interrupt your reverie?"

"My thoughts were of trifling importance. I was pondering my own inconsistency: I enjoy your unpredictability, while I rely on Watson's dependability."

"I may be unpredictable, my dear Sherlock, but I trust I am always dependable."

"You make an excellent point," I conceded.

Her hand squeezed mine. "I promise to be careful," she repeated. "Besides, a grieving, middle-aged woman hardly presents much of a threat."

"A woman who withheld important information about her daughter. Do not underestimate her, Bea."

"I will take all care, and you do the same. I'll see you later."

"Ah, that reminds me. I thought to see my brother later. Would you care to join me?"

"I should be delighted. Dear Mycroft. I have missed him."

CHAPTER TWELVE

Bea left me at the corner of St Aquinas Street. I watched as her carriage trundled away towards Hampstead, then I strode down the street looking for number 8, where Mr Kyle resided. It surprised me to see how picturesque and well-tended Lestrade's home appeared. I do not know why I should be surprised. His wife is a formidable woman and, by all accounts, earns a considerable fortune from her baking business. No doubt they could afford a full complement of household staff. The three-story, red-bricked terrace building boasted no front garden, but the black and white tiles that decorated the entrance to the house gleamed and a number of colourful plant pots added a charming touch. The curtains of white lace shone like freshly fallen snow. Everything spoke of taste, affluence, and comfort.

Number 8, across the street, presented a smaller, grubbier version of the same building. Its miniscule courtyard was piled with rubbish, and the curtains looked a dull grey colour, though I suspect they had once been as white as the Lestrades'.

I knocked on the door and waited. After several minutes, I heard the sound of shuffling footsteps. The door opened and a man who had once been young and hearty stood before me, grey, haggard, and in a state of something that may have been pain or anguish or some ghastly combination of the two.

His hands and neck were those of a young man, certainly under the age of forty, but if one judged solely by his face, you'd think him closer to sixty. His eyes as they met mine seemed ancient.

"Yes?" he said in a trembling voice.

"Mr Kyle, my name is Sherlock Holmes. I am a friend of Inspector Lestrade's. He asked me to look in on you and see if there is anything you need."

The eyes brightened for a moment. "That's such a kind man. Always ready to help a neighbour. Come in, do. Can I get you a cup of tea? I'm afraid we're out of coffee."

"Thank you, no, I just ate."

His gait was curious, he shuffled slowly, bent over at the waist, with his left arm wrapped around his midriff. As he walked, his body emitted a cloud of noxious gases.

He fell back rather than sat in the tired armchair and indicated that I should sit in the greasy chair opposite him. A thought, as unwelcome as it was unbidden, invaded my mind: There but for the grace of God went Watson. I supressed a shudder at the thought.

"Thank you for your time, Mr Kyle. I will not keep you long," I said. "I can see you are in a lot of pain."

"I'm always in pain these days," he said. "My gut's been all but destroyed. But I get by." He forced a smile. "I get by. Please don't rush off, Mr Holmes. I am glad to have company. Best thing for me is to keep my thoughts away from my own miseries. Tell me, how is Lestrade? I haven't seen him for a few days. Rushing off on some case or other, I expect."

"I am afraid Lestrade is rather under the weather, Mr Kyle. He had his gallbladder removed and is recovering in St. Bart's Hospital."

"Oh, the poor man. Never a word did he say about his illness, and he must have been in a fair bit of pain, himself. Always busy looking after others, he is."

This notion of Lestrade took me by surprise, I confess, but, of course, I don't know him that well outside his professional capacity.

"I should add that I am working on a case that has its roots in South Africa. Lestrade thought you might be able to give me some information."

"Of course, of course. Any help I can give you."

"I am looking into the murder of some nurses who worked in one of the hospitals and the camp at Bloemfontein. They came back to England around the same time as you. I wondered if you may have met them or know something of them."

"Nurses murdered, you say? That's dreadful! Who would do such a thing? Angels of mercy they were, Mr Holmes, angels, and no mistake. What were their names?"

I told him, and a look of dismay overcame him.

"Oh, no, oh that's dreadful. They were on the boat with me, Mr Holmes, and no one could have been kinder. Pretty Miss Dixon used to read to me. She had a rough time of it on the boat, made her sick to her stomach like, but she'd never complain. Spent most of her time looking out for us poor wounded blighters. She looked forward to going home, she said, but upset that she'd not been able to see the job through.

"Now, Miss Lysander scared me to death at first, but no one could be kinder. She took it on herself to change my dressings three times a day. Frightful job, what with half my guts hanging out, but she'd chat away about all sorts of different things to keep my mind off it. By the time we reached the dock, she'd become a big favourite, not only with me, but with the other lads, too. One of my mates, Jocko, said, 'I wouldn't want to wed her, Harry, but there's no one I'd rather have looking after me when I am sick.'"

"That's interesting. And Miss Reid?"

"Well, I didn't see as much of her; I heard she'd been poorly. She came out on deck once or twice but did not stay long."

"How did the three women get on, did you see?"

He thought carefully, his wound forgotten. "Well, you never saw three women more different from one another. Miss Dixon: all charm and prettiness, good for reading a book or holding a man's hand, but not so much with dressings and

142

suchlike. Now Miss Lysander for all her stern look, never seemed troubled by the worst of wounds. As I say, we saw little of Miss Reid, but she seemed to think herself a leader of the group; Miss Dixon, in particular, sought her advice and deferred to her. Miss Lysander didn't spend a lot of time with either of them."

"Did they say anything about why they were returning home?"

"Not that I recall. I did once hear Miss Dixon complaining to Miss Lysander about the way they'd been treated by the military and the senior nurses. Miss Lysander shrugged it off, but Miss Dixon seemed vexed. I never heard Miss Reid talk about it but, as I say, I didn't get to see much of her."

"Had there been much talk about them when they were in Bloemfontein?"

"Perhaps, but I was too sick to notice. I'm sorry, Mr Holmes."

"Not at all, Mr Kyle, you have been enormously helpful. Did you ever hear about some of the Boer dying in the Bloemfontein camp because there weren't enough staff to look after them?"

"No, I'm afraid I paid little heed to anything but my own health during that time. I will say, though, people died by the dozens every day there. Mostly women and children, you know. Supposed to be a place of refuge for them after their farms were destroyed." A look of anger flashed across his face. "That's us, you know, Mr Holmes. Our idea of British fair play. Burn women and children out of their homes and then round them up like cattle and watch them die in these camps full of awful diseases. Shameful, Mr Holmes. Not the Britain I know."

"I understand your feeling. Indeed, I cannot imagine there are many who would disagree with you. Is there anything I can do for you before I go?"

"I shouldn't think so but thank you kindly. My missus should be home soon enough."

He insisted on walking me to the door. As I opened it, he said, "Green might be able to help. Now I think of it, no one would know more about it than he would."

"Green?"

"Jerry Green. He's a reporter based in Bloemfontein. He knows everyone and everything that's going on. He's a decent chap, too. A man of honour, which is rare in his profession, I'm sure you agree. You could write to him at the camp and I'm sure he'll send you a full report."

"That's a capital idea. You have been of enormous assistance, Mr Kyle. Thank you."

*

I walked up the road and took a cab to Hampstead Heath. Mr Kyle, both his stories and his condition, weighed heavily upon me. If the fellow lived in the Marylebone area, I would suggest he attend Watson's clinic, but his being on the other side of the river made it difficult. Perhaps Watson might know of someone in Kyle's neighbourhood who might be able to help. And this fellow Green; if he covered the events in Bloemfontein, he might be an excellent source of information. I would send him a telegram as soon as possible.

These thoughts so occupied my mind that I arrived in Hampstead before I knew it.

I dismissed the cab and stood behind a tree not far from Mrs. Dixon's door. I had a long wait. Almost an hour passed before Beatrice emerged. Mrs. Dixon stood at the door, shaking Bea's hand for an inordinate length of time. I could not hear their conversation from where I stood, but the tone and their stance seemed cordial. Bea left, and the door closed behind her. She walked down the street in my general direction. When she came within a few feet of the tree behind

144

which I had hidden, she said, with some amusement, "Since you're here, you may as well escort me to our next appointment, Sherlock."

I laughed. "I am losing my touch if you could spot me so easily."

"Oh, you may console yourself that I did not, in fact, see you, but I know your nature. I looked for you when I left Mrs. Dixon's home. I thought you would be most likely to pick the tree for your hiding place."

I chuckled with delight. Of all the people I have ever met, Bea is the only one other than my brother I have never been able to fool. Not that I often try to do so.

We walked in silence weaving through the streets until we reached the Finchley Road where we caught a growler. Beatrice had told her driver not to wait.

"Whitehall," I told the driver.

Bea smiled. "I do hope your brother will not mind our barging in on his day."

"I daresay he can spare five minutes." I replied. "Did you discover anything?"

"I learned a lot about Alice and her life in South Africa. Yes, I think I have uncovered a lead or two.

"Mrs. Dixon greeted me warmly, and almost immediately began to ask questions about Alice and her time in South Africa. She gave me tea and listened as I told her a tale about working in one of the camps, and later in one of the hospitals. 'I did not know Alice well,' I said. 'But I could see she was popular with both the other nurses and the officers.'

"At that, her face clouded, and she said, 'The less said about those officers, the better. They were no gentlemen. All of this is their fault.'

"I cannot say if she meant the nurses being sent down or something else. I tried to eke some more information out of her, but she clammed up at that point. After a time, the conversation turned to the conditions at Bloemfontein, and she dropped her guard a little.

"She said, 'Worked to the point of exhaustion, they were, and no gratitude. Refused a few hours break. Outrageous!'

"She then added, 'I couldn't ever get Alice to tell me the full story about that night. She felt guilty about it, you know. I blame that Nurse Reid for being a bad influence.'

"At that point, I expressed surprise that Meg should be described in such a manner. 'Really?' I said. 'Everyone spoke of her as the most reliable and conscientious nurse who could be found,' I said.

"Mrs. Dixon reluctantly admitted that Meg might have only been trying to look out for the other women, but, she said, leaving the camp without permission was 'not the wisest decision.'"

Bea added, with some amusement, that this was as close as Mrs. Dixon came in expressing any criticism of her beloved daughter.

"'Oh, I know Alice shouldn't have gone along with it,' Mrs. Dixon added, 'but her nature made her more a follower than a leader. And probably they'd have had nothing more than a slap on the wrist, had it not been for those deaths and the Boer making such a fuss about it.'"

This certainly tallied with Mr Kyle's story.

I went on to tell Bea what I had learned from that unfortunate gentleman. She heard me out in silence. When I concluded, she said, quietly, "I may have misread Meg, or perhaps she behaved rather differently with her cohorts than she did with me. Or perhaps her illness may have made her meeker than usual."

"There are many possibilities," I said. "And you know, I still think we must not judge her too harshly. As Watson said, war has an impact on everyone. If the others were, as Mrs. Dixon said of Alice, easily led, Megan may have felt she had no choice but to become a de facto leader. She may even have been encouraged to do so by her nursing superiors."

"Yes, that's possible," Bea agreed. "Meg never spoke to me about her experiences in South Africa, except to say nursing staff were desperately needed, and that she bitterly regretted being unable to contribute. I suggested that with the proper care she might regain her health sufficiently to return there, or at least return to some form of nursing in Scotland."

"Yes, that sounds reasonable," I said, then added, "but I admit, I know nothing about nursing as a form of employment. Surely there must have been some jobs that even she would be able to manage?"

Bea nodded. "I thought so, too. Megan said that while all the doctors she had seen agreed she would never be up to the rigors of nursing again, she had excellent references from the nursing sisters with whom she had worked, as well as several physicians. In fact, one of the sisters in South Africa had arranged a position for her in a Dumfries hospital. It was, Meg said, less arduous and more appropriate for her condition."

"That's interesting," I said. "I surmise she remained on good terms with some of the staff at least."

"I thought so too," Bea said. "Here's what puzzles me, though: Meg implied that she had been sent home because of her health. She never mentioned any misconduct."

"Well, not all people are as forthright as Miss Lysander," I said. "Under the circumstances, I suppose I cannot condemn either Reid or Dixon for dissembling about the reason for their return. Indeed, if they believed themselves to be the injured parties, they may well have thought their silence was justified. In Megan's case, in particular, I suspect she may have resented the toll her service had on her health, and I cannot say I blame her."

Bea fell into a brown study, and I indulged myself in observing her. How remarkable that it is almost four years since I met her. When did she become so essential to my — I

147

will not say happiness. Equilibrium, then. Between her and Watson, I feel balanced. A clock whose pendulum has been finely calibrated. Not, of course, that I need either of them. I functioned extremely well on my own for a significant portion of my life. I could again; I merely choose not to.

She raised her eyes to meet mine and smiled. I found myself flushing slightly as she realised that I had been observing her.

"Did you manage to persuade Mrs. Dixon to give you the other letters?"

"I'm afraid not. She mentioned that you had asked for Alice's correspondence, and she had given you everything she had."

"But you didn't believe her."

"Not a whit."

As we rode past the elegant Mayfair homes on our way to Whitehall, the conversation turned to the king and Bea's time with him. Although she spoke with her usual discretion, I concluded that his spirits swung from jubilant to morose, but only his most intimate acquaintances were privy to his moods and his thoughts.

"The difficulty, I think, is he is overwhelmed, not by his duties, which he anticipated, but by the demands of so many other people. Everyone wants something from him."

"No wonder Mycroft feels so undervalued."

"He does?" Bea seemed genuinely surprised.

"He thinks the king does not hold his opinions in any esteem, unlike our late queen. She admired my brother, and he proved his worth to her many times."

Mycroft came hurrying forward to greet Bea. He kissed her cheeks in the Continental style and ushered her to sit in the best seat beside the fire. His aide, Gillespie, brought up coffee and scones to, "help her ladyship keep the cold out." Bea says this attention is because they are so unused to seeing women in the office, not because of any particular fondness for her. Utter nonsense, of course.

"How fares our new king?" Mycroft said when we three sat together by the fire.

"I confess, I feel rather sorry for him," Bea said. "He is surrounded by so many sycophants and beggars, and he does not yet know whom to trust. I have advised him — rightly or wrongly — that until he gets to know people better, he would do well to be sceptical of everyone."

She reached out and squeezed my brother's hand. "Give him a little time, dear Mycroft. It will not take long for him to realise what a wonderful support you are, and how wise." She lowered her voice. "Indeed, I have been effusive in my praises of your inestimable worth. I doubt it will take long for his majesty to reach the same conclusion."

"Do you have a particular issue of contention between you?" I asked my brother.

"No, but I disagree with the current government regarding this war in South Africa. They are advocating continued involvement; I am encouraging a withdrawal."

"Prime Minster Salisbury is unlikely to agree to that," I said. "In any case, the king cannot be seen to take sides."

Bea said, "That's true, Sherlock, but he can certainly make his displeasure known to the PM. The trouble is he wants to please everyone."

Mycroft bit into another scone and brushed away the resulting rain of crumbs. "I fear Beatrice is right, Sherlock."

It troubled me to see his spirits so low; even more so that he did not do a better job of disguising the fact. However, nothing could be gained by probing further.

"He will understand your worth in time, Mycroft. Let him get to know you. I know he's likely to be somewhat dubious about your support in the beginning; our late queen spoke so highly of you, that it makes him nervous. Most people whom the queen trusted were not friendly towards her son."

"I have heard that the queen treated him badly," I said.

"Oh, quite dreadfully. She never forgave him for her husband's death — as if poor Bertie gave Albert typhus — but she could not see the absurdity of the accusation. Mind you, she could be harsh with all her family."

I nodded, remembering the peculiar circumstances of our marriage. If it had not been for the queen's insistence that Bea marry, my life might be very different today. Fortunately, we were able to persuade Her Majesty that I was a worthier choice than the cad she had originally chosen.

Bea continued to console my brother. "Just give the king a little time to get to know you, Mycroft. He's no fool, despite what some people think, and he has a strong sense of fairness. It will not take him long to appreciate your worth."

He patted her hand, and I could see her words moved him. "Thank you, Beatrice," he said, his voice unusually husky.

With an effort, he regained his equilibrium and said, "What news, Sherlock?"

I explained how I had ruled out Amberley and Lord Walton and offered my theory about Qualtrough.

"I can well believe it. The fellow is a scoundrel," he said.

"You do not seem terribly impressed with him, Mycroft," Bea said.

"My brother once saw him commit an act of barbarism," I explained, "and he has never forgiven him."

"Good heavens! What did he do?"

Mycroft eased his back and said, "Not long after Qualtrough started working for me, I caught him in a most despicable act. He had left the office a few minutes before me and did not know I followed so close behind him. Out on the street, I saw a miserable looking mongrel yapping at him, a skinny, hungry-looking creature. Qualtrough kicked it half way across the street."

Bea's hand went to her mouth. "Oh, that's dreadful!" she exclaimed. "Did the poor thing survive?"

150

"No. It landed under the wheels of a passing growler."
Mycroft's lips became a thin white line of outrage. "No one but a monster abuses an animal," he said. "Never trust a man like that."

Trying to bring the subject back on track, I said, "How well do you know Sir Nigel Royston, Mycroft? Is he a temperate fellow?"

Mycroft fell silent for almost a minute. He has a mind like that of a master chess player.

"I have always found him rather unpredictable, even volatile at times. I would not look for help from that quarter, not without proof."

"Watson is going to speak to Dr Baxter. I think we can agree that's the most appropriate first step."

At length, the conversation moved on. "I know I have had you focus most of your attention on Qualtrough, Sherlock, but in light of your news, I suppose we ought to widen our search."

"I think that's for the best. Now, tell me, how are you? You look tired."

"I am," he said. "I feel I have not had a moment to breathe since December. Between the queen's death and this damnable war. Begging your pardon, Beatrice."

"Under the circumstances," she said, smiling, "I should think damnable is the mildest epithet you might resort to." She buttered another scone and handed it to him. He broke off his diatribe and smiled at her. I wonder if I, too, am as malleable in her clever hands.

"Your brother tells me things in South Africa are grim, indeed," she said. "I am sure he told you that Mrs Hudson's niece and two other women were murdered by a man from that region, or so it seems. We can, at this stage, only speculate as to his motive, but it seems connected to the service of these three women."

151

"It's a sorry situation all round," Mycroft said. "I am not sanguine about sending young women with no experience of life into a war zone. Some are performing admirably, it is true, but others, presented with their first moment of freedom, have run amok."

He rose and went to his desk and found a handful of documents. He placed them on the table before us. "These are reports from Bloemfontein and various other medical departments in South Africa. As you can see, the conditions are grim."

Beatrice and I read the reports. She said, "Why are things so deplorable? Surely more help can be sent."

"There are financial matters. The government is reluctant to spend more than they must. Besides, we — that is to say, the government — is hoping the Boer will surrender soon."

"I am astonished that so many young women have gone to serve in the nursing corps," Bea said. "And I do not understand why they are valued so much less than the young men who are soldiers."

"Women do not go into battle," my brother pointed out. "They are kept as safe as possible."

"Do not treat me like the dolts who work for you, Mycroft," Bea replied sharply. "The women live in appalling conditions, with little to eat. Some assist the ambulance crews, and they work as hard as any of the men. Surely they deserve appropriate recompense."

"You mistake me for the government, my dear sister. I do not entirely disagree."

They stared at each other, and anyone who did not know them as well as I would assume that they detested each other. I, however, could see their deep mutual affection.

"I should mention the disparity in treatment when I next speak to the king," Bea said, her voice as icy as I have ever heard it.

152

"By all means." Mycroft seemed unperturbed. Amused, even. She glared at him, and he laughed.

"Children, children," I said, "we seem to have wandered off the subject."

"If you don't think conditions in South Africa have played a part in these murders, you are as misguided as your brother," she snapped. I am still unsure if that were meant for me or Mycroft. It seemed we were equally guilty in her eyes.

My brother eased his considerable bulk back into his armchair. He elevated his foot on a stool and rubbed the leg for a moment before saying, "Of course I don't mean that, Beatrice. But you must see that a man's role in war is far more dangerous than that of the nurses."

Bea said nothing, but I could see from the stubborn tilt of her chin that she did not agree.

"These reports are indeed alarming," I said, bringing the conversation back to the point. "It appears that the circumstances in which these nurses are placed are utterly deplorable."

"It is at least tolerable in some of the hospitals," Mycroft agreed. "At least there they have access to clean water and are generally safe from the fighting. However, the concentration camps are another matter."

"How so?" Bea asked.

"Some, like Bloemfontein, have been established near stagnant waters. As a result, diseases such as typhus and dysentery are widespread and impact not only the Boer inhabitants, but also the staff. Furthermore, not enough staff are assigned to cope with the numbers of people who need care, I'm afraid. Not nearly enough."

"With all the reports you receive from South Africa, Mycroft," Bea continued, "Have you come across a story about three nurses being dismissed for allegedly attending a party?"

He shook his head. "No, I would remember if I had, I assure you. This was in Bloemfontein?"

"Yes."

"I'm afraid not. Of course, my reports focus on battles and military operations."

"Have you come across a journalist by the name of Green?" I said. "He's currently based in Bloemfontein."

"Jerry Green? Yes, indeed. A fine man, good mind and strong morals. He's highly respected. What is your interest in him?"

I explained that he had been suggested as a source of information about those women. Mycroft heard me out and said, "Yes, I would concur. Green knows just about everything that is happening in the region, and you may be sure of a meticulous account."

"I sent him a telegram requesting information."

"It may take a little time for him to reply. He spends a lot of time away from the camp following the troops on manoeuvres. However, when he does reply, you may be sure that his report will be comprehensive."

I could see my brother giving looks at the piles of papers on his desk. Beatrice rose and offered him her hand. "Please don't be cross with me, Mycroft," she said, gently. "I know what a good man you are, and I know this appalling situation is not of your doing."

"I am glad to be friends again," he said warmly, shaking her hand. "And I am glad you know that while I may be curmudgeonly at times, you have my undying respect and affection."

"Please come to dinner on Sunday, so I may make up my ill manners to you."

"It is worth a squabble to dine at your table," he said, smacking his lips.

*

154

When we returned to Baker Street, we found that Watson had returned from his afternoon with Baxter.

"I 'happened' upon him in the Furlong Club — it caters to people interested in horses, racing and so forth. Baxter likes the odd flutter. He had already had a fair bit to drink by the time I arrived; I gather his horse had done well, and he persuaded me to help him celebrate his winnings. I explained our concerns and he is troubled by the idea. He will run the necessary tests as soon as possible."

CHAPTER THIRTEEN

25th February

I awoke to find the flat oddly quiet. Usually, I hear the hum of a conversation between Mrs Hudson and Watson, or, worse, some dreadful music hall melody being savaged by Maisie. This morning, all was still, beyond the usual distant rumble from Baker Street. As my bed chamber is at the back of the house, I am spared the worst of the din.

I lit my first cigarette of the day and contemplated the comparative silence. I realised what was missing. Or, rather, who. Surely Bea had not left already. The sound of her laughter is one of the first things I hear when I awaken.

Setting that puzzle to one side, I realised that I could smell coffee. I threw on my dressing gown and shambled out to the sitting room.

"Sleep well, Holmes?" Watson greeted me from the breakfast table. I swallowed an oath and growled "perfectly soundly" in reply.

"The coffee is fresh, and the food is hot. Maisie, would you bring some eggs up for Mr Holmes?"

She bobbed and nodded, then hurried off.

At my surprised look, Watson added, "Maisie has a sore throat. I have advised her to rest it for a few days."

He took a bite of toast and smirked at me. "It's nothing to worry about, you know," he said. "I'm sure she isn't too far away."

"I cannot imagine what you mean."

His smile grew broader. He held the morning newspaper in front of his face and added, "Oh good. I thought you might be worried about her."

156

I sat down and poured a cup of coffee from the pot, added milk, and stirred. I determined not to let Beatrice's absence get the better of me. I could see Watson knew more about the matter than I did.

I managed to drink one cup of coffee before I surrendered. "Oh, the devil take the woman! Where is she, Watson?"

He lowered the newspaper and managed not to chuckle, though his mirth danced in his eyes. "She is downstairs talking with Mrs Hudson."

"You might have simply said so."

"I just did." And, unperturbed, he continued to eat his eggs and read the newspaper.

Maisie returned with my breakfast. I thanked her, and she nodded again before leaving in the same silence with which she had arrived.

I ate an egg and a slice of toast and drank my coffee. I certainly had no intention of hunting the woman. For twenty minutes, I sat and paid attention to my breakfast. That done, with a casual, "I have an errand to run," I hurried down the stairs, my ears burning with the sound of Watson's chortles. I reached the landing before I remembered that I was still in my nightclothes.

Bea sat in Mrs Hudson's little kitchen with our landlady. I felt curiously excluded by virtue of my sex. "Excuse me," I said, "I did not mean to intrude."

"You're not intruding, Mr Holmes," Mrs Hudson said. "Sit down and let me see if those scones are done."

Oh, heavens, not more food.

A few minutes later, Beatrice and I were sitting alone, eating buttery scones and drinking more coffee. Mrs Hudson claimed that she had something to do and bade us make ourselves welcome in her snug kitchen.

"The letters from Mrs. Reid arrived," Bea said, "and I started to go through them. I found them a little confusing

157

between Megan's penmanship and her Scottish idioms, so I sought Mrs Hudson's assistance."

She took one of the letters from the stack and set it before me.

"This one, for instance," she said. I frowned at it, perplexed. "I asked John, but he seemed no less confounded than I."

"Yes, I can quite see why."

"I have written down the translations here." She handed me her notebook.

"What have you learned? Anything of note?"

"Not yet, no. Mrs. Reid kindly sorted them into chronological order, and I have read the first few where Meg talks about her journey and arrival in South Africa. She is an interesting correspondent. Her turn of phrase reminds me so forcefully of her conversation."

"I think leaving the letters in your safe hands is the best thing I can do. I gather you have been working on these for some time."

Her eyes crinkled in amusement. "Yes, of course. I have been up since six."

"Oh. What time is it now?"

"Ten-fifteen."

"Oh."

"Go away, Sherlock. Let me continue to decipher these mysterious letters. I shall let you know if I find anything of interest."

I returned to the apartment and found Watson still sitting at the table reading the newspaper. With as nonchalant an air as I could muster, I asked what his schedule looked like for the next few days.

"I am cutting back my hours over the next week. I shall be working half-shift on days when I am at the clinic, and I shall be taking a few days off, too. The clinic has hired two more

158

physicians, sprightly young fellows. I thought I might prove more useful here."

"I could certainly use your unique insights and expertise, my dear Watson."

I proceeded to tell Watson about Mr Kyle. He listened quietly before observing, "As you say, Holmes, it is unfortunate that he lives on the other side of the river. It's not a great distance, I know, but travelling over the bridge when he is so unwell, especially at this time of year, would be very unpleasant for the man. I am not familiar with any services in his area, but Beatrice might. She is a veritable encyclopaedia of information regarding charities."

"Thank you, Watson, I shall ask her when she comes back up. That poor fellow's suffering troubles me. I cannot forget it."

"I suspect he is not long for this world, Holmes. Men with those sorts of injuries do not fare well. Frankly, I'm surprised he's lasted so long. The best we can do is try to keep him as free from pain as we can."

Watson made himself comfortable at the table with his writing things. I picked up my file on the Holland case. Perhaps coming to it with fresh eyes might reveal something that I had previously missed.

As I delved back into the file, Bea returned. It was already time for luncheon.

"Well?" I said, as she joined me at the table. "How did you get on?"

"Meg's letters make for grim reading, Sherlock," she said. "My word, the things those women endured. We already knew of the privation, the overwork, and the terrible disease, but the conditions there are beyond deplorable. The women became accustomed to the poisonous insects and the snakes, but I don't think Meg or any of them became reconciled to the threats of violence from both the Boer and even our own soldiers. Those men were out of their heads, most of them, but even so. Some nurses were punched, kicked, or spat at during the time they were there. Meg does not address any incidents that involved herself, but she does say that the only one who seemed to escape serious injury was Alice Dixon. Meg attributes this, rather cynically, to Alice's blonde curls and winning smile."

"Hm. Have you come across anything yet that would shed light on the murders?"

"Not yet. I've been reading the letters in chronological order. If you prefer, I can do the reverse."

I thought about that for a moment. "No, I think continue as you are going. I would not wish to miss a salient point because it is buried in one of the earlier missives."

"So, what is on the agenda today?" Bea asked.

"I am going to see Lestrade," Watson said.

"You're a good friend," she told him, as she buttered a roll. "As are you, Sherlock."

I shook my head. "I feel I still have much to learn. I spent too much time alone as a young man and I never learned that easy manner of discourse that seems to come so naturally to you and Watson."

"We may have more experience in that manner," she said, "but your instincts are superb."

"Here, here!" Watson said. "Mrs Hudson has not stopped singing your praises regarding how you comforted her when she learned of Megan's murder. 'No one could have been kinder or more supportive,' she said. Indeed, I suspect if she had been given a choice between you and me at that grave hour, she would have chosen you without hesitation."

At my frankly sceptical look, he added, "I am used to offering kindness and commiseration; they are essential components of my profession. I flatter myself that I am a good friend and an honourable man, but I am no Sherlock Holmes. Thanks to years of practice, I say all the right words, and I am unquestionably sympathetic. You are sometimes awkward and find it difficult to offer the right words, but the words you do offer are all the more precious for being so heartfelt. In you Mrs Hudson and, indeed, all of those in need, find a champion. If you give your word to solve a puzzle or bring justice to those who have been wronged, there is no one who would ever doubt you."

"Absolutely!" Bea added. "You, my dear Sherlock, are the knight valiant; Watson, dear though he is, remains your page."

"And honoured to be so," he added.

I confess these extraordinary compliments much moved me. As usual, I could find no words to reply, but had to settle for squeezing Bea's hand and nodding at Watson.

With Watson visiting Lestrade and Bea engrossed in Megan's letters, I decided to see what I could learn about Edward Wainwright, Mycroft's senior clerk.

He is about thirty years of age, married to a supportive woman, and father to a pair of schoolboys and an infant. They live in a small house on the river end of Savoy Hill.

As luck would have it, I spotted Mrs. Wainwright pushing the pram down the hill to her house, the two boys in tow. I hurried over to open the doors and helped her with the pram. I claimed to be a businessman in London for a few days and had got a bit lost. Could she direct me to Whitehall?

The harassed woman offered the service of her sons to show me the way. They know the area intimately, she said, since their father works there. She invited me to take tea and spoke with considerable pride about her husband. No finer man nor father ever breathed, if she were to be believed.

Later, as the boys, Frederick and Michael, escorted me to Whitehall, they revealed more than they realised about the family's finances, their father, and how he enjoyed working for the government.

"He works for a great man," Frederick said.

"The king?"

161

They chuckled. "Well, him too, I reckon, but no, Mr Holmes. He runs the whole government."

"Does he, indeed?"

"No better man than Mr Holmes, that's what our dad says."

Well, if this is to be believed, Wainwright is not our man. I've asked Little Mac to keep an eye on him over the next few days, but I don't have any great expectations. I suppose I should be happy that I can cross another suspect off my list. Unless, of course, the list is wrong.

CHAPTER FOURTEEN

26th February

I felt that I had just retired when someone hammered on the door. I donned my dressing gown and hurried downstairs. A policeman with a message from Inspector Morton. Could I meet him at the Queen's Arms Hotel on Jacob's Island in Bermondsey? A carriage was waiting.

I hurried upstairs and roused Watson. As he dragged himself out of bed, I dressed warmly and pulled on stout boots. Finally, I slipped my weapon into my pocket. I have often found calls after midnight come with an element of risk, and Jacob's Island is dangerous at any time of the day or night.

"Where are we headed, Holmes?" Watson asked, as he pulled on his coat. I told him and he frowned. "That hell-hole?" He, too, slipped his army revolver into his pocket. "Someone should have burned that damned place to the ground years ago."

"It's not as bad as it used to be, but it's best to be prepared," I said.

"What time is it?"

"A little after one."

He tied up his boots. "I hope the racket didn't wake Beatrice."

"She went home just after you retired to bed. She said she has a dinner to prepare for Mycroft. I don't understand all the palaver that goes into a simple meal; it's not like she is the cook. Are you ready?"

"Yes, yes. I'm coming,"

We rode in near silence along the banks of the river. Even within the confines of the carriage, I could feel the icy wind sting my face. I tried not to anticipate the reason the good

163

inspector had summoned me from my bed, and I Watson from his, but I could not help but speculate that perhaps the foul murderer from South Africa had been apprehended at last.

I chided myself. I know better than to draw suppositions without any evidence. I attempted to let my thoughts work in a more productive manner. I pondered Mycroft's business with his alleged spy and tried to formulate a plan to investigate the business.

The carriage turned onto Hickman's Folly, one of the worst streets in that most evil part of the city. For all the nonsense in the newspapers about its rehabilitation, its evil reputation still clings. I saw Watson cover his mouth with his handkerchief. A moment later, we came to a halt.

Despite the lateness of the hour, Watson and I stepped out into a crowd of neck-stretchers. "Murder," I said, softly.

The lamps were lit in all the windows that overlooked the street. As I stepped out into the damp night, I breathed the stench of the river at low tide, and the stink of poverty, neglect, and despair.

Constable O'Brien stepped through the crowd and shook our hands.

"Sorry to bring you out on a night like this, Mr Holmes. But the Inspector knew you would want to see this for yourself."

He led us through the dingy hotel foyer and up the narrow staircase. None of us spoke until we were inside the poky room on the top floor, staring at the grotesque sight before us.

The room looked tiny, scarcely bigger than a closet. An unmade narrow cot sat in the corner, and a dresser stood opposite. Layers of dust covered almost every surface, and cobwebs hung from the yellowed ceiling. Some sort of sticky substance, strawberry jam, I thought, from the smell, lay mixed with bread crumbs on the one creaking dresser.

In the midst of all this hung the thing that had once been a man. A stout rope formed a noose around the neck, and the

164

body dangled from the curtain rail. The angle of the bloated purple face suggested that his neck had not been broken.

"Mr Holmes, Doctor," Morton greeted us. "His name is Arno Cobbledick. We found his passport in his pocket. Native of South Africa. There's a suicide note on the dresser."

The note, a scrap of surprisingly expensive paper, was brief:

> *"I am not sorry for what I've done. They were evil and deserved to die. I will be with my wife and babies now.*
>
> *AC."*

What a curious declaration. Without lingering on the thought, I turned my attention to the corpse. I estimated his age as around forty. Slender but muscular, around 5'7" tall, if one could judge in such circumstances. His eyes were open in that opaque stare so characteristic of the dead; petechial haemorrhage attested to his manner of death. Almost-healed scars covered his face and hands, a legacy from one or more of his victims. His collar-length blond hair matted on his skull. He wore a bedraggled pair of trousers and a grey jumper. His bare feet bore that terrible purple colour of lividity, likewise his hands.

Without saying a word, young O'Brien found a chair from somewhere and set it before me so that I might examine the neck in situ.

"Thank you, Constable," I said.

For several minutes I examined the knot, the skin, and the hands. Some distant part of my mind noted Watson talking to the policemen.

"You're rather out of your jurisdiction, aren't you, Inspector?" Watson said.

165

"We were following a tip that placed our bird from the Dixon murder here," Morton said. "The coat hanging on the back of the door is stiff with old blood. It's several days old, if I'm any judge. The blood, I mean."

Having learned all I could from the hanging corpse, I had the policemen help me cut down the body and lay it on the floor. This made it easier to examine in more detail.

The face seemed oddly innocent, as if this murderer were only a boy, although Morton said he was forty-three.

Despite his appearance and his dreadful death, I felt no sympathy for him. My only regret was that he had not lived long enough to face trial for his foul deeds.

As my focus remained on my task, I scarcely registered Morton saying, "O'Brien, go and tell the men to be ready to transport the body to the morgue as soon as Mr Holmes has completed his examination."

Cobbledick's clothing looked cheap and inadequate for the harsh English winter. He wore a thin knitted jumper, in the fibres of which I found threads of long silvery hair. He also wore a pair of grey worsted trousers. A tattoo of an eagle decorated his left forearm. His short nails were intact, as were his hands. However, several rough scratches covered the length of his right index finger.

"Did you find a ring?" I asked.

"A ring?" Morton said. "No, Mr Holmes, but we haven't touched the room; we were waiting for you."

"I am much obliged to you. What about a knife?"

"No, sir."

I set the matter aside for a few moments and resumed my examination of the body. I found what I was looking for on the back of his right shoulder.

"Watson, come and take a look at this," I said.

He knelt down beside me and peered at the pinprick.

"He was injected with something," Watson exclaimed. "It's badly done. Whoever did it, most likely had never used

166

a syringe before. Mind you, if he'd been resisting, that could have made the administration difficult. He certainly didn't do it himself, not at that angle."

I nodded in agreement. "Indeed. As he was right-handed, he'd have injected his left arm."

Watson nodded in agreement.

Morton squatted down beside us and took note of my findings. "Ah, how do you know he was right-handed, Mr Holmes?"

"You will observe the right hand is fractionally bigger than the left; the muscles are more developed on the right side, too."

"So, someone helped him commit suicide?"

"This wasn't suicide, Inspector; it was murder. Heinous, cold-blooded murder."

"What about the note?"

"I knew at once that Cobbledick did not write it. It is in a woman's handwriting, and the notepaper is expensive and slightly scented with bergamot. I'm sure you'll agree that none of those elements suggests this fellow."

"Is this the man who killed Meg and the other women?" Watson said.

"I believe so." I said. "He certainly matches the description. If our theory of the motive is correct, we shall need to verify his relationship to the dead woman and children in the Bloemfontein camp. I am awaiting confirmation of the names from South Africa.

"The killer wore a ring with the head of an eagle on his right forefinger. You can see from the scratches on this fellow's hand that someone tore a ring from that finger. Since the dead man's name, Arno, means eagle, I suspect that's the relevance of the symbol."

"There's also the matter of the missing knife," Morton said.

"Yes, quite."

I looked around the room as Watson began his own assessment of the body. "The fellow's been dead for long enough for rigor to become fully developed," he said. "At least four hours, I'd say."

"Puts the time of death around ten o'clock," O'Brien observed, newly returned.

"Death was due to asphyxiation; the spine is intact. Ghastly way to go. It would have taken several minutes."

"Indeed," I said, as I went through the dresser drawers. "The killers either wanted him to suffer or were incompetent."

"Killers?" Morton said.

"Two. A man and a woman." I handed him the hairs I retrieved from Cobbledick's jumper. "You can see the woman's footprints clearly by the window. Fortunately for us, the housekeeping in this establishment is worthless. I believe it was the woman who injected the fellow."

"What with?" Morton asked. "Any thoughts?"

"We cannot be sure without an autopsy, but I suspect curare."

"Oh, how dreadful!" Watson cried.

"Curare?" the inspector said.

"It freezes the muscles," O'Brien said. "Paralyses them."

"Well done, Constable," I said. "That's perfectly correct."

"But it didn't render him unconscious?" Morton asked.

"No. He would have been fully aware of what they were doing to him," I said, "but helpless to stop it. That's why there are no scratch marks around his neck. Even a genuine suicide will claw at the rope. Of course, it's possible the drug was some sort of tranquilliser that knocked him out. The surgeon should be able to tell us. You might want to look around for a syringe. I doubt they will have discarded it; such things are expensive. If, by chance, you do find it, be careful not to stab yourself with it. And we also need to see if we can find his knife. The ring, I believe, is gone."

"Is it possible that this was a robbery, Holmes?" Watson said. "Not that the fellow had much, but in this neighbourhood…"

"They came prepared, Watson," I said. "They brought the syringe and the rope with them. No, they came to kill; robbery was a mere matter of opportunity."

As we searched the room, Morton caught O'Brien up on what he had missed.

"Extraordinary to think of a woman being involved in something like this," the constable said.

"It's hardly unheard of," Morton replied. "You recall that case in Fall River, Massachusetts, a few years ago?"

"They found Lizzie Borden not guilty," O'Brien said.

I smiled. Yes, he would make an excellent inspector.

As I had expected, we did not recover the syringe, but I found the knife.

"There it is," I said. "Under the dresser. You should just be able to reach it, Constable."

His long fingers easily caught the deadly knife by the handle and handed it to me. "A savage looking thing," I said. "As I had previously speculated, the blade is some seven inches in length, sharpened on both sides like a bayonet."

"That can't be blood on the surface, surely?" Watson asked, indicating the smear of red on the blade.

"Strawberry jam," I said. "Probably his dinner."

"He spread jam on the bread using the same knife that he had used to murder three women?" O'Brien said, looking a little green.

Morton drily replied, "Well, he probably wiped it first. It's a savage looking thing. Standard issue for the Boer, do you think, Mr Holmes?" He handed it to me.

"I doubt it," I said, "It looks handmade. I surmise that the blade had been part of a bayonet that he or some cohort converted into something more manageable. The handle is carved from bone and, yes, coated in animal hide."

169

"How did it get under the dresser, do you suppose?" Watson said.

"Would you care to speculate, Constable?" I said.

"I imagine a fellow like Cobbledick would have the knife in his hand when he opened the door. When he saw the woman, he believed she posed no threat and he let down his guard; he dropped the knife when she injected him. It slid unnoticed under the dresser and was forgotten after the murder."

"Oh, well done!" Morton said, patting his blushing colleague on the back.

"Yes, indeed, Constable. I suspect you're perfectly correct."

Since I had completed my examination of the body, a group of officers loaded the corpse of Arno Cobbledick onto a stretcher and took it away. Watson and the two policemen stood in the hallway while I gave the room a final appraisal. It did not take long.

The space resembled a prison cell, longer than it was wide, perhaps seven feet across by some nine feet long. An unsavoury bed stood to the right of the door, and opposite it slumped a dresser of indifferent style and substance. With the body gone, we could clearly see the grimy window flanked by a pair of yellowing curtains. The window faced the Bermondsey Wall.

Cobbledick's coat, stiff with dried blood, hung from a hook on the back of the door. Swallowing my distaste, I searched the pockets and found a railway ticket stub dated 12 February, a return fare from Keighley in Yorkshire to London. A relic of Kathryn Lysander's murder. I handed it to Morton, along with an assortment of coins, both Stirling and South African, and a number of wood chips, presumably from the dead man's whittling. Of more interest was a thin wallet. This contained a £20 note, and a newspaper clipping about the deaths of a woman and her two children in the Bloemfontein camp. I handed it to O'Brien without comment.

"Well, if we needed any more proof that this is our bird," Morton said, "I believe this is it."

"Nothing much in here," I said, as I examined the contents of the dresser. "Two pairs of trousers, one stiff with dried blood, two shirts likewise spotted, and a woollen jumper that used to be blue."

Finally, from under the bed, I retrieved a small valise. This contained some exceedingly dirty underwear, a grimy shirt, and another jumper. In the pocket of the shirt, I found a poorly made fake British passport in the name of Norman Lincoln. I doubted this would have facilitated the fellow's plan to flee the country.

More compelling was the newspaper cutting that lay folded inside the passport. This featured a photograph of three women in tropical nursing uniforms standing together on blanched and dusty steps. Beneath the picture, the caption read, "Alice Dixon, Kathryn Lysander, and Megan Reid, three of the thousand British nurses serving in the Boer conflict."

"British Nurses aid their troops," read the headline. Someone had underlined the names and circled the faces of the women.

"All the dead women," Morton said, when I handed it to him.

"It explains how he learned the nurses' names," Watson commented.

I refrained from pointing out that it raised as many questions as it answered: How had Cobbledick determined that those three nurses were the ones deemed responsible for the death of the woman and children in South Africa? More importantly, how had he learned where they lived? Indeed, how did he know they had returned to Britain, and were not still in Bloemfontein? But he did know. A newcomer to the country, with demonstrably few resources, and yet he had

171

managed to find all three of these women in a matter of days. Curious.

"Any final observations, Mr Holmes?" Inspector Morton said.

"Regarding Cobbledick's killers? There were two, and one is a woman. Given the angle of that injection wound, I would estimate that she stands approximately five feet-four inches tall; she is in good health; and has excellent upper body strength. She may be of middle age with grey hair, or she may be younger with pale, silver-blonde hair."

"Ah..." O'Brien said.

"You have a question, Constable?"

"Yes, begging your pardon, Mr Holmes. How can you be sure those strands of hair weren't there before the murder? Is it possible — I don't say likely — but mightn't they belong to Cobbledick himself? Or some sort of, um, visitor?"

I nodded approvingly. "Both excellent and on point observations, Constable O'Brien. These strands, as you see, are long. But while Cobbledick's hair is longer than an Englishman would wear, it is, nonetheless, considerably shorter than this strand. In addition, neither he nor any of the victims had hair of that colour, so we may rule them out. As to some sort of, ah, paid companionship, I would surmise that as the man was grieving for his wife and children, he would be unlikely to let any woman get close enough for her to lose not one but two threads of hair on his jumper. And while I admit that a woman of the night is possible, it is discounted when you observed that the hairs smell faintly of rosewater. That would be a rarity for a prostitute, I'm sure you agree."

"Thank you, Mr Holmes." O'Brien looked a little embarrassed.

"Keep asking questions, Constable. That's how we learn, don't you agree, Inspector?"

"I do indeed, Mr Holmes."

"What of her companion?" O'Brien asked.

172

"You tell me," I said, delighted to watch the young man working things out. Watson leaned against the wall, an amused look on his tired face. I suspect he was remembering how I put him through these paces when we were first acquainted.

"He's tall," O'Brien began. "Since he could hang the dead man up from that curtain rail, perhaps an inch or two taller than you, Mr Holmes. Strong, too. Lifting a dead weight, especially of a fully grown man, takes some muscle."

"Good. Anything else?"

Morton watched in silence, his eagerness for the younger man to succeed evident in his blue eyes.

"I think he was the muscle, and the woman was the leader."

"Why do you think that?" Morton asked.

"Well, a few things." O'Brien frowned, trying to explain the thoughts that had brought him to this conclusion. This is more difficult than people realise; sometimes the brain works at such extraordinary speed, that one reaches a conclusion without quite remembering how one got there. Of course, being able to retrace those mental steps is essential.

"Everything suggests the male was the muscle. He probably held Cobbledick still while the woman injected him. If he were in charge, he wouldn't have bothered bringing the woman with him. He probably wouldn't rely on the injection either; he'd have just bludgeoned the fellow to death. Also, I think he took the ring from Cobbledick's hand."

"Because?" I urged.

"Because? Why, because Cobbledick was a slight fellow, but he had fingers like sausages. From his hands, I believe he once worked as a blacksmith.

"That ring on his index finger wouldn't have fit a woman unless she were stout; but it would fit on a man's hand. The violence used to tug that ring off his finger seems more like something a man would do. Women are funny; they'll have

173

no problem watch a man strangle to death, but they'll shy from causing him unnecessary pain by tugging forcefully on a piece of jewellery."

He fell silent. The inspector opened his mouth to say something, but I silenced him with a brief shake of the head. O'Brien wasn't done yet.

"There was no reason to take the ring. The fellow wanted it and took it. That tells me that he has no self-control. I think the woman knew this and she may have kicked the knife under the dresser for that reason. She didn't want the man to stab the victim and spoil the fake suicide."

"Well done!" I cried. "Oh, you have done exceedingly well, constable. First rate. I think you have hit on all the important aspects."

"All we have to do now is find out who this pair is," Morton observed.

"And update Sergeant Thorne," I said.

"I have done so. He said he was too busy to join us and asked that we continue to work the case."

"Very well," I said. "Have you interviewed the desk clerk yet?"

"Not yet."

The man in question, one George Snood, was a recalcitrant, weasely looking fellow, who made me think of Lestrade, if Lestrade were corrupt and vile, rather than a man of honour. His narrow eyes darted from one to the other of us when we returned to the foyer. He had furtively slipped some sort of sweet into his mouth when he saw us coming. This added to his air of guilt.

Morton began the interrogation.

"You were on duty all evening?" he said.

"Since six o'clock," he admitted with the greatest reluctance. He seemed to feel that even confirming his name might put him in danger of arrest. Morton, both intelligent and experienced, let the silence linger until Snood couldn't bear it

174

any more. Defensively, he added, "We work twelve hour shifts, like. Six to six."

I saw Watson cover his smirk with his hand.

"Did your guest on the top floor receive any visitors?" Morton continued.

The shifting eyes turned down to the desk top. "I didn't see no one," he muttered.

Morton slammed a beefy hand onto the desk before him, making the rodent-like fellow jump.

"Lying to me will earn you a spell in the clink, and while you're in there, we shall tell all your clients how cooperative you have been."

"Oh, Lor, don't do that, guv. He ain't had no one in there that I ever saw, honest."

"Not even this evening?"

Again, the long pause until Snood, seeing the increasing irritability on our faces, said, "I didn't stay by the desk the whole time. Some of the lads was 'aving an argy-bargy, outside like. I wanted to see what were going on so I just stepped outside for a bit."

"What time was this?"

"Uhm, 'round eight-ish, I'd say. P'raps a few minutes afore."

O'Brien was taking careful notes of the conversation, much to Snood's discomfort.

"How long did this 'argy-bargy' go on?" Morton continued.

"Don't know. Not long. I mean, it died down, and I thought I'd go back inside, but it started back up again."

"Let me put it another way. What time did you go back inside?"

"Uh, around half-past."

"Did you see anyone go into the hotel — if hotel is the word — during that period?"

"No. I mean, no, sir. I didn't see no one."

175

Morton looked at me, and I added my own questions to the clerk. "Did the fellow in that top room ever have any visitors?"

"Not that I ever saw, sir. Kept himself to himself, if you know what I mean."

"When did he move in?"

"Uh, last Friday, I think." He made a show of examining the register. "No, Thursday. I remember now. The 21st, it were. See, 'ere's where 'e signed."

I examined the register and frowned at the name, Norman Lincoln. The handwriting was shaky and almost illegible. The 21st was the day after Alice Dixon's murder.

"What did he look like'?"

"Pretty filthy. I reckon he'd been sleeping rough. Nasty cough, 'e 'ad, 'ad the shakes pretty bad too."

"DTs?" Morton suggested.

"He didn't smell of drink," Watson said, "and I didn't see any bottles in the room. More likely it was malaria."

"What's that?" Snood said.

"A terrible disease," Watson said. "Like the worst influenza."

"Can it kill yer?"

"Oh, heavens yes. Horrible way to go."

Snood shivered and Watson smiled genially at him. For all his presenting himself like Mr Morality and Kindness, he does not flinch from going for the jugular when he feels it is called for. To be fair, though, he doesn't do it often, and only when he finds someone truly unbearable.

"Who was involved in the brawl?" I asked.

Snood blinked, thrown by the sudden change of subject. "Uh, I'd say about everyone. Usually, it's just a couple of 'em, but tonight it seemed like it were everyone."

"Who were the ringleaders?"

"Dunno." The narrow eyes dropped down to the counter.

"This man is Sherlock Holmes," O'Brien said softly. "Reckon you ought not cross him."

The weasel's face drained of its scant colour, leaving a waxen image. "Red Boy and Spitter," he stuttered.

"Charming names," Morton muttered under his breath.

CHAPTER FIFTEEN

It took almost an hour of frustration and slamming doors to find the pair, but at last we managed to locate them. While Morton and O'Brien took Spitter down to the corner to question him, Watson and I talked to Red Boy outside the hotel. He was a pale, lanky youth. I suspected he was no older than thirteen. Eventually, this story emerged:

Some woman dressed all in black with a veil over her face and a fellow as "big as two 'ouses" offered the pair ten shillings each if they would create a distraction. The lads were happy to accept.

As soon as Snood — or Snoop, as they called him — had come out of the hotel and made himself comfortable watching the melee, the strange couple slipped inside.

Half an hour later, the pair returned, and the woman paid the two men. She still wore the veil over her face, but a strand of silver-blonde hair had fallen loose and lay upon her shoulder.

"Did she seem old?" I asked Red Boy — whose real name, I learned, was Raymond Boyd.

"Not young but not old neither. Somewhere in between."

"Go on."

He sighed heavily, as if we were keeping him from some important business.

"She moved easy enough, like she were still youngish. Her back were straight and her hands were smooth. She wore no rings nor jewellery that I saw."

"Good man!" I said. "You have excellent powers of observation, don't you agree, Watson?"

"Absolutely!"

Despite himself, the young man preened. His pimpled face blushed deeply, explaining his nickname.

"I'll tell you something else an' all," he continued, "That dress weren't hers."

"No?"

"Naw, it had been taken up, like it belonged to a taller lady, but the shoulders were too wide for her. I reckon someone taller than herself had that dress. It were decent quality, too. Silk, maybe. Oh, and she wore black gloves afore she went into t'otel, but not when she came back out."

"Now, that is excellent. What about her voice? Did you notice anything about it?"

He frowned, unwilling to admit any lack in his thus-far commendable skills. Suddenly he smiled, looking like the boy he actually was, "It were young; like, not creaky like how old ladies sound. And she weren't from London."

"No?"

"Manchester. I got an uncle what lives there and I recognised the accent."

"Splendid! You know, it is remarkable to find a man as young as you so observant. I warrant half our police forces couldn't do so well. Tell me, what about the big fellow with her?"

"A bit of an imbecile, I'd say. Couldn't make a move without her telling him. Had those flat sort of features that you see on people who have trouble thinking."

"Probably Mongolism," Watson suggested. "Did he talk at all?"

Red Boy frowned, thinking. "Not words," he said at last. "Sort of grunts. She seemed to understand him though."

"I don't suppose you noticed if he had any tattoos or wore any jewellery?"

"When they came back out, he had a ring. Thick gold signet ring with an eagle on it. Spitter offered 'im a shilling

179

for it, but 'e sorta growled." He smirked. "Spitter took that as a no."

"Thank you, Red Boy. I mean that sincerely. You are a first-rate witness." I handed him a sovereign and he grinned. I added, "Here is my card. If you find yourself in a spot of bother, you may call me and if I can help you, I will."

He stared at it as if I'd handed him a diamond from the Crown Jewels.

"Cor, thanks, Mr 'olmes," he said.

"If you think of anything else, I'd be obliged if you would let me know."

*

By the time we returned to Baker Street, the silvery dawn had crept over the buildings. I opened the door and found that the maids were already at their work. I asked Maisie if Mrs Hudson were awake yet.

"Yes, sir," she said in a soft voice, remembering her throat. Followed instantly by, "No, sir."

Watson interrupted before I could lose my temper. "Maisie, will you please ask Mrs Hudson if we may speak with her for a moment?"

She stared at us in that infuriating slack-jawed way she has.

"Now!" I said.

She turned and scarpered.

"You frighten the girl, Holmes. Have you never heard that you catch more flies with honey than with vinegar?"

"Why should I want to catch flies?" I replied.

"You can be exhausting sometimes."

Before I could argue the point, Maisie returned. "Please, sir," she whispered, "Mrs Hudson says will you come back, sir."

We found our housekeeper in her sitting room, a maroon dressing gown over her night gown, and her hair still in a sleeping bonnet.

"We are very sorry to disturb you, Mrs Hudson," Watson said. "Would you prefer we come back later?"

"Not at all, not at all. Sit down, please. Maisie, bring us a pot of tea, there's a good girl."

We sat down on the small sofa, and I tried to suck back my impatience as the fire was stoked, the kettle boiled, and Maisie resumed her insufferable humming. It didn't help that Watson seemed unperturbed by these proceedings. He made idle chatter with Mrs Hudson, about what, heaven only knows. Finally, finally, the tea was poured, the maid dismissed, and Mrs Hudson said, "You have more questions for me, Mr Holmes?"

"In point of fact, we have news, Mrs Hudson. The man who killed Megan and the other nurses was found dead last night. He, too, had been murdered."

She stared at me, her hand to her mouth, and her brown eyes filled with tears. "You found him! Oh, God bless you, Mr Holmes, I knew you would."

Before I could confess that I had little enough to do with finding the fellow, Watson said, "He has been working on the case day and night, Mrs Hudson."

"With a lot of help," I demurred.

"Tell me what happened, Mr Holmes," Mrs Hudson said. "Who was this man and why did he kill all those poor girls?"

I gave a carefully edited account of the South African, aided considerably by Watson.

"So he blamed the nurses for the deaths of that woman and her babies?" Mrs Hudson summarized. "I can understand his anger, but why take it out on those poor women?"

"Perhaps they seemed like easy targets, Mrs Hudson," Watson said. "No doubt there are many questions we will never be able to answer."

181

At last, Mrs Hudson stood and said, "I shall send word to my sister, Mr Holmes. She will be as grateful as I am to know this man will harm no one else."

"There is one point, Mrs Hudson, for my own curiosity alone: Can you ask your sister if Megan knew anyone in Manchester? We believe whoever killed Cobbledick had ties to that city."

"I will, of course, Mr Holmes."

At last, with the topic exhausted, I fled to my room. I threw myself on my bed and surrendered to oblivion.

Around one o'clock I awoke feeling more than usually bleary eyed and with no sense of having rested. It is the curse of my mind that it cannot let go of a problem until it has found a solution. As a result, I tossed and turned all through the morning hours, my thoughts continually exploring possibilities and looking for things I had overlooked. Unfortunately, I had insufficient information at my disposal to arrive at any sort of conclusion. I feared that I had reached a dead end.

Eventually, I gave up. I bathed, dressed, and went into the sitting room. Maisie, still humming, brought up a pot of coffee and a tray of food. I expected her to scurry away after she had performed her task, according to her custom. To my surprise, however, she said, "Mr Holmes?"

"Ah, yes, Maisie?" I said, trying not to sound too intimidating.

"Just, I, um."

I swallowed back my urge to demand she get to the point. Affecting a show of patience, I poured the coffee and waited.

"Thank you, sir," she said, in a rush. "For helping Mrs Hudson, I mean. She's been ever so kind to me. And, um, thank you, sir. God bless you."

Upon delivering these extraordinary words, she fled.

The smell of coffee drew Watson down from his room. I poured him a cup and we dined in silence for several minutes.

At last, he said, "You look dreadful, Holmes. Did you not sleep?"

"No, at least, not well. I feel I am at an impasse on both these wretched cases."

"I've been thinking about that," he said. "What do you say to a visit to Mrs. Dixon? We ought to let her know that the man who murdered her daughter is dead. Perhaps the news will encourage her to be more forthcoming."

"I am sluggish indeed, my friend. That is an excellent suggestion. I cannot imagine Mrs. Dixon will be any more willing to cooperate with us, but it is certainly worth trying."

*

We were neither of us in any mood to hurry, and so it was a little after two by the time we arrived at the prim little house in Hampstead.

"Oh, it's you," she said, as she came into the hall and dismissed her maid.

"We have some news, Mrs. Dixon," I said. "May we come in?"

With a heavy sigh, she brought us into her sitting room. She did not sit, nor were we invited to do so.

"We have found the man who murdered your daughter and the other nurses," I said.

At that, Mrs. Dixon dropped heavily into an armchair. With a belated wave of her hand, she invited us to sit, too. "I hope he hangs," she cried. "Why, why did he have to hurt my precious girl? Did he say?"

"He's dead," Watson said in a flat voice.

"Dead? The scum! He deserved to come to trial; to dangle at the end of a rope. I hope he died in agony."

"It was a violent death," I said. "I'm afraid I cannot speak more plainly."

She dabbed at her tears. "I pray he suffers for all eternity," she said between sobs. "Evil, wicked man."

"We are truly sorry for your loss," Watson said in his most gentle voice.

"Unfortunately, our investigation has not yet concluded," I added. "We need to be sure this fellow did not have any accomplices and, if he did, bring them to justice."

"Why do you think he had accomplices?"

"He is or, rather, was a South African by the name of Arno Cobbledick. Though he had never been in England before, as far as we know, he managed to track all of these women. I believe someone was helping him."

"Do you think other women may be in danger?" For the first time since I met her, Mrs. Dixon seemed concerned for people outside her own sphere.

"We have no way of knowing," I said. "It's possible this person has ties to Manchester. Can you think of anyone your daughter may have mentioned who lives or lived there?"

She thought deeply and I had no doubt she was giving the question her fullest attention. When she raised her head, I could see the answer already in her eyes.

"I'm sorry, Mr Holmes. Alice had friends from all over, and she received letters from so many people. I will go through the rest of her correspondence and see if I can find anything that may prove helpful."

"Thank you, Mrs. Dixon, I would much appreciate it."

"How much do I owe you, Mr Holmes?"

"Not a farthing. I undertook the case for personal reasons."

She walked us to the door and, to my surprise, shook my hand, and Watson's. "Forgive an old woman, gentlemen," she said. "I am not ungrateful."

*

On our way back to Baker Street, Watson said, "Would you mind leaving me at the clinic, Holmes? I should like to see how things are progressing with the new staff."

I was happy to do so but felt less enamoured at the thought of returning to Baker Street and continuing to ruminate with no new information to direct my thoughts. After I bade goodbye to Watson, I had the cabby take me to Wimpole Street.

I found Beatrice in her study, an untouched cup of tea on the desk, and a small tower of books and papers before her.

"So, he's dead," she said, by way of greeting.

Thus am I repaid for all the times I made what appeared to be a singular observation to some mystified client.

"Mrs Hudson, again?" I said, trying not to look put out.

"The afternoon newspapers, in fact. most of the accounts were positively ghoulish, though none of them mentioned the murdered nurses. Your doing?"

"Yes, I asked Inspector Morton to keep that quiet. I suspect Cobbledick may have had an accomplice and I do not want to alert him or her."

"Her?"

I recounted the events of the night in close detail. She poured a cup of tea for me from the pot as I spoke and heard me out in silence.

"So, we are left with another mystery," she said, setting down her own cup. "None of the people related to the victims would seem to make acceptable candidates for his killer; neither Mrs. Dixon nor Mrs Hudson fit what we know of the description, nor do they have Manchester accents. Then there is the mysterious hulking brute who accompanied the woman."

"And this is where we seem to remain," I concluded.

"Perhaps not. I telephoned Baker Street about half-an-hour ago looking for you. As you were out, I spoke to Mrs Hudson for a few minutes. She said her sister had telephoned her a short while earlier to discuss Meg's funeral arrangements. Mrs Hudson told her the news, and Mrs. Reid asked her to pass on her thanks to you.

"Mrs. Reid also said she had been thinking about the person called 'E' who sent the postcards, and she thinks it might be a Mrs. Goodrich. She believes the woman's first name is Eleanor. She said Meg went through her nurse training with the woman and they became good friends. Mrs. Goodrich abandoned her training in order to marry, but she and Meg remained in contact."

"Ah, good news at last!" I cried.

"So it appears. I still have more than half of Meg's letters to read, but thus far, they are exceedingly circumspect. Perhaps Mrs. Goodrich will know more. By the bye, Mrs Hudson says Mrs. Goodrich came to visit Meg a few times over the holidays. They spent several hours talking."

"One of the most frustrating elements of this case has been trying to glean bits of information from people who either keep their secrets or have little enough to share. I hope Mrs. Goodrich will be more forthcoming."

She smiled sympathetically. "I take it you have not yet heard from South Africa?"

"In point of fact, there was a telegram from Green waiting for me when I returned to Baker Street this morning. He has been 'up country', he says, and will put together a comprehensive report. I should expect it in a few days."

"Well, that's something."

She finished her tea and rested her head on the back of the sofa with her eyes closed. The sunlight filtering through the lace curtains cast gentle patterns on her cheeks.

"Do you have an address for this Mrs. Goodrich?" I asked.

"Yes. She lives in Tally Ho Corner in North Finchley."

"Hm, it's still early enough to visit, I think," I said. "Will you join me?"

Beatrice rose and rang for the maid to bring her a coat. "I would dearly love to come with you," she said, "But I promised to bring Lestrade some books and snacks. I shall send him your love," she added with a twinkling smile. "Why don't you telephone to see if Watson can join you?"

I was surprised to find Watson at home already, his business at the clinic having taken far less time than he had anticipated. He would be happy to accompany me, he said. Bea's carriage stopped by Baker Street to pick him up, and then we left her at St. Bart's.

"Begone, woman!" I said, in pretended outrage. "Abandon us for the inspector."

"No doubt Holmes and I can manage on our own," Watson said, smiling.

"You have certainly managed long before either of you ever knew me. I wish you good fortune, gentlemen."

She was still laughing as she hurried up the hospital's steps.

*

A little after four o'clock, we two old stalwarts set off. I gave Bea's driver the address of 33 Castle Road, and we were on our way. Bea always keeps a couple of rugs in the carriage, and Watson and I made good use of them. It was a far more comfortable journey than we would have had in a hansom.

Throughout the entire cab ride, Watson expounded on the delights of the name of the place and speculated that the people of the region must be fine hunters. He regaled me with tales of some long-forgotten coach company that had once kept stables in the area. "Sixteen horses, Holmes! Can you imagine the stench?"

I mercifully drifted off somewhere in the middle of his dissertation about the French origins of the phrase *tally-ho*. (Note to self: Do not let Watson read *The Anglo-Saxon*

Review. He tends to remember the most trivial and useless pieces of information. An hour or two with my own monographs or even the police jotter would be of far greater benefit to him.)

In any event, I managed to fall asleep as my friend continued to wax lyrical on any number of nonsensical matters. When I awoke at last, I found we were on the Finchley Road heading north. I gave the driver further instructions to Mrs. Goodrich's address. I wished I could nod off again, but I remained sadly awake for the rest of our journey. As we travelled, I was compelled to listen as Watson thundered on about flowers and the architecture and goodness knows what. I honestly marvel at my patience sometimes. No one can imagine what I have to endure. Not until we finally arrived at our destination, did he exhaust his lexicon of superlatives. With considerable relief, I asked the driver to wait for us, and we walked up the winding garden path.

The young maid who answered our knock was a slender girl, perhaps eighteen years of age, with a halo of blonde curls. Watson, who harbours a curious fascination with blondes, smiled winsomely, introduced us, and asked if Mrs. Goodrich were available.

"I'm afraid she's not here," the maid said. "She's away on holiday."

"Ah. Can you tell us when she left?" Watson took over the conversation, seeing the dispirited look on my face.

"Mm, yesterday morning around nine o'clock."

"Damnation!" I exclaimed.

The maid flushed a deep colour. At a glare from Watson, I apologised profusely.

"Can you tell us where she went?" Watson asked in his most soothing manner.

"Aye, Sir, she left me a copy of her itinerary."

Watson quickly made note of all the dates and locations and, with that in hand, we returned to the carriage and endured the interminable journey back to Baker Street.

Darkness had fallen by the time we returned. We found Beatrice sitting by the fire reading one of my monographs.

"I thought you were busy preparing for Mycroft's special dinner," I said.

"That's why my staff are so excellent; they can manage perfectly well without me. I wanted to hear what you learned from Mrs. Goodrich. From your faces I gather the outing was not successful."

"She is away on holiday." I flopped down into my seat, unable to hide my irritation.

"In February? She must be a hardy soul. Where has she gone?"

"To the Kentish coast."

"The coast in this weather? Not hardy so much as foolhardy. She will not be gone forever, Sherlock," Beatrice said, making a noble, if fruitless, attempt to contain her mirth.

"How did you get on at the hospital?" Watson asked her. "I'm sure Lestrade was delighted to see you."

"He was. He's getting better every day. The doctors are hoping to release him home by the end of the week if he continues to make such good progress."

"Well, that's splendid news, don't you think so, Holmes?" he said.

"Harrumph."

"When did Mrs. Goodrich leave for her holiday?" Bea asked, and I could tell she had something on her mind.

"Yesterday. We missed her by one day." I handed her the itinerary.

"The garden of England," Watson mused in that dreamy voice he reserves for pretty women and bucolic scenery. "That's what they call Kent, you know. She went with some

189

friend of hers and is not expected back for another two weeks."

"I know how reluctant you are to leave London, Sherlock," Bea said, "but, you know, Kent is not so far. You could take a train and speak with Mrs. Goodrich there. Stay overnight and return the following day. I am sure Watson would be happy to accompany you if you'd rather not go alone." Beatrice smiled at me in her most roguish manner.

"I suppose that's better than waiting for the woman to return," I grudgingly replied. "Watson, how would you feel about a trip to Kent?"

Before he could reply, Bea added, "Alternatively, Sherlock, if you would rather not leave the city, I could go and see her on my own. I might bring my maid; I'm sure poor, long-suffering Mary would be glad of the break, especially with the way my cook has been acting while she prepares Mycroft's dinner. Since Mrs. Goodrich is travelling with another woman, they may not be comfortable to be accosted by two men, even ones so worthy as Mr Sherlock Holmes and Doctor John Watson."

I was not amused at my plans being scuppered and Beatrice essentially taking over. However, I had to admit she had a point.

"Your maid has the easiest job in Christendom," I said. "When would you leave?"

Beatrice looked up from her examination of the itinerary. "According to this, the women should be staying in Canterbury until tomorrow morning and going on to Deal in the afternoon. They will be staying in the Castle Hotel on Beach Street until the end of next week, so that is where I shall hope to rendezvous with them."

"Well, it's a possibility, but I think I should come with you," I said. "Oh, but Mycroft's case—"

"Yes, and his dinner," Bea said, "I know. I can leave the following day, on Sunday, the third. I can manage perfectly

190

well on my own, Sherlock. You must keep your obligation to your brother." I recognised that look. Sometimes I wonder if my wife is not distantly related to a mule. Before I could remonstrate, however, Watson said, "I can take over Mycroft's case for a few days. You can instruct the Irregulars, Holmes, and they can report to me. I will follow up with Baxter and take it from there.

"It might be nice for the two of you to have a little break in the charming Kent coast. It is quite beautiful. It's supposed to be unseasonably mild and dry over the next few days, too."

Beatrice is too much a lady to snort in disparagement, but I could see the look of ire in her intelligent eyes.

"I will not come if you would rather travel alone," I said, "But a break does sound pleasant."

"A break? From London? Please! Sherlock Holmes hardly ever leaves the city save under the spell of a beguiling case."

"This is a case," I pointed out, "and I owe it to Mrs Hudson."

"As you wish. We shall leave first thing Sunday morning. I had better go and make arrangements."

"I hope you are quite pleased with yourself, Watson," I said, after she had left.

"Look on the bright side, Holmes. At least now you'll have time to pay another visit to Lestrade."

His face resembled a feline that had recently dined upon a canary. "I shall have the flat all to myself for several whole days. Bliss!" He held the newspaper up before his face, but I could still hear his chuckles.

I cannot think how I have endured the fellow for so long.

CHAPTER SIXTEEN

27th February

I spent the day working on the Holland case. I have pored over the list of likely suspects and added a couple of known occasional visitors. I cannot be sure, of course, if they were in the office on the days in question, but neither can I rule out the possibility.

Sir Edgar Lyons is, of course, a man of high distinction, but his family fortune has dwindled in recent years thanks, primarily, to his wastrel son. Despite this, he remains an ardent representative for his constituency. I added him to my list, because in addition to his financial incentive, he and Mycroft have engaged in some fierce arguments over the years.

I contrived to encounter him as he trudged up the Mall. Bea had loaned me the use of her carriage and driver for the day. We stopped beside him, and I offered him a lift.

Given the slanting rain and the battered state of his umbrella, he accepted with alacrity.

"Useless," he said, indicating the umbrella. "I am much obliged to you, Mr Holmes."

"Not at all, Sir Edgar. It is such a deplorable day, not fit for man nor beast. I say, I wonder if you might be free to do me a small favour?"

"If I can," he said.

"I am going to the Savoy to observe a rather unpleasant fellow. I'm afraid if I go alone, I might draw too much attention, but if you were to accompany me." He nodded his understanding. I added, "I would be happy to repay you for your time by standing your luncheon."

The thought of a free meal, and at the Savoy, was more than he could resist. He smacked his lips and accepted instantly.

Of course, once we reached that elegant establishment, I had to find a suitable individual to "observe." Fortunately, I immediately espied the odious Dr Appleby sitting in the shadow of a palm near the entrance to the Grill.

I asked the waiter for a table that would allow me to observe the fellow — or, at least, appear to — whilst conducting my real business of speaking with Sir Edgar.

Since I was in a mood to be magnanimous, I ordered steak and suggested my guest do likewise.

As we shared a bottle of wine, I inquired after his son.

"I will tell you, Mr Holmes, I have spent many sleepless nights worrying about Charles. He was a giddy youth, and a reckless young man. However, a little over a year ago, he met Lady Gwendoline Derby at some art exhibition, and it was love at first sight for both of them. She has been a remarkable influence on him. He settled down and has returned to Oxford to complete his law degree."

"He always had an excellent mind," I said honestly. "I imagine he will do well in that field."

"Thank you, yes, I must agree. It broke my heart when he abandoned his studies, you know, especially as he was so close to graduating. However, he has only three months left, at which time he means to propose."

"What splendid news! Lady Gwendoline's family is highly influential. I am sure her father will be happy to find a suitable position for his son-in-law. I assume they are happy about the match?"

"Well, there was some hesitancy at first, but Lord Derby sees Charles's determination to succeed and has warmed to him. It has been the making of my boy."

I did not allude to the considerable fortune Lady Gwendoline inherited from her late mother, or the even greater wealth she should one day inherit from her father. A fortuitous match, indeed.

As we dined, Sir Edgar said, "Tell me, Mr Holmes, how is your brother? I have not seen him for some time."

"He is well, thank you. You have not been to the office of late?"

"I stopped in once or twice after the queen's death, but unfortunately I missed him both times." He leaned forward and dropped his voice, "Please tell him to be careful. I have heard rumours that someone has been speaking ill of him to our PM. All of it lies, of course, but I suspect they saw the queen's death as an opportunity to unseat him. You know, for all the times he and I have sparred over a number of issues — indeed, we never seem to agree on anything — I have immense respect for him. Do please tell him to be careful, won't you?"

*

I was surprised to find Watson already adorning his usual place by the fire when I returned to Baker Street.

"I came home after I stopped in to check on Lestrade," he said. "He asked me to thank you for helping his friend Kyle. I gather the visiting nurse and the weekly delivery of groceries have made a big difference."

"I hope you pointed out that the visiting nurse was arranged by your good self, and the groceries are all down to Bea. I did no more than mention the poor fellow's plight to both of you."

I told him about my afternoon, and we reluctantly crossed Sir Edgar off the suspect list. My fears that the disappearance of the Holland documents were meant to discredit Mycroft seem to have more merit than I should like.

No word from Baxter yet. Watson says we must be patient.

28th February

I spent the day investigating some of the other suspects on Mycroft's list, starting with his chief clerk, Edward Wainwright. Though not wealthy, he is financially secure. He studied law at one of our more prestigious universities and left a lucrative practice to go into government service ten years ago. Other than his dreadful dandruff, he doesn't seem to have a mark against him. I have learned everything I can about him, but he seems a blameless, dedicated public servant. If he is guilty of any wrongdoing, it is a closely guarded secret.

As for Qualtrough, the lads have been taking turns following him to and from the office. Unless the weather is particularly bad, he usually walks. Thus far, he always takes the same route. I have instructed the boys to tell me at once if they see him diverge from that.

Long Mac has had the task of watching McDuff and Burnett virtually alone. Poor boy has had to immerse himself in tennis and pretend he wants to learn how to play. Fortunately, it's too early in the year for him to have to make good on that. At least since McDuff and Burnett are hardly apart, it's easy enough for one boy to keep an eye on them. They even share a flat together on Bury Street between Green Park and St. James's Square. The flat has been paid for by McDuff's father, a wealthy and rather tyrannical fellow from what I have heard, and McDuff junior is his only son. Could treason be the young man's way of rebelling against a rather despotic father? Perhaps.

While the lads are scattered all over the city keeping watch on the suspects, I "happened" to come across Sir Cuthbert Redmond in the chambers of Westminster. He is one of those men who is charming to women but speaks contemptuously about them in the company of other men. If the rumours are true, he has made a number of conquests. He is just shy of six feet tall, with thick black hair that hangs in waves to his collar.

Rather unfashionable, but this air of poetic indifference seems to endear him to many. He is, however, highly intelligent with an impeccable education. As the fellow is independently wealthy, if he is stealing the nation's secrets it is not for financial gain.

"I say, Holmes," he greeted me cheerily, "What are you doing in this den of iniquity?"

"I had hoped to speak to Secretary Baines," I said.

"Ah, has that old rascal been up to some skulduggery? It's always the quiet, stolid type you have to watch, eh?"

"Sorry to disappoint, Sir Cuthbert, but I'm hoping he can give me some background information regarding South Africa. A number of young nurses who had recently returned from there have been murdered, and I am looking into the case."

His countenance changed. "Oh, what a clod I am! That's quite dreadful. And here I am making foolish jokes about a good man. You mustn't take me too seriously, Holmes. Baines is a jolly decent chap. To tell the truth, I am a little jealous of him."

"You are? Why so?"

"Because he is a model of propriety and is always taken seriously. No one ever takes a dolt like me seriously, not that I can blame them. My late father always said I would be a good man when I grew up. Alas, I am still waiting."

"You are too hard on yourself, I'm sure," I said. "Your work on behalf of the Education Act is exemplary."

"You are much too kind, Holmes. It's no more than any man would do, I'm sure. How is your brother?"

"He is well, thank you. Rather disconsolate about the queen's death."

"Aren't we all? Send him my regards, won't you? It seems an age since I last enjoyed his company. Such a remarkable man. Oh, look, there's Baines now."

I followed his gaze to see the slightly stooped form of that old man slowly descending the polished wooden stairs to where we stood in the lobby. He shook my hand and nodded a little absent-mindedly when I asked if I might speak with him.

Minutes later I was in the secretary's office with its panelled walls and Persian rugs, talking about the Boer War and the murders of the women. Baines hemmed and hawed but promised to ensure I received whatever documents I needed. "Of course, the nursing services are outside my realm of influence, so I cannot promise anything; however, you may be sure of whatever assistance I can lend you."

Though I usually find him a strictly business-like fellow, today he seemed in a mood to converse. He plans to retire soon, and happily shared his plans with me. As with the other suspects before him, I could see nothing that would suggest he was Mycroft's spy. Indeed, he is the epitome of the English gentleman.

As we walked out of that illustrious building together, he said, "We place too much emphasis on the machinery of war. We need to focus on making peace. I know your brother would agree."

I left Westminster torn between relief that a man Mycroft respected was not a blackguard, and annoyance that my investigation led nowhere.

Rather than returning home, I stopped by Bea's house in Wimpole Street. She seemed happy to take a break from her many responsibilities and invited me to spend the evening with her.

Over dinner, she asked if I could not find an excuse to stay in Mycroft's office until the villain is caught, but she reluctantly concurred that I am too well known there.

1st March

This morning saw the arrival of a most unexpected visitor. Ray Boyd, or Red Boy, came bearing news.

"I got to thinking, Mr Holmes, that just because the lady spoke like she were from Manchester it didn't mean that she lived there. Anyway, I asked a few questions, and found the cabby who took her and the big lad from the Queen's Arms Hotel to Marylebone Station. I know a lad what works there, and he told me he saw them get on the train to Manchester."

"That shows great initiative, Boyd," I said. "Well done."

I did not tell him that he had actually fared far better than the official police. They had also tried to get this information but failed.

"Well, you treated me fair and square, Mr 'olmes. Not too many do that, and I wanted you to know that I appreciate it. Oh, and one other thing. That lad, the big fella, you remember I said 'e seemed a bit simple to me? I've an uncle lives in Manchester. 'e's a priest in St. Barnabas's church, and 'e spends a lot of time with lads like that. I reckon if you describe the fella to Father Boyd, 'e might know where to find him."

He handed me the man's name and address. One thing I can say for this case, it doesn't lack surprise.

I thought for a moment and said, "You saw him, Boyd. Come with me."

Fortunately, Peter Gallagher was home and ready to take a break. My young friend seemed fascinated by the paintings he saw, and he asked a dozen questions, to the quiet amusement of the artist and myself. At length, I explained why we were there.

"I've never thought to be a police artist, Mr Holmes," Gallagher said, "But if it will help you, I am happy to give it a try. Well, young 'un, you describe the fellow to me, and I will try to capture his likeness."

The entire process took no more than half-an-hour. The likeness, according to Boyd, was perfect and he stared amazed at the portrait Gallagher produced.

"That's 'im!" he cried. "Cor, What a marvel!"

With the sketch carefully rolled up and tucked inside my coat, I added, "One last item of business before I leave, Mr Gallagher. It's about that Oxford Street painting you were working on when we last spoke…"

2nd March

What a splendid evening! Beatrice outdid herself, though of course she gives all credit to her staff and, in particular, to her cook, Mme. Chabon.

Bea fussed over Mycroft and made sure he had as much to eat and drink as he could wish. Even Mme. Chabon came into the dining room to ask if everything met with my brother's approval, and they chatted for some time in French. Bea looked quite pleased with herself, and who could blame her? Although I am not a gourmand like my brother, I do enjoy good food when I have the opportunity to savour it, and this was one of the finest meals I have ever eaten. Certainly, it surpassed anything I have ever been served in one of her late majesty's banqueting halls. The trout, lime sorbet, tournedos à la bordelaise, and so forth were superb, but it was the dessert that won the accolades. We were offered a choice between lemon tart with Chantilly cream, and opera cake. Mycroft with little persuasion, accepted both.

After dinner, Bea indulged our requests for her to play the piano, and treated us to a considerable range of pieces, from Mozart to Scott Joplin. That "Maple Leaf Rag" she had told me about is delightful. I can quite see why she enjoys playing it.

Later, we retreated to the library. This is my favourite room in Bea's Wimpole Street home. I believe it is a favourite of Mycroft and Watson, too. The selection of books is quite enviable; leather and gold covers fill every shelf. One wall is dominated by a substantial fireplace, and on this occasion a merry fire burned within. Fuelled by good food, brandy, and cigars, we sat to enjoy one another's company and conversation. Unlike most such post-prandial gatherings, the lady joined our masculine company.

"Have there been repercussions regarding those missing documents, Mycroft?" Watson asked.

My brother swirled the golden liquid in his glass before replying. "Not that we have learned. However, since both the stolen documents pertain to the plans for a submarine that is being built, we might not learn of any sabotage until it is too late."

"Lestrade tells me that Scotland Yard is starting a fingerprinting service some time this year," Watson said. "Is there no way you could print everyone in the office?"

"Not without drawing the suspicions of everyone in the building," Mycroft said. "I mean for it to happen eventually, to have all government employees fingerprinted, but we are not there yet. As to the stolen documents, discretion must be our watchword. Right now, the thief does not know he is suspected. I want to keep it that way. The challenge is to find him red-handed."

"If there is any way I can help, Mycroft, please let me know," Bea said.

He smiled at her with a rare look of affection. I cannot remember the last time he looked at anyone like that, not since we lost our mother, I think.

Conversation turned to politics, and segued to art. Bea is as knowledgeable about both topics as my brother and I. I was a little surprised to discover that she is a great admirer of Peter Gallagher's. She attended one of his exhibitions in the Haymarket a few years ago, and even purchased one of his paintings.

"It's in the cottage, Sherlock," she said. "That night-time view of the Thames that's hanging in the study."

"Ah, the one with the red boat? Yes, I remember, it's an excellent piece. I thought his style seemed familiar."

Eventually, we all succumbed to fatigue. As has become our custom, Mycroft spent the night in one of Bea's guest rooms that she has taken to calling 'Mycroft's room.' The other is occupied by Watson. Bea and I had already packed our bags in preparation for our journey to Kent in the morning. It was, therefore, a most contented group who retired for the evening.

CHAPTER SEVENTEEN

3rd March

I have never determined how she manages to achieve it, but Bea was in her carriage reading a guide book about Kent, long before any of we three gentlemen joined her.

"We shall drop you at your lodgings, Mycroft, if that is acceptable, and the driver will take Sherlock and me to the railway station. Finally, if you do not object, John, he will take you home to Baker Street."

"Actually, Beatrice," Mycroft said, "I wonder if the good doctor would care to join me in the Diogenes Club so we may discuss our strategy."

"I would be delighted," Watson said.

With all these trivialities arranged, it was not long until Beatrice and I finally sat in our private carriage on the train. As we left the smoky city behind us, I said, "I did have a thought about how we might catch Mycroft's spy, but I have not yet had the opportunity to put it into practice. I should welcome your opinion."

2 p.m.: Deal, Kent

We are in Kent, and I am happy to say Beatrice is in excellent spirits. Although I do not, as a rule, like leaving that great metropolis called London, in this instance it seems essential. After a week of almost constant frustration, the change of scenery can only — Good heavens! Is it possible my mind has become so used to Watson's incessant utterances about the "delights" of the countryside that I echo the same banal sentiments even in his absence? I mentioned this to Beatrice and, rather than sympathise, she laughed for so long I thought she might do herself a mischief.

Following Mrs. Goodrich's itinerary, we found rooms in the small hotel where she is staying. It appeared clean, genteel, and quiet. Besides, it boasted a splendid view of the sea. As I checked us in, Beatrice inquired about her "good friend" Mrs. Goodrich. We learned that the woman had checked in but was currently out walking with her companion.

Other than a giddy amount of floral fabric, wallpaper, and carpet, I found our room pleasant enough. Due to its location on the second floor and at the front of the building, it offered a wonderful view of the roiling sea. The thick grey clouds met the churning waves in a monochrome haze, rendering the horizon line invisible. The maid told us that when the weather conditions are favourable, one can see all the way to France.

The temperature felt milder than I expected for this time of year at the coast, but I was pleased nonetheless to see a fire blazing in the hearth.

I sat on the narrow window seat and with the aid of a pair of binoculars I could see two women walking along the strand some distance away. I could not be certain they were Mrs. Goodrich and her companion, but it seemed likely.

Bea spent several minutes taking photographs of the view. It has been quite some time since she was last able to indulge her hobby, so I kept my impatience at bay.

Once she was ready, we went out to take a small tour of our own. I have not been to this location before, and I must admit, at least within the privacy of these pages, that it is a perfectly charming area despite the remarkable preponderance of drinking establishments. There is a wide street before our hotel, beyond which lies an equally broad promenade. I gather this is where kiosks and amusements are set up during the summer months. Further up the beach we found a number of boats sitting in the sand, lest we forget that many in this seaside town rely upon the fruits of the sea for their livelihood.

Bea and I had thought to take a stroll along the pier, but the wild wind decided us against it. Instead, we made a round of the streets away from the beach and found small parks, quirky laneways and those gravity-indifferent buildings that seem so plentiful in England. The types that slouch against their neighbours, or, worse, appear as inverted triangles. Watson would be charmed.

Despite the hard ground, spring was starting to make an appearance. I have forgotten — by choice — the horticultural lessons that were forced upon me as a boy, except those that are relevant to my particular sphere of interest. It is no idle boast to say my knowledge of the various types of tobacco is peerless, and no one possesses a more comprehensive repertoire of poisons. Beatrice, however, who has read more books than a spinster librarian, and whose memory may match my brother's, was happy to regale me about Culpepper's herbal lore and the health benefits of garlic. After we had rambled for an hour or so, it began to rain, and so we took shelter under a tall tree.

"It's wonderful to be able to breathe the sea air," Bea said. "Much as I love London, some part of me always aches for the coast. Oh, how I long to just jump in the sea and splash about like a child."

I laughed. Her mixture of irritation and longing made her seem much younger than a woman of her maturity.

She offered me a shame-faced smile. "It makes me a difficult companion, I fear. I am sorry, my dear Sherlock."

I laughed. "It is your willingness to reveal your honest feelings, even those that many would deem unwomanly, that makes you so delightful a companion. To me, at least; I cannot say that would be true of all people."

She laughed too. "Oh, I have missed you. But, damn you, you have made me laugh and with that all my irritation has evaporated. I say, I believe the rain has stopped."

"Would you like to go back to the hotel? It is getting late."

"Oh, may we eat first? I'm famished!"

We found a small café not far from the hotel and dined on fresh cod.

Back at the hotel, we relaxed and enjoyed a leisurely few hours before we needed to change into our evening attire and go downstairs to the dining room. Beatrice looked splendid in some shimmery blue thing. I think we made quite a handsome couple.

We sat not far from the fire in the dining room. After our long walk in the cold and wet I felt pleasantly warmed. Beatrice had regained her usual lively temperament, something I welcomed even if it did mean I could expect some raillery. Perhaps I flatter myself, but I believe that I have become better equipped to handle her gentle teasing since we first met.

The dining room looked full, surprisingly so, given the weather and the time of year. In response to my question, the waiter said the restaurant was popular with locals, particularly on Sunday evenings. He promised entertainment would begin shortly. I chuckled at Bea's look of alarm.

As we dined, we kept our ears open to determine which of the ladies sitting nearby was Mrs. Goodrich.

A moment or two later, someone two tables over cried, "Oh, Eleanor, whatever have you done?" The conversation was lost for a moment, consumed by laughter and the discussion of others in the room, then the same, loud lady said to the waiter, "I'm afraid Mrs. Goodrich has upset the water jug. I told you to speak nicely to it, Eleanor!"

There was no mistaking the culprit. Mrs. Goodrich was tall, with thick black hair worn in some unfortunate style involving braids, and she was attired in a gown of what Beatrice calls forest green. The lady had a loud and raucous laugh, which incited a variety of responses, from tuts and frowns, to broad smiles.

The ladies sat no more than ten feet from us. As they were still on their appetiser, I deduced that they had been seated only moments before us, and so we found no difficulty in keeping up with them.

As the pudding was served, the hotel's owner, a corpulent gentleman by the name of Amberley, announced that it was time for what he called their "musical appreciation" evening. I forced my face to reveal nothing while Beatrice suppressed giggles.

"Oh, heaven help us!" I groaned.

"You should volunteer to play," she said. "You're a splendid violinist."

"And you are an accomplished pianist," I countered. "I am sure the assembled would far prefer to hear you."

Unfortunately, it was not Beatrice's delightful piano playing that greeted us, but a rather humdrum plonker and a woman whose talents may have been many, but, sadly, did not include musical ability. We were treated, if that's the word, to a selection of "ditties" by Messrs Gilbert and Sullivan as well as an attempt at an aria from *Cosi Fan Tutti*. One must, I suppose, applaud the courage such an endeavour undoubtedly took, if not the dubious talent behind the effort.

About fifteen minutes into the session, we observed Mrs. Goodrich and her companion leaving. The handkerchief to their mouths might have assayed to convey illness, but the shaking of their shoulders made it clear they were consumed by laughter.

Beatrice and I, by silent agreement, followed suit. We waited until we were halfway up the staircase behind the two ladies, when Bea succumbed to giggles.

The two ladies, only slightly ahead of us, paused and turned.

"Was that not dreadful?" Mrs. Goodrich exclaimed, still laughing.

"Horrible, horrible," Bea said, shaking with mirth. "Bless the poor thing. Someone should discourage her from all such displays in the future."

"For the good of mankind," Mrs. Goodrich's companion added.

"I say," Mrs. Goodrich said, "There's a charming little sitting room on the top floor with a fireplace and a wonderful view. Would you care to join us?"

"Oh, please do," added her friend. "There are few enough people with a sense of the ridiculous. One must cling to the few one meets."

"We'd be delighted," Beatrice said.

The upper lounge was deserted apart from ourselves. A fire crackled cheerfully in the grate, and we were not at all dispirited despite the rain lashing against the window.

The waiter arrived at our table within seconds of our arrival, and we ordered a bottle of Bordeaux.

"Oh, thank heavens for the quiet," Beatrice said fervently.

"Such a relief after that din," Mrs. Goodrich's companion said. "You know, I have never heard 'Poor Wandering One' sung in that key before."

"Those keys," Bea corrected to peals of laughter.

"Appalling," I agreed. "I wish Bea had commandeered the piano before that, ahem, person."

"You are a pianist, ma'am?" said Mrs. Goodrich.

"An exceptional talent," I replied, smiling at Bea's blushes. "My apologies, I should introduce us. This is Lady Beatrice, and I am Sherlock Holmes."

"*The* Sherlock Holmes?" exclaimed Mrs. Goodrich. "Why, you must be clairvoyant! We were just speaking of you this morning. Excuse me, I am Mrs. Eleanor Goodrich, and this is my friend Miss Joyce Adams."

"Holmes is not clairvoyant, although he often seems that way," Bea said. "Did you have a mystery to be solved?"

207

I admired the casual way she led into the topic. It seemed so natural a question to ask.

"Yes, indeed," Mrs. Goodrich replied. "A good friend of mine was recently murdered. As bloody and wicked a crime as I have ever heard of."

"You mean, I think, the case of Nurse Megan Reid," Bea said. I was surprised at her frankness. Had she not been cautioning restraint? Still, the two women did not seem particularly troubled by the revelation.

"Why, it is not only Mr Holmes who is clairvoyant!" exclaimed Mrs. Adams. "How on earth did you know that?"

"I must confess, ladies, we came here hoping to speak to you," I replied. "Nurse Reid's aunt, Mrs Hudson, is my landlady. She already engaged me to look into this tragedy. I hope you will forgive us interrupting your holiday on such an unpleasant matter."

"Of course!" Mrs. Goodrich replied. "Sweet Megan was the dearest of my old friends. Even though our paths led in different directions, we stayed in touch. I am happy to help any way I can. You do not object, Joyce?"

"By no means." The woman's eyes glittered with excitement, and I could see that, for her, this was no more than a game. Mrs. Goodrich, however, seemed genuinely upset at her friend's death. Her eagerness to assist lay in nothing but genuine friendship and a hunger for justice.

Bea sat back and sipped her wine as I reviewed the facts of the case as I had uncovered them.

"I have never met any of the other nurses you mention, Mr Holmes," Mrs. Goodrich said when I had finished. "However, Meg wrote to me about all her adventures after I left nursing school. I feel I know them as well as I do my own family."

"What can you tell us about them?" Bea said. "The more we understand them, the greater the likelihood we can determine why all these unfortunate women died."

"Of course, I shall tell you all I recall. I should add, too, that I saved all of Meg's letters. I will be happy to give them to you if it helps."

As Bea offered effusive thanks, I thought, "Oh heavens, not more letters!"

"I am puzzled about one thing," Miss Adams said, "Why does it matter if the killer is already dead?"

"An excellent point," I said. "But as I told Bea, I cannot ignore the possibility that there is more to this story than we know."

"I am happy to trust to your judgement, Mr Holmes," Mrs. Goodrich said. "Let me see, Alice Dixon. I should preface my comments by saying Meg never spoke ill of anyone, but she expressed concerns about Nurse Dixon's suitability to serve as a nurse, in a war environment, at least. From some of her stories about things Dixon had done, I understand the girl could be flighty and unreliable. She'd been raised by her mother alone; her father died when Dixon was an infant. Her dear mama utterly spoiled her, and the girl lived for parties and shopping. She went into nursing in hopes of marrying a rich doctor, a plan that met with her mother's approval. Not that I can talk. I left nurse training to marry a doctor, but that was not my plan. Mind you, I would have made a dreadful nurse."

"Nonsense," Miss Adams said. "I'm sure you are far too hard on yourself, Eleanor."

"Your insight is invaluable," I said. "Please go on. What of Kathryn Lysander?"

"A hard woman to read, I gather, but an excellent nurse. She had a waspish tongue, and didn't suffer fools, but she could be very kind to her patients and to the nurses she respected — though I gather there were precious few of the latter.

"Lysander told Megan that she grew up in a violent household. Megan added that the woman bore many scars

209

from her father's abuse. She didn't trust many people, just Megan and one or two others. However, Meg said Lysander's patients always spoke highly of her."

"Did that include the Boers?" Bea asked.

"No, no, our own boys. I don't think Lysander cared much for the Boer. They were 'the enemy,' even the infants. Odd behaviour, if you ask me. Not what one would expect of a nurse."

"It's not unusual in wartime," I said. "My friend Dr Watson is the kindest man I have ever known, but he has made the same observation about his service in Afghanistan. Sympathy is reserved for one's own side, save under the most extreme circumstances."

"I can understand that of soldiers," Mrs. Goodrich said, "but nurses? A nurse is nothing without compassion, Mr Holmes."

"Do you know why the nurses were sent home?" Bea asked.

"Yes, I do, and I'll get to that. But first, I want to be clear that the doctors sent Meg home because her health had deteriorated so badly, and no other reason. As for the others, well, I suppose you've heard about that wretched dance?"

"We have heard a little, but we should like to hear it from you," I said.

Mrs. Goodrich thought for several seconds, choosing her words carefully. At last, she said, "Several nurses had been invited by the First East Lancashires to a dance. They were eager to attend as they had endured weeks of dreadful labour and little time off. They were supposed to get additional staff, but for some reason or other, that had not happened. The nurses were exhausted and, frankly, aggrieved by their treatment. They were angry when they were denied permission to attend, and three of them decided to go anyway.

"If they'd been gone for just a few hours, they might have got away with a slap on the wrist, but they didn't return until

210

the next day. To make matters worse, some Boers had died during their absence. Frankly, I suspect those poor souls would have died anyway, but the story found its way into the papers and blame fell upon the nurses. Matron, like many before her, did nothing to protect her staff. There followed a sham of an investigation, and the three were sent down."

Bea and I exchanged a glance. I voiced our puzzlement in a question: "I'm sorry, Mrs. Goodrich, you said three nurses were sent home?"

"That's right, the three who attended the dance: Dixon, Lysander, and Reed."

"I thought you said Meg went home because of ill health?" Bea said.

Mrs. Goodrich seemed as baffled as we and then said, "Well, you know about Reed, of course."

"That's why we're here," Bea said. "To look into Meg Reid's death."

"Oh, oh, I understand. You don't know!" Mrs. Goodrich said. "Not our dear Meg, the other one. Our Meg was Megan Reid. R-E-I-D. But I mean the other nurse called Margaret Reed, with a double-E. She sometimes called herself Meg just for mischief, I think. Margaret went to the dance with Dixon and Lysander. It is she who was sent down."

CHAPTER EIGHTEEN

"Another nurse!" I exclaimed.

"I'm sorry, I thought you knew," Mrs. Goodrich went on. "Though she and Meg — our Meg — had almost the same name, they couldn't have been more different in temperament. Margaret, as I shall call her for the sake of clarity, was tall, powerfully built, and in her mid-forties. I understand that she came to South Africa with considerable experience, but this didn't seem to inspire confidence in either her supervisors or the other nurses. I don't think Meg liked her."

She sipped her wine before adding, "You must understand, Meg never spoke ill of anyone, no matter the provocation. Even if Margaret were dreadfully unkind to her, she wouldn't have said a word about it. What I'm telling you is from reading between the lines, as it were."

4th March

A fine day has dawned with blue skies and mild temperatures. Bea has gone for a walk with Mrs. Goodrich and Miss Adams. I am not sure if it's because she's hoping to learn something more or because she genuinely enjoys their company. I ate breakfast alone in my room and spent the morning thinking about everything we learned last night. I knew something was missing from the story of the three nurses, now we have some idea what it is. The problem is where do we go from here? Mrs. Goodrich does not have Nurse Reed's address so it may be difficult to find her. That is, if she is still alive.

I confess, when we retired last night, I had all but made my mind up that we should return to London as soon as possible so I could begin my search for this nurse. I am also well aware of my obligations to Mycroft. However, though she made every effort to disguise it, I could read Bea's disappointment quite clearly on her features. Her holidays must seem doomed to curtailment.

We were in her "cottage" in Sussex when word came of the queen's imminent death. I think Bea's grief surprised her. While their relationship could sometimes be fraught, she had great fondness for the old woman. Besides, as her godmother, the queen was almost the only family Bea has, besides me and, I suppose, Mycroft.

In the space of a moment, our quiet walks along the beach ended. Bea ordered her staff to ensure my comfort, and to arrange her transport to the Isle of Wight so she could say her goodbyes. A sad and sudden end to a blissful time.

Consequently, I felt reluctant to remove her from this much-needed break, but she rejected my suggestion that she remain here with Mrs. Goodrich and Miss Adams. We compromised by agreeing to stay in Kent until after luncheon. Perhaps when these cases are resolved, we might take a proper holiday together. I would like to return to Sussex; the cottage is charming, the food excellent, and the air fresh. It is, besides, not so far from London that I cannot easily return if necessary.

Bea returned with her cheeks flushed from her walk and her hair tumbling free of its pins to decorate her shoulders. As she brushed out her tresses, she said, "Mrs. Goodrich had a splendid notion, Sherlock. She suggested we write to the Matron over the Bloemfontein camp and ask her for an address for Nurse Reed."

"Yes, that is an excellent idea," I said. "I shall send a cable before we leave Kent. Did you learn anything further from her?"

"No; not, I suspect, because there is no more to tell, but I think Mrs. Goodrich feels she must be circumspect around Miss Adams."

"We may need to follow up with her after she returns to London. What time do you want to dine?"

"I just need to freshen up and try to do something with my hair. Shall we aim for 12:30?"

About twenty minutes later, looking every inch the sophisticated and titled London lady, Bea neatly packed her bag. As I watched her, I said, "I am sorry to take you away so soon, Bea. I know you were enjoying yourself."

"The case comes first. Perhaps we may return another time."

"Certainly, if you wish it. Indeed, while you were out walking with the ladies, I wondered if we might return to Sussex for a week or two when this case is done. Well, this and Mycroft's case."

"Oh, what a lovely idea! I do love the cottage."

She finished folding and placing the last garment and strapped the bag closed. Then, sitting in the armchair said, "Speaking of Mycroft's case, I have been thinking about that."

"Yes?"

"I wondered: what if you could plant someone in the office who could keep an eye on things there?"

"I had thought of that. However, there is still the matter of the murdered nurses to consider. Besides, all of Mycroft's staff know me too well."

Beatrice smiled. "They don't know me."

*

Later, as we sat on the train, we debated the subject. I felt uncomfortable with the idea of Bea working in the government office, even with Mycroft so close at hand. My brother is an exceptional man with many talents, but an agile defender of young women is not one of them. Bea tried not to laugh at the image but could not help the unladylike snort that resulted. I confess, I, too, chuckled at the thought.

"Sherlock," she said more sombrely, "you have been exhausting yourself trying to treat these two cases with equal attention. You must allow that I can keep better watch on Mycroft's office if I am close at hand. It will also afford you the freedom to devote yourself entirely to investigating these murders."

I thought about her suggestion for a moment. She did, indeed, make an excellent point. However, I thought of one more objection. "You have already been seen in Mycroft's office." She said nothing, and I added, "I need to give the matter further thought and, of course, we would need Mycroft's approval. In principle, however, I admit it might work."

"I'm sure it will, Sherlock. After all, no one in the office save for Mycroft knows that you and I are married. I can claim to be a family friend — it has the virtue of being true — and say that I have recently fallen on hard times. I can play the part of the secretary to ease some of Mycroft's burden, which would be an additional benefit."

"You have made your point," I said. "I will call upon Mycroft this evening at the Diogenes Club. Ultimately, it must be his decision."

"Excellent," she said, smiling broadly. "What time do we meet him?"

"We? The Diogenes Club does not permit women."

Her smile grew broader. "Oh, Sherlock, you worry too much."

*

The train made good time and we reached London a minute or two before five. I argued with all the logic at my disposal; I flatter myself the clarity of my thinking is

215

undiminished, and my arguments as forceful as ever; however, Bea refused to be dissuaded.

Well, I thought, it would no doubt amuse Mycroft, and at least Bea would hear for herself his answer.

I arrived home to find Watson sitting by the fire reading a book.

"I had hoped you would take a little longer, Holmes," he said in a reproachful voice after we exchanged greetings.

"We have a new lead on the case, as well as a plan to catch Mycroft's spy red-handed. Do you have any news?"

"I have heard from Dr Baxter. He reports no change in condition, but he has finally been able to obtain some samples for testing."

"Why did it take so long?"

"The gentleman seemed reluctant to cooperate. Still, it's done now. Tell me your news."

For the next hour, I updated him. He was astonished to hear about Margaret Reed.

"Why, that explains so much," he said. "Like Mr Kyle's report of the woman on the boat journey back from South Africa."

"Precisely. Bea kept saying all those stories of Meg being harsh and unpleasant seemed at odds with what she knew of the woman; she may have been right. Many of those tales pertained to Margaret Reed, not Meg."

"How do we find her?" he said. "Or is she dead, do you think?"

"We have insufficient evident to form a hypothesis. I have sent a telegram to South Africa to see if the matron can give us an address for her."

"It's unfortunate Megan lost her address book," Watson added. "Mrs Hudson said she had always kept one, but it went missing some time between her illness and her return home."

"Went missing, or was stolen," I said.

*

I telephoned Mycroft and told him to expect two visitors to the Diogenes Club at 8:15. He, I think, assumed I would attend with Watson, and I did not correct him.

I chuckled when a young man about town knocked on my door at 7:30. Bea appeared in a perfectly fitted black suit, a crisp white shirt, and a bowtie. The dark brown wig in the latest style fit perfectly. She completed the disguise with a pair of tortoiseshell spectacles.

Watson gasped with amazement.

"Bea? It is you, isn't it? Why, that's quite something."

"You make a bonny young man," I said. "What name should I call you?"

"I thought Ben. Ben Edwards."

"It's nice to meet you, Mr Edwards. Well, shall we?"

The Diogenes Club glittered under a bright moon, and soft light gleamed through the tall windows. The doorman, who knows me well, admitted me and my "friend" without demur. We waited in the Stranger's Room until my brother joined us.

"Sherlock, it's good to see you. I expected you bring the good doctor. How d'you do —" Then he gaped in utter astonishment as he recognised the "young man."

For a moment, I expected him to roar in fury. Though seldom seen, my brother has a fierce temper at times. However, instead, he threw back his head and laughed loudly. Several minutes passed before he could regain his equilibrium. He wiped tears from his eyes with his handkerchief and beamed with delight.

"Splendid!" he cried. "Utterly splendid. I think you both deserve an excellent dinner, but first, by your leave, I have some news, as, no doubt do you."

We had the room to ourselves and sat by the fire.

"A letter went missing some time this afternoon," Mycroft said softly. "Another important directive from the Foreign

217

Office and included a copy of Kitchener's itinerary. It turned up two hours later in exactly the right place. I've no idea where it had been during those missing hours. I would have contacted the good doctor if you had not telephoned to let me know you'd be joining me for dinner.

"This matter requires your full attention, Sherlock. I know, I know, the murdered nurses' case is unpleasant, but surely the official police can handle it. Besides, I happen to know the killer is dead."

"You are right, at least to a point, Mycroft. However, there are still many questions presented by the case, and these, I fear, are beyond the official police, for all they have developed over the years."

"But we do have a suggestion," Bea put in.

"Well, sister-mine," he said, smiling at her. "Do not keep me in suspense. Tell me, what is this suggestion?"

"We, your brother and I, that is, thought I might work in your office as a temporary secretary. I can come as myself or, perhaps preferably, as Ben Edwards whom you see before you this evening. I can observe the staff and visitors, and the documents that come into the office. I am sure you agree it is best if we catch the culprit in the act."

"Yes, indeed. And you are willing to do this, Bea — excuse me, Ben? I should warn you, apart from the, ah, skulduggery element, the job itself is quite tedious."

"If it will help you, dear Mycroft, and serve the country, I have no hesitation in offering my services. It also allows Sherlock to continue to work on his case. Everyone gains."

"Yes, indeed," Mycroft said, rising, as a staff member appeared at the door indicating our table was ready. "I think it is a splendid solution. Excellent, Ben. I shall be delighted to welcome you to the office. You have my word, Sherlock, I shall take excellent care of her."

"I do not doubt it," I replied softly, "but whoever is spying on your office may prove dangerous. Please promise me you'll be careful, Bea."

"I will, Sherlock. I promise."

CHAPTER NINETEEN

5th March

Beatrice has gone to Mycroft's office or, rather, "Ben" has. I am torn between amusement and concern. I know she will be careful, but I cannot help my disquiet. Whoever the spy may be in Mycroft's office, I have no doubt they will be dangerous if crossed.

Mrs. Goodrich sent word that she has directed her maid to send me all the letters from Megan. I am hoping they will arrive in this afternoon's post. Watson is back working in the clinic, and I am at a loose end until those letters arrive. I've never known a case with so many damned letters.

Bea has suggested we meet with Princess Christian and see if she can shed any further light on the events in Bloemfontein. As Her Highness is the president of the Army Nursing Services Reserve, I think the suggestion has much merit. Her Highness may be able to offer insights that we could not find elsewhere. I have still received nothing from Green, but I suppose one should not judge delays in receiving wartime post harshly.

*

This afternoon, I called in on the clinic but found Watson dealing with some medical crisis. I returned to Baker Street and spent a little time with Mrs Hudson and told her about the mysterious Margaret Reed. Even with the coffee and cake, however, that did not take as long as I might have liked. In the end — oh how the mighty have fallen! — I took myself off to St. Bart's to visit Lestrade.

I found the inspector in high good spirits. He is now allowed out of bed and is to be discharged home tomorrow.

"It still hurts," he said, "but compared with how it felt before the operation, it's pretty tolerable."

"When do you expect to return to work?"

"It will be up to my doctor, but I am hoping it won't be more than a couple of weeks. Between ourselves, Mr Holmes, I am not anxious to spend more time at home with my wife than I must." He chuckled. "Don't misunderstand me, she's a fine woman, but she must be constantly doing something and that is not restful for a man. Worse, she is so busy with her baking business that she is getting notions that I should quit the force and work with her. Am I not in enough pain?"

I could not help but laugh. Mrs. Lestrade is a force of nature.

"I quite understand," I said.

For the next half-hour, I updated him on the nurses' case, which kept us both engaged until visiting hours ended.

*

I did not return to Baker Street until almost five o'clock. I picked up the afternoon post from the hall table and noted the package of letters from Mrs. Goodrich. In addition, I received a parcel from South Africa, the long awaited information from Green. A feast or a famine, as they say.

I opened Green's parcel first.

Dear Mr Sherlock Holmes, (Green wrote)

I apologise for the delay in responding to your request. As I mentioned, I had gone up-country with one of the battalions, and we were away from the camp for several days. Upon my return I set about putting the

221

information together as you requested. I could have sent you some cuttings from various newspapers, and I have, indeed, included some, but in the interest of clarity, I thought to write a report of the events as they unfolded. Where I am uncertain about various incidents, I have been clear about that fact in my report. If my information came from hearsay, I have noted that, too. I am anxious that the details I am sharing with you are as truthful and accurate as possible.

Bloemfontein was the first of the camps, of the major ones anyway, to be established. It is also one of the largest, bigger even than the nearby town of Bloemfontein from which it derives its name.

The British took the town in March 1900, but refugees began arriving even before then. The camp is a hideous place, about two miles from the town, and it affords no protection whatsoever from the fierce sun that beats down on the tents every day.

As of January this year, an excess of 2000 souls lived in the camp, and that figure increases daily. I tell you this that you may better understand the ghastly conditions in which those nurses found themselves.

Privations were such that, in the early days, as many as twelve persons shared one tent. Furthermore, as there is no fuel, the Boer women scavenge for green bushes and mule

222

dung with which to make a fire. Things are little better with our people. For instance, many of the nurses begged the authorities for things as basic as soap and facilities to boil water — this last being essential due to the ever-present typhus. They did get some meagre provisions eventually, but everything seems to take so long.

Many of the inhabitants of the camp are women and children. The nurses, not only British, but also Australian and Canadian, do their best, God bless them, but disease runs rife through the camp, and many of the Boer women and their children are ill. Not only typhus, but dysentery and measles are rampant. The death numbers are dreadful, and yet, to the credit of the staff, the mortality rate is considerably less than it has been in other camps. Despite this, the camp hospital has an evil reputation. For many of the Boer, the word 'hospital' is synonymous with 'murder.' Frankly, I can see their point.

As you can imagine, with new refugees arriving daily, there is a constant need of medical attention. The nurses work twelve-hour shifts routinely, and seldom are granted time off, unless they fall ill. They are assisted by orderlies and auxiliary staff, most of them Boer.

By September, the staff who had arrived early on, which includes the nurses you listed, were frustrated, exhausted, and demoralised. When an army troop invited them to a social event, they were keen to go. There are a number of stories about whether the nurses had been given permission or not. The senior staff are adamant that permission had been refused, but Alice Dixon and Kathryn Lysander claim to have been told that they might attend. I have no proof, but I strongly suspect that a Miss Margaret Reed misinformed the other two. In any event, the three opted to go. They might have escaped with a scolding, but unfortunately, one of the Boer women, a Helena Cobbledick, and two of her children were gravely ill. During that night, the mother and the children —a boy, Herman, and his sister, Lizzie — died of measles. The little girl's photograph, taken after her death, appeared in the newspapers and subsequently circulated among the Boer as evidence of British cruelty and indifference. I have sent you a cutting about these deaths to give you an idea of how the incident was reported.

As the event threatened to become a major incident, the authorities felt they had no choice but to make an example of the three women. Accordingly, Dixon, Lysander, and Reed were dismissed and sent home.

I'm afraid that I know little about the dead woman's husband beyond the fact that he was a Boer whose homestead had been burned to the ground, and I believe his six other children died around that time. One can only imagine his fury. He went by the name of either Arno or Arnold Cobbledick.

You asked particularly about Megan Reid. I happened to have met her on a number of occasions. I found her to be a quiet, dedicated young woman, spending herself beyond wisdom. She suffered a number of health problems including a severe heart attack. Doctors ordered her to rest, but the night when the three nurses left the camp, she felt obliged to return to duty. As a result, her health became irreparably damaged, and she could no longer continue her work. Reluctantly, the administration sent her home.

Finally, I pass this one with no idea of its veracity, so you may make of it what you will: Rumour has it that the three nurses who attended the party stayed away all night. Upon their return the next day, they claimed that they had been so exhausted that they had fallen asleep, then, when they awoke, could not find anyone to give them a lift back to the camp. Some believe that they engaged in immoral behaviour with the soldiers.

I hope this is helpful, Mr Holmes. I would like to discuss the murders with you when I return to England; I have no idea at present when that may be.

Please let me know if you need anything further.

Sincerely,

Jerry P. Green

I read Green's report three times and pondered the contents. The accompanying article read as anti-British propaganda, but in light of the terrible death-rate in the Bloemfontein camp, it would prove difficult to refute. Green also included the article Cobbledick himself had possessed, the one that included the photograph of the three dead nurses.

At least now we have some facts. As Mrs. Goodrich said, it was Margaret, not Megan who attended the party. Arno Cobbledick shared his surname with the woman and the children who died. It may, of course, be a common name in South Africa, but I think it too much of a coincidence. Still, Inspector Morton is following up with the South African authorities for confirmation of the relationship between our murder victim and that unfortunate woman and her children.

I penned a brief letter of thanks to Green for his assistance then, setting the report aside, I settled back on the sofa and sorted Megan's letters to Mrs. Goodrich into reverse chronological order. I assumed the most recent letters would be of more use to my case than the older ones.

Unlike the letters to her mother, these missives contained none of the Scottish and Gaelic idioms that had so vexed Bea. I noticed a distinct change of tone in these letters to a friend she genuinely liked, compared with those sent to former colleagues. She exuded good sense, wit, and endless patience. My only complaint lies with the quality of her penmanship. I must assume she acquired illegible handwriting from too much time with physicians. I am bewildered that Bea and Watson can read her writing without any apparent difficulty.

The most recent letter is dated just two days before she died. This much I gleaned:

Thank you, dear Eleanor, for your most recent postcard. I am glad you are over that cough. It sounded most unpleasant. How attentive Edward is. You are fortunate to have found so kind and gentle a husband. As you know, not all physicians fall into that category.

You will be pleased to hear that I have been feeling far better these past few weeks. I find I can walk to the church without becoming short of breath, and this despite the cold, wet weather we have been experiencing. I begin to hope I may be able to return to nursing when I go home to Scotland. It may only be part time, but even that is an improvement over what I expected when I left South Africa.

Alice Dixon wrote to me a few days ago. She is hoping to get a job in her local hospital. I fear her chances may be poor given the reason she returned from South Africa. She seems to think the subject will not come up, but I cannot imagine any potential employer not asking about one's most recent experience, can you? I suppose she might lie. I would like to think better of her than that, but, frankly, I don't have much faith in her integrity. I suppose I should admire her consistency. She has never made any secret of her desire to marry a physician. If she spent as much time tending to her patients as she does her face — but that is unworthy. She cannot help who she is, I suppose.

I have heard nothing recently from Kathryn Lysander. I do hope she is well. My last letter from her revealed a deep sadness and despair that troubles me. Of the women who went to the dance that night, she alone exhibited any regrets. Indeed, she admits to suffering from chronic insomnia and wretched nightmares on those rare occasions when she does sleep. I confess, I, too, have nightmares. I than Heaven that my ill health enables me to sleep.

Kate found employment in Yorkshire, and I am delighted for her. I gather the work is hard (is nursing ever easy?), but she feels a deep sympathy for the patients in her care. She is less impressed with most of the staff. They have not worked anywhere but in England and that makes them ignorant of the situations in which Kate and the men in her care found themselves during their service. I invited her to come and visit me when I go home to Scotland. I think it would do us both good to talk about those terrible days. No one can truly understand unless they were there. We are not all gifted with such sympathetic friends as you, my dear Eleanor. I fear poor Kate is often seen as surly and ill-tempered, but I see a different side of her. She is blunt, certainly, and she has a sharp temper at times. However, there is such kindness and sympathy for her patients and the few friends she has, that I am inclined to be more charitable towards her.

You asked about (illegible) Margaret Reed. I have not heard from her at all since I returned, neither, to my knowledge, have the others. It's odd because she always seemed to see herself as the leader of the group when we were in South Africa.

There followed the usual valedictions and promises to keep in touch. I sat and contemplated the contents I had read. It revealed something about the group dynamics that I had not previously realised, to wit, that the previously unknown Margaret Reed saw herself as group leader; the recriminations and despair of Lysander; and the frivolity of Alice Dixon. And what of Meg Reid herself, I wondered. How did she fit into this tidy little group?

As I stood pondering this, the door opened, and Watson joined me at the fire.

"Ah, the letters have arrived," he said. "I hope they contained some good news. I could use some after the day I've had."

I refused to take that bait. I have made the mistake before about asking my friend to tell me about his day. Instead, I handed him the letter I had just read.

"She is a charming correspondent, is she not?" he said.

"Indeed," I replied indifferently.

He gave me a look and continued to read. "Interesting what she says about Nurse Lysander. The woman seems to have been deeply troubled. I must say, I am surprised she found a nursing job after being sent down from her post. Mind you, having seen that facility in Yorkshire, I don't doubt they were desperate for staff, and a Nightingale nurse would be welcomed."

"What exactly is a Nightingale nurse, Watson? How does she differ from any other kind?"

"Well, the Nightingale nurse is trained in the manner prescribed by Florence Nightingale. She understands the importance of cleanliness, fresh air, proper nutrition, and so forth. Other nurses — who are becoming fewer by the day — have no training at all. Some of them, to be sure, are competent, kind, and even efficient, but those are the exceptions. Most hospitals nowadays look for the Nightingale nurse because they know they will get someone whose work is of the highest standard. Mind you, some nurses of my acquaintance feel the late Mary Seacole did even more for the education of nurses than even Nightingale."

"So are there Seacole nurses too?"

"No, unfortunately not. And before you ask, I do not know why, though I suspect it may have something to do with Miss Seacole being a woman of African descent. It should not matter, but it seems to."

He looked so tired that I almost suggested he go to bed. I knew from experience, however, that he would balk at the idea. I decided to continue the conversation in hopes that it would help him to shake off whatever gloom had descended upon his spirts.

"After everything we've heard about the care given by some nurses in South Africa, does it not seem to you that there was little professionalism in their behaviour?"

He lit a cigarette and inhaled deeply before replying. "In some cases, that is true. However, I think we can agree that the circumstances are exceptional. Besides, you cannot judge all those women by the mistakes made by a few." Watson stretched his back and yawned.

I winced at the cracking sound his spine made. "Yes, that's true," I said. "I received the report from Green. He makes no bones about the conditions in Bloemfontein. You will find his letter most illuminating."

He read it through in silence, nodding and murmuring in agreement as he worked his way through the pages.

I waited until he had finished before adding, "Oh, by the by, Lestrade says hello and is happy to report that he is going home tomorrow."

"Good evening, gentlemen," a soft, feminine voice came from the door.

I turned and beheld Beatrice standing in the doorway, a faintly mocking look on her face. She looked as weary as I have ever seen her.

"Did Mycroft work you too hard?" I said, recovering my humour.

"He certainly kept me busy," she agreed. "But Mr Qualtrough had me running hither and yon all day. He's a fussy little man with delusions of competence. That is to say, he sees himself as Mycroft's successor, but he cannot even keep a simple list of five items in his head for more than fifteen seconds."

"Did you have a chance to ascertain the likelihood of his being the spy?"

"I think it exceedingly unlikely. He prefers to hand off tasks to other people rather than handling them himself. This is his habit, as several people told me, and that, combined with his inability to remember important details, seems a poor personality trait for a spy."

"It could be a ruse," Watson said. "A way of covering his behaviour."

"He has worked in Mycroft's office for years and his reputation followed him from the Ministry of the Treasury."

"So why would they assign him to Mycroft?" Watson continued, "if he were so ill equipped for the task?"

"In part, I am told, because Qualtrough's father-in-law, Sir Nigel Royston, demanded it. As Mycroft handles all the details himself it minimizes the amount of harm the fellow can do. On the other hand, it adds considerably to your brother's burden, Sherlock. He is worn ragged, poor man." She smiled. "I did suggest to him, in Qualtrough's hearing, that he should take a holiday and no doubt his assistant could handle everything in his absence. Oh, you should have seen the look on that pipsqueak's face! Mycroft and I had a good laugh about it later."

"Pipsqueak?" Watson said.

"Oh, one of young McDuff's words. It means inconsequential, I believe."

I could see Watson making mental note of the word for future usage.

"Have you formed any theories about the identity of the spy?" I asked.

"After one day? No, my dear Sherlock, not yet. Between learning the routine and keeping up with the work, I scarce had time to breathe. I have, however, met most of the staff. Wainwright is the senior clerk. A pleasant enough fellow with an unfortunate dandruff problem. I think him an unlikely spy; his unhappy affliction marks his presence everywhere he goes. He is, however, highly competent and an excellent worker. He seems devoted to Mycroft. It is Wainwright who does most of the work that Qualtrough ignores. He strikes me as kind and is generally well-thought of, except by the aforementioned Qualtrough. The two do not get along and, indeed, seldom speak to one another.

"Gillespie, you know. He has served as Mycroft's doorman for many years. While he has ample opportunity to help himself to any number of documents, I believe he is too stalwart a fellow to betray either his country or his senior officer. His respect for Mycroft is enduring. Unlike the rest of the office, Gillespie is aware that there is a spy. His outrage is

232

something to behold. I should not like to be near him when the culprit is unmasked."

"What of the others?" Watson asked.

"There are two junior clerks, McDuff and Burnett, inseparable and rather giddy. They seem to spend ninety percent of their time discussing tennis."

"And do they work the other ten percent?" I asked.

"Oh, heaven's no! They only work about one percent of the time; the remainder is spent discussing McDuff's father, whom he abhors." Bea shook her head when I offered her a glass of sherry. "I cannot stay, alas," she said, and continued:

"There is a pool of other junior staffers, each with a responsibility for a different region. There are about thirty of them. Their sphere of activity seems limited. They all work together in the same room and report directly to Wainwright. None of them seems a likely suspect.

"There are also the regular visitors. These are the ministers and under-secretaries from the various offices or departments who have reason to visit Mycroft to discuss any number of issues. These people come into the office several times a week. There are dozens of them. I'm afraid it will take some time to narrow the list. Now, if you'll forgive me, gentlemen, I must retire. I promised Mycroft I would get into the office early in the morning to go over some files with him."

CHAPTER TWENTY

6th March

I spent the morning reading Megan Reid's letters. I found little in the way of new information but having a better idea of the four participants gave me a clearer insight into the women's experience. I have also managed to arrange an appointment with Princess Christian, thanks to Beatrice. Her highness is the president of the Princess Christian's Army Nursing Service Reserve (PCANSR). Bea suspects that the princess will know about the incident in question and may be able to find the address of Nurse Margaret Reed, and perhaps even some background information. A telegram arrived from South Africa this afternoon saying that all records of previous staff have been sent back to the headquarters of their own country.

Progress, albeit slowly.

Watson returned at five o'clock and we dined together. As last night, Bea did not arrive until almost 11 p.m. To my surprise she was in merry spirits and gave the impression of having imbibed some potent drink.

"M took me to dinner at the Diogenes Club," she said. "It amuses him to see everyone treat me as a young man, and none the wiser."

"M?" I said.

"Mm. That's what everyone in the office calls your brother. It is a term of respect and affection, I think."

"I think you have been having a wonderful time working for my brother," I said, rather irritably.

"I have," she agreed. "I like being with clever people, and I like being busy."

"And how does your investigation progress?" Watson asked with a tone of amusement in his voice.

"It moves forward slowly. An important document came in today, something highly confidential and marked 'eyes only' for M. I kept close watch on it, and I noticed three individuals try to get their hands on it over the course of the day. Wainwright, the senior clerk, asked about it; I told him I was processing it. A while later, one of the clerks, a fellow named Anderson, said he needed to copy it. I told him that M had made it clear to me that there were to be no copies made of the document. And this afternoon, Sir Cuthbert Redmond stopped by from the Home Office and asked if we had received it. I told M about all these queries."

"Please stop calling my brother 'M'," I said testily. "I believe you are inebriated, Beatrice."

"Just good spirits," she replied with a smirk.

7th March

Bea had left Mycroft's office early returned to her home in Wimpole Street to transform herself back into a respectable married woman (though that fact and is known only to a trusted few). We ate a late luncheon and then rode in Beatrice's carriage to Windsor for our appointment with the princess.

We arrived at precisely at four o'clock, and our hostess did not keep us waiting. She presented as a practical, no-nonsense sort of woman in her fifties. She greeted Bea with no-nonsense affection and the two spent a few minutes discussing various family members and acquaintances. At length, the princess said, "Beatrice, I read about the deaths of these women newly returned from South Africa. So dreadful. Murdered, you said?"

Bea nodded to me, and I took up the tale, explaining how we knew for a fact that three nurses were now dead at the hands of Arno Cobbledick, a Boer.

"I see. Well, if the killer is dead, what do you need from me?"

"We have learned that there is a fourth nurse," I explained. "A woman called Margaret Reed whose last name was spelled differently from Megan's. We need to make sure she is safe and well."

The princess frowned. "Is this not mere curiosity, Mr Holmes? Since the killer is dead, I don't see why it matters; the woman is either alive or not. Either way, there will be no trial."

"Sherlock likes to be thorough, Helena," Bea said. "There are still some pertinent questions about this case, for instance, how the killer found the three nurses that we know of."

"Do you think Nurse Reed revealed that information?"

"Not necessarily, Your Highness," I said. "She may have been misled or even be completely uninvolved. We cannot tell until we ask her. Of greater concern is the chance that Cobbledick did not act alone. If he had an accomplice, more nurses may be at risk."

"I see. Well, of course I am happy to help in any way I can, but I must insist on your discretion, Mr Holmes. The formation of an official board of nursing is essential if we are to establish and maintain uniform standards of care, as well as to ensure our nurses are granted a professional status. This will benefit not only the young women who enter the field, but all the patients in their care. I confess these events in South Africa could present a serious obstacle to that goal.

"I have here a personnel sheet for Nurse Margaret Reed. In addition, I have the report from Sister Devereaux, who conducted the investigation into the South African event and the people concerned. I hope you will find both useful, Mr Holmes."

"You are most kind, Your Highness," I replied. "I appreciate you taking time out of your busy schedule to help us with this matter."

"Of course, Mr Holmes. I am relying on your discretion."

"You have my word, Your Highness" I replied.

Once we were snugly ensconced in Bea's carriage, she said, "Do you believe Margaret Reed has been murdered or had some part in the murders?"

I hesitated to reply. Often, I have found it is easier to think contrary thoughts than it is to try to verbalise them.

"It would be a mistake to theorise with so little information. Certainly, either of those scenarios may be correct, or neither. She and Cobbledick may have never crossed paths, for all we know."

"How did he get the addresses of those three women?"

"Perhaps from someone in Bloemfontein. Unfortunately, there are some questions to which we may never learn the answers."

She snuggled under the warm rug and remained silent for a moment. I could, however, almost hear her mind working. After a few minutes she said, "Have you met Helena before — Princess Christian, I should say?"

"I saw her at a dinner I attended in the late queen's presence some years ago," I said, "but we did not have an opportunity to converse. You and she seem on excellent terms."

"Yes, I like her. She has her father's curious mind and her mother's determination. Of all the queen's children, she is the one I like best."

"More than the new king?" I said, in mock affrontery.

She laughed. "Ah, you have learned how to tease as well as be teased. Excellent! In fact, I am fond of Bertie — that is, his majesty, but he never forgets he is a man, and a woman is a woman. Every conversation with him is coloured by that perspective. With Helena, we are simply people together." She laughed. "You are eager to begin reading those papers, I see. Do not let me distract you."

I smiled. She was, of course, perfectly correct, and so I began to read the documents the princess had given us. As I finished each page, I passed it silently to Bea.

"'A natural leader with considerable clinical skills, who would do well to remember that she is not infallible. She is often guided by her emotions, and this impairs her judgment,'" she said, reading from Reed's personnel sheet. "Oh, and someone added this after the dance party event: 'Can, on occasion, lead less experienced nurses astray due to her strong personality and sometimes questionable judgement.' Hmm, it seems the South African hierarchy placed primary responsibility for the actions of the three nurses on Reed's shoulders. She certainly seems like a strong personality."

Bea read the pages as I handed them to her, and she exhaled in a huff of irritation.

"Whoever wrote this report has a tenuous grasp of truth and impartiality," she said, drily. "Thank goodness we had a less jaundiced account from Green."

"Yes, indeed. I suppose it is useful to see how the nursing reserve corps is presenting the events. 'While one may excuse the nurses' need for a brief respite following their weeks of unbroken labour, one cannot pardon their absence for the entire night,' I read. Curious."

"What's that, Sherlock?"

"There is no mention of the Cobbledick family or the demise of the mother and her children. A strange omission given that this event was the alleged reason the nurses were dismissed."

"How curious. An attempt to dissuade anyone from investigating that event, I suppose. By presenting the nurses' unauthorised absence as a lack of judgment and the sole reason for their dismissal, it looks as if the leadership in South Africa are being firm and highly moral."

"Quite," I said. "I suppose that is one reason Nurse Lysander found a job in Yorkshire; even Dixon had a job of sorts. No doubt the omission benefitted them in one way; in an interview, the nurses could claim that they were exhausted due to the rigors of war. With staff in short supply, they should not be long out of work.

"More importantly, we now have Margaret Reed's last known address. Another element I find curious."

"Mm, Manchester," Bea said. "Naïve of me to hope that she lived in Marylebone. When would you like to go? It's a bit late now to take that journey; it's almost six o'clock."

"Tomorrow morning will suffice."

She hesitated and I wondered at her frown. "I am supposed to work with Mycroft tomorrow, but I'm sure he'll understand if I have another commitment."

"I can go alone," I said. "Watson has been working in the clinic all week and he is worn out."

By the time we returned to Baker Street, we found Watson waking from a nap on the sofa. The newspaper lay sprawled over him, and he jolted awake when we opened the door.

"Good nap, John?" Bea said, hiding a smile.

"Yes, thank you. I'm not sure why I feel so lethargic today."

"I understand you have resumed working long hours at the clinic. I'm sure that must take a toll."

"Sad cases," he said, adjusting his clothing as he sat up. "Those poor wretches have been through so much. It would horrify you to see their injuries."

"I hope you are not overdoing things, dear John. Your commitment to the care of these men is commendable, but you cannot forget your own health."

"Thank you, Bea. I assure you I am perfectly well, only a little tired. I feel much better for the nap, and I am not on the schedule again until next week, so that should set me to rights.

239

"Oh, before I forget, Holmes, Baxter stopped by the clinic to let me know that all the tests were negative."

"Damnation!"

"That's good news, surely?"

I tried to keep my reply as non-committal as I could. Watson, knowing better than to push the matter, said, "So, tell me, how did you get on? Was Princess Christian able to help?"

"We have an address for Nurse Margaret Reed," I said. "She lives in Manchester, in the Victoria Building. I plan to go to see her tomorrow."

"Oh. You don't want me to come?"

"I thought you might like to have the chance to rest, my dear fellow," I replied. I could see his disappointment, though he tried to hide it.

"It's hardly arduous," he said, "Sitting on a train."

Bea swallowed a grin. "Well, I think if John does not object, Sherlock, you would find his presence invaluable. After everything we have heard about Margaret Reed, I think it would be as well to go accompanied by a man who handles women so adeptly."

"Well, I am glad you both have arranged everything to your satisfaction," I said feeling thoroughly disgruntled. "You need hardly involve me at all."

"I'm sorry, Sherlock," Bea said. "Do you mind?"

These emotional matters are tempestuous waters and I do not trust myself to navigate them. "No," I said, "No, of course I do not mind." Though, in fact, I could not be sure how I felt.

"Isn't Manchester where Cobbledick's killer lived?" Watson said.

"Well, the pair took the train there, but whether that is where they reside, I cannot say. Still, I take your point; it does seem rather coincidental that Miss Reed should live in the same city."

"What about the incident that precipitated this whole event?" Watson said, moving on. "What have you learned?"

Bea handed him the report and he read it out loud:

> *An Investigation by the Nurses' Activities Committee into the alleged dereliction of duty and abandonment of post by Nurses Margaret Reed, Alice Dixon, and Kathryn Lysander.*
>
> *Last month, on the thirteenth of September (Thursday), Nurse Margaret Reed approached me to ask if she, Kathryn Lysander, and Alice Dixon might have the following Saturday (15th) evening off in order to attend a dance party being thrown by the 1st East Lancashires. Lysander and Dixon were rostered for the day shift in the camp, and Reed the night shift.*
>
> *Given the late notice and the lack of available staff to replace them, their request was denied.*
>
> *I later learned that the aforementioned three nurses had appealed my decision to Matron. They were again denied permission to take the night off for the aforementioned reasons.*
>
> *However, on the morning of Saturday 15th September, one of the orderlies, Edward Moorhouse, informed Sister Channing that none of the nurses had reported for duty. She sent word to Hospital No. 8 requesting assistance, but while they were amenable,*

nurses would not be available until the following morning. Given the extreme needs of our patients, and despite her recent, life-threatening illness, Nurse Megan Reid offered to work the shift alone. This she did, with assistance from Sister and the orderly.

Subsequently, Nurse Margaret Reed also failed to report for her night duty shift and, as a consequence, Nurse Megan Reid ended up working a double shift to the serious detriment of her health. Orderly Moorhouse voluntarily stayed to work the night shift with her.

Sister Channing later confirmed that the three nurses in question had indeed left the camp, contrary to the orders of senior staff.

Compounding the issue is the fact that the three nurses in question did not return until 1300 hours on Sunday. Nurse Reed intimated that they were all so exhausted that they had fallen asleep at the party and did not waken until late the following morning. They had some difficulty getting a lift back to the camp. It should be noted that upon their return, none of the three seemed capable of giving an acceptable account of themselves, and it appeared that they were inebriated. One can only surmise what they had been up to during the night. It is my opinion that their conduct did not become ladies much less members of the Princess

Christian Reserve Nursing Service. It is the opinion of the investigating panel that the three are guilty of dereliction of duty, and of abandoning their post.

In the interest of justice, it is only fair to note that none of the women in question has had a day off in almost a month. In addition to this, they have been working 12-16 hour days in the most trying circumstances. While the committee agrees that this is unfortunate, it does not, in our opinion, mitigate their abandoning their post, particularly as replacement staff had already been requested. Furthermore, it should be remembered that Nurse Megan Reid, who ended up covering a vast number of patients alone and worked a double shift to cover for her errant colleagues, is recovering from serious health problems. This incident has, unfortunately, had a serious impact upon her health, and it now seems inevitable that she will have to leave the service and return home. This is a tragedy, not only to Nurse Reid, but to the service. She represents the very best of what a nurse should be, and we can ill afford to lose nurses of her calibre.

Of the three nurses who went absent without permission, only Kathryn Lysander has apologised and requested to be allowed to stay. Her observation that the shortage of Nightingale staff will negatively impact the patients is noted. However, the committee feels that all of the nurses betrayed the watchwords of duty and respectability, and all should be dismissed from service. We feel it would be unfair to make an exception for one and not the others.

Signed on behalf of the Nurses' Activities Committee by Sister J.D. Devereux. Sunday, 21ˢᵗ October, 1900: Bloemfontein Hospital 8, South Africa.

Watson frowned and set down the document. "There isn't much there we didn't already know, but it feels far more condemnatory laid out in this stark manner."

"Yes, it is cold and blunt as one might expect of a military ruling, though I confess I would have expected more compassion from a nursing service."

"Even in nursing, discipline must be maintained," Watson said. "The service had no choice but to discharge them."

"At least it completely exonerates Meg of any wrong doing," Bea added. "I think her mother would find comfort in that."

I agreed. "The worst part of this, in my opinion, is that the selfishness of those three women led, in part, to the deterioration in Meg's health that necessitated her return home."

*

For several hours I sat up reading Meg's letters. I found myself immersed in the picture she drew of life in South Africa. Deprivation widespread, hunger commonplace, disease rife. Almost everyone spoke of the Boer with hatred,

244

something Meg found distressing. She took the "all God's children" approach, which I find commendable under the circumstances. Despite being an excellent nurse, it appears that she came in for a fair amount of berating and hectoring from some of the other staff. Perhaps, surrounded as she was with violence and death, sneers and scolding did not seem so important.

However, one incident concerning Margaret Reed seemed to distress her particularly. Meg had spent the previous two weeks in hospital due to another bout of dysentery; upon her discharge, she was assigned to the night shift with Reed. From what Watson has told me, I believe the night shift is generally quieter than the day shift. "Although that can change in an instant. All it takes is one emergency to throw the entire night into chaos."

Meg and Margaret Reed were making their rounds when they were accosted by a group of men. The nurses were harangued and pushed around. Meg tried to placate the intruders, pointing out that the nurses were there to administer care to the sick. Margaret, on the other hand, decried the men in the most passionate and, it seems, unladylike language. As a result, the incident, which may have passed without injury, escalated, and one of the men punched Margaret in the face. There followed a number of kicks and punches and only the arrival of a small group of armed soldiers saved the women from a most horrible fate. No sooner had the situation calmed when Meg suffered a heart attack. Margaret had sustained several contusions and lacerations, and a sprained shoulder. They rushed Meg to the infirmary, and she subsequently spent several weeks convalescing. During this period the physicians and senior management decided that they could not risk her health further and told her she was being discharged home.

Margaret Reed spent the night in the infirmary. Doctors released her the following day with orders to stay off work for the following two weeks.

Upon her release, it seems that Margaret became skittish about working the night shift and took pains to avoid it. Further, it appears that her contempt for the Boer had escalated into utter hatred.

Less than a month after Margaret's return to work, Dixon told her of their invitation from the soldiers. Curiously, that night, the night of the dance, should have been the first night shift she worked since that violent incident. Meg does not specifically state that this influenced Margaret's insistence on accepting the officers' invitation, but it is evident that she is of that opinion.

Again, though Meg does not say so, it appears Margaret Reed's argument that all the staff had been working long hours for weeks was disingenuous at best. While it may well have been the case for Lysander and Dixon, she had returned to duty a mere three weeks earlier. Even supposing she had worked the same hours as the others, she could not have been as fatigued as they, given the extent of her recent sick leave. (I have no doubt Watson would disagree with me on this point.)

Once she heard about the event, Margaret became obsessed with attending. She began to importune every sister in the hospital trying to persuade them to let her go. When her efforts proved in vain, she decided to attend anyway, and persuaded the others to join her.

Meg wrote,

> *Most of what I am telling you now I learned after the event. I had been discharged from the hospital back to my tent, and, as I remained so unwell, I seldom encountered the gossip that is so prevalent in all medical establishments.*

246

On the day of the dance, Orderly Edward Moorhouse, told me that Lysander and Dixon had not reported for their shift as scheduled. The nurses who were going off-duty had sent him to report their absence to Sister, but he wanted to cover for them if he could. (Unlike many of the orderlies, Mr Moorhouse is an absolute treasure and always tries to help the nursing staff.) He came to ask my advice. Although I felt, and indeed, still feel quite dreadful about it, I knew he had no choice but to report their absence to Sister. At the time, I fretted that they had fallen ill. It never occurred to me that they had gone absent without leave.

About twenty minutes later, Sister Channing came to see me looking vexed. 'I've sent to the hospitals to see if they can send some replacement staff, but at this late notice, it is unlikely. Those girls have gone to that wretched dance!'

The lack of staff presented a crisis not only for the patients for whom we were responsible, but also for the reputation of the entire nursing corps. Although my physical condition remained poor, I could not ignore the situation, and so I told Sister Channing that I would work the shift. She initially refused my offer, but when it became evident there were no other options, she agreed. With her help, and that of Mr Moorhouse, we managed to get through a difficult evening. Sadly, we lost a woman and two of her children to a variety of illnesses, but their deaths were expected.

Sister Channing, bless her, had already worked sixteen hours in a row. She could not have been kinder to me, though, of course, I could see how furious she felt about the nurses who had gone absent without leave. She dismissed any sense of guilt I felt in having Mr Moorhouse report their absence and pointed out that she would have observed the women's absence when she made her rounds. Furthermore, Sister spoke to the patrolmen at the gate and thus confirmed that the three had left the camp. The men had already reported the incident to their own Commanding Officer.y the time the night shift rolled around, and neither Nurse Reed nor the other nurses had returned, I had volunteered to stay on duty with the assistance of Mr Moorhouse. Sister Fox would assist me as much as she could. I must say, the senior nursing staff proved extremely kind and supportive. That said, I felt utterly spent by the time the morning came and had to be carried to my quarters. I still blush to think of it.

I slept for the longest time. I did not waken until two days later and found myself back in the infirmary. I then learned that Reed, Dixon, and Lysander had been suspended pending an investigation. Fortunately, a *new group of nurses had arrived, and that helped the staffing levels considerably.*

As I am sure you will remember, Eleanor, you cannot beat a hospital for gossip, and, as you can imagine, this is magnified on a war front. Being back in infirmary meant I got to hear all the rumours that were circulating. I soon began to hear that the three blamed me for reporting them and were furious.

I asked to see them. Kate could not have been kinder. She took full responsibility for her actions. She should know better, she said. She told me that Rosemary Godwin had agreed to swap the shift with her, but, apparently, changed her mind but did not let Kate know. When asked, Rosemary completely denied the agreement. (I hate to speak ill, as you know, but Rosemary, being a bit of a duffer, often fell foul of Kate's sharp tongue, so I cannot help but think that Rosemary hoped to get Kate in trouble.) I digress. Kate apologised for being in part responsible for me having to work the shifts and my subsequent relapse. She hoped I suffered no ill-effects as a result.

Dixon never came to see me, but Reed did, and she ranted at me so long and so loudly that Dr Stewart evicted her from the room.

Her tirade reduced me to tears, and I feel I shall never recover from her excoriating remarks. I must put aside my letter now, as the doctor will be here shortly to examine me. Oh, Eleanor, they mean to send me home. I am so afraid that I will never nurse again.

Sister Channing tells me that there will be a hearing next week. I am expected to answer questions about that awful evening, and I rather dread it. I hate to get my colleagues in trouble, but I must speak the truth.

Pray for me, dear Eleanor, and all those who suffer in this dreadful war. What will happen to these poor, dear people?

Your devoted friend, Meg.

An appalling situation, indeed. Whilst I can understand the women wanting to take a little time to themselves, but surely their responsibilities and duties should come first. I wonder what Watson will make of it.

CHAPTER TWENTY-ONE

8th March, 3:15 p.m.: Manchester

Those of us who live in London are always startled to find other cities contain their own sort of vibrancy. The hustle and bustle of central Manchester easily equals that of the capital. Trams, carriages, and omnibuses dominate the streets, while people throng on the pavement. The buildings are, in the main, built of a striking red brick. Bea, who seems to possess more irrelevant information even than Watson, informed me that these are made from Accrington Red bricks, hence the vibrant colour. For reasons known only to herself, she added, with wry amusement, that there are an estimated 11,000 hansom cabs in London alone, not counting other vehicles, and several thousand horse-drawn omnibuses culminating in an approximate 50,000 horses trudging through the streets each day. "That's a lot of manure, don't you think?" she concluded. I cannot imagine what made me think of that. The stench, probably.

Watson and I arrived this afternoon to find the city in the middle of a downpour. We found a cab outside the train station and within a matter of minutes alighted outside a clean and modest hotel in Victoria Street. By the grace of some divine power or mere good fortune, we were able to get a room which afforded a direct view of the Victoria Building where Miss Reed lives. The compromise is that we must share a double room; Watson insists I sometimes talk to myself in my sleep. Absolute rubbish! I can attest, however, that he snores loudly enough to be heard over the average brass band. Still, it's only for one night, so I suppose we can put up with each other for that long.

I made enquiries at the front desk and learned that Miss Reed owns a sizeable apartment on the top floor of the building opposite. A woman of means, then. With the assistance of a few shillings, the concierge told me that our window faced her. Excellent!

As Watson unpacked his bag, I sat by the window, my glasses trained on the window opposite. Unfortunately, thanks to the lace curtains, I could not see much. However, after about ten minutes of careful observation, and with the rain stopped, the curtains were drawn back by a young woman in maid's attire, and she opened the window.

"Holmes," Watson said.

"Hm?"

"Holmes?"

"Yes, I hear you. What is it, Watson?"

"Luncheon. Come on. You cannot change anything by sitting there staring across the street."

Before I could reply, the maid closed the curtains again. Though they rippled lightly in the breeze, I could not see beyond them.

I swallowed back the arguments that rose to my lips. I knew from long experience that I could not win this disagreement. Besides, as I could not see anything, I may as well indulge him. I slid the binoculars into the desk drawer and followed Watson downstairs. Not far from the hotel, we found a small restaurant with excellent service and edible food, which is to say Watson enjoyed it. I drank a cup of coffee that had pretentions of being Turkish.

Knowing my eagerness to get back to work, Watson did not delay. "What's our plan, Holmes?" he said.

"I think we should simply go to see Miss Reed. We will say that we were concerned for her well-being. After that, well, we shall have to wait and see."

After our meal, we crossed the street to the Victoria Building and had to walk around the triangular shaped edifice to the Deansgate side in order to gain admittance.

We were accommodated by a friendly and exceedingly helpful doorman. He was a tall, hulking fellow, obviously a retired soldier. I could see at once that he had been married for a long time and had at least three grandchildren. A swimmer, by his complexion, and a regular churchgoer.

"Whittaker," he said, "Lionel Whittaker. What may I do for you gentlemen?"

"I am Sherlock Holmes. This is my friend and colleague, Dr Watson," I said.

A young man stopped and asked the doorman for directions to the nearest public convenience. The doorman responded with admirably detailed directions before turning back to us.

"Sherlock Holmes and Doctor Watson, by Jove!" he said. "Well, my, it's an honour to meet you gentlemen. An honour and a privilege." He shook Watson's hand energetically. "Always good to meet another retired soldier."

"What regiment?" Watson asked, his cheeks aglow with enthusiasm.

"The 7th Queen's Own Hussars," the doorman said.

"Were you, indeed? You were in India?"

"Aye, though not for long. Got bitten by a ruddy snake — begging your pardon — and sent home not six weeks after I arrived."

"You're lucky to be alive," Watson said. "I didn't last too long in Afghanistan, myself."

"Excuse me," a woman said, "Mr Peters? He's expecting me."

"You'd be Miss Walcott? Yes, ma'am. Mr Peters is on the third floor. Number 306. Do you need the lift?"

"I wouldn't set foot in one of those contraptions if you paid me," she replied with a snort.

After the door closed behind her, Whittaker turned back to us and said, "How may I help two of the finest men in England?"

"We were hoping to see Miss Reed," Watson said.

A look that might have been distaste flickered across the man's face, but another interruption forestalled his reply.

Moments later, Whittaker turned back to us. "This is a bad time to talk, gentlemen," he said.

"Could we meet you after your shift?" Watson said.

"I should like to, but I have to go to the hospital this evening, and I have an early shift again tomorrow. Perhaps tomorrow evening?"

"It shall have to wait for another time, I'm afraid," I said as I shook his hand. "No doubt we shall be back in Manchester in the near future. I wish your grandson a speedy recovery."

He blinked, examined his appearance, and smiled at the small stuffed kitten that peeked out of his pocket. "Astonishing. Quite remarkable. I shall look forward to meeting you again, gentlemen. You'll find Miss Reed on the fifth floor. You need to go through the building to the Victoria Street side and take the lift up. Her door directly faces the lift, number 508. Oh, and make sure you close the gate tightly. We've been having a problem with the latch."

We bade goodbye to Whittaker and pressed the button for the lift. As we waited for it to descend, Watson said, "I spotted the stuffed animal, but how did you know that it was for a sick grandson?"

"Why else would he have the toy with him? He obviously brought it with him from home because he would not have had time to go shopping during his lunch break."

"It could have been for a son."

"Not so, Watson. He has been married for at least thirty years. He wears a silver tie pin to which pearls were later added. Silver being the traditional symbol of twenty-five years, and pearls for thirty."

"What about a granddaughter?"

"The kitten had a tag attached that said, 'To Charlie.'"

We stepped onto the lift and Watson pushed the button for the fifth floor. As we rose up the building, he said in a lofty voice, "You realise he could have been married twice, and his second wife is much younger."

Our arrival on the fifth floor rescued me from having to make a response.

*

The top floor of the Victoria Building featured a stylish landing with wood-panelled walls, and a deep-pile red rug upon the floor. The light streamed in from a tall window adjacent to Miss Reed's flat. Upon inspection, I found that this boasted a splendid view of the bustling city and our own humble hotel room directly opposite.

We knocked on the door and introduced ourselves to a maid with striking copper-red hair and the most perfect emerald eyes I have ever seen. Her eyelashes and brows were so light as to be almost invisible. She admitted us into the large bright sitting room where the curtains continued to waft in the gentle breeze and went to fetch the mistress. A few moments later, the woman herself emerged leaning on a cane and assisted by her maid.

Margaret Reed is tall, at least as tall as Watson, but frail. Though I would put her age at around forty, she appears much older. Her once-fair hair is now mostly silver, and I noticed several bald spots under the thin strands. A complicated-looking sling encased her right arm and positioned it with the hand towards her left shoulder. She also wore a neck brace. Not surprisingly, her face looked pinched and drawn, like one who has suffered a long-standing illness. She moved slowly, leaning heavily on a cane, and, with some help from the maid, eased herself into a well-cushioned armchair.

At her invitation, we sat on the sofa facing her. The pale blue eyes, flecked with green and centred by small pupils, met mine without hesitation. I observed that her left hand looked coarse and red, a nurse's legacy, I suppose. Though I surmised she could hardly be more than forty, something about her reminded me of withered leaves falling unheeded in the December snows. She greeted us politely and sent the maid to fetch coffee.

"It is kind of you to take the time to see us, Miss Reed," I said.

"I have heard of your work, Mr Holmes," she said, "And, of course, yours, Dr Watson. I cannot imagine what help I can offer you, but you may be sure I will do all I can."

"We wanted to talk to you about the murder of several of your colleagues," Watson began in his soft, gentle voice. "I'm sure you read about it in the newspapers."

"I did. So awful. I rather lost touch with them after we returned home to England, but we were close for a while."

"When you served in South Africa?"

"Yes. I'm sure I don't have to tell you, Dr Watson, that serving together in wartime forges close bonds. That is no less true for women than it is for men."

"Since you were all cohorts," I said, "We were concerned for your safety."

"I understand. I am fortunate to be as you see me. Have you found him, the wretched man who committed these atrocities?"

"Yes," I said. "Dead."

"He took his own life out of guilt?"

"He was murdered."

She fell silent and I could not read her face.

"What can you tell us about the women?" I continued, "Your former colleagues?"

She smiled sadly. "Probably less than you might like. People behave differently when they are away from home. And really, if the killer is dead, what does it matter, now?"

"I like to be thorough," I said as smoothly as I could. "Besides, the families are still looking for answers. The motive, in particular."

"Well, I will tell you what I can, with the caveat that young women away from home, all that freedom makes them giddy, some of them, anyway. They were all considerably younger than me, so you must forgive my rather maternal attitude towards them."

"We are most obliged for your insights," I said.

"I dislike speaking ill of the dead, but dissembling will not help you. I found Alice Dixon to be a spoiled young woman. She did not like getting her hands dirty; I cannot imagine what she thought nurses do. But she wanted to marry a doctor, so I suppose she thought it worth the trouble. I found her an indifferent nurse, more concerned with her appearance and self-indulgence than caring for those poor, wounded and diseased men. She wasn't unintelligent, just single-minded in her goals. If she had committed to being the sort of nurse our patients needed, she might have done well, I think. She did not lack compassion, and I confess the patients seemed fond of her.

"Kathryn Lysander seemed very much her opposite: dedicated, intelligent, and one of the best in terms of knowledge and technical ability. In short, a dedicated nurse, like Meg. Though where Meg embodied kindness, exceptional knowledge, and limitless charity, Kathryn could be abrasive and no-nonsense. Still, the patients seemed to love her and, to be fair, regardless of how acerbic she could be with her colleagues, she showed exemplary kindness and gentleness to those in her care. She told me once that she understood suffering. I did not doubt it. Poor woman bore scars on her face and arms, old, but still painful, I'm sure."

257

"Did she say where she had acquired them?" Watson asked.

"No, and one didn't like to ask. There were lots of rumours: a violent husband, an abusive father, but no one knew for sure. In any event, her own experiences made her a compassionate and hard-working nurse. Even the most horrific wounds did not seem to trouble her; she treated every man without demur. I often thought she would have made an excellent doctor. She frequently observed details that the physicians missed."

"That cannot have warmed the doctors to her," Watson said.

"True. Where Meg would have drawn the same thing to their attention, she'd have done it in an innocent, 'please explain it to me' way that no one could take issue with. Kathryn, on the other hand, would march up to whatever poor physician vexed her, her hands on her hips, and accuse him of incompetence before he'd even had a chance to observe the patient for himself.

"The patients loved her for it; they saw her as their advocate, an avenging angel. Kathryn didn't care what anyone thought of her. She did what she believed to be right, and the devil take the consequences."

"As in her going absent without authorisation?" I said.

Her face did not change expression. If anything, I would say she froze, but only for an instant. Almost at once, she managed to offer a semblance of a smile and said, "Kathryn and I agreed that requesting to attend the dance should not have been so extraordinary. We had all gone to similar events in the past without any problems. Certainly, the nursing sisters did not approve; I knew the behaviour of some of the younger nurses left something to be desired, but what can one expect when young women are far away from home for the first time and without any real supervision?"

"But in this instance," Watson said, "there were large numbers of nurses who were sick, leaving those who could care for the patients much reduced in number. Surely you and the other nurses felt a duty to those in your charge?"

"What about our duty to ourselves? From what I've read, Dr Watson, you have served in a war zone. What sort of care can you expect a nurse to deliver if she is exhausted and starving? Our supervisory nurses could have requested additional staff from other hospitals for a few weeks so we would have a chance to rest and recover, but they refused to do that. At least, not until after the dance when the staffing became critical. They were negligent in their treatment of us. They told us we were replaceable, and yet they refused to replace us. We were all sick of it." She paused and smiled at the maid who brought in the coffee. "Thank you, Iris," she said. For a few moments, attention must be taken with domestic matters; coffee had to be poured, sugar and milk offered, also food of some variety.

Eventually, clutching her half-filled cup in a slightly trembling hand, she added, "I won't distress your sensibilities by discussing our living accommodations, particularly while we are eating.

"I should add, too, that we did not leave the camp willy-nilly. We had asked other staff to trade shifts with us. Lysander, I believe, had been promised by another nurse that she would work on her behalf. I'm not sure about Dixon."

"And you?" Watson asked in that gentle voice that has won him so many admirers.

"It wasn't my responsibility. The sisters were being paid to manage the rosters. If they'd done their job properly, there would not have been such shortages."

"How did Meg end up taking a shift the day of the party?" Watson said. "I understand she had been unwell."

"She chose to," Miss Reed replied. "I imagine one of the sisters complained about having no one to cover the shift, and

Megan volunteered to do it. I heard that her doctor recoiled from releasing her to duty but felt he had no choice under the circumstances. Some orderlies had been requested to return to the camp from other hospitals, but they would not arrive until morning. The Sister should have taken care of the matter much sooner."

She sipped her coffee slowly, her trembling hand making it difficult. "I understand from your point of view we must seem like villains, gentlemen," she continued. "But if the staffing had been better managed, no problems would have arisen. The issue lay not with our alleged dereliction of duty, but with our supervisors' incompetence."

Without looking, I could feel Watson's frown. There were few crimes he abhorred more than dereliction of duty whether it be by a soldier or a doctor or nurse.

"How did you get injured?" I asked. "Did it happen on the front?"

"Yes. A group of Boer assaulted me one night. I still don't know how I escaped with my life."

"That must have been terrifying," Watson said. Despite the gentleness in his voice, I could hear the undercurrent of disapproval.

"Terrifying," Miss Reed replied. "Megan and I were on duty in the camp. Most of the people were grateful for our care, but some, well, they saw us only as oppressors. A group of men became aggressive, and they focused all their hatred on me. Thank heaven some soldiers happened by when they did. I cannot think how it would have ended if they had not. I spent two weeks in the infirmary, and I haven't been the same since."

"Was Meg injured in the attack, too?" I asked.

With a haughty look she said, "No. They didn't lay a finger on her."

"I take it your injuries have become more troublesome since your return home?" Watson said.

"Yes, I sustained nerve damage of the right shoulder. Later, arthritis set into the joints and is much aggravated by the cold weather." She sipped her coffee. "Some days are better than others. I suffered a terrible episode about three weeks ago. The pain became unmanageable, and I ended up spending the night in hospital."

"Do you remember what day?" I asked. It is three weeks exactly since Cobbledick died.

She frowned and shook her head. "Iris, what day did I go into the Royal Infirmary?"

"It was a Tuesday, Miss Reed. You remember, I had gone to the market and brought home those lovely lavender salts you like. You were planning to take a bath in them to ease the pain but ended up having to go to the hospital instead."

"That's right. I don't know what I'd do without you, Iris. Thank you."

The maid refilled our cups, and Watson resumed his topic. "What set them off?" he asked. "The Boer, I mean."

"If you mean, did we provoke them? No, certainly not. There weren't too many men in the camp; most of the occupants were women and children. I've no idea where those men came from. All I know is that they felt angry and put-upon. The fact that we were women made us easy targets for their anger."

"Excuse me, I did not mean to suggest that you had instigated the attack; I meant, had they been drinking, or had some event in the camp angered them."

She released her anger in a slow exhalation of breath. "I'm sorry. I suppose I am still not over the event. My sleep is still troubled by terrible nightmares."

"I quite understand."

"To answer your question, nothing had aggravated them that I know of. Megan often observed that the Boers' living accommodations were appalling, and that is true, but it doesn't justify their behaviour, in my opinion."

261

"Were there no men on duty with you?" Watson persisted.

"Yes, at least theoretically. An orderly called Moorhouse had been assigned to that shift, but he claimed he had dysentery and had to answer a call of nature. In any event, he did not show up until after the incident."

"Unfortunate," Watson said, "but I suppose it could not be helped. What became of the men who assaulted you?"

"Nothing, as far as I know. They were threatened with detention, but that meant nothing to men like that. The soldiers who came to our aid escorted us back to our base and saw that we received the medical attention we needed."

"Both of you? I thought Meg escaped injury?"

"She didn't have a scratch; no one would harm a hair on her precious little head. Saint Megan. She did have a bad reaction afterwards, though, with her heart and breathing affected, so they admitted her to the hospital too. Oh dear, I sound like a cat, don't I? Poor woman suffered the most awful health, and the senior sisters took terrible advantage of her kindness and sense of duty.

"The night of the attack came only a few days after Meg had been discharged from the infirmary after treatment for dysentery. I suppose I am annoyed because she seemed to blame me for the assault. Not that she made any direct allegations; she wouldn't do that. But she said I should have just played along, and that you had to know how to talk to those bounders. She may have been right; I can be too bull-headed for my own good."

"Did the nurses have any enemies that you know of?" I asked. "Do you know why a man called Arno Cobbledick might have sought out your friends and killed them?"

"Cobbledick?" she said. "The name is familiar. I think we had a patient by that name. A woman, terribly ill, and her children too. Perhaps they were related?"

"We believe so."

"Oh dear. I'm afraid the enemy made quite the production about us, that is, the British, treating the Boer with disdain and cruelty. I can only suppose this fellow listened to those allegations and believed them. I really cannot think of another reason why he would have sought those three nurses out because they didn't have anything to do with that poor woman's care. That is, Meg would have looked after her, but I am sure she did everything in her power to help her and the children."

We left shortly afterwards, thanking Reed for her time. As the door closed behind us, I smiled to see Watson bristling so much he might have made a fine hedgehog.

"You are upset with the way the women were treated, Watson?" I said as we rode down in the lift.

"Yes, of course; what civilized man would not? But it's not that which irks me, Holmes. There is something about that woman I find utterly disagreeable. It's telling that she took the brunt of the assault, allegedly, while Meg remained untouched."

"Allegedly? You do not believe her account?"

"Oh, I'm sure there is some truth in it, but I doubt her injuries were to the extent that she claims. She says she was signed off duty for two weeks; that suggests a soft tissue injury. Had she suffered broken bones, she would have been unable to work for much longer a period."

"Do you think she lied to the doctors then, or is lying to us now?"

"Neither, necessarily. She may, at the time, have merely wanted to make a point about how vulnerable the nurses were, or she may have been suffering real pain or shock. I suppose it's possible, too, that her injuries were more severe than they first appeared. But that problem with her right arm, her neck, and her difficulty walking seem much too severe to be related to mere soft tissue injuries that occurred half a year ago. It's not only the injuries, either. Her colour is poor, and I believe her pain is genuine." He pursed his lips as he looked at me. "I see that none of this surprises you."

Watson's much-overlooked perspicacity amused me. I pushed the gate open, and we stepped out into the lobby. Even the stench of the wet street beyond felt like a relief after the claustrophobic atmosphere of that flat. We waved at the busy Mr Whittaker as we left the building and joined the bustling throng on the street.

"Back to the hotel?" Watson said.

"Not yet. I want to visit the infirmary."

CHAPTER TWENTY-TWO

In the cab, Watson said, "Holmes, I hate to admit it, but there is no way she could have killed Cobbledick, not with those injuries. However, the casual way she mentioned her alibi seems suspicious."

"Ah, you spotted that. Yes, and how she conveniently mentioned the name of the hospital so we could confirm."

"On the other hand," Watson said, "It's possible that she merely wanted to be helpful. Her needing to ask the maid when she had gone into the hospital may have been perfectly legitimate. She is an irksome woman. I wonder why she became a nurse. I'll tell you one thing, though, she is addicted to laudanum."

"The pinpoint pupils, the trembling hand? Yes, I drew the same conclusion. I suppose that gives some credence to the theory that she did suffer from some physical trauma."

"Not necessarily, Holmes. Laudanum can be given for a number of reasons, dysentery, for instance."

The journey to the Royal Infirmary took less than fifteen minutes. By the time we arrived at the big red building (another one!), the rain had stopped.

It took some time to find someone who could confirm Reed's admittance to the hospital. Thanks only to Watson's status as a doctor, and a junior physician who greatly admired his writings, were we allowed to see the records.

"She came in around 4 p.m. on that Tuesday," Watson said, interpreting the bewildering hieroglyphs on the page. "Complaining of intractable pain. Tenderness and swelling noted at the third cervical vertebrae and right shoulder. Radiculopathy to the right hand. They admitted her overnight and administered an injection of morphine. By the following morning, she said she felt somewhat better having slept all night following the injection. The attending physician voiced reluctance to discharge her, but she insisted. Her maid came in a taxi and escorted her home."

"Well, that's clear enough," I admitted. "Not that I expected anything different."

By this time, I could see that Watson was flagging. It had been a long day, and for all his bravado about a train journey not presenting any challenges to his stamina, I could see he needed to rest. In addition, I needed to think. I had much to consider.

*

I settled myself by the window of the hotel room smoking the first of what I expected would be several pipes. Evening slipped into night, but I hardly noticed. Watson, utterly done in, poor fellow, had needed little persuasion to lie down for an hour or two. It took me a moment for my mind to register a curious groaning sound. I turned to see Watson tossing about in the bed. I confess my initial reaction was annoyance. I dislike having my reverie interrupted, but my irritation lasted no more than an instant. As he grew louder and more agitated, I understood why he had been so fatigued of late. He suddenly screamed, "Oh God, his head! He has no head! Jock! Jock!"

"Watson!" I cried, gently shaking him. "John! Come now, wake up. It is a nightmare, that's all. Watson!"

With another cry he sat up in the bed, shaking convulsively, bathed in sweat. "It's all right," I said, trying to soothe him. "You're safe. Watson, you're safe. I won't let any harm come to you."

"Holmes!" he cried, coming to his senses. "Oh, dear God!"

I put my arms around him and held him until he'd calmed. It is only in retrospect that I thought to be surprised by my own behaviour. In the moment, however, it felt natural and, thank God, it had the desired effect.

"Take a breath," I said. "That's it. I will get you a glass of water —"

"No! No, Holmes, please, don't leave. Just, please, just stay here with me a minute."

I stayed still, and eventually his trembling stopped.

"Sorry," he said. "What a fool I am."

"On the contrary, you are the wisest man I know. Are you sure you're feeling better?"

"Yes. Yes, thank you, Holmes. Just a nightmare. I'm sorry I disturbed you."

"It couldn't matter less. Do you want to talk about it?"

"Good heaven, no!"

I wanted to press, but I could see nothing could be gained, not at this juncture. Perhaps later, when he calmed.

"Have you been enduring these dreams every night?"

"No, not every night." He met my eyes and managed an embarrassed smile. "But often enough."

"Watson, perhaps you should consider leaving the clinic. You're ruining your health —"

"No, no, Holmes. The clinic needs me. I'll take that water now, if I may."

I poured him a glass from the carafe on the dresser. He downed it in almost one gulp.

"Thank you. I used to get these all the time, every time I fell asleep, I woke again screaming. It hasn't been this bad in years."

"What helped you get better the last time?"

"You did." The embarrassed smile flashed briefly. "Sharing 221B with you, working on cases together. It helped me to realise that my life did not have to be over, and there were other ways I could make a difference in the world."

*

About an hour later, we went downstairs to the restaurant in the hotel. We managed to find a corner table, quiet and secluded. To appease Watson, I ordered a full meal, as did he. At least his appetite hadn't been affected. I also ordered a bottle of scotch.

"A glass would do, Holmes," he said, mildly, as I poured for him.

"We shall take the bottle to our room."

Since the war and his nightmares were obviously forbidden subjects, I spoke at some length about the operas of the great Guiseppe Verdi whose recent death is such a loss to the world of music.

"I am, I confess, rather partial to *Rigoletto*. It is a musical triumph, and I defy any man not to hum along to *La donna è mobile*." I demonstrated for good measure and smiled to see Watson roll his eyes. "Of course, Bea prefers *Nabucco*, I have heard her sing *Va Pensiero, Sull'ali Dorate*. She has a pleasant voice though, of course, it is untrained."

"I've been thinking about those nurses," Watson interrupted abruptly. He certainly knows how to capture my attention. "I believe Kathryn and Megan volunteered to serve because they felt a genuine compassion for the injured and the sick; Alice Dixon focused on her quest to meet and marry a physician. However, Miss Reed does not seem to fit into either of those categories."

"True. She is an anomaly," I agreed. "She is obviously wealthy enough that she never needed to work. Is it possible she merely felt called to serve?"

"Oh, come, Holmes, you met her. Did she strike you as the serving others type?"

I smiled and he realised I was merely amusing myself.

He laughed. "Well played, sir," he said. More sombrely he continued, "I have known some nurses who enjoy being in a position where they can bully and abuse others. Oh, I'm not saying that is she; in fact, she may have been very different in the early days of her career. But I would not rule it out. Her lack of concern for Meg, indeed, for all her former colleagues, is quite telling."

"That does seem more likely," I agreed. "She has a strong personality; not the sort of woman who seems interested in serving others in any capacity."

We fell silent as the waiter cleared the table. We took the bottle and our glasses to our room and did not resume our conversation until we were inside.

"The whole thing is a muddle," Watson said, as if there had been no interruption, "Why did Cobbledick focus on those nurses out of all the other people in the camp? How did he get to England, and more to the point, how did he find out where the nurses lived? How did he mix up Meg and Margaret? How did Margaret come by her injuries? Who killed Cobbledick and why?" He paused and yawned so loudly I half expected his jaw to crack.

"Enough for tonight," I told him. "It's bedtime for you."

"It isn't that late, Holmes. Why, it's not even nine o'clock."

"A good sound night's sleep will set you to rights. Come on, Watson. You know I'm right."

Watson looked at his bed in distaste but proceeded to get himself ready to retire. With a huff of annoyance, he lay down and said, "I'm not even sleepy."

I turned down the gaslight and returned to my seat by the window. I lit a cigarette and said softly, "I have nightmares too, Watson. Or rather, the same nightmare, over and over. I am falling off the Falls with his hands at my throat. I can feel the spume and smell the water, but there is nothing beneath us but the abyss."

"Not surprising," he said. "Moriarty came closer to ending your life than anyone, plus he forced your lengthy exile from England. Why did you never tell me about them?"

269

"Probably for the same reason you never told me about yours, Watson. One doesn't like to seem weak, or a coward. Besides, in daylight, it feels as if one is safe and well, and one doesn't like to be reminded of those terrible dreams."

For several minutes he remained silent. I continued to smoke my cigarette and thought he might have fallen asleep, but at length he said, "He was a young orderly who sometimes worked as my assistant. Jock. He came from Edinburgh, nice lad, barely seventeen years old.

"We, Jock and I, were escorting two wounded men back to the base when the enemy opened fire. We took cover behind some boulders and fired back. Imagine it, Holmes: two medical men and a couple of wounded men facing an untold number of enemies.

"The firing was very heavy and some of the enemy were shooting over the very rock that made our shelter. The onslaught seemed endless and Flynn, one of our patients, was crying out in pain from a leg wound. Try as I may, I could not stop the bleeding. I bound dressing over dressing, but each became soaked so quickly. Too quickly. As the blood dripped onto the ground, it hissed and congealed on the heat of the stones.

"The other patient, an Irish lad named McDermott, insisted on fighting at our side despite his wounds. For about fifty of the longest minutes of my life the gunfire shattered the peace of that godforsaken dune. I heard a whistling sound, the sound of a bullet flying close by my ear. I felt something warm spray my cheek. I turned and saw, Oh God!"

"Go on, Watson. It's the only way to overcome it, as well you know."

"Jock's head had been shot off, the entire right side. In my nightmares, though," and his speech faded.

"His entire head is gone?" I finished.

"Yes."

270

"What happened to McDermott and the other wounded soldier?"

"The three of us made it back to camp, thanks to the timely arrival of a platoon of the 66th Berkshires. McDermott had lost two fingers, and the other man, Flynn, died the following day of the wounds he received previously. I escaped without a scratch."

We fell silent. I struggled for something to say. Then, in despair, returned to the topic of "Tally-ho."

"Did you know," I said, "that after the success of the Tally-Ho coaching service which you mentioned the other day, many other companies sprang up using the same name?"

I turned to look at him, but he was sound asleep.

*

9th March, 8:30 a.m.: Manchester

Watson slept soundly for the rest of the night, I am happy to say, and for more than ten hours. He desperately needed it, poor chap.

I have been sitting by the window, smoking, for most of the night, thinking about the case and what we have learned so far. While there is no doubt that Arno Cobbledick murdered the nurses, I cannot find his connection to Margaret Reed. There is a missing link somewhere. What takes us from Cobbledick to the dead women? Did he contact Reed, or did she get in touch with him? How did he identify the nurses? What part did that newspaper article we found in his hotel room play? Is that how he mistook Meg for Margaret? It's possible. What really caused Reed's injuries? And, not least, who murdered Cobbledick and why? I will not feel this case is finally closed until I can put all the pieces together, to my own satisfaction if no one else's.

Watson seemed quite himself when he woke up. After we broke our fast in the hotel restaurant, we walked to St.

271

Barnabas's Church. The rain had stopped, at least for the moment, so we enjoyed a dry if rather grey walk.

Father Boyd looked no more than seven-and-twenty. Impossibly young, and even more impossibly trusting. He would be delighted to help us, he said. He insisted on bringing us into his rectory, or whatever they call those places, and gave us tea. Watson accepted his cup with delight, saying he found the hotel's offering substandard.

"I don't know this lad," the priest said, pointing at the picture, "But I know lots of people who work in the field helping fellows like him. I'll show it around and I'm sure I shall find someone who knows him. It might take a few days, mind."

I handed him my card with my telephone number. "We expect to return to London this evening. Call any time and reverse the charges. I am most grateful for your assistance."

"Not at all, I am happy to help. Tell me, how is that nephew of mine? He's a good boy, is Raymond, but I worry about him since his dad died last year."

"He seems to have surrounded himself by a gang of youths of poor character. It is a pity, because he is bright and eager to learn."

The young priest looked troubled. "I shall have to bring him to Manchester," he said, "though what I shall do with him, I have no idea."

Between them, Watson and the priest drained the teapot. It pleased me to see a return of the brightness in my friend's eyes that has been missing for some time.

*

"Where now?" my friend said, as we walked back the way we had come.

"The local constabulary, I think. I should like to see if they know anything about Miss Reed."

272

"That seems a long shot," Watson said. "She would have needed a clean record to be accepted into nursing school. Still, it's worth a try, I suppose."

The police station lay hard by, and we arrived in a matter of minutes. A stodgy fellow who introduced himself as Inspector Pellow offered the usual "honoured to meet you" palaver, though I did not trust the suspicion in his eyes.

Over a cup of appalling coffee, he told me that he had lived in Manchester all his life and knew Miss Reed by reputation.

"Not that she'd have anything to do with a man like me, you understand," he said, "with her being quite the lady and me being nothing more than a working lad. Anyway, most people know her family, what with her father being wealthy, and her being his only kin, she inherited everything upon his death."

"When was that?" Watson asked.

"About fifteen years ago. He served as a local politician and was greatly admired as a humanitarian; however, we officers saw a rather different side of him."

"Oh?"

"There were rumours. Nothing ever substantiated, you understand, but many believed that he had an unsavoury interest in little girls."

I tasted bile in my mouth and saw the blood rise in Watson's cheeks. He sucked in his lips in what I recognised as an attempt to avoid releasing an oath.

"Did you find evidence?" I asked.

"No, only whispers. I and many of my colleagues believed it, but we could never catch him. He felt unsavoury."

"Had he ever been inappropriate with his daughter?" Watson said.

"She never said anything, but the rumours were disturbing."

"What happened to him?" I asked.

273

Pellow leaned forward and in a lowered voice added, "Gentlemen, what I am going to tell you is just a rumour. There isn't a scrap of evidence to prove it. If you tell anyone I said this, I shall deny it."

"You may count on our discretion," I said.

"Thank you. About fifteen years ago, Mr Reed took his daughter to Heaton Park Lake for a few days. They went annually. Locals said he could easily have afforded a trip to the sea, or to London, or could even have taken her abroad, but I 'spect he didn't get rich by splashing on luxuries. Anyway, off they go to the lake and on their first day there, he rents a boat and takes her out on the water."

"Was this usual?"

"Yes, indeed, Mr Holmes. Same thing every year. Anyway, no one knows for sure what happened, but somehow Mr Reed ends in the water. Miss Reed said he tried to reach for summat and lost his balance."

"It could happen," I said, "what makes you doubt it?"

"The big black bruise on the fellow's head. Daughter claimed he'd banged into the boat, but most of us reckoned the bruise looked the exact size and shape as an oar."

"What did the surgeon say?"

"Accidental death. Miss Reed sat there, demure as a nun, and no one could believe her capable of such a thing. Murdering her father, indeed! Not she! We knew though. Coppers, I mean."

"Fifteen years ago, you said?"

"About that. Mind, she were no nipper at the time, nearly thirty, if she were a day. If the stories about him were true, I'd have thought she'd be too old for the dirty bastard — begging your pardon."

"Perhaps she was, but one is never too old for revenge," I mused. "If our suspicions are correct, her fury and outrage may have been building for many years."

274

"She may have even thought she had a responsibility to protect other young girls," Watson added. "I suppose we shall never know."

"Anyway, she sold that big house she'd lived in with him and moved into that hotel on Victoria Street," the inspector continued. "Next thing is she wants to do some good, so she trains as a nurse. Fair number of folks had a bet against her making it, but blowed if she didn't succeed. I'll say one thing for her, she's determined. Like her father in that respect. Next I hear she's off to South Africa to do her bit for 'our boys'."

"Does she have any intimate acquaintances?"

"I doubt it. Too stuck up. I'd say the only one who knows anything about her is that maid of hers. Too cheap to pay for a full staff, for all the money she's got."

"We met her yesterday, and she seemed to have a number of disabilities."

"Seemed being the word all right. The cane comes and goes, though I suppose she could have good days as well as bad."

"Yes, she said as much."

"In fairness, I will say she has seemed much worse of late. It's been increasingly difficult for her. I saw her in one of the shops a couple of weeks ago and her hand looked so crooked she could barely use it to open her purse. And she's not an old woman, as I say."

"She does seem much older than her years," Watsons said.

"Aye, she do at that. She had hair like honey not so long ago. Before she went to South Africa, I mean. Hung down her back to her waist, they say. Not an unattractive woman at all. Now, though," he shook his head. "I 'spect she had a hard war, as they say."

"No doubt."

We thanked the sergeant and left.

Over luncheon in an out of the way pub, Watson said, "What do you make of that, Holmes?"

275

"A lot of hearsay, but it does explain something about her air of self-possession and detachment."

"She's had to learn to protect herself," he said, sipping his beer. After he wiped the foam from his mouth he added, "One of those more sinned against than sinning, perhaps. It doesn't make her more likeable, but at least it explains something about her behaviour."

"Other than the small matter of patricide," I said.

"Assuming it's true."

"You doubt it?"

He shook his head. "No, I'm sure it's true. What about you, Holmes?"

"It would, as you say, explain much about her. However, it remains hearsay. We should remember it, docket it. It may, perhaps, prove useful later."

"What now?" Watson said.

I looked at my pocket-watch. "I think we have done all we can at present. I suggest we return to the hotel and pack our bags. We may leave as soon as we wish."

"Excellent."

CHAPTER TWENTY-THREE

10th March, 2p.m.: Baker Street

For all its smoke, noise, and bedlam, London is still a relief. Beatrice arrived after dinner. Watson and I took turns telling her about Manchester. She listened in her usual intelligent silence until we finished and said, "Well, I'm sorry I missed it. Margaret Reed seems like an interesting woman. Do you honestly believe she murdered her father?"

"There is no proof, but it seems probable," I said. "It would certainly explain much about her behaviour."

"Poor woman must have been driven to extremes," Watson said. "Such a horrible crime, to murder a parent. Unforgivable in the eyes of many."

Bea seemed lost in her own thoughts for several minutes. When at last she became aware of the silence she said, "Apologies. What you said, John, about something being unforgiveable reminded me of a conversation I had with Megan not long before she died.

"I had come here to see you, Sherlock, and I met her in the hallway downstairs. We exchanged the usual perfunctory greetings, but I observed that she seemed troubled about something. I asked her if I could do anything for her, and she said, 'Do you think there are some sins too terrible to be forgiven?' You know I am not particularly religious, so the question disconcerted me. I told her that I did not know, and suggested she talk to her minister."

"Do you think she did?" Watson said.

"I have no idea. You spoke to the minister after the murder, didn't you, Sherlock? Did he give you any indication?"

"No, indeed. I focused primarily on the murder itself. He led me to believe he didn't know her well, but he may have felt a need to be circumspect."

"I cannot think why I did not recall that conversation until now," Bea added. "It's funny, isn't it, the way the mind works?"

"Perhaps your woman's intuition at work?" Watson suggested.

"Watson may have a point, Bea. You know, I have often found my intuition has a profound impact in the solving of problems. How many scientists have made remarkable breakthroughs because they listened to their instinct? I am sure you have found the same thing in medicine, Watson."

"Yes, indeed. It happens far more often than one might imagine."

"And you think my instinct is trying to tell me something now, Sherlock?" Bea said.

"Perhaps. It's certainly worth following up."

"If the nurses learned that Reed had murdered her father, that might be sufficient reason for wanting them dead," Watson said.

After a brief and fruitless debate on that topic, the conversation turned to Mycroft's office. Bea assured us that there had been no further activity.

"That's good, isn't it?" Watson said.

"Up to a point. Unfortunately, it means that everyone in the office, barring Mycroft and I, remain under suspicion. It's an untenable situation."

I smiled at the mischievous look on her face. "You have a plan," I said. "Is it the one we discussed?"

"It is, indeed. Mycroft and I have made a document of our own and spread the word that it contains a vital update to the submarine plans, invalidating everything that came before it."

"What is in the plans that will narrow the suspect list?" Watson said.

"It's not anything that is in the plans, but what is *on* them."

I laughed. "You and my brother make a fine pair of desperadoes. Tell Watson what you have concocted."

"Just a little compound of methylene blue dye," she said. "It goes inside the folder with the papers. We have made sure it is invisible to the naked eye."

"But anyone who touches it will find their hands turn blue," Watson said, and joined in my laughter. "That's splendid!"

"We had toyed with the idea of using itching powder," Bea continued, "but we realised anyone's hands might itch for any number of reasons. The blue dye will be much more difficult to explain. I started to think about it when Mycroft said he wanted to catch the culprit red-handed," she chuckled. "He agreed that blue-handed works just as well."

"Excellent!" I said. "When does your plan go into action?"

"Tomorrow morning. The 'letter' and its folder have been prepared and it will be delivered to Mycroft's office in the morning. It will come with an 'eyes only' stamp so none of the assistants will be allowed near it. I will place it in the safe, and make sure enough people know what it is. Then we will wait."

I laughed. "I would dearly love to come to the office in the morning and see how it plays out, but I mustn't tip off the thief. I must be content to hear all about it later."

"I must go," Bea said, rising. "I have a busy day ahead of me."

I walked her downstairs, and we stood talking in the hallway for a short time. "I never knew what it meant to be employed," she said, "nor to spend my days in some worthwhile activity. My godmother, may she rest in peace, frowned on anything other than charity work for young ladies."

"And the king?"

"Oh, he doesn't mind. I finally may do as I wish. I am still awed by the thoughts of such freedom."

As she turned to leave, I caught her hand and said, "If I find the minister cannot help us, perhaps we should visit Mrs. Goodrich. I suspect she knows more than she told us. A lot more."

*

11th March

Watson is back in the clinic this morning and so I ate breakfast alone. In the distance, I could hear the usual cacophony: the traffic as it rumbled through Baker Street, a door banging, and Maisie somewhere downstairs singing a plaintive Celtic ballad. The song suits her voice far better than her usual music hall ditties. I asked her about it when she came to fetch the breakfast things.

"Oh, it's a tune my wee brother sings at home. Kevin has a grand voice, and you'd love to hear him sing. It's called *The Mountains of Mourne*, and it's about how much we miss Ireland when we're away from it."

"Well, it's a lovely melody."

As she piled the dishes onto the tray, I said, "Do you get homesick, Maisie?"

She nodded. In a voice thickened by tears she added, "I do, aye. It's Kevin's birthday today, and I miss him, and all my brothers and sisters."

With her mood surprisingly clinging to me, I donned my coat and gloves and set off to St. Thomas' Church. Fortunately, I found the Reverend Cyril T. Cleghorne in his study. He greeted me warmly, shook my hand, and invited me to join him in a cup of tea.

As we sipped the surprisingly good Darjeeling, I told him about Arno Cobbledick and my theory regarding his motive for killing the nurses.

"Poor women," he said, shaking his head. "Poor women. What could have poisoned his heart to commit such a dreadful act?"

"What we have learned so far, Dr Cleghorne, is that three women, colleagues of Megan's but not Megan herself, attended a party while they were serving in South Africa. This, despite the fact that they had been refused permission to attend. During their absence, a woman and two children died. Though we are still awaiting confirmation, it appears that this man was husband to the woman, and father to the children."

"It is certainly understandable that he should harbour such resentment. Understandable, if regrettable. But from your tone, Mr Holmes, I suspect there is more to this story."

"I believe there is, all my instincts tell me so. However, what that might be." I met his clear, blue eyes, and read his sympathy and understanding.

"And you believe I can help you? Well, I certainly will if I can."

"It is a delicate matter," I said, over the rim of my teacup. "And were it not a matter of seeing justice done for these poor women, I would not dream of asking you."

"Please, if I can be of any assistance. I am not a priest, after all. We do not have the concept of confession as a sacrament, though, of course, one tries to be discreet."

"I understand, Dr Cleghorne; it is not only ministers who must be discreet." He nodded sympathetically, and I continued. "We have learned that another woman, a person called Margaret Reed, also served in South Africa at the same time as the other ladies. I wonder if Meg said anything to you about her?"

"Not by name, Mr Holmes, but she did mention to me a woman that she described as forceful and sometimes lacking in judgment. Do you think it might be the same person?"

"It certainly matches her description. Can you tell me what Megan said about her?"

281

He remained silent for several moments then set down his teacup. "Well, with the understanding that we cannot be certain that we are speaking of the same woman, I can tell you that Miss Reid did once ask me what one's responsibility would be if one believed a that a peer was behaving in an immoral manner. I told her she should tell the individual that she found such behaviour troubling and why. I emphasised that she should speak in as gentle and forgiving a manner as possible. Then it would be up to the individual to take heed or not."

"And she said, 'was behaving' implying some ongoing the activity?"

"To the best of my recollection."

I thanked him for his time, and, with his assurance that he would keep me in his prayers, I left. I found my mind distracted and my mood still oddly dejected. With a concerted effort, I focused on the case. From what Cleghorne said, it seemed that Meg's conversation with him did not relate to Reed's alleged murder of her father, nor the nurses' unauthorised absence from the camp, but something more insidious. Something ongoing? Of course, if she did mean Reed, it may have been merely a matter of her attitude. I am hopeful that Mrs. Goodrich knows more. If not, this may become one of those cases that Watson never writes about, the ones that end up going nowhere. Dear God, I hope not! I should not be able to face Mrs Hudson if I failed so terribly though, to be fair, I believe that good lady is satisfied enough.

Both this and Mycroft's damnable case seem to drag on and on. Every time I think I have got to the heart of either matter I find yet another layer underneath. It feels more like archaeology than detective work.

I needed a walk, and as the day remained dry and bright, I set off to Hampstead Heath. While Morton and O'Brien had closed the case on Dixon's murder, that of Cobbledick remained open. I hoped they might have news.

282

Fortunately, both were at the station and seemed pleased to see me. I politely rejected their offer of coffee and joined them in the station's sitting room, telling them about recent developments in the case.

"I can request the file on Reed's father, Mr Holmes," Inspector Morton said. "I doubt it will tell us much, but you never know."

"Better than rumours and speculation, in any case," O'Brien added. I agreed wholeheartedly.

I stayed for an hour, and before I left, I invited the two men to stop by Baker Street this evening after their shift for a glass of brandy. They were both happy to accept. (This is Watson's doing. He is turning me into what our American friends would call a glad-hander despite my strongest resistance.)

The weather, in typically British fashion, had changed by the time I left. A savage breeze tore the leaves from the trees and stippled the budding daffodils with careless hailstones.

I took a cab home.

Maisie, still humming, though more cheerfully this time, handed me an enormous basket of fruit and some messages when I came in. The basket came from Lestrade and his wife and included a thank you note to all of us for being so kind and visiting so regularly.

I set it aside and made myself comfortable by the fire, with two other notes in hand. Before I had even opened the first envelope, Watson returned from his shift and graced his customary chair opposite me.

"A gift from Lestrade?" he said, immediately opening the basket and taking an apple. "What does he have to say?"

"A thank you to all of us." I handed him the note.

"That's very thoughtful," Watson said. "He seems to be recovering nicely."

"Yes, he'll be back to his usual level of mediocrity in no time."

"Tut, Holmes, that's not kind. Lestrade has come a long way over the years. You've been a wonderful influence on him."

Watson thinks I don't see when he is laying on the compliments. I gave him my most long-suffering look and received nothing but a smirk in return.

The letter I opened came from Jerry Green. He confirmed that Arno Cobbledick had been the husband of the unfortunate woman and children who died. He included an article about the scandal which included a photograph of the distraught man. Green added, "The Cobbledicks' two babes died at the same time, as I think you know; but they were the last of what had been a brood of eight. Enough to damage any man's mind."

After dinner as I sat pondering what we have learned so far, the door opened, and a rather windswept Bea entered. She seemed in high good spirits. Both her exuberance and her appearance spoke of an eventful day.

She all but leaped on the sofa, laughing. "Oh, Sherlock, you should have been there, it was glorious!"

"Tell us."

CHAPTER TWENTY-FOUR

She took the glass of sherry I handed her, shrugged off her jacket, and told her story.

"Mycroft and I spent the last few days creating a document that purported to completely revise several aspects of the submarine. Unadulterated piffle, of course."

"Cleverly designed to shake out the spy," Watson said with a chuckle. "I gather it worked?"

"Like a charm! Mycroft and I let a couple of the juniors hear us discussing the letter and the importance of keeping it under lock and key. McDuff and Burnett, in particular, are chatterboxes, and we knew they wouldn't be able to keep the information to themselves."

"I hope they don't usually have access to anything of any importance," Watson said, aghast.

"Not usually, and then only when it serve's M's purpose. There are times when news cannot be disseminated in the usual manner. This is an excellent case in point. When we need to share news but on a completely unofficial basis, using juniors like McDuff and Burnett is an excellent way to proceed.

"Anyway, Mycroft made sure everyone knew he'd locked the document in his safe. With that done, he spent the next several hours in various meetings around the building. I turned away several visitors who arrived in hopes of seeing him. The day rather dragged, and from my vantage point — I have a desk at the end of the hallway that leads to his office — I could see anyone who attempted to slip into his room.

"A little after two, Sir Edgar Lyons arrived, but when I said Mycroft was in a meeting he asked, first, how long he might be. When I said I didn't know, he said he wanted to leave something for him. I offered to take care of it. He agreed, and left.

"Only moments later, Malcolm Amberley stopped by. I have seen healthier looking cadavers. He is all bone, and his flesh is so yellow he looked like a walking candle. I had a similar conversation with him. When I replied that I did not know how long Mycroft would be, he asked if he might wait for him in the office. I agreed. He stayed for the best part of an hour. I checked on him after a while and brought him some coffee. I found him asleep in the armchair by the fire. I confess, for a moment I thought he had expired, but he woke and took the cup.

"I asked if I could help with anything, and he said he was retiring and wanted to thank Mycroft for all his years of help. I did not doubt his sincerity, and I asked Gillespie to send a message to M to take a short break from his meeting.

"Mycroft returned a few minutes later and he and Amberley spent about twenty minutes together in his office, before the poor man left. Mycroft checked his safe and nothing had been disturbed.

"Mycroft returned to his meeting, and around four o'clock a third visitor arrived."

"Let me guess," I said, "Sir Cuthbert Redmond?"

"Quite so. He said he had an urgent matter to discuss with Mycroft. I explained about M's meeting, whereupon Redmond asked if he might leave a note in M's office. I acted as if I were distracted by the pile of papers on my desk and told him that would be all right."

"He remained in the office for a good ten minutes. When at last he returned, I could see the tell-tale discolouration blossoming on his hands. Of course, I pretended not to notice, and told him that the back stairs were closed due to some sort of spill that needed cleaning up. He nodded and went down the front staircase as usual. As soon as he left my sight, I pressed the buzzer on my desk to alert Gillespie that we had found the villain. That done, I hurried after the fellow."

I chuckled, imagining the scene. Watson looked slightly perplexed.

Bea continued, "I reached the front hallway and saw Redmond being searched by the security men and the false document recovered.

"Mycroft arrived at that moment and looked so gleeful at the wretch being discovered at last, I half expected him to dance a jig." She laughed.

"The culprit did not realise he had stolen a fraud?" Watson continued.

"No indeed, but I doubt he did more than glance at it. He would have been too fearful of being caught in the act." Bea sipped her sherry.

"So, what happened?" Watson asked.

"Gillespie and the security men had cornered Redmond as he reached the door. He bristled, as you can imagine. How dare mere underlings accost him! Who were they to search him, etc., etc. Of course, it took only a matter of moments before they found the document hidden in his pocket. I have never seen Mycroft so angry. I cannot repeat the language he used to castigate the fellow. Redmond of course, tried to bluff, but by now he noticed his hands and knew the game was up."

"I cannot believe it of a shadow minister," Watson said. "The bounder!"

"I haven't told you the worst of it," Bea said, her delight vanishing like the sun behind a cloud. "That foul-minded, facinorous, treasonous snake he said he didn't do it for the money, nor even for any sense of moral obligation, but because he hates Mycroft and wanted to be rid of him."

"What!" Watson's appalled look no doubt reflected my own.

"Why?" I said when I recovered my power of speech. "What does he have against my brother?"

287

"Nothing," Bea said, "Or at least, nothing he could point to. All I could gather is that he is exceedingly jealous of M. He said, and I quote, 'That fellow who runs the government with no thought to his own prestige is everything I hold in contempt. He is so noble, so esteemed, the essence of the English gentleman. Who can blame me for despising him?'"

"Monstrous!" Watson cried. "What sort of, whatever you called him, Bea, could hold a man's morality against him?"

"He will serve life," I said, "and consider himself lucky not to hang. While my brother continues to grow in influence and esteem, Redmond will rot in a cold, damp cell. I hope Mycroft is not too distressed."

"I think he might have been, but Wainwright punched Redmond's nose, and Gillespie hit him with a rather deadly-looking paperweight."

Despite my distress for my brother, I could not help but laugh at the picture. "Well, at least you retained some decorum," I said.

She coughed. "I, um, had the remains of the blue dye in a canister and I sprayed it in his face. I must say, he looked a sight: A blue face, bloody nose, and a rather large bump on his forehead, added to which, he stood in the midst of Mycroft's staff, and I think they'd have torn the fellow to bits if the police had not intervened. As they led Redmond away in cuffs, he added tears to his facial concoction.

"With that excitement over, Mycroft shouted for order, and some semblance of normality resumed."

"Where was Qualtrough during all of this?" I asked.

"I have no idea," she replied. "He left early to run an errand, he said, and he had not returned by the time of Redmond's arrest. I suspect an afternoon assignation.

"Oh, what a pity you could not have been there, Sherlock. It was your plan, so you should have been able to see the conclusion."

"I knew the thief would not act if I were present since I am far too well-known in Mycroft's office. Even with a disguise I could not risk it. In any event, it all worked out splendidly. My congratulations, Bea."

"Well, at least Long Mac can give up his pretended interest in tennis," Watson said.

"Ah, speaking of that," Bea added, "you may be interested to hear McDuff has tendered his resignation. His father has put his foot down and insists Junior concentrate on learning the family business."

I laughed. "I'm sure Long Mac will be glad of the reprieve, though I doubt Mr McDuff is happy about it.

"Bea, how is Mycroft?"

"He says he is relieved that the spy has been caught, and I know he appreciated the support of his staff, but, oh, Sherlock, he looked so hurt. I wish I could help him, but he has all his defences up."

For a moment we all fell silent. At last, Beatrice, in a more sombre frame of mind, said, "What about you, gentlemen? Sherlock, did you learn anything further from your meeting with the Reverend Cleghorn?"

I related our conversation and she sat quietly, thinking. She shares with Watson a talent for silence. She sits and thinks and has an extraordinary capacity to see situations from a number of angles. It is one of the things that makes her such a formidable chess player.

"When do you go to visit Mrs. Goodrich?" she said.

"I thought to go tomorrow, if you are free," I said. "Since you and she seem to have hit it off so well, I think it would be best if you were present. You do not object, Watson?"

"By no means. I have more than enough to keep me busy."

Beatrice hesitated. "I have no objection to accompanying you, Sherlock. Indeed, I should like to be present. However, your brother has asked me to attend a meeting at the office tomorrow. He wants to discuss the repercussions of

Redmond's treason, and to put in place a system to prevent such a thing from happening again."

"Tomorrow evening, then? I will send a message to Mrs. Goodrich to see if she is amenable to our visit."

"That should be acceptable." She held out her glass and I refilled it. "And you, John," she said. "How were things in the clinic today?"

"Busy as usual, but we managed to stay on top of things. After a slow start, the new doctors are finally settling in, and the new nurses, too."

"Excellent news," I said. "Bye the way, Bea, did you find out how Redmond managed to get into the new safe?"

"I gather Qualtrough 'borrowed' Mycroft's keys and made Redmond a copy," she replied, her lips white with anger and contempt.

"For a small fee, of course," Watson suggested.

"I doubt the fee was so small," I replied. "What about after the safe was changed?"

"It seems Qualtrough got in touch with the safe company and said Mycroft wanted a spare set of keys, just to be on the safe side. Oh, and in order not to inconvenience anyone, he collected the spare key from the company himself."

"Bounder!" Watson exclaimed.

"This is, of course, from Redmond's account," Bea added. "Whenever Qualtrough returns he may have a different story."

I heard a knock at the door below and said, "Ah, will be Inspector Morton and Constable O'Brien. I asked them to stop by this evening."

Sure enough, a few moments later, a flushed Maisie brought the two men to our room.

"Can I get you some coffee, sirs?" she said.

I noted with amusement that she never took her eyes off young O'Brien.

She hardly heard my answer, but the moment the constable thanked her, she rushed away to do his bidding. I caught Watson's grin and tried to force my own face to behave.

"Gentlemen," I said. "Come in and sit down. Bea, may I introduce Inspector Morton and Constable O'Brien who have been such assets in handling the Dixon case? Gentlemen, this is Lady Beatrice Jacoby; Dr Watson you have already met."

The two men shook hands with Bea. I felt a moment's twinge of sympathy for poor Maisie. O'Brien seemed utterly charmed by my lady.

Bea is remarkably at ease with people. Not even Watson can match her ability to invite confidences. I sometimes envy her ability to talk to street urchins and royalty in the same interested and gentle manner. So it proved on this occasion. She chatted easily with the two men and seemed fascinated by everything they had to say.

Morton told her about his wife and his two children. She had to know their names, ages, birthdays, and so forth. It all seemed of extraordinary interest to her. She paid no less attention to O'Brien, asking about his home and family, his career ambitions, and any number of other inconsequential matters. He looked delighted to indulge her, awed by her consideration.

Maisie returned with the tray and O'Brien rushed to help her, whether he wished to prove himself a gentleman to the maid, or because he hoped to impress Bea, I could not say.

For a few minutes, the pair spoke in hushed tones to one another, and it took me a minute to realise they were speaking Gaelige.

Eventually, Maisie dragged herself away, and our conversation turned to the case.

Bea said, "Holmes is fulsome in his praise of your handling of this dreadful case, gentlemen. Constable O'Brien. I have no doubt you will rise to the top of your profession."

291

He blushed to the roots of his curly brown hair.

I managed not to snort.

"In fact," said Inspector Morton, "Young O'Brien received word just this afternoon that he is being promoted to sergeant."

"Oh, that's splendid, excellent news!" I cried.

Watson and Beatrice wasted no time in adding their congratulations.

"Now all you need is a wife," Morton said with a wicked grin, obviously enjoying his young colleague's embarrassment.

After the coffee, they accepted the brandy, and regaled us — well, mostly Bea — with details of some of their cases. She seemed all eager attention and admiration. What intrigues me is that there is nothing false in her behaviour. She would be just as awed if she were listening to the king talking about a new bill Parliament had passed.

After their coffee, brandy, and cigars, the two policemen left. As the door closed behind them, I heard Maisie singing some cheery music hall ditty. Nice to have some joy in the house again.

*

I was getting ready for bed when there came a loud hammering at the door. As the rest of the house had retired, I went down and answered it.

"Quinn?" I said, "What is it?"

"It's happening, Mr H," he said. "That beggar Qualtrough just broke into Hale's on the Tottenham Court Road. I left Little Mac watching 'im and came to tell you."

I hollered up the stairs for Watson. He leaned over the banister and asked what was happening. Within a matter of minutes, he and I were dressed and in a cab on our way to Mayfair. I sent Quinn to Scotland Yard to fetch a policeman.

Little Mac stood waiting outside Qualtrough's house when we arrived.

"'e just went in, Mr H," he gasped. "Not mor'n a minute ago."

"Good lad. Get your breath. The police should be here in shortly."

Using my own set of skeleton keys, I opened the door, and Watson and I crept inside.

"Shouldn't we wait for the authorities?" Watson whispered.

"It might be too late by then. Time is against us."

Softly, softly, up the stairs we climbed. On the first floor landing, we paused and listened. The sound of footsteps came from above us.

Up we climbed, and at the second floor I could clearly hear the sounds of Qualtrough's voice coming from a room at the front of the house. Watson and I immediately flung the door open just in time. I saw the fellow leaning over his cowering wife, a syringe in his hand.

"Help me!" the woman cried in a frail voice.

"Drop that!" I demanded.

He froze and stared at me. Realisation dawned in his furtive eyes, and he began to quiver.

Watson carefully took the syringe from his hand, just as Inspector Bradstreet and a gaggle of uniformed men charged into the small room.

Qualtrough, weeping, pathetic, offered no resistance. He continued to insist he meant only to help his poor wife, but no one, least of all the lady, believed him.

CHAPTER TWENTY-FIVE

12th March

I spent a good part of the night at Scotland Yard, helping Bradstreet question their prisoner.

I left in time to get a few hours' sleep, and after a solitary breakfast, I went to Mycroft's office.

"He's just finishing up a meeting with his staff, sir," Gillespie said. "Shouldn't be too much longer."

"I don't mind waiting," I said. "How are you, Gillespie? I understand you were quite the hero yesterday."

He shook his head. "I wouldn't say that, sir. The nerve of the fellow — a knight of the realm, no less — to commit treason. And the things he said about your brother, sir! Outrageous! No finer gentleman in the kingdom than Mr Holmes, saving your good self, sir.

"To tell the truth, the real hero was Mr Wainwright. Gave that villain a bloody nose, he did, and would have laid him out if the security men hadn't pulled him off. I wouldn't have thought he had it in him."

We both laughed. At that moment, his buzzer sounded, and Gillespie picked up the receiver. After a brief conversation he said, "You may go right up, Mr Holmes."

I found Mycroft and Bea in my brother's office.

"Ah, brother Sherlock," he greeted me, "I gather you have adventures of your own to relate."

"I do, but first I want to hear about your own escapades. I gather you had quite an eventful day yesterday."

He recounted the story I had already heard from Bea. "The plan worked like a charm," he concluded. "And that pipsqueak — oh, dear, now I'm talking like young McDuff — shall never see the light of day again save through prison bars.

I am grateful to you, Sherlock, and to you, Beatrice, for your help. I confess I found the matter quite distressing."

"Well, it's over now. You must feel gratified to see how well regarded you are by your staff. I wish I had been here to see it though, as Gillespie said, I would have flattened the worm."

Mycroft managed a smile, but I could see the pain in his eyes. Before I could say anything else, he said, "Now your story, Sherlock."

I so no point in arguing with him and so I complied and related the events of last night.

"Why didn't he just use arsenic like everyone else?" Mycroft said. "A digitalis injection seems unduly elaborate."

"He knew that arsenic could be easily detected, and that his father-in-law would immediately suspect him. His wife is being treated with digitalis for her heart, and he hoped a large injection of the same drug would be interpreted as an accidental overdose if it were discovered in the autopsy. If blame were levelled, suspicion would fall on Dr Baxter. A thoroughly wicked plot."

"Where did he get the drug?"

"Hale's Chemist on the Tottenham Court Road. Those keys let him into the building and the medication cabinet."

Bea said, "Where did the keys come from?"

"Qualtrough says he bought them from a man whose name he has conveniently forgotten. He had them made."

"John said they had a ribbon attached," Bea said. "Did you find out why?"

"Qualtrough said the keys had the ribbon attached when he received them. I suspect the man who made them used the colour to distinguish this set from any others he may have made. That is speculation, of course."

"But surely he could have simply distilled digitalis from some foxgloves?" Mycroft said.

"Simple for you or me, but your secretary is not a bright fellow. He thought it easier to get into the pharmacy, steal what he needed, and leave no trace."

"It would have worked, too, if you had not anticipated him," Bea said. "Do you think his paramour — what's her name, Mrs. Burns — knew?"

"I doubt it. Despite her behaviour regarding men, she is essentially an honest woman. I think she would have been appalled to think what he had planned."

"I told you I had him pegged as a heartless blackguard," Mycroft said. "You will own that I was right about that."

"You were, indeed, Mycroft."

"Well, why don't you both let me get back to work? Take this lady out of here, Sherlock, and feed her. She has been too busy to eat."

"Mycroft —"

"Hush, brother mine. I am perfectly well, I assure you. True, I felt rather irked yesterday by that villain's comments, but the loyalty of the people around me has reminded me how fortunate I am. Away with you, now, and let me get to work."

*

Bea and I took a cab to her home, and she transformed herself back into a high-born lady.

"I am not convinced Mycroft is as resigned as he claims," she said over luncheon. "I am worried about him."

"Perhaps when the Cobbledick case has been concluded," I said, "when we go back to Sussex, would you object to bringing him along?"

"No, indeed. I had a similar thought. When did he last have a holiday?"

"Not for years. When he finished in university, I think."

After our meal, Bea's driver took us back to Tally Ho Corner. (Watson still chortles when he hears the name; he can be such a boy at times.)

At first, Beatrice seemed unusually quiet, and I thought her fatigued after her long days as a working woman. But as we turned up the Finchley Road, she said, "I am sorry to be so out of sorts. I just feel rather sad to be leaving Mycroft's office. It's one of the few times in my life when I have felt useful."

"You have proved your usefulness to me time and time again," I said. "Not to mention the fact that you do not need to dress up as a boy but can simply be yourself."

She made no reply but fell back into her reverie. I gave her a few minutes to indulge her thoughts before adding, "I have no doubt Mycroft will miss you, too. I am sure your presence took a great deal of the burden from his shoulders."

"I cannot disagree. I worry about him; there are so the many important matters for which he is responsible."

We turned the conversation to other topics. Bea is well-read and versed in any number of subjects. For the rest of the journey, we discussed the Lizzie Borden case in Massachusetts. It has been on my mind since O'Brien mentioned it that night we found Cobbledick.

Our discussion took us all the way to Mrs. Goodrich's house. Upon our arrival, I gave the driver some coins to get himself some coffee and asked him to return for us in an hour. As he left, Bea and I walked up the quaint garden path and knocked on the door.

"Come in, miss, sir," the blonde, curly-haired maid said. "Mrs. Goodrich is waiting for you."

"How good it is to see you both again," our hostess exclaimed, rising from her chair and coming forward to greet us. "I hope you did not find your journey too tiresome."

"Not in the slightest," Beatrice said. "You have a lovely home, Mrs. Goodrich, and a perfectly charming garden."

"Oh, how kind of you. Sit down, please, and make yourselves comfortable. Gertie, bring us some coffee, there's a good girl."

We sat in the still-sunny living room. The women made idle conversation about roses until the maid had served the coffee and then been dismissed.

"How do you get on investigating the deaths of my dear friend, Meg, and her colleagues?" Mrs. Goodrich asked as she lifted her coffee cup.

"Our progress is slow, but not without points of interest," I said. "Indeed, a matter has come to our attention just recently and we wondered if you might be able to elaborate on it."

Mrs. Goodrich's grey eyes, sharp and knowing, met mine. "Does it have a direct bearing on the murders?"

Beatrice replied, "At this stage, we dare not make any assumptions regarding what is pertinent and what is not. Mrs. Goodrich, I knew Megan, not as well as you, to be sure, but enough to be see her as an honest, gentle-hearted soul. You may be assured that Mr Holmes and I will treat anything you tell us in the utmost confidence."

Our hostess placed her cup in its saucer and sat in silence for several moments. At last, with a glance to the door, as if to be sure she would not be overheard, she said, "Tell me, what you need to know."

"Thank you, Mrs. Goodrich. You may count on our discretion," I said. "Since we last met, I have been to Manchester to speak with Margaret Reed. She is alive and, I shall not say well, but certainly not —" I broke off as a thought struck me.

Some part of my mind registered that Mrs. Goodrich seemed about to say something, but Beatrice forestalled her with a gesture.

I cannot say how long I remained lost in my reverie, in that thrill of excitement that I always feel when the pieces start falling into place. I managed to set the thought aside and return to the matter at hand.

"Forgive me," I said. "An idea occurred to me, and I fear I allowed it to momentarily distract me but let us continue with the purpose of our visit.

"Mrs. Goodrich, in the days before her death Megan asked both Beatrice and a local minister if some sins were too great to be forgiven. At first, I thought she meant a singular event, but I have come to believe she referenced an ongoing practice."

I heard an intake of breath and glanced at Bea. From her flushed cheeks and the brightness of her eyes, I saw that she had reached the same conclusion.

"I think I know what you mean," Mrs. Goodrich said, looking uncomfortable. "But it is difficult to discuss."

Bea added gently, "Miss Reed — Margaret — frequently performed a service that might have earned her an extended stay in prison, if caught. It had nothing to do with the nurses' failure to report to duty, or any such infraction. Mrs. Goodrich, if we are correct, this is why all those women were murdered, not because of the Cobbledick deaths. Will you help us?"

Our hostess flushed a deep red, all the way down her neck. For an instant, I thought her embarrassed, but the blaze in her eyes could be nothing but fury. She leapt to her feet.

"Good God!" she cried. "She did it! That evil, wicked woman!"

"We are right, are we not?" Bea persisted. "Margaret Reed is an abortionist."

CHAPTER TWENTY-SIX

We were almost on the outskirts of Hampstead before I settled my thoughts.

"How did you know?" I asked her.

"I'm not sure," she said. "I think perhaps your phrase about it being an 'ongoing practice' started the pieces tumbling into the right places in my mind. As soon as I thought of it, it answered all the questions. I remember when Meg asked me the question, I wondered why she seemed so conflicted. Now, though, I realise that she could probably see both sides of the matter, both the illegality and the desperate need of those unfortunate women who required Margaret's help."

That aspect had not occurred to me, I confess. It is not a subject I have ever given much thought. However, I now remembered so many unfortunate women who died in the birth of a child they could not care for, or a child conceived by force — Oh, Alice Dixon! Damnation! Why did I not think of that sooner? Alice had been pregnant and undergone an abortion. The piece lay right there in front of me. All those mysterious hints and secrets that no one would say out loud.

The taste of the brandy Mrs. Goodrich had poured for all of us still burned in my throat and I recalled the secrets she had revealed to us.

"I would have told you when we first met in the Lake District, but I would not broach such a topic in front of Joyce," she said. "She's a nice enough woman, but it's not a topic ladies discuss, certainly not in public."

"We quite understand," Bea said.

Mrs. Goodrich managed to calm herself down and filled in some of the gaps:

300

"As you may be aware, when they worked in that awful concentration camp, the nurses were assigned to share a tent. I cannot speak for the other women, but Megan had been moved around a few times. She adapted quickly to so many situations, and her remarkable understanding of infectious diseases meant that her skills were often in demand.

"Although there were new nurses arriving every week, the ones who had been there longest did get to know one another. Meg had worked with the other three women at various times and had also met them at social events and tutorials.

"One night, Kathryn told Meg that Margaret had helped one of their colleagues who had fallen pregnant.

"'Help, how?' Meg said.

"'Margaret is going to abort the foetus,' Kathryn said."

Mrs. Goodrich paused to refill her glass. Bea and I declined.

"I can imagine Meg's reaction," Bea said, trying to urge the conversation along.

"She felt so conflicted. She had been raised to believe abortion is a sin, but she also knew that there are times when there is no other alternative."

"I do not remember seeing her mention this in her letters," I said.

"No, she did not write about it. I went to visit her over Christmas and brought her a small gift. We talked for a long time."

Her face took on that dreamy expression as she remembered. After a moment, she shook off her reverie and continued.

"Meg had been raised with strict religious values and a strong sense of right and wrong. I should add that I, personally, have no great abhorrence of abortion; I have seen the horrors that await unwanted children and their mothers. However, I sympathised with Meg's sensibilities. Is any of this helpful?"

301

"More than you can imagine," I said.

"I'm not sure I understand Meg's conflict," Bea said.

"Meg worried that Margaret continued the practice, even here in England," I surmised. Mrs. Goodrich nodded in agreement.

"She wondered if she should report Reed to the authorities," she explained. "Of course, if she had done so, and if Reed had been convicted, it would have meant a life sentence, and of course it would have impacted others besides."

Mrs. Goodrich refilled our brandy glasses before she continued.

"You know about that wretched dance. Well, here's the part of the story that you may not have heard: The women did not return to camp until the following morning. They claimed that they were so exhausted that they had fallen asleep. However, Kate told Meg that Alice had disappeared during the evening and neither she nor Reed could find her.

"Alice showed up the next morning, bleary eyed, dishevelled, and rather disoriented. She refused to answer questions about what she'd been doing or where she had been, and the others decided to let the matter go.

"However, about a week before they were shipped out, about five or six weeks after the dance, it became evident that unfortunate girl had fallen pregnant. She insisted that her behaviour had been unimpeachable, and that she had no recollection of being intimate with any man. Indeed, she didn't remember where she had spent the night — or claimed she didn't. She was distraught. All her dreams had come crashing down. She would never find a husband now, and her nursing career must end in disgrace. She would never get over the shame even though, she said, she had done nothing wrong.

"Since the three disgraced nurses were considered *personae non gratae*, they were assigned to the same tent, though they were free to come and go as they wished. When

302

she felt well enough, the doctors discharged Meg to the same tent. She said she slept most of the time. The other nurses came and went, and Meg didn't pay much heed. However, one night the other three left the tent together. Meg thought nothing of it and went back to sleep. The next day Dixon seemed unwell and told her that she'd suffered a miscarriage. Meg suspected what had really happened. She questioned Kathryn and she confirmed it."

"That Reed had aborted the foetus with Lysander's assistance?" Bea said.

"Exactly."

"Kathryn confirmed that Reed had performed an abortion on Dixon, and she had assisted. Meg felt troubled and pondered reporting Reed, but Lysander pointed out she could not do so without destroying Dixon's reputation and incriminating Kathryn as the assistant. Despite her misgivings, Meg agreed to stay silent, though she continued to feel the burden of guilt."

"Though her hands were clean, so to speak?" I said.

"She felt strongly that her silence made her complicit."

"I understand." Bea did indeed look as if she understood. In hindsight, I suppose I did too, although the ways of women remain something of a mystery to me, I can imagine what the situation must have felt like to all those involved. I wonder if Watson will see things the same way.

"I believe the matter continued to distress Megan even after she returned to Britain," Bea continued. "Even I, a stranger, could tell that something weighed on her mind."

Mrs. Goodrich nodded. "She certainly continued to feel burdened by her knowledge. I reminded her that the women involved could simply deny her allegations and she had no proof."

"That is true," I agreed. I had the same thought about Cobbledick's death.

303

"Do you know if Meg told Nurse Reed how she felt, Mrs. Goodrich?"

"Yes, Lady Beatrice. They evidently had a long conversation about it at some point before they returned home. Nurse Reed made the case that she offered help to women that others would ignore. She felt strongly that without her assistance, these unfortunates would be in dire circumstances. To be fair to Megan, she understood that and, I think, even sympathised with it. If she had not, I believe she would have gone to the authorities immediately. She felt there ought to be some other way to help those poor women. Margaret Reed pointed out that even in England our orphanages are overfilled and, of course, it wasn't always due to immoral women. There were women like Nurse Dixon who had been violated."

I wondered as she said that if Reed herself had ever needed such services. If she had indeed been a victim of her father's depravity, I thought it possible, even likely. More than that, it made her interest in nursing and her continued concern for other women understandable.

"We only have Dixon's word for that," Bea began.

"She did not remember what had happened to her, Lady Beatrice, which means she could not consent. For whatever it is worth, Meg believed her. Nurse Dixon had been, as they say, saving herself for the right man. To discover she had been, ah, compromised distressed her deeply."

"Perhaps she should not have drunk so much," I said, somewhat acidly. "She is not — or rather, was not — a child. She should have shown more responsibility."

"That may be true," Bea answered, "but there are drugs that can be put into drinks by unscrupulous men in order to make a woman, ah, compliant. She could even have been given alcohol in a fruit juice. We have no way of knowing."

"Quite so," Mrs. Goodrich agreed.

"I take it Nurse Reed made no promises about giving up the practice?" Bea said.

"I don't believe so, and frankly, I doubted Meg would have believed her if she had."

"We did not find any letters from Margaret Reed in Meg's correspondence. Do you know if they remained in touch?"

"I know Meg sent her a Christmas card but, to the best of my knowledge, she heard nothing back."

"So they exchanged addresses?" I asked.

"Yes, they all did." She pursed her lips and added, "Not long before their boat arrived in England, Meg's address book went missing. She suspected Reed had stolen it perhaps believing if Meg didn't know how to find her, she would be safe."

"That obviously did not work," Bea said, "if she sent Margaret a Christmas card — Oh!"

"What?" Mrs. Goodrich asked.

"Reed had perhaps comforted herself with the belief that she would be safe if Megan didn't know where to find her. But when she received the Christmas card, she would have known her theft had not worked."

We could not be certain, of course, but I believed Bea was right. Mrs. Goodrich looked ill.

Bea added, "They were such different people, and other than Meg and Katheryn, I don't see them staying in touch. However, I'm sure they all exchanged addresses for form's sake."

I again thought about how Cobbledick had found out where all the nurses were and, in particular, how he mistook Meg for Margaret. Yes, the pieces were coming together. I must return to Manchester.

"Did Megan ever mention an orderly by the name of Moorhouse?" I asked.

"Yes, she thought highly of him."

"He was the man on duty the night of Reed's assault by the Boer, I understand."

"That's right. Reed blamed him for contributing to her assault. She reported him for leaving his post. The poor man had dysentery and had to visit the convenience; he shouldn't even have been working. Thanks to Margaret, they suspended him unpaid for two weeks. He would have been dismissed, but Meg spoke on his behalf as soon as she became aware of his plight. The suspension alone meant a hardship to him. He alone supported his family."

I saw the light in Bea's eyes and knew she had followed my reasoning. "Do you think that he might have had access to Margaret Reed's address?" Bea said.

"That, I could not say," Mrs. Goodrich replied. "I suppose it is possible."

Turning to me, Bea said, "Even if he had access, would he have passed that information on to Cobbledick?"

"Meg told me that Mr Moorhouse felt sympathetic towards the Boers. He had many friends from among them," Mrs. Goodrich said.

"It seems likely that this is how Cobbledick obtained Reed's address," I said. "Moorhouse held a grudge against Reed and Cobbledick probably played down his intent; he may have said he wanted to demand compensation from her. Moorhouse saw no reason to deny him."

"That holds," Bea said. "Yes, I think you've hit on the truth, Sherlock."

"It certainly rings true," I said. "Thank you, Mrs. Goodrich, your help has been inestimable. You may be sure we will treat everything you have said in the strictest confidence and will share it only with those who need to know."

Bea's carriage sat waiting for us by the time we were ready to leave. Mrs. Goodrich shook our hands and asked us to let her know the outcome of our investigation.

As we travelled down the Finchley Road, Bea said, "Assuming Moorhouse gave Cobbledick Reed's address, how did he locate the others?"

"I have been thinking about that," I said. "When we went to see Reed, Watson and I noted her injuries. She tried to tell us that these were the result of the Boer assault, but Watson felt that the severity and the subsequent complications were not consistent with that event. I surmise that, contrary to her statement, Cobbledick had indeed visited her."

"But he assaulted her, and did not kill her," Bea argued. "That doesn't fit with his later behaviour towards the other nurses."

I shook my head. "I am not sure he had intended murder from the outset. Perhaps Reed herself goaded him into murder. No, hear me out. Cobbledick goes to see Reed. Perhaps he intends to assault her, and she is indeed injured. However, she manages to convince him that he had the wrong woman. More than likely, she kept that newspaper cutting we found in Cobbledick's room. She gave it to him as a sort of 'proof' that he had the wrong 'Meg Reid.'"

"And she worried that Megan might report her abortionist activities to the authorities, so this seemed a way of both saving herself, and being rid of a threat. Yes, I can understand that. But what of Lysander and Dixon?"

"No doubt Reed would consider them an unfortunate price she must pay, or perhaps she believed they were as great a threat as Meg. In any case, she willingly sacrificed them in order to save herself."

"That's depraved," Bea cried. "Black-hearted!"

I agreed. We fell silent. I mused over the day's revelations and pondered my next steps. There were still questions to answer: Even if Reed had protected herself from Cobbledick by giving him her friend's address, she could not have killed him, not alone. She had help, but from whom?

307

We arrived back at Baker Street after dark. I invited Bea in, but she opted to return home. I realised, belatedly, that neither of us had spoken for most of our journey.

"I must apologise for my reverie this evening, Bea," I began.

"Oh, Sherlock, I confess I did not notice. I was lost in my own thoughts. I shall come see you tomorrow if I may." She smiled. "Don't do anything further about the case without including me, will you?"

"You have my word."

I found Watson adorning his usual chair by the fire reading a book when I let myself into the sitting room. I updated him on our discoveries and my theories. He heard my account in his usual attentive manner. "A real conflict between the two Miss Reeds," he said when I concluded. "Both strong-willed women, both certain of their positions, and neither willing to change."

"I am curious, Watson. What advice would you have given Megan if she had asked you?"

He thought about it for a moment. "I suppose I would have told her to consider the greater evil: the termination of a pregnancy or compelling a young woman who might be in desperate straits to give birth to a baby she neither wants nor can afford. You know, people always see death as a terrible thing, and most of the time it is, at least some of the awful deaths we have seen. But sometimes it's a merciful release. Take Harry Kyle, for instance."

"Who? Oh, Lestrade's neighbour. Yes, I must admit, every day is a burden to him, poor fellow."

"No, he died this morning. Given how much pain he'd been in and how constricted his life had become, I have no doubt he greeted death with welcome."

"Poor fellow. I hope he is at peace now."

Long after he went to bed, I sat up trying to put the pieces together. There is still something missing, but I cannot think what it might be.

CHAPTER TWENTY-SEVEN

13th March

I woke late and after breakfast, sat in my seat and read the newspapers. Beatrice arrived midday and Mrs Hudson appeared a few moments later with a fresh pot of coffee. Anything for Her Ladyship.

As Watson had left for the clinic, Bea and I had the place to ourselves.

"I wanted to talk to you about some things," she said, seriously.

"You can talk to me about anything," I assured her. "Do I take it this has to do with Mycroft and your time in the office?"

"In part. I feel I am frittering my days away, Sherlock. I have a good mind and I am not untalented. While the queen lived, my options were severely circumscribed. However, the king is far more liberal. During the time that I spent with him, he made it clear he would support me in anything I wanted to do."

"You are too hard on yourself, Bea. You have done so much for so many people: the Irregulars have a safe place to sleep and adequate food; Watson is able to help those poor former soldiers in the clinic; to say nothing of what you have done for me."

She smiled in reply, but I could see my words had not appeased her.

"What do you have in mind?" I said. "You know you can count on my support, too."

"Thank you, Sherlock, I did not doubt it." She sipped her coffee and placed the cup carefully in the saucer before saying. "Mycroft has asked me to continue to work for him.

Not as Ben, but as myself. I would function as his personal secretary but would have responsibilities far in excess of most secretarial staff. He has promoted Wainwright to senior administrator. He will get a welcome pay increase and be responsible for the entire office. I must say, the staff members are delighted, and Wainwright himself is overwhelmed with happiness."

"And you want to continue to work for Mycroft," I said, seeing the glow of excitement in her eyes, and answering her question.

"I do, yes. I've thought about other things: going to university, devoting myself to my music or my photography. But working with Mycroft offers me an opportunity to have a real impact on the world. Not to mention that it would help Mycroft, too."

"Does this mean my brother has decided to stay on in his role?"

"Not yet, but he will." As if she were changing the subject she added, casually, "I have an appointment to see His Majesty this afternoon to let him know my plans."

I smiled at her devious grin. "You are a mistress of organisation," I said. "I would not dare to question you."

Mrs Hudson arrived carrying a tray and proceeded to clear the breakfast dishes. She was humming some tune that she had picked up from Maisie.

"Are you sure there is nothing else I can get for you, Lady Beatrice?" she said.

"You're very kind, Mrs Hudson," Bea said. "To quote my late, and much-missed father, I have partaken of an adequate sufficiency this morning."

"Her Ladyship needs to keep her energy up today, Mrs Hudson," I said. "She is seeing the king this afternoon."

"Oh, my! Isn't that wonderful? Will you have time for luncheon before you leave?"

"No, thank you, Mrs Hudson, this excellent coffee is all that I need. You know, His Majesty has a hearty appetite and will, no doubt, insist I dine with him." She made a point of taking an appreciative sip of her coffee before saying, "Has Sherlock told you that he should have Megan's case wrapped up in just a few days?"

"I shall never be able to thank you enough for all your doing, Mr Holmes," Mrs Hudson said. "You're the kindest man in England."

Bea managed to keep a straight face until the good woman went back downstairs, upon which she erupted in laughter.

"Poor Sherlock," Bea said, "able to face any danger without turning a hair, but a word of appreciation completely discombobulates him!"

After Bea left, I went back to Mayfair and asked to speak with Mrs. Qualtrough. The butler, recognising me, stared in astonishment, but showed me into the library without demur.

The lady, pale and trembling, sat by the fire with her father, Sir Nigel Royston. He greeted me warmly.

"It is you I have to thank for saving my beloved girl from that villain," he said, shaking my hand. "I will never be able to repay you."

"I am happy I could help," I replied. "How are you, Mrs. Qualtrough?"

"Please don't call me by that dreadful name," she replied. "You may call me Henrietta. I think you have earned the right to use my Christian name."

"I am honoured."

She sent the maid scurrying to fetch coffee and sat back in her chair. When I saw her the night her husband had tried to murder her, I had thought her small and frail. Now, sitting by her father, I observed she possessed his same strong features and much of his height. She wore her black hair parted in the middle and coiled up on her nape, giving her a rather severe look. Other than her pallor, she did not look particularly delicate.

"How did you discover my wretched son-in-law's plan?" Sir Nigel said.

I replied with a carefully edited explanation. While investigating another matter, I had occasion to observe the fellow and grew suspicious of him. A chance remark suggested his intentions to me, but I had no proof. I kept a close watch and acted after he broke into the chemist's.

I could see that neither father nor daughter were completely satisfied with my explanation but, happily, they did not press. Over coffee, Sir Nigel said his daughter would move back home and the Mayfair house would be put up for sale.

A short while later, I rose to leave.

Sir Nigel walked me to the door and handed me a cheque.

"I know you were not employed to save my daughter's life, Mr Holmes," he said, "but she is all I have, and I am grateful beyond words. I am horrified to think what that brute had planned."

The cheque was extraordinarily generous, and I pocketed it with pleasure. It is a most welcome addition to my bank account.

After I left the bank, I visited all the Irregulars and gave each of them a guinea bonus for their exceptional work. By the time I returned to Baker Street, Watson had returned.

"This is early for you," I said.

"Yes, indeed. With the new staff, I feel quite a gentleman of leisure."

The sound of unusually gay singing rose from the hallway below. Mrs Hudson came up to say dinner would be only a few minutes.

"I'm famished, Mrs Hudson. What smells so wonderful?" Watson asked.

313

"Salmon and colcannon, Maisie's idea since it will be St. Patrick's Day on Sunday."

"Ah, that explains Maisie's gleeful singing."

"Yes, I told her she might take Saturday and Sunday off. She has plans to celebrate with young Mr — I should say Sergeant — O'Brien."

"Maisie? But she's only a child," I protested.

The pair laughed. Mrs Hudson replied, "She twenty years old, Mr Holmes. Many lassies are married by her age."

"They'll probably ask you to be best man at their wedding," Watson said, and they laughed most heartily at my horrified reaction.

"Colcannon?" I asked after Mrs Hudson left.

"Traditional Irish dish made of cabbage or kale and mashed potatoes."

At that moment, the telephone rang in the hall below. Father Boyd.

"I have been able to identify that young man you were looking for," he said. "His name is Eddie Fitzgerald. He's twenty-seven and feeble-minded, poor lad. He lives in the St. Joseph of Cupertino home in the Groton area."

"What can you tell me about the institution, Father?" I asked.

"It's probably the best of its sort in the county. The staff are excellent, and the boys are treated with all kindness and humanity. Unfortunately, it is, as you might expect, rather expensive."

"Do you know who is paying his way?"

"I don't, I'm afraid."

"Never mind. Thank you for your help, Father. I greatly appreciate it."

After I hung up the telephone, I updated Watson and was surprised to find that he had heard of the facility.

"It's highly regarded, Holmes. Their methods of treatment are considered the best of their kind. They offer the poor souls

314

they care for every opportunity to develop to the best of their abilities. The staff do not believe, as so many do, that children with these difficulties cannot learn. It merely takes longer, and more imaginative teaching."

"Commendable," I said. "Well, I mean to return to Manchester tomorrow. I think this case is finally coming together. Are you available to come with me?"

"I wouldn't miss it!"

"Splendid! I need to put some things in place. It would not do to arrive ill-prepared."

"I understand. Shall I call that hotel where we stayed last time, and see if they can give us the same room?"

"Yes, do."

I spent the rest of the evening putting plans in motion. I had expected the various telephone calls, telegrams, and so forth to take much longer than they did, but thanks to a considerable amount of help from friend Lestrade, intensely bored with his convalescence and eager to be of use, everything came together in a matter of hours. Bea, alas, was not free to join us, but she wished us Godspeed.

*

I retired early, but found my sleep troubled by peculiar dreams. I do not recall many of the details now, but in one, I swam in a vividly blue sea. At some point I realised that it was not a sea at all, but methylene blue dye. Next came a waterfall of red water which, strangely, did not blend with the blue, but formed pools of red within the sea. Somewhere, I heard Mycroft's voice saying, "That's your problem, Sherlock. You are far too concerned with how things look, rather than how they are." At that, I woke up, tired and perplexed, to see I had retired no more than thirty minutes earlier.

I must make an effort to get some rest.

15th March: Baker Street

The journey to Manchester passed without incident and we arrived just before noon. Watson and I were delighted to be met at the railway station by Morton and O'Brien, both as fresh-faced and eager as a pair of schoolboys. (I maintain that the latter is far too young to start courting young girls. I kept that thought to myself, of course. I am not quite the social duffer Watson pretends. Also, Bea threatened me with a scolding if I was "unkind" to the fellow.)

"I don't know how you arranged for us to be here, Mr Holmes," the inspector said, "but we are delighted to join you."

"You have both contributed so much to this case, gentlemen," I said, "and Inspector Lestrade agreed you should participate in what I hope will be the conclusion. I understand you are soon joining that illustrious group of detectives, Inspector Morton."

"I am, Mr Holmes, and if I know anything, Connor here will soon join me."

The newly promoted sergeant flushed. "I am lucky to have such a mentor," he said, sincerely.

"Well, gentlemen, come and join Watson and me at our hotel, and we will tell you our plan."

As the two policemen insisted on helping us with our bags, we walked the short distance to the hotel.

Our room seemed cramped, filled, as it was, with four robust men, but somehow we managed. The officers heard me out in breathless silence.

"So you think this Eddie Fitzgerald is the one who hanged Cobbledick?" Morton said.

"And stole his ring. It is the ring that will seal his fate," I said.

"But why?" O'Brien said. "Someone must have put him up to it."

"The blonde woman, I surmise," I said. "I cannot imagine the boy needed much persuading."

"It doesn't seem right that a boy with his mental infirmities should be faced with the same justice as the rest of us," Watson said.

"Well, not that I have any concern for Cobbledick," Morton answered, "but he is as dead as if he were murdered by any man of average intelligence. The fellow is a hazard, Doctor."

When the subject turned to Reed, Morton told us he had seen the report of her father's death.

"We arrived here in Manchester last night," he said, "and Inspector Pellow had the file available. I can see why they took no further action. The surgeon attributed the cause of death to drowning, and at least three witnesses swore they had seen the woman crying for help and trying to reach the man in the water."

Watson nodded. "I suppose with drowning being the official cause of death, they didn't pay much attention to the bruise on the fellow's head."

"The surgeon did mention it, Doctor," O'Brien said, "But he said they could not prove it was anything other than an accident."

The conversation returned to our plan of attack, then, once we were ready, we set off in a carriage that the officers had borrowed from the Manchester constabulary.

It did not take long for us to reach the St. Joseph of Cupertino home. Although O'Brien and Morton were in civilian clothes, their occupation was obvious. Many heads turned as we walked up the path that traversed the rich green lawns.

Inside the building, however, the illusion of civility fell away. Screams, grunts and howls, while distant, filled the antiseptic corridors with deep distress.

317

A nun who identified herself as Sister Isadore brought us into her office. We found Father Boyd waiting. The two heard us out with expressions of grave concern.

"We don't have many problems with Eddie, as a rule," the nun said. "He's usually a sweet young boy. There are things he enjoys, and we try to reward him with them when he behaves well. The only things he seriously dislikes are baths."

Someone brought the boy — man, I should say — to the office. He was a massive, hulking brute of a fellow, at least six-foot-six, with arms as big as most men's thighs. He came shuffling in, his head hung down, and stood by the door, not looking at anyone. Something glittered on his hand.

"That's an interesting ring you have there, Eddie," I said. "May I see it?"

"Mine!" he cried.

"I'm not sure where he found that," the nun said. "He's been wearing it for about two weeks now. It doesn't even fit him properly, not even on his little finger."

"He stole it from the body of a man he murdered," I said. I ignored Watson's shocked look. I thought it important for everyone in the room to remember who we were dealing with.

The fellow suddenly seemed to notice us, and he started shouting, "Out! Out! Out!" But whether he wanted us to leave, or wanted to leave the room himself, I could not say.

"That's enough, Eddie," the nun said. He instantly fell silent but rocked back and forth, his head hung down.

"We need to know who pays for his treatment, Sister Isadore," Morton said.

"The secretary handles those things," she said. "A moment, and I will review the record."

"Did you enjoy your trip to London, Eddie?" Watson said, placing a restraining hand on my arm. "Did you go on the train?"

318

"Choo-choo," Eddie said. "Big train." He looked at Watson and for the first time I saw his intensely green eyes. Green as emeralds.

Swimming in a sea of methylene blue, and the red not mixing with it. *You're too focused on how things appear rather than how they are, Sherlock.* Mycroft's voice echoed from the dream as the last puzzle piece slipped into place.

"His sister," I said. "His sister is Iris. Does she pay for him, or does her employer?"

The nun looked up from the fat register. "You are correct, Mr Holmes. Miss Fitzgerald is his sister, and her employer, Miss Reed, pays all of Eddie's fees."

"Would you like to take a ride with us in a carriage, Eddie?" Watson said, his voice still gentle. "You can see the horses. Do you like horses?"

"Gee-gee," Eddie said, and made a clip-clopping sound.

I felt a sudden rush of sadness for the boy-man who had no chance to live a normal life, but immediately after came a surge of fury for those who would take advantage of such a vulnerable young man and have him commit murder for them.

Watson, thank heaven, remained calm and gentle in his dealings with the fellow. Thanks to him, we were able to bring Eddie outside without any difficulty. Not until he faced the prisoner transport vehicle did the hulking fellow become agitated. It took two uniformed officers as well as the London policemen and me to secure him in manacles and lock him in the van. Morton managed to retrieve the ring and handed it to me.

"An eagle's head," I said. "It was unquestionably Cobbledick's; I saw the imprint clearly on Dixon's face."

"Are you all right, Watson?" I asked as the van drew away.

He shook his head. "It's disgusting," he replied after a moment. "That boy had no ability to deliberately kill. He did

319

simply as someone told him. No doubt they gave him that accursed ring as a reward."

"I agree, Doctor," Morton said. "He does not pass what our barristers call the McNaughton Rule, or the requisite intent to kill. I am sure he will be all right."

"Reed is paying for his treatment here. What if she will not, or cannot do so any longer? What happens to Eddie?"

We had no answer and remained silent.

Looking at his pocket watch, Morton said, "It will take time for the local constabulary to get Eddie settled. Perhaps we should get lunch now while we can."

"I agree. Watson?"

"Yes, that's a good idea."

We found a small inn and dined on roast chicken. None of us seemed to have much appetite, although the food seemed perfectly adequate. We did not linger. Within half-an-hour, we were heading back to the police station.

"Ah, Mr Holmes, gentlemen," Inspector Pellow said. "We found exactly what you were looking for. It's in the Harpurhey area. If you are ready, we can go there now."

"And Eddie?" Watson asked.

"Still creating havoc, I'm afraid. We would do well to give him time to calm down."

For as well as I know London, I know little enough about Manchester beyond the main thoroughfares. I did once spend some time on McBride Street, but it is many years since. Pellow's driver, however, drove us unerringly through the warren of side streets and alleyways, until we stopped at a nondescript building amid a cluster of warehouses and factories.

"An inauspicious façade," Watson said.

"True. However, if our surmises are correct, it has been used for inauspicious purposes."

In fact, the interior of the building looked very different from its exterior; scrupulously clean, smelling of antiseptic, with a hospital trolley in the middle of the room, a number of medical books on the shelves, and a glass-fronted cabinet against the wall contained an array of horrifying-looking medical instruments.

"These books all pertain to abortion and women's health," Watson said.

"And there is no question that Margaret Reed owns this place?" Morton asked.

Pellow shook his head. "She owns the building. Of course, we cannot say when she was last here, but there is no doubt as to its purpose. Furthermore, we found several men who say she terminated their wives' pregnancies contrary to their — that is, the men's — wishes. They are willing, even eager, to testify against her."

I could see Watson's distress. What makes that good man so constant is that his conscience is neither complicated nor corruptible. He is as honest and as plainspoken as a monk. More so, for some monks, in my experience, frequently dissemble.

"This seems a roguish way of treating the woman. I understand she has done some wicked things, Holmes, but this smacks of, of." He shook his head and said no more.

"Of what, Watson?"

"Of cheap tricks. I'm sorry, I know what she did, but surely, we can arrest her for that?"

"Either way, sir, she's going to prison," Pellow said.

We returned to the station in silence. I understood Watson's concern, even shared it to some extent, but if I could not prove Reed guilty of aiding and abetting the murders of three nurses, this was the next best thing. She wouldn't hang, but at least she'd be off the streets.

321

CHAPTER TWENTY-EIGHT

It has been a long and extraordinary day. Watson said he feels we have stepped through the looking glass. Upon my query, he referred me to a book. While I am not familiar with the work in question, I must admit that I do feel thoroughly discombobulated and at odds with myself. Everything about this wretched case riles my emotions, something to which I am not accustomed.

After we left the clinic, as I suppose we must call it, we went to the Victoria Building. Pellow, with all the bombast of his kind, insisted on bringing half a dozen uniformed officers. I saw O'Brien shake his head in either amusement or irritation, and I nodded in agreement.

If Mr Whittaker felt bemused to see his lobby filled with so many policemen, he did not show it.

"Forgive us for taking up so much of your time, Mr Whittaker," Watson said. "We shall keep this as brief as possible. Holmes?"

"Mr Whittaker," I said, "has Miss Reed ever been injured since her return from South Africa?"

He nodded. "Yes, indeed, Mr Holmes. Not long after she came home, no more than two weeks later, I'd say, she came staggering into the lobby one afternoon covered in blood. She said she had been set upon by a ruffian just up the road. If it hadn't been for her maid, young Iris, I cannot imagine what would have happened.

"We were in the middle of a storm, one of the worse I've seen. I stayed in the foyer so as not to get drenched, otherwise, I would probably have seen it happen.

"Anyway, Miss Iris helped Miss Reed into the lobby. Soaked, they were, and so much blood dripping on the floor.

"Miss Reed, she sat in my chair, ever so calm. She had a swollen left cheek, a black eye, and any number of cuts and bumps and bruises, still, not a word of complaint out of her.

"'Iris,' says she, 'We dropped all the packages. See if you can gather them up.'

"'Yes, Miss,' says Iris, and off she runs out into the storm.

"It took me a few minutes to realise that Miss Reed didn't want to worry her.

"'Mr Whittaker,' says she, 'can you see if Dr Goldfarb can attend me? I fear I am badly hurt.'

"Dr Goldfarb is a retired physician who lives in the building. He is always happy to help the other tenants. I called him at once, and he came down to the lobby. After a cursory check, he asked me to help him carry the lady to her flat. We helped her to lie down on the sofa and the doctor examined her. She refused to go to the hospital or to call the police, though Goldfarb and I urged both.

"Said she, 'Let it be, I beg you, gentlemen. I prefer to forget it.'"

"Thank you for your help, Mr Whittaker," I said. "I would be obliged if you would keep our conversation to yourself. Do you know if Dr Goldfarb is home?"

"My pleasure, gentlemen. Dr Goldfarb should be home at this time of day, aye. His flat is 506."

"You have been enormously helpful, Mr Whittaker," Watson added. "I do hope your grandson has a full and speedy recovery."

"Thank you, gentlemen. I'm glad to have been of service."

As we waited for the lift, Watson said, "That was a generous tip you gave him, Holmes."

He spoke in that voice that never fails to embarrass me. Bea often asks why I feel uncomfortable to be caught doing some small kindness for others. I tell her it is because it means nothing to me.

"But it's a great deal to the person who receives your largess."

I felt uncomfortable now and did not reply. Watson, to my surprise, patted me on the shoulder. "You're a good man, Holmes," he said. "You're allowed to accept the appreciation of others."

"Hospitals are expensive," I muttered. "And you were quite generous yourself."

"We were talking about you."

He really is impossible.

We stepped off on the fifth floor and Pellow sent the lift back to the ground floor so it would be immediately available for his men.

We discovered Dr Goldfarb's flat just across the hall from Miss Reed's. The door opened within moments of our knock and a slight, bearded fellow wearing spectacles stood before us. He blinked in surprise at the sight of two London gentlemen and three police officers on his threshold. I thought it fortunate he could not see the additional half-a-dozen uniformed men we had left in the hallway.

"Dr Goldfarb?" I said. "My name is Sherlock Holmes. This is my friend and colleague, Dr Watson. These other gentlemen are police officers. I wonder if you have a few moments to discuss a case with us?"

He seemed puzzled but welcomed us in quite genially. "It is an honour to meet you, gentlemen," said he. "Please, sit down and make yourselves comfortable. May I offer you some refreshments? Tea, coffee?"

"Nothing, thank you," I said.

His flat reminded me of 221B. The stacks of books, the smell of pipe tobacco, newspapers and journals on every surface.

We sat on a brown Chesterfield, dislodging a black and white cat that gave us that contemptuous look all felines seem do so well.

Dr Goldfarb, his glasses on the end of his nose, smiled genially. "I must say, I have read your stories with great interest, Dr Watson. What a lesson in logic and deduction they present."

Watson, slightly pink around the ears, smiled and nodded. He went on to introduce the subject of why we were there.

"Yes," the doctor said. "Mr Whittaker asked me to tend Miss Reed after she sustained an assault by an individual a few months ago."

"I understand she had some pre-existing injuries," Watson said. "No doubt this attack served to aggravate those problems."

The doctor nodded and took his time answering. After some moments of rumination he replied, "You probably know that Miss Reed served as a nurse in South Africa. When she came home towards the end of last year, she told me that the injuries and illnesses she had suffered during her time there had ended her service. I confess that I observed no evidence of long-standing illness, but I had no reason to examine her. However, after this recent attack, her limitations were unquestionable. Yes, quite profound. She suffered any number of contusions, lacerations, stab wounds, a severe dislocation to the right shoulder joint, several broken fingers, and a fractured pelvis. The villain had pulled out great chunks of her hair, too, causing great damage to the scalp. I fear it will never grow back. Poor lady: a woman's hair is her crowning glory."

"From what you're saying, I assume her right arm remains weak," Watson said.

"I fear she will never recover the full use of it, or of the hand. She also has difficulty walking, thanks to the injury to the pelvis. I shudder to think what might have happened if young Iris had not been there. The girl has been a blessing. Not only has she helped considerably with Miss Reed's care, but they have become good friends into the bargain. I do hope that man who caused such mischief has been apprehended."

"He is dead," I replied. "Murdered."

"Oh, dear," said the doctor. "A harsh penalty, to be sure."

"We believe he murdered three women, colleagues of Miss Reed's," Watson said. "I suppose it is a case of the punishment fitting the crime."

"Goodness me, yes. Wickedness. Absolute wickedness. Those poor women. All nurses, too?"

"Yes, and all recently returned from South Africa."

"Poor women. May their memory be a blessing. And poor Miss Reed, too, to lose so many friends following her own injuries."

At the door, Watson said, "Thank you for your time, Dr Goldfarb, you have been a font of information. Ah, we would prefer it if you didn't mention our conversation with Miss Reed. No need to upset her."

"You may count on my discretion. Poor lady has had so much to cope with since her return home, but she is strong, you know, remarkably strong. No doubt she has had to be."

"Do you know how long Iris has worked for Miss Reed?" I said.

"Oh, many years. Let me see, they moved into the building about ten years ago, and Iris came with her from wherever Miss Reed had lived before. Iris stayed here when Miss Reed volunteered to go to South Africa. She served as a live-in housekeeper, I suppose."

"You are familiar with Iris's brother?"

"Poor Eddie, yes indeed. I believe he stayed with the two women for a short time when they lived in the other house. I gather Miss Reed paid for him to receive special care."

We stepped out of the cosy flat into the hallway. The glare of electric lights hurt my eyes following the soft lamps of Dr Goldfarb's home. Beyond the big window, I could see that Manchester had fallen into evening, and only lights in the shops and on the streets pierced the darkness of the city. I had lost all sense of time. Indeed, I could not have said with any certainty that it was still Thursday.

As the other men stood by, I knocked on Reed's door. A moment later it opened and a young maid, a white cap on top of her vivid red hair, greeted us.

"Yes, sir?"

"We need to speak with your mistress, Iris," Watson said.

"Now? Miss Reed is quite unwell, sir. Can it not wait until morning?"

"No," Pellow said, pushing past her into the flat. "It cannot."

Reed lay upon the sofa, her face grey with pain, her once-blonde hair sticking like commas to her heavily perspiring forehead.

Pellow, with the same bluster and aggression that Lestrade used to show, barged up to the woman and bellowed his arrest and read the charges. Reed merely looked at him with glazed eyes, her laboured breathing continued.

Watson pushed forward and felt her pulse. He shook his head and turned angrily to Iris. "What did she take?"

"She didn't take anything. I gave her a shot of morphine."

"How much?"

"Enough to send her to sleep," Iris said.

Watson rose to his feet and glared at her. "Enough to kill her, you mean, you stupid girl."

To my horror, the maid smiled. "You have the wrong woman, gentlemen," she said. "I saw you all coming, marching across the street like an army. I knew what you were thinking: that my dear Margaret took care of those women and that awful Boer. But you're wrong. She knew nothing about it. I did it."

Pellow snapped, "Nonsense. You couldn't have known —
"

327

"That those nurses knew about her performing abortions? Of course I knew. Margaret keeps no secrets from me. She told me all about them. She said they were her friends, that they would never betray her. But I knew they were dangerous. I couldn't think what to do, and then Providence sent that cutthroat to me. I put him on my list, too, for attacking my dear girl.

"I managed to fight him off; I'm stronger than I look. Years having to fight off my brother — well, that doesn't matter. I saw the brute run into the pub up the road. Once I got Margaret safely indoors, I went to find him. He hadn't left. He stood there in the pub, sheltering from the storm. I told him I'd give him the proof that he had the wrong woman, and where to find the real ones. He agreed to meet me early the next morning. I wrote down their information from Margaret's address book, and I took a newspaper cutting she had brought home about her three friends. He thanked me. I asked him to stay in touch. I said I would give him money.

"After he finished off the last nurse, he wrote and told me where to find him. He asked if I would send him some money. Instead, I went to see him."

"And brought your brother," O'Brien said.

"Eddie is harmless. I brought him to help me and keep me safe. A woman travelling alone, you know?"

Her smile made me shudder.

"Did she know?" I said. "Margaret? Did she know what you did? I'm sure she must have suspected when you coloured your hair."

"Yes, she suspected, but no more than that until you came to see her. She knew what I'd done. Oh, she would never have betrayed me, any more than I would betray her. You don't know what an awful life she had, the things she endured. I couldn't let you arrest her and lock her away."

She turned and knelt down by the sofa and caressed the dying woman's hair. "She's not just my employer, you know.

She's my friend, my sister, my darling girl. Rest easy, my pet."

"Iris Fitzgerald," Pellow said, as he produced a set of manacles, "I am arresting you —"

"Not yet!" she cried. "It will only be a moment or two."

At that moment, Reed gave a final gasp, and, so quietly, simply died. Iris kissed her forehead and stood. "May I get my coat?" she said.

Pellow nodded.

O'Brien stared at the Manchester policeman with an expression of loathing.

"Aren't you afraid of her escaping?" Morton said, his sarcastic tone reflecting O'Brien's expression.

"How? We're on the top floor, and I have officers in the lobby."

But at that instant, we heard the apartment door open. We all ran after her, but we were too late. Iris had jerked back the gate from the lift and thrown herself down the shaft. She landed with a sickening thud on the roof of the cabin below.

CHAPTER TWENTY-NINE

23rd March

I feel I have done nothing over the past week but sleep. I cannot think when I last felt so exhausted.

This afternoon, Watson and I had luncheon together. He is looking much more relaxed since the new staff has settled in. He is sleeping better, too, I am happy to say. He brought me up to date on the things I have been missing.

Mrs Hudson has gone to Scotland for Meg's funeral. Bea gave her all of Meg's letters so our landlady may safely return them to the girl's poor mother. Bea also returned the letters we received from Mrs. Goodrich and Mrs. Dixon.

Bea has been kept extremely busy in Mycroft's office. I gather she is enjoying being a working woman, and I have no doubt that Mycroft is delighted to have her help.

With the deaths of Iris and Reed, nothing remained to link Eddie to Cobbledick's murder other than the ring and that on its own would be useless. Morton returned it to him, and, over Pellow's objections, saw that Eddie was released to the home.

We later learned that Margaret Reed had left her considerable fortune to Iris and she, in turn, left everything to her brother. At least he is no worse off than before, beyond the loss of his sister.

Lestrade is back from his convalescence and has resumed his work at the Yard. He reports that Inspector Morton is proving an outstanding addition. They both have their eyes on O'Brien and plan to bring him into their division as soon as they can. O'Brien continues to woo Maisie and I must say, I see a great improvement in her. She is no longer the scatter-brained girl who drove me almost demented with her silliness. She has blossomed — to use Watson's phrase — into an intelligent young woman. An astonishing development, but extremely welcome.

Father Boyd has found a house for Raymond Boyd and his mother in Manchester. The lady will do some light work for the parish and be well looked after in return. Raymond will go back to school. He came to see me before he left the city and seems to be looking forward to the change.

I shall now take a walk and call upon my wife at the office. Good heaven, how that sounds!

*

30th March: Sussex

I have been wanting to return to Bea's 'cottage' again, but initially I had expected it to be just us two. That said, it is unexpectedly pleasing to have my brother and Watson here.

"A proper Easter family celebration," Bea said. In spite of my initial grumbles, I must say, I am enjoying sharing this delightful home with people whose company I most enjoy.

My brother has regained his vigour and enthusiasm ever since Bea began to work in his office. This evening, he and I walked along the beach together, enjoying the sound of the waves and the peace of the day. I commented that I could not remember when he last seemed so well.

"You have your wife to thank for that, Sherlock," he said. "After a tenuous beginning when the men in the office seemed unwilling to take her seriously, she has become their de facto leader. Not only does she serve as my primary assistant and takes many of the meetings that were eating into my time, but she serves as a stabilising force for the younger men. Wainwright, too, is a tower of strength. I had not realised how much misery Qualtrough brought to the office."

"And your issues with the new king?"

"All resolved. I had a meeting with him last week, just the two of us. He apologised for not meeting me sooner, and he spoke fulsomely of my work. Yes, I think I shall have no further difficulties from that quarter."

I thought, but did not say, that I saw Beatrice's hand in this development.

"That's splendid. It must be a great relief to you," I said.

"It is, indeed. And what of you, brother mine? You seem at home here."

"In a peculiar sort of way, being here feels like remembering a childhood I never knew."

He fell silent a moment before saying in a droll voice, "You realise that makes no sense at all."

I laughed. "No, it doesn't, and yet that is how it feels.

"You know, this year started so badly. First, the queen's death, and Bea being called away to help our new king, and Watson spending so much time at the clinic. On top of that, there was the distress Megan's death and that wearisome Holland case. For a time, I felt quite abandoned. You know, it's funny, Mycroft, but like you I have spent so much of my life keeping the human race at an arm's length. To find myself, at my age, surrounded by people who care about me, and for whom I care in my turn, took me by surprise. It may be only March, but this year has taught me not to take the people in my life for granted."

"Forgive me, brother, but I would not have expected such maudlin piffle from you."

I shared in his laughter. "I quite understand your saying so. Oddly, it was Lestrade's illness that forced me to think about the value of these people in my life."

"The policeman? As I recall, Sherlock, you were never too fond of him."

"Oh, we have certainly had our fraught moments, but over time I have come to realise that I have grown used to him. Indeed, I would miss him if he were no longer around."

We stopped and gazed out across the water. Mycroft's breath sounded laboured. Listening to him huff and puff, I realised we should return to the cottage.

"How is Lestrade?" Mycroft asked, more out of politeness than interest, I think.

"Quite back to himself," I said. "Delighted to return to his work. A couple of weeks ago, he sent an enormous basket of fruit to Watson and me by way of a thank you. Mostly it was to Watson for insisting he go to the hospital. Evidently, the outcome could have been extremely serious if he had not done so."

"Peculiar gift."

I snorted with laughter. "For you and me, certainly, but I believe it's quite common for many people. Anyway, we gave most of it to Mrs Hudson."

"She's a stalwart lady, your housekeeper. How is she getting along?"

"Better. Learning the full story of what happened to those nurses and, in particular, how well Megan acquitted herself, has been of great comfort to her. At present she is in Scotland with her family."

We fell silent and revelled in the distant sound of the waves.

"I say, Sherlock, is this not a splendid place? So quiet and peaceful."

"It is indeed. The cottage, as Bea so entertainingly calls the house, is perfectly splendid. I find myself more able to relax here than anywhere else."

"That painting you gave her is quite magnificent. A Gallagher, you said?"

"Yes. I saw him paint it, well, part of it. Oxford Street in the snow. That picture in the library of the Houses of Parliament is one of his, too."

"That's a much more appropriate gift than fruit," he said with a chuckle. "Anyway, I appreciate your kindness in inviting me and the good doctor to stay."

"All Bea's doing. A family get-together she called it. I'm impressed you felt comfortable enough to leave the office."

"We're not so far away from London, and the telephone lines shrink that distance still more. Do them good to see how much they depend on me."

"It's getting rather chilly," I said. "Well, Mycroft, what do you say we return to the house for a hot buttered rum, and you can try to beat me in a game of chess?"

"Lead on, Sherlock."

END

Historical Notes

Great Warrior is a work of fiction, but I have tried to be as faithful to historical events as possible. In case you are curious about some of those details, here is some more information.

1901
With the death of Queen Victoria in January, Britain underwent a radical change, though change had been coming for some time. The fogs remained, but gaslight belonged, for the most part, to the past. Electricity and telephones transformed the lives of the wealthy, though the poor remained as disadvantaged as ever. Automobiles added to the feeling of modernity. When Edward VII took the throne, the country felt the shackles of the repressed Victorian era were over. Many would later view this period as a golden age or the calm before the storm that was World War I.

Second Boer War (1899-1902)
One of the things that preoccupied society at the turn of the century was the Second Boer War. It is remembered for the infamous 'scorched earth' policy, concentration camps, genocide, and guerrilla warfare. It cost Britain £210 million (which would be £25 billion today), 120,000 casualties and 22,000 dead. Most deaths were due to disease and poor medical provision.

Conan Doyle in South Africa
Having been rejected by the army, Arthur Conan Doyle travelled to South Africa as a private citizen and went to work in Langman's private field hospital. Virtually upon arrival, the hospital was overrun with men suffering from typhoid. On top of that, the location suffered fierce thunderstorms, and the tents that formed the hospital were knee deep in mud and

faeces. Doyle believed that the typhus inoculation he received while on route to South Africa had saved his life.

Doyle subsequently wrote *The War in South Africa: Its Causes and Conduct*. It is an account of his own experiences and something of an apologist report of the British war with the Boer. The book was published in 1901.

Nursing in 1901
While the medical profession had begun registration in 1858, it took several more years before nursing leaders could establish professional status of their own. Princess Helena, daughter of Queen Victoria, played a pivotal role in legitimizing the profession until she was forced to hand her role to Queen Alexandra after Victoria's death in 1901. However, Helena retained the presidency of the Army Nursing Reserve.

Almost 2000 nurses served in the Second Boer War, along with nurses from Australia, New Zealand, and Canada. 23 nurses died due to diseases contracted.

The Nursing Registration Act was finally passed in 1919.

John Phillip Holland and the birth of the submarine
Holland, born in 1841 in County Clare Ireland, began his initial designs for what would become the first submarine while he was in hospital recovering from a broken leg. His initial designs were rejected by the US Navy, but this did not prevent Holland from continuing to work on his idea. In May 1897 he launched Holland VI, a craft that could run underwater for considerable distance. The US Navy purchased this model. The Royal Navy commissioned the Royal Holland 1 in 1901 and this was built in top secret. She was launched on 2 October, 1901.

The McNaughton Rule
Is the litmus test by which the sanity of defendants is determined. Established in 1843, Section 84 IPC explains: "Nothing is an offence which is done by a person who, at the time of doing it, by reason of unsoundness of mind, is incapable of knowing the nature of the act or that he is doing what is either wrong or contrary to the law."

Sir Edward Marshall Hall (1858-1927)
A renowned barrister and orator who was also admired for his wit. He was particularly famous for his impassioned defence of women who had been abused by men.

The Victoria Building
Manchester's Victoria Building was erected in 1877. It formed a triangle in the middle of Deansgate to the west, Victoria Street to the East, and St Mary's Gate at the rear. The Victoria Hotel occupied the fifth floor. The building was in the Gothic style with a brick façade. It was destroyed by fire on December 22, 1940.

www.ingramcontent.com/pod-product-compliance
Lightning Source LLC
Chambersburg PA
CBHW072053020726
47501CB00003B/567